Also by Paige Tyler

UNDERCOVER
WOLF

PAIGE
TYLER

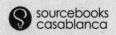

sourcebooks
casablanca

With special thanks to my extremely patient and understanding husband. Without your help and support, I couldn't have pursued my dream job of becoming a writer. You're my sounding board, my idea man, my critique partner, and the absolute best research assistant a girl could ask for. Love you!

Published by Sourcebooks Casablanca, an imprint of Sourcebooks
P.O. Box 4410, Naperville, Illinois 60567-4410
(630) 961-3900
sourcebooks.com

Printed and bound in Canada.
MBP 10 9 8 7 6 5 4 3 2 1

CHAPTER 1

Paris

Harley Grant ran her hands down her little black dress as she climbed the steps in her surprisingly comfortable platform heels and walked into the crowded nightclub. The throbbing techno beat immediately made her sensitive ears ring and she winced. She'd have a splitting headache in five minutes. Loud noises always did that to her, which was one of the many reasons she hadn't been to places like this since turning into a werewolf eight years ago, when she was a junior in college.

Out of the corner of her eye, she saw her STAT teammate and fellow werewolf Caleb Lynch glance at her with concern on his face. Tall and muscular with brown eyes, his dark blond hair always looked like he was running his hands through it. "You okay?"

"Yeah, I'm good," she said, raising her voice a little to be heard. "I hate loud music, that's all."

Caleb nodded, clearly not as bothered by it as she was. Then again, Caleb was an omega werewolf. While he might be as big as a house and as strong as a bull, his senses weren't anywhere as sensitive as an alpha's, like she was.

"It's not the music I'm worried about," he said, taking in all the people around them with a frown. "I'm not a fan of big crowds. Being packed into a place like this when the shit might hit the fan at any second makes me twitchy."

Control and temperament were another thing that differentiated alpha werewolves from omegas. Harley had dealt with some anger management issues right after her change, but Caleb would have to deal with them for the rest of his life. When he lost it, he really lost it. As in people ended up bruised and bloody—or dead. It was something everyone on the Special Threat Assessment Team was helping him work on, but it wasn't easy. The list of things that could set him off seemed to grow by the day. Apparently, crowded nightclubs were the newest trigger.

"I think you can relax," Harley said as they moved deeper into the club, the music getting louder with every step until she could practically feel her body vibrating. "You're menacing enough that most people will be more than happy to give you space. And if the vague intel we got is any indication, I doubt we're going to run into any trouble tonight. More likely we'll walk around for a few hours, then head back to the hotel in time for the jet lag to catch up to us."

Caleb looked skeptical at that. She supposed they'd know soon enough.

"Okay, Jake," she said, hoping the support techs had been right about the tiny microphone concealed in her necklace working in the loud club. "We're in."

"Roger that," Jake Huang, their pack alpha/team leader murmured over the radio. "Jes and I are heading toward the private rooms upstairs. Misty and Forrest are near the band, trying to work their way backstage. That leaves the dance floors for you and Caleb, as well as the lower levels, if you can figure out how to get to them."

"Copy that," Caleb said, then looked at Harley. "I gotta admit, wandering around looking for something suspicious that'll lead us to the kidnappers or their captives, both of which might or might not be supernatural, isn't much of a plan."

Harley would like to say he was wrong, but Caleb had hit the nail on the head. Twelve hours ago, she and the rest of the team had been back home in Washington, DC, hanging out at Jake's place, enjoying some downtime after their first mission together, when their boss had called about a possible human-trafficking ring operating out of Paris that might involve supernaturals. With little more than that to go on, they'd immediately caught the next flight to France, where a support team met them with weapons and other equipment.

But going into unknown—not to mention possibly dangerous—situations was what being part of STAT was all about. She and her teammates ran around the world sniffing out threats to see if they were common everyday bad guys or scary things that went bump in the night.

"I'm with you there." Harley scanned the people around them, who were gyrating under the colorful strobes on the nearby dance floor while strategically placed black lights found the fluorescent paint on the exposed parts of their bodies. She wondered what constituted *suspicious* in a place like this. "Let's hope we get lucky."

Caleb only grunted in reply.

As they made their way through the club, Harley realized it was one thing to memorize a floor plan on a piece of paper, but a completely different thing to figure out where you were in that same building when it was filled with people. Within minutes, she had no idea where she was in relation to the entrance and even less idea how much more area they needed to explore. The place was much bigger than it looked in the drawing.

"We'll cover more ground if we split up," she said to Caleb.

From the scowl on his face, Harley knew his first instinct was to say no. Not because he thought she was wrong about being able to cover more ground on their own, but because he was worried about letting her search alone. Even though they'd only been working together for a few weeks, he'd already become like a big brother to her. It was sweet in a bittersweet kind of way, since she'd long ago given up on her real family.

"The sooner we find these people, the sooner we can get out of here," she added before he protested. "We're in Paris. Don't you want to look around a little before McKay puts us right back on a plane home? Besides, we'll be in constant radio communication. If I run into trouble, you can be there in seconds."

He still seemed resistant to the idea, but after a few seconds, he relented. "Okay, but don't do anything crazy, all right? At the first hint of danger, I want you on the radio. Not once something happens, but the second you get a funny feeling, okay?"

Harley nodded. "You, too."

Another grunt.

Giving him a smile, she slipped into the crowd before Caleb could change his mind. It wasn't that she didn't like being part of STAT or working with Caleb. On the contrary, she loved hanging out with her teammates. But she'd been on her own for a long time. Depending on other people was something she would have to get used to again.

She wandered through several smaller rooms, each filled with mobs of dancing people, pulsing music, and flashing lights. Harley tried to ignore the extraneous and focus on the details, looking for anything that suggested there was a human—or supernatural—trafficking ring working out of the club.

As she moved from room to room, she depended on her eyes to lead the way. As a werewolf, she should have been putting as much trust in her nose and ears, but she wasn't a big fan of that. While her boss, Nathan McKay, had hired her because of what she was, she wasn't keen on using her werewolf abilities. Besides, they were kind of unreliable anyway. Sometimes, she could smell a pizza delivery vehicle from half a mile away. Other times, she could barely smell her own perfume. Then again, maybe they were so inconsistent because she didn't make use of them. But since she refused to hone them, at the end of the day, her ears and nose were going to do what they wanted.

Which was why she was a little shocked when a familiar scent tickled her nose. She smelled a werewolf. And it wasn't Caleb or Jake. Even with her less-than-reliable nose, she knew that for sure.

What were the chances of another werewolf in the club *not* being connected to an alleged supernatural trafficking ring?

Harley stopped and sniffed the air, trying to be as subtle as she could. Then she was moving again, intent on tracking the scent to its source. Should she radio the team about her discovery or wait until she had more information? As sketchy as her nose was, it was possible the other werewolf had been in the club days ago and she was simply picking up residual scent.

She wove through the crowd, circling dance floors and around tables, then moved through an archway that led to a set of dimly lit concrete stairs and the lower level Jake had asked her and Caleb to find. She absently listened to her teammates reporting in over the radio, saying they still hadn't found anything. Tuning them out, she focused on her nose, trusting it to lead her down the steps even as she lost the trail more than once.

There was yet another dance floor downstairs, this one filled with people moving to a much less chaotic rhythm than those on the level above. There were fewer flashing lights, too. That should have made it easier to scan the room and locate the source of the scent that had drawn her down there, but nobody stood out.

Maybe she was completely wrong about the scent.

Maybe it wasn't a werewolf at all.

Then she caught a glimpse of someone out of the corner of her eye that made her snap her head around, but she didn't see anyone. Sure she'd seen something, she skirted the outside of the dance floor in that direction. She was starting to question herself again when she spotted a tall, attractive guy with broad shoulders, casually disheveled brown hair, and scruff on his square jaw. He was circling the dancers on the floor in much the same way Harley was but in the opposite direction, keeping pace with her so they stayed exactly opposite each other.

Yeah, like that's a coincidence.

A little voice in the back of her head told her to get on the radio and call Caleb and the rest of her teammates, but she ignored it, too mesmerized by the handsome man across the room from her.

Every few seconds, piercing blue eyes locked with hers, making something inside her—maybe her inner wolf—feel a sensation she didn't recognize.

Even if she hadn't picked up on the scent, Harley would have known he was a werewolf from the graceful, animalistic way he moved.

He was a predator, no doubt about it.

Was he a kidnapper as well?

She wanted to say he'd never do anything like that, which was an asinine thing to consider about a man she'd never met.

Tired of stalking in circles, Harley stopped, turning carefully to keep her eyes on the big werewolf as he moved closer. She wasn't sure, but for a brief moment, she thought she caught sight of what might have been a smile tugging at his sensuous mouth.

The other werewolf—an alpha most definitely—strode past the last few people separating them and came to a halt a few feet away. Harley couldn't ignore that the man in front of her was possibly the most gorgeous guy she'd ever seen.

Which pretty much guaranteed he was one of the bad guys. Because that was how her luck worked out when it came to the opposite sex.

Harley took a single step forward and felt a tingle in her stomach when he did the same, that dangerous smile showing up again. She took another few steps toward him when his head whipped to the side. She looked that way, too, trying to see what had attracted his attention, and caught sight of two men slipping behind a black velvet curtain covering a section of the far wall. The second guy cast a furtive glance over his shoulder before disappearing.

That isn't suspicious at all.

She turned back to the alpha werewolf, but he was already striding in that direction. She quickly followed, knowing she should call the rest of the team, but once again, her instincts insisted she hold off. By the time she slipped behind the curtain, all she saw was another set of stairs. The mysterious werewolf was nowhere to be found.

She paused long enough to slide a hand under her dress and pull the small frame Glock 9mm from the tiny holster strapped to her upper thigh, chambering a round as she started down the steps, rather proud of how comfortably she handled a loaded weapon. Considering that before joining STAT she'd never even held a gun, she thought she was doing rather well.

From down below, she heard the rhythmic sound of rapid footsteps along with the soft murmur of voices but no music or partying people or anything else to make her think this was a part of the dance club open to the public. Whatever the hell those two guys had come down here for, it probably wasn't on the up-and-up.

Lit only by three low-watt bulbs mounted in cobweb-covered fixtures hanging from the rough stone ceiling, the room at the bottom of the steps was filled with crates, racks of empty bottles, and bags of trash. The dim glow was barely enough to throw shadows, but Harley didn't need a lot of light to see the werewolf standing a few feet away, his broad back to her, a pistol down at his side.

"You always bring a gun when you go to a nightclub?" he asked without looking at her.

His voice was as deep as she'd imagined it would be, a little rough with a hint of a British accent, like he'd traveled extensively for much of his life and lost a bit of the distinctive sound over time.

"A girl has to be careful these days," Harley said, smiling even though she was standing in the middle of a filthy storage room twenty feet underground with an alpha werewolf who'd probably lured her down here with kidnapping in mind—or worse. "I've heard big cities can be dangerous."

The man turned to look at her, blue eyes piercing even in the dimness as they slid up and down her body. "If you think it might be dangerous, why come to Paris? And all the way from America, if I'm not mistaking the accent."

The Brit's perfectly sculpted nose lifted a little, his nostrils flaring the slightest bit, like he was trying to take in a scent he found tantalizing. Harley knew he was picking up her pheromones and couldn't help wondering what she smelled like to him.

Did he like her scent?

Did she care if he did?

"You know the song 'Girls Just Want to Have Fun,' right?" She approached him slowly, glancing around and trying to figure out where the other two men had gone. "Maybe visiting potentially dangerous places is how I have fun."

"Strange hobby," he said, his voice dropping down an octave to practically make her tummy vibrate…as well as regions a bit farther south. "I prefer reading, but whatever. You do you."

Harley lifted a brow, lowering her gun to a safe position. "Is that what you're doing down in this dank, dark room?" She stepped to the side a little, making him circle to the right as they resumed the little dance they'd done upstairs. "Looking for a good book?"

He snorted, coming to a stop again a few feet away. "We both know that's not what I'm doing down here any more than you're here looking for some fun. So, as entertaining as this banter is, I think it's time we get on with what really brought us here."

Harley was almost disappointed but knew the man was right. While she'd enjoyed their verbal jousting, she was here for more important things.

"Do you know if the men you followed down here are supernatural in any way?" she asked. "Or are they normal bad guys holding supernatural victims captive?"

The British werewolf's eyes narrowed, and Harley was worried she'd made a big mistake assuming he was aware of creatures besides werewolves out there in the world. But then he shrugged. "I'm not sure how much you know, but the situation is more complicated than that. While those two guys you saw weren't anything special, I'm almost certain there are other supernaturals involved and that at least one of the people they kidnapped is, too."

There was a lot to unpack there, but the implications were staggering. Supernaturals working with humans to kidnap other supernaturals?

Harley was about to ask him that exact question when she was interrupted by a loud scraping sound coming from the far end of the room. She stared in shock as the whole wall slid to the side. What the…?

The werewolf immediately lifted his weapon and pointed it in that direction. She did the same, grimacing as a smell hit her in the face so hard she almost choked. With her nose, that was saying a lot. But it was hard to ignore the stench of mud and stale blood. It was nasty as hell.

Three men stepped into the room. Two of them were the guys the Brit had said were *nothing special*. The third guy, on the other hand, was definitely supernatural. Not quite as big as Caleb, he was damn close. But the thing that nearly froze her solid as she stood there were his flat, black eyes. Cold and dead, they reminded her of a shark's. Before she even saw him move, he took a gun out of his jacket pocket and pointed it in their direction with a hiss, displaying more teeth than any human should have.

Because the thing obviously wasn't human.

Gunfire lit up the darkness, bullets filling the air. Harley felt one slice through her waist and another burn a line of fire across her right shoulder. She ignored the pain long enough to put a round through Dead Eyes's chest, then she was diving to the floor, rolling as she hit and coming to a stop behind a knee-high crate before emptying her magazine into the other two men with him.

Her werewolf partner had focused on Dead Eyes, too, putting five more bullets in the creature. It didn't seem particularly bothered by the holes in its body or the dark blood pouring out.

Harley scrambled for the extra magazine strapped to the inside of her thigh along with the gun holster, then called for backup over the sounds of gunfire, warning teammates about the creature she was up against. As Caleb and Jake asked for additional details, she popped up from behind the crate to put a few more bullets in Dead Eyes. That was when she realized the British werewolf was calling for backup on his own radio.

She hadn't expected that but was secretly thrilled at the possibility he was one of the good guys.

The two men who'd come in with the creature were dead, but Dead Eyes didn't seem to care as he leaped over them and ran through the doorway, the wall beginning to slide closed behind him.

Harley and the British werewolf ran for the door at the same time. Instead of trying to slip through the opening that was getting tinier by the second, he grabbed the two dead men and shoved them into the door's path, stacking them on top of the other. There was a crunch and a pop, but the wall stopped, leaving a foot and a half gap.

"What the hell was that thing?" Harley asked as the werewolf scooped up one of the dead guy's weapons and handed it to her, then took the other man's before searching them for spare magazines.

"I have no bloody clue." He tossed her one of the magazines he'd found, then darted his head through the gap in the wall to look into the darkness beyond. "But we don't have time to wait around and figure it out. Whatever that thing is, we have to assume it's involved in these kidnappings."

Harley didn't hesitate to follow when he slipped through the opening and into the stairwell, knowing he was right. The creature they'd filled full of holes was down there somewhere right now, either trying to escape with his victims or killing them to clean up the evidence. Either way, they couldn't wait for backup.

As they ran down the long, uneven staircase, sounds and

random scents from below bombarded her senses. Shouts of anger and confusion were interspersed with screams of terror and pain. The smells were myriad and unusual, and there were way too many of them for her untrained nose.

"We're on our way, Harley," Jake said over the radio. "Hold your position."

At least that's what she thought he said. The reception got crappier the farther underground they went, and she couldn't be sure of anything that came through her earpiece, but Harley swore her pack alpha said something about chopping off the creature's head. Or maybe he'd said hand? Both options sounded extreme.

It was pure bedlam at the bottom of the stairwell as a handful of heavily armed men moved to confront her and the other werewolf. Behind them, more bad guys were dragging half a dozen prisoners out of a row of cells along one wall. Two of the captives were resisting, but the others seemed completely out of it, like they were drugged. Dead Eyes was standing in the middle of it all, shouting orders in a deep voice that echoed off the stone walls even as blood continued to pour out of him in black, sluggish rivulets.

Harley and the Brit were forced back into the stairwell by a storm of bullets. A werewolf could take a lot of punishment and still keep going, but a bullet through the head or heart would kill them as quickly as anyone else. And unlike the fairy tales, the aforementioned bullet didn't have to be silver. But retreating wasn't necessarily a bad thing. All they needed to do was hold the stairs and keep Dead Eyes and his buddies from getting past them with the prisoners. It wouldn't be long before Jake and the rest of her team found them, then they could finish this.

But the next time Harley poked her head out to take a quick look, that hope died. The bad guys were headed to the far end of the long room with their captives, and if her faulty nose wasn't lying to her, there was a scent of fresh air coming from that direction.

"Crap, they're getting away!" she shouted. "There must be a

back exit out of this place. They probably have transportation waiting for them."

The Brit snarled and cursed, which sounded almost sexy with that accent of his.

"Cover me," he said.

Before she even realized what he was doing, he was up and running out of the stairwell straight into the hail of gunfire. Cursing, she loaded a fresh magazine in her weapon, then followed, firing rapid shots at the armed men facing them, focused on trying to hit as many as she could.

The British werewolf closed on the shooters so fast Harley could barely keep up with him. Under his long overcoat, his body twisted and spasmed in a partial shift she'd never even attempt, his claws and fangs extending even as he continued to fire his weapon. Even though he got hit multiple times, he still kept running toward them.

Within seconds, they were both in the middle of a group of bad guys. The large automatic pistol they'd gotten off the dead guy earlier locked back on an empty magazine. She flipped the pistol backward to hold it by the barrel, ready to swing it like a club.

"Go after them," the British werewolf said, ripping out a man's throat with claws that had to be an inch and a half long. "Save as many of the captives as you can."

She didn't want to leave him to fight on his own, but she also couldn't let the traffickers get away with the prisoners. Dropping the borrowed handgun she pulled her 9mm out and ran as fast as she could, praying she didn't get a bullet in the back for her trouble.

When she got to the archway at the end of the room, Harley slowed as she realized it opened into a tunnel. It was dark in both directions, but she headed up the ramp, sure that's where the fresh air was coming from. Dead Eyes's stench seemed stronger in that direction, too.

Harley raced up the incline to the end of the tunnel and

cautiously stepped out into an underground parking garage where she saw two vans disappearing up a ramp and a third starting its engine even as a man in a ragged leather jacket carried an unconscious woman toward the open back doors. Harley sprinted toward it, wishing for once that she could shift enough to run as fast as any other werewolf. But she'd never been able to do that, which meant she probably wouldn't be able to catch the man before he made it to the back of the van with his captive.

Sliding to a stop, Harley lifted her weapon, hoping she'd hit the guy and not the woman. She squeezed the trigger slow and steady, just like Jake had taught her, and hit the bad guy in the leg. He went down, the girl tumbling from his arms.

Harley hurried toward the downed man and van still idling. If she reached it, she might be able to save a few more prisoners. But then a young guy with long black hair hopped out of the back of the van and came at her, a knife in his hand.

She barely had enough time to mutter a curse before he suddenly disappeared into thin air. Half a heartbeat later, the guy popped back into existence right in front of her, thrusting the blade into her chest at the same time he rammed into her with the impact of a Mack truck. Her 9mm went flying before she could even think about pulling the trigger.

Hitting the concrete floor so hard she bounced and slid five feet, she fought off the urge to lie there and wait for the pain to subside. She had to find her weapon.

She rolled onto her side and saw her gun a few feet away. Unfortunately, the guy with the long hair was heading straight for her with that damn knife again. She lunged for her weapon, coming up with it and spinning around to fire all in one smooth move. But the man disappeared before the bullet reached him and it ricocheted into the darkness as the slide of her weapon locked back on an empty magazine.

Oh crap.

The man popped back into view by her hip, the blade coming at her throat. She threw a hand up to block the knife only to see the man jerk sideways as the sound of gunfire filled the parking garage. A split second later, he disappeared again, reappearing beside the guy she'd shot in the leg and the still unconscious girl. He moved to pick her up, but the other guy shoved him away.

"Leave her," he said. "We don't have time. We have to get out of here."

The guy with the long hair hesitated but then helped his partner in crime up and got him into the van, which immediately sped away. Groaning, Harley started to get to her feet as she heard footsteps coming in her direction. She turned to see Caleb, Jake, and the British werewolf running toward her. Jes, Misty, and Forrest were right behind them, along with two men and a woman she didn't recognize.

Jake reached her side first, concern in his dark eyes. "You okay?"

Harley nodded. "Yeah. I'm fine. Check on the girl."

Giving her a nod, Jake hurried over to the unconscious woman, Jes joining him.

Caleb frowned at the knife wound, the top of which was visible above the V-neck of Harley's dress. It had stopped bleeding and was already starting to close up. "You should have called for backup sooner."

She nodded. "I know. Go see if Jake and Jes need help."

As he strode off, albeit reluctantly, the British werewolf sauntered over, mouth curving.

"Don't take this the wrong way, but you're bloody awful at this werewolf thing."

"Yeah, I'm aware of that." She held out her hand with a smile. "I'm Harley Grant by the way. Any chance you're the one who kept that guy from stabbing me again?"

His handshake was firm, his warm skin sending a little tingle through her. "Sawyer Bishop. And yes, although I can't take too much credit since I didn't get here in time to stop him from doing it the first time."

"That's okay," Harley said, realizing she was probably grinning like an idiot and had absolutely no idea why. Sure, he was cute, but seriously? "You're here now. That's all that matters."

CHAPTER 2

"ARE WE GOING TO TALK ABOUT WHAT HAPPENED LAST NIGHT?"

Sawyer wondered when someone on his MI6 team was going to bring that up. The question seemed to bounce off the walls in the silent hotel conference room, and he turned away from the window he'd been gazing out for the past twenty minutes to look at his teammate, Elliott Lloyd. Between the breathtaking view from the tenth floor and thoughts of the beautiful female werewolf he'd run into at the club, he was a little distracted at the moment. It was all he could do to think about anything else since setting eyes on her.

"What's to talk about?" he asked, trying to sound casual even though he was tense as hell. "We went up against a crew of human traffickers and got our arses handed to us."

Stocky, with blond hair, the team's medic/equipment specialist eyed Sawyer like he was crazy. His other two teammates, Rory Higgins and Erin Nichols, were doing the same. Afraid they'd see the nervousness on his face he was trying desperately to hide, he turned back to the window, forcing himself to concentrate on the scenery.

Sawyer had been to France more than a dozen times during his years in MI6, but he'd usually been rushing to get somewhere else—or getting shot at. On those occasions when he'd been fortunate enough to spend more than a few hours here, it was always in some safe house in the middle of nowhere. He'd never stayed at a hotel as nice as this one, that was for sure.

Straight across the Seine, the Eiffel Tower threw shadows in the late-morning sun, with the Arc de Triomphe a little to the north and the big glass pyramid of the Louvre a mile to the east.

He couldn't see it from where he was standing, but the Bastille district and the club they'd been at last night was somewhere in that direction, too. He couldn't help wondering if he'd get a chance to see any of this beautiful city someday, or whether this was the best he could ever hope for.

"Don't act like you didn't see that woman get up and walk away after having a knife shoved halfway through her chest," Elliott said in exasperation. "And that was after getting shot at least twice judging by the holes in her dress. She shouldn't even be alive right now."

Sawyer was trying to come up with a reasonable explanation for that, in between breathing a sigh of relief that his teammates had apparently missed his own gunshot wounds, when Erin Nichols, their weapons and tactics specialist, let out a short laugh.

"I don't know why you're so worried about the woman." Fair with shoulder-length, curly, red hair, Erin was sitting in the same chair at the conference table she'd commandeered when they'd gotten there—the one with the best view of the door. Like she was worried someone was going to kick it in and attack them. "I'm more interested in knowing how the guy who stabbed her was able to disappear from her side one second and show up again fifty feet away. That shouldn't be possible."

Sawyer opened his mouth to answer but was interrupted by a loud snort. He turned around again, this time to see Rory Higgins, the team's intel analyst and resident computer geek, shaking his head. A redhead like Erin, his light skin was even paler than usual. He looked plain wrung out.

"Maybe it isn't possible, but we all saw it happen," Rory said. "I think we need to accept last night was about something beyond the possible."

Erin's gray eyes narrowed suspiciously. "Like what?"

Rory glanced at each of them in turn before looking down at the floor. In that one second of eye contact, Sawyer saw a mountain of doubt and uncertainty. "I was thinking maybe something...I don't know...supernatural?"

Sawyer was stunned Rory had gone there. Had he had a run-in with something strange he'd never told them about? If the room had been quiet before, now they were in that hearing-a-pin-drop category.

"Supernatural?" Erin stood, moving closer to where the rest of them were, an incredulous look on her face. "Please tell me you didn't use that word with Weatherford and the other agents during the post-mission interview."

Rory didn't answer, but his sheepish expression said it all.

Sawyer sighed. Clarence Weatherford was their team's section chief at MI6. Weatherford rarely left the comfort of his London-based office, and as far as Sawyer knew, the man hadn't been in the field for almost four years. But after the report Sawyer sent in immediately following what happened at the club, saying they'd had a run-in with an American covert team and that something unexplainable had occurred, Weatherford had been on the first plane to Paris. Sawyer hadn't revealed that three of the Americans were werewolves, but since he knew his teammates had gotten to the garage in time to see Harley get stabbed, he had to at least mention the guy who could disappear at will. When Weatherford had asked pointed questions, Sawyer had been honest about the guy with the freaky, black eyes and all the teeth, too. There was no way he could hide that he and Harley had put more than half a dozen bullets in the guy—there was blood everywhere—or that the thing had simply walked it off afterward. Not when there was a good chance his team might end up running into the creature again in the future.

"Don't rag on him too hard, Erin," Sawyer said. "How else do you describe a guy who seems like he can teleport in the blink of an eye?"

Erin looked like she wanted to argue, but Sawyer cut her off.

"Look. The guy with the knife wasn't the only strange thing in the building last night. There was another man, I guess you'd call him, with flat black eyes and a mouth full of razor-sharp teeth. I shot him six times and the female agent from the American team got him a couple more. Any one of those bullets should have killed him, but he shrugged them off like they were nothing."

Elliott and Erin exchanged skeptical glances while Rory went even more ashen.

"He was probably wearing some kind of fancy tactical vest," Erin said, the words casual, like she wasn't implying he'd missed something so obvious. "With all the exotic materials out there these days, they can make those vests so light, it's hard to tell someone is wearing one under their clothes."

"That doesn't explain the teeth," Rory pointed out.

She folded her arms with a shrug. "Dental implants."

Sawyer had to fight the urge not to roll his eyes. "Erin, I watched blood pour out of the guy from those gunshot wounds. I'm talking pints of it. And the razor-sharp teeth were as normal and human as yours right up until he hissed at us."

"Hissed?" Elliott repeated, the expression on his face giving away how lost he was at the moment. "What, like a cat?"

"No, definitely not like a cat," Sawyer said, correcting him. "And yeah, he hissed at us."

Before his teammates could come up with anything to say to that, a familiar scent tickled his nose. The perfect combination of vanilla custard and raspberries he was quickly coming to associate with Harley. She was in the hallway and coming this way. For some crazy reason, his heart sped up a little.

Harley wasn't alone. He picked up several other scents, including the two male werewolves from her team and Weatherford. None of their scents were as distinct—or as enticing—as Harley's. Then again, what could compete with his favorite dessert? Or the woman herself. In some crazy way, it was like he and Harley had known each other for years. Then again, after last night, maybe he needed to recalibrate his definition of crazy.

The door to the conference room swung open, and Weatherford walked in leading Harley and her team along with an older man in an expensive suit. Sawyer didn't recognize him, but there was something about him that screamed *covert agent*.

Since Sawyer hadn't paid much attention last night to the other people Harley worked with, he figured he should probably do it now. But no matter how hard he tried, he couldn't take his eyes off her. She'd traded in the dress he'd seen her in last night for jeans and a simple red blouse. With long, wavy, blond hair and blue-gray eyes that locked with his the moment she stepped through the door and refused to let go, could anyone blame him? Her creamy skin was like porcelain and her bubblegum-pink lips had to be the most kissable he'd ever seen.

She wasn't simply beautiful.

She was mesmerizing.

Sawyer regained his focus in time to see Weatherford motioning everyone toward the table. Sawyer quickly grabbed a seat, hoping Harley would sit directly across from him so he could keep gazing at her without anyone else knowing what he was doing. Bollocks, he felt like a sodding teenager.

It didn't work.

Before Harley could pull out the chair opposite Sawyer, one of her teammates grabbed it and she had to take a seat closer to the end of the table, leaving Sawyer sitting across from the big werewolf with the dirty-blond hair. For whatever reason, the guy didn't seem to like him. In fact, if the expression on the man's face was anything to go by, murder was currently being considered.

What the bloody hell is that about?

As soon as they were all seated, Weatherford introduced everyone on both teams, finishing with the man in the expensive suit and glasses standing beside him.

"This is Nathan McKay, head of the joint FBI-CIA Special Threat Assessment Team—aka STAT. The FBI part handles domestic missions while the CIA portion focuses on international ones. The *special* part of the moniker is because they tackle cases involving supernatural creatures."

Even after everything he and his teammates had been talking about moments before Weatherford had arrived, Sawyer could tell their boss's words caught them off guard. As the silence stretched out, he noticed Harley and the other two werewolves—Jake and Caleb—were regarding him curiously. They probably couldn't understand why Erin, Rory, and Elliott were so freaked out over the term *supernatural* considering they had one on their team. That was because Erin, Rory, and Elliott didn't know he was a werewolf, something he spent every day making sure they never found out.

While the American werewolves mentally chewed on that, Sawyer took the opportunity to size up the rest of the STAT team. Dark-haired Jes Ridley was human and carried herself like an experienced field agent. Interestingly enough, her scent was intertwined with Jake's, which could only mean one thing—they were a couple.

They weren't the only ones. Clean-cut Forrest Albright and the very unique-looking Misty Swanson were also clearly a couple. Sawyer was pretty sure Forrest was human, but he couldn't say he was as confident about Misty. Her violet eyes and long, purple hair—which something told him were natural—made him think she was some kind of supernatural, though he wasn't sure what.

Beside Sawyer, Erin let out a derisive snort.

"No offense," she said in a tone that plainly suggested something offensive was on the way. "But I don't buy any of this bloody supernatural stuff. And if anyone in this room does, they're barmy. I'll admit, last night was a little out of the ordinary, but everything in that parking garage can be explained rationally."

McKay pinned her with a hard look. "Normally I wouldn't care about your opinions on the existence of the supernatural, but with our respective agencies deciding they want MI6 and STAT working together on this, I need to change your thoughts on the subject quickly."

Sawyer was so busy wrapping his head around why MI6 would team up with STAT, he barely noticed the look McKay threw Jake's way. It wasn't until the other werewolf pushed back his rolling chair and stood that he realized that Jake was going to shift. Right there in front of everyone.

No effing way.

But that's exactly what Jake did, his upper canines elongating at the same time that his eyes glowed vivid gold and claws extended from the tips of each finger.

The response from his team was predictable.

Elliott shoved away from the table so fast his chair flipped over; Rory froze solid, eyes wide in shock; and Erin jumped up, pulling her Glock from the holster just behind her right hip before backing up to put extra space between her and the werewolf across the table from her.

"What the hell are you?" Erin demanded, pointing her weapon at Jake even as she moved back a little farther so she could keep an eye on all of the Americans at once. She glanced at Sawyer. "And how the hell can you sit there like this is no big deal?"

"Put your gun away and sit down," he said calmly. "You aren't going to shoot anyone."

Even though he was confident Erin wouldn't actually pull the trigger, Sawyer still sighed in relief when she lowered her weapon and holstered it before finally sitting down again. On the other side of Sawyer, Elliott took his seat as well. This only reinforced his decision to hide his secret from his teammates all these years. It would have absolutely sucked arse if Erin pulled a gun on him like that.

Weatherford stood there looking pissed as hell—and maybe a little embarrassed, too. Harley and the rest of her STAT team didn't seem too happy, either. McKay was the only one who didn't appear rattled by Erin's little temper tantrum.

"Jake is a werewolf. So are Harley and Caleb," McKay said.

On the other side of the table, Caleb grinned, flashing his fangs, while Harley simply tugged the neckline of her blouse aside to show them the barely discernible scar left from the stab wound last night.

"STAT has learned that when you're dealing with supernaturals, it's best to have a few on your side. While we have no idea what that man with the knife was, we do know the other creature was a vampire. And taking them down is impossible without having a werewolf or three on your side." McKay leveled his gaze at Sawyer, his expression unreadable, before looking at Rory, Elliott, and Erin in turn. "Luckily, now you do."

CHAPTER 3

"SINCE WE'LL BE WORKING TOGETHER, MAYBE WE SHOULD compare notes while we're waiting for the girl we rescued to come in," Sawyer said cautiously, like he was concerned the suggestion might upset the fragile peace that had finally taken hold in the conference room. "Particularly how we both ended up in that nightclub last night."

Working together.

That might be easier said than done, Harley thought. But that was what McKay and Weatherford wanted them to do.

"Track down these supernatural creatures, figure out what they're planning to do with those prisoners, and put a stop to it," McKay had said before he and Weatherford had left.

Apparently her boss and his counterpart in MI6 had missed the fact that no one in the room trusted each other. Then again, considering Erin had been ready to shoot Jake a few minutes ago, trust might be the least of their problems.

Harley was still musing over that when she caught the delectable scent of cinnamon coffee cake on the air. It was so mouthwatering she looked around, trying to see if there was a plate of goodies she'd missed, but there wasn't. For the thousandth time, she cursed her crappy nose.

She glanced over at Sawyer to see him regarding her with those captivating blue eyes of his. She thought she'd imagined how handsome he was because there was no way any guy could be so goodlooking, but he was even more gorgeous than she remembered from last night. It was all she could do not to spend the entire time staring at him. But Erin and the two men on his team were already suspicious of her and her werewolf teammates. If she kept eyeing

Sawyer like he was that yummy piece of coffee cake she kept smelling, they might think she wanted to eat him up.

The notion was so enticing, she wanted to crawl across the table and over to him so she could do just that.

Harley stifled a moan and forced herself to focus on the real reason she and her team were there—forging a working relationship with MI6.

She didn't know how long Sawyer and his team had been working together, but after his teammates' display when Jake partially shifted after they'd sat down, she could understand why he hadn't told them what he was. That must suck. Not to mention being exhausting as hell. While she wasn't a fan of using her abilities, at least she was on a team full of people who would be okay with it if she did.

Thankfully, none of her STAT teammates had spilled his secret.

"About a week ago, our analysts learned that an officer with the French National Police filed a report from a tourist who claimed to see several men dragging some people from a van into a tunnel near the river," Jake said. "The witness said he saw one of the victims toss his kidnapper ten feet through the air and into the side of a building."

Sawyer nodded. "I can see how that might get your attention."

"There's more." Jake leaned forward, resting his forearms on the table. "At the same time National Police were dealing with the kidnappings, they were also investigating the disappearance of two people from the club we were in last night. A few days later, they found both of those people floating in the river drained of blood. The medical examiner said they'd been stabbed, then dumped in the water where they bled out, but after running into that vampire last night, I think we all know that isn't what happened."

"You mean that thing with all the teeth Sawyer said he ran into," Erin said.

The redhead might be on the fence when it came to this whole supernatural thing, but it was obvious her interest was piqued when it came to the idea of vampires. She might not think the same after coming face-to-face with one of the things. Harley was going to have nightmares about the creature she and Sawyer ran into.

Jake nodded. "Yeah, that thing."

Sawyer looked at Harley. "Did you know that's what we were chasing when we went after it?"

"No," she said. "That was as much a surprise to me as it was to you. McKay mentioned they existed, but it's one thing to hear about a vampire and another to deal with one in real life. I completely blanked on what that thing was even when Jake shouted over the radio about how to kill it."

Harley left out the part about Jake being pissed at her afterward, saying how stupid it had been to go after that creature without any of her STAT teammates for backup. She couldn't say much in her defense, especially since she wasn't sure how to explain that she'd been completely comfortable with Sawyer—a man she'd never met before and didn't know anything about—watching her back.

"So how do you kill a vampire?" Elliott asked. Of Sawyer's teammates, he seemed the one most accepting of the possibility of them working together. Or maybe he was better at hiding his discomfort than the others. "Sawyer said he and Harley put at least eight bullets in the thing and it didn't slow down at all."

Jake snorted. "They could have shot him twenty more times and it still wouldn't have stopped him. The only way to kill a vampire is to take off their heads or rip out their hearts. Though trapping them in a building and burning it to the ground also works."

"If vampires are so tough to kill and they have all those damn teeth, why didn't that one go after Sawyer and Harley last night, instead of turning tail and running away?" Erin asked.

"Because werewolf blood is like acid to a vampire," Jake said, his gaze flicking to Sawyer. "The damn creatures are scared to death of getting our blood on them."

Sawyer seemed as intrigued by that as the rest of his MI6 team and Harley wondered if he was replaying the fight from last night. Was he thinking they might have been able to take down the vampire if they'd known that?

"Okay, so that's the deal with a vampire," Elliott said. "What about the guy who could make himself disappear? What do you know about him?"

Jake sighed. "Our intel people back in DC are digging through everything they have as well as talking to an expert on the subject of supernatural creatures, but so far, we've got nothing. I have no idea how we'll deal with him next time other than to suggest none of us go anywhere on our own. The guy is less likely to get the drop on you if there's someone watching your back."

Harley could vouch for that.

"What about MI6?" she asked, looking at each of them before settling on Sawyer. "How did you know about the trafficking ring?"

Erin and the other two British operatives looked at Sawyer, clearly waiting to see what their team leader would say. Harley got that. Management might want them to work together, but neither side wanted their closely guarded secrets getting out.

"We didn't," Sawyer said after a moment. "Three weeks ago, my team and I were in Mexico City chasing down a guy who broke into the MI6 classified records repository in Buckinghamshire. We were there to track him down and interrupt the information transfer with whoever hired him, then grab them both and get back what he took."

"Do you know what kind of information he stole?" Harley asked.

Sawyer shook his head. "No. The archives hold everything MI6 has ever written down, recorded, videotaped, or collected. It could have been anything from files related to ongoing operations, old case reports, financial documents, even personnel records for retired operatives."

Harley suddenly had a vision of the huge warehouse in *Raiders of the Lost Ark*, except MI6's was filled with mountains of paperwork.

"We followed our guy to the northern part of the city to what we assumed would be the site of the exchange, but when we got there, he was nowhere to be seen," Sawyer said. "We split up to search the area and a little while later, I found him and several other men trying to kidnap a woman. I ran toward them, and by the time I got there, the guy we'd been chasing was dead and the other men escaped with their captive, who just so happens to be the same woman we rescued last night."

Jake frowned. "What led you to the club?"

"Pure luck," Sawyer said. "We got a tip that a man fitting the description of one of the kidnappers had been spotted there."

From the way Sawyer glanced at his teammates, Harley got the feeling he was leaving a lot of the story out to keep from revealing he was a werewolf. Jake must have realized it, too, because he didn't press for details.

"If the guy who broke into the MI6 repository was working for the traffickers, why kill him?" Caleb asked.

"I don't think they did," Sawyer said. "I think the woman they kidnapped did."

Wait. What?

Harley glanced at her teammates to see that they looked as confused as she was.

"What makes you think that?" she asked.

"I was still a hundred meters away, so I couldn't see exactly what happened, but as they were dragging her toward their vehicle, there was a bright flash of light. It blinded me, and by the time I could see normally again, our suspect's body was smoldering on the ground."

That wasn't what Harley had expected. She'd assumed they'd struggled for a weapon and it had gone off. "Smoldering?"

Sawyer nodded. "Yeah. Like something—or someone—toasted him."

Jake shared a look with Jes. "You think the girl we rescued possesses the ability to burn someone?"

Sawyer opened his mouth to answer, but Erin spoke before he could.

"Not burned as much as fried. Like the guy'd been hit by lightning or touched a high-voltage electrical line. His skin was charred, but he also had lacerations like you'd see on someone after electricity from a bolt of lightning leaves the body."

Harley's mind was still spinning from that horrible image when the door of the conference room opened and Tessa Reynolds, one of the STAT agents with the support team, walked in with the kidnapping victim she and Sawyer had rescued last night. Petite with wavy, dark hair and soft-brown eyes, the woman was maybe twenty-three or twenty-four. She'd been unconscious since last night thanks to whatever drug the kidnappers had given her. Harley had been a little concerned she hadn't woken up yet and was relieved to see she was okay. Looking at her, it was difficult to picture the girl frying anyone with a bolt of electricity.

"This is Adriana Perez," Tessa said. "I told her a little bit about what happened last night at the club, but thought you could fill in the rest, Jake."

Harley's pack alpha nodded. "Thanks, Tessa."

Giving Adriana a reassuring smile, Tessa walked out of the conference room, leaving Jake to make the introductions. When he was done, he gestured to the empty seat on the other side of Harley.

Adriana hesitated, looking at each of them a little nervously before pulling out the chair and sitting down. "I can't thank you enough for what you did last night. If you hadn't been there, I can't even think what would have happened to me." She tucked her hair behind her ear, the pulse in her neck visibly fluttering. "I'm almost afraid to ask, but were you able to rescue my boyfriend, too?"

Harley exchanged looks with Sawyer, silently wondering if he'd left out the part about Adriana's significant other. As if reading her mind, he shook his head.

She turned back to Adriana. "Boyfriend?"

"Kristoff Neumann. We met while I was being held captive." Eyes pleading, Adriana reached out and took Harley's hand in both of hers. "He's tall and blond and has the most perfectly beautiful face you'd ever want to see. Please tell me you got him away from those evil people."

Anguish and hope poured off Adriana in waves, tugging at Harley's heartstrings. She could easily imagine how two people being held captive and fighting for survival could fall for each other. She wished like anything she could say they had rescued her boyfriend, but she couldn't lie.

"I'm sorry," she said softly. "You're the only one we were able to rescue. Whoever was holding you captive escaped with everyone else. They would have taken you, too, if I hadn't shot the guy with the ragged leather jacket who was carrying you."

Tears filled Adriana's eyes, her heart beating so fast Harley could feel the thrum of the girl's pulse through her palm. All at once, she began to hyperventilate. Harley opened her mouth to say something to calm her down, but the words caught in her throat as sparks suddenly shimmered and danced across Adriana's skin while her dark hair floated up in the worst case of static frizz in the history of the world.

Harley had half a second to hear Sawyer curse as he and everyone else at the table jumped to their feet right before a crackling sound snapped in the air. Body tingling like she'd stuck her finger in a light socket, Harley flew backward out of her chair and smacked into the wall with a thud.

Sawyer's fangs and claws slid out as he ran over to catch Harley before she tumbled to the floor. He knew he had to get his crap together and pull his fangs and claws back in before his teammates saw them and lost their bloody minds, but that was easier said than done as he gently lowered Harley to the carpet, her strong staccato heartbeat the only proof she wasn't dead. Her eyes fluttered open, a groan escaping her beautiful lips, and relief coursed through him.

"Are you okay?" he asked urgently. "Can you hear me? Say something if you can."

He felt more than saw someone drop to a knee at his side, but he was more than ready to ignore whoever it was. That was, until a big hand came down to settle over the top of his where he was holding Harley's shoulder. That was when Sawyer realized Jake was hiding his fully extended claws, protecting his secret.

Sawyer appreciated the gesture even as he cursed himself. He hadn't lost control in years, not since the first few months after the change. But seeing Harley flying through the air like that had set him off like nothing he'd ever experienced. Closing his eyes for a moment, he took a few deep breaths, forcing his claws and fangs to retract as everyone else in the room descended on them.

"Crap." Harley pushed herself up into a sitting position and looked down at her hands in confusion. "What the hell was that? My body feels like I took a bath in novocaine."

"I'm so sorry!" A panicked Adriana was suddenly on her knees at Sawyer's side, tears running down her face. "I didn't mean to do that. It was an accident."

Sawyer's inner wolf went on alert again as Adriana reached for Harley's hand and he had to clench his own into fists to keep himself from stopping her. What the hell was wrong with him? Fortunately, everyone else was focused on Harley and Adriana, completely unaware of his internal struggle to keep his crap together. It was easier to do when Adriana pulled her hands back, like she knew she shouldn't touch anyone.

"What happened?" Harley asked Adriana. "I was holding your hands, and the next thing I know, I'm on my butt."

Adriana flushed, looking contrite. "Sometimes when I get nervous or scared, I lose control and zap people. When you said you shot the guy in the leather jacket, I lost it. I...I guess I was afraid the people who kidnapped me might get angry at what you did to one of their own and take it out on Kristoff."

"Do you think you can stand up?" Sawyer asked her.

Harley nodded, taking the hand he offered and letting him help her back to her chair. Sawyer ignored the questioning glance Erin threw his way. Instead, he held out the other chair for Adriana, gesturing for her to sit. She stood where she was, arms wrapped around her middle, eyes darting toward the door like she wanted to bolt.

"Relax," he told her. "Harley's okay and we all know you didn't intend to hurt anyone."

"I know," she said. "It's just that I keep thinking about Kristoff and..." Her voice trailed off, her eyes glistening with tears again.

"Harley only shot the guy with the leather jacket in the leg," he explained. "I honestly doubt the kidnappers will hurt your boyfriend as a way to get back at us. He wasn't even there when it happened."

Adriana chewed on her lip as she considered that, then nodded. Sawyer wasn't sure she believed him, but at least she sat down beside Harley again.

"How long have you been able to do this thing with the electricity?" Sawyer asked, taking his own seat again.

She didn't answer right away, and when she finally spoke, her voice was soft. "It started when I was fourteen. At first, it was only little sparks when I got excited. Like when you walk across the carpet and touch a doorknob. It was a joke with my family at first, but it got progressively stronger as I got older. If I got scared, nervous, or something startled me, the electricity would come out.

My family helped me hide it as much as they could, and over time, I got better at controlling it. But I still messed up and hurt people I never wanted to hurt. That was when I realized I couldn't stay with my family anymore. I left my home in Taxco, thinking I could disappear in a place as big and crowded as Mexico City, and for more than two years, it seemed to work. Then it didn't."

"What happened?" Sawyer asked.

"A woman showed up at my apartment claiming that a man in Europe wanted to hire me." Adriana looked down at her hands clasped in her lap. "I immediately knew there was something wrong because I never applied for a job in Europe. She said the man was aware of my special abilities and would pay me an insane amount of money if I worked for him. When I said I didn't want the job or to use my abilities, she took out a phone and told whoever she called that I was resistant and she needed help. I freaked out and ran."

Sawyer heard the girl's heart beating a mile a minute and knew she was reliving that moment. He was all too familiar with the adrenaline surge that came with memories like that when the fear and anxiety made it feel like you were right back in the thick of it.

Adriana took a deep breath, a frown creasing her forehead. "I thought for sure I'd escaped, but a man caught up with me before I got more than a couple blocks from my place. He just kind of showed up out of nowhere right in front of me. I tried to fight, but another guy came to help and they both dragged me toward a van. I was more terrified than I've ever been in my life and I completely lost it. The electricity inside me kept building until I thought it might tear me apart. When I zapped the men, the flare of light was so bright it blinded me and I collapsed."

"What's the next thing you remember?" Harley asked.

The girl lifted her head to look at them. "Waking up in a dingy room. I didn't know where I was or how long I was out of it. My head was spinning so much I could barely stand up. At first, I thought I'd hurt myself from channeling all that power, but the man guarding my cell told me they'd drugged me. He said that since I hadn't wanted to do it the easy way, they would do it the hard way."

"How long were you held there?" Sawyer prompted when she paused, lost in thought again.

She shrugged. "Maybe a day. They drugged me regularly and everything was sort of a blur after that. I vaguely remember riding in a few trucks, but there were some long plane rides, too, and an endless procession of dark holding rooms. A week ago, they brought me to the club where you found me last night. I didn't even know I was in Paris until Tessa mentioned it this morning."

"How did you meet Kristoff?" Harley asked.

Adriana's lips curved, her dark eyes dancing a little with happiness. "On the plane from Mexico City. He was amazing. He made sure the guards gave me something to eat and drink and even got them to leave me alone so I could wash up in privacy. I don't think I would have made it without Kristoff. He was like my guardian angel."

Sawyer hoped for her sake they could rescue her boyfriend along with all the other captives. "What about the other prisoners? Were they with you from the beginning like Kristoff, or were they here in Paris when you arrived? Did you get a chance to talk to any of them and learn why they'd been kidnapped?"

"We picked up two of them on one of the stops between flights," she said slowly, as if she was trying to remember. "The rest were already here. They were kidnapped because they're all like me."

Sawyer froze along with Harley and everyone else in the room. It was Jake who finally shook off the shock first and asked the question that was on the tip of Sawyer's tongue.

"You mean all the other captives can control electricity like you?" the alpha werewolf asked hesitantly, like he was trying to work through the implications of what she'd told them.

Adriana shook her head. "No, they aren't like me in that way. None of them can control electricity. But they all have special abilities. One girl could hear what a person was thinking if she touched them. Another one could start fires with her mind. An older man from Serbia not much bigger than I am was so strong he could bend the metal bars of his cell. Well, he could if he wasn't drugged. The guards took him and the mind reader away earlier in the week. Most of the other captives wouldn't talk about what they could do because they were too scared someone would use the information against them, but I'm certain every one of them was special in some way."

"Do you know where they took the strong man and the mind reader or what they did with them?" Harley asked, concern etched on her face.

Sawyer didn't have to try that hard to know what Harley was thinking. Like him, she was probably worried whoever had kidnapped them had killed them.

"I'm not sure where they took them," Adriana said. "I overheard the guards talking about a lot of different cities, but I'm not sure if that was where they were heading or where they'd come from. But I heard enough to know they were planning to sell the people. They mentioned an auction where rich people go to buy oddities."

Sawyer thought he was ready for anything, but he'd been wrong. Bloody hell. There was someone out there collecting supernaturals and putting them up for auction. He suddenly wondered if any of the people they'd kidnapped had been a werewolf. What would a collector of human oddities pay for a werewolf? It was too insane to even think about.

"The guards told me that I'd end up on the auction block, too, if I didn't fall in line and take the job the woman had offered me," Adriana added. "The way they said it made it obvious the auction wasn't a place I wanted to be."

"Adriana, you said you overheard the guards talking a lot, right?" Harley asked.

The girl nodded.

"Would you be willing to sit down with Tessa and our other intel analysts to go over what you remember from your captivity? It's possible you know more about what they're up to than you realize."

"Of course," Adriana said. "I'll talk to anyone you need me to for as long as you need me to. But only if you promise I can go with you when you rescue the other captives, so I can help get Kristoff back."

On the other side of the table, Jake gave Sawyer a questioning look. Sawyer wasn't sure taking Adriana with them was a good idea, but they needed information. And if he was being honest, he wouldn't mind having someone with her abilities along on this mission, either. He nodded at Jake.

A moment later, everyone but Caleb left the room, eager to finally get some sleep. The big werewolf looked at Harley questioningly.

"I'm going to hang around downstairs for a little bit," she told him. "I'll see you later."

Caleb hesitated, his blue eyes darting to Sawyer, his expression unreadable. Mouth tight, he gave Harley a nod, then walked out, leaving her and Sawyer alone. Now that they were by themselves, the raspberry-and-cream scent was even more powerful, not to mention definitely mouthwatering.

"You aren't tired?" he asked, walking around to where she stood on the other side of the table.

She smiled, tilting her head to the side a little to look up at him. "I am a little, but I'm also hungry, and I can't sleep on an empty stomach. Besides, I'm in Paris with a few hours to spare, which means I can get to sightsee before we go after the bad guys."

Sawyer returned her grin. "You want to catch a few of those sights together, then have dinner?"

Harley's smile broadened, her blue-gray eyes twinkling. "I'd like that."

It was scary how happy that simple answer made Sawyer.

CHAPTER 4

"You realize there's no way we can see the Louvre, Notre-Dame, the Eiffel Tower, walk the Champs-Élysées and still have time to get something to eat, right?" Sawyer asked in that sinfully perfect accent of his as they strolled toward the Seine River. Behind them, the late-afternoon sun bathed everything in soft light. "You're probably going to need to trim down your wish list and focus on where we can go on foot."

Harley groaned in despair but knew Sawyer was right. As much as she might want to spend the rest of the day exploring the city, they weren't going to have time. The truth was, Jake could call any minute to say they were on the move. She didn't want to waste time riding a bus or taking a train to get to one of the farthest tourist sites and end up missing everything.

"What do you think we have time to see?" she asked.

"Well, we could cross the river and walk along the south side until we get to the Eiffel Tower, then hang out there for a while before following the river to the Pont Alexandre," he suggested. "From there, we can take the bridge across the river to the Champs-Élysées and pick a restaurant we like."

There was no way Sawyer could know it, but that was the perfect itinerary. The Eiffel Tower was number one on her must-see list, and it was hard to go wrong with any tour that included the shops along the Champs-Élysées. She'd never admit it, but she had a serious thing for designer shoes. She didn't actually own any because there was no way she'd ever pay that much money for a pair you couldn't run in or wear in the snow, but it was still fun to look. And where better to window-shop for shoes than Paris?

"Sounds good to me," she said with a smile.

The stroll along the river was absolutely breathtaking. Not only was the weather perfect, but there was also something awe inspiring about walking past buildings and bridges that were older than a lot of countries in the world, including the U.S. Harley could practically feel the history under her feet.

When the elegant-looking bridge, Pont de Grenelle, came into view with its copy of the iconic Statue of Liberty, they both pulled out their phones to snap some pictures. Harley almost laughed, thinking how completely normal they appeared. Like they were simply two tourists out seeing the sights. Except they were about as far from normal as anybody could get. Then again, given everything Adriana had told them, maybe there were a lot more people in the world who were *far from normal* than anyone had ever thought. Maybe she and Sawyer weren't so different from everyone else after all.

Harley looked around at the people they passed. The laughing teenagers, the young man with his pastels and easel painting a bridge called Pont de Bir-Hakeim with the Eiffel Tower in the background, the old couple holding hands and smiling. How many of them were *special*?

"Do you think any of these people are like us?" she asked Sawyer when they stopped to take in Île aux Cygnes, the man-made island in the middle of the river. Lined with trees, the walkway with its many benches looked perfect for whiling away the hours.

Sawyer didn't say anything at first, his attention fixed on the people moving along the narrow island a few hundred feet away. He wore the same long overcoat he had last night, and damn if it didn't look good on him. When he finally turned to her, his expression was curious. "Are you asking if there are any werewolves around? The answer is no. We'd be able to smell them."

Harley almost snorted. Sawyer might be able to smell them, but she doubted she ever would. She might have been able to pick up a fellow werewolf's scent in the confined space of the club last night, like she'd done with him, but out in the open like this, with the breeze swirling around all over the place? Not a chance.

Although, oddly enough, she could still pick up that same delicious scent of cinnamon coffee cake she'd smelled in the conference room. Her nose really was freaky.

"What if they aren't werewolves?" she pressed. "What if they're special like Adriana? Would we smell them then?"

He regarded her thoughtfully. "Adriana has a specific scent like any other human, but she definitely smells human."

"What about Misty?" she prompted. "Does she have a distinctive scent?"

Misty smelled human to Harley, but that didn't mean much of anything.

"Should she?" Damn, Sawyer's accent even made confused sound sexy. "Is she special like Adriana?"

Harley nodded, wondering if she should be outing Misty's hypercool ability. "She can communicate with computers and other kinds of electronic devices. Like a Vulcan mind meld, except with an inanimate object."

She thought Sawyer would be as surprised as she was when Misty had first demonstrated her talent, but he merely lifted a brow. "That's useful." His mouth twitched. "Although I have to admit, I'm more of a *Doctor Who* than a *Star Trek* fan. But for the record, Misty smells human, too."

Harley considered that as she eyed the tourists and they started walking again. "So we could be surrounded by people like Adriana, Misty, or even that jerk with the knife."

The memory of the guy who could disappear and reappear at will made her wonder how worried they should be about that.

Sawyer didn't seem concerned, though. "We could be, but I'd like to think our werewolf instincts would tell us if any of them were dangerous."

Up ahead, the Eiffel Tower came into view as they moved past the bridge. Even from this distance, the structure was something to behold.

Harley let out a little snort. "You have a lot more faith in your wolf talents than I do. I was lucky to figure out the vampire was bad news and that was only because I saw all those teeth."

"It can be tricky when you're new to the whole werewolf thing," Sawyer said as they paused across the street from the Eiffel Tower. They both had to crane their necks to see all the way to the top, but it was worth it. Up close, it was truly spectacular. "I know my instincts got better over time. How long has it been since you went through your change?"

Harley doubted that was the issue, and even though she knew the exact date she'd turned, she did the math in her head anyway for the hell of it. "Eight years. I was twenty when I turned."

When Sawyer didn't say anything, Harley looked away from the gorgeous gigantic tower in front of her to see him standing there looking a little uncomfortable. It wasn't hard to figure out why.

"Let me guess," she said drily. "You've been a werewolf for less than that, right?"

"Yeah." He gave her a sheepish smile. "I turned four years ago. But I don't know much about our kind, so maybe it's less about time and more about experiences. Being part of MI6, I kind of had to figure out how to make this thing work for me—fast."

Considering she'd spent the vast majority of her time as a were-wolf completely ignoring that part of herself, she imagined Sawyer was probably right, though she doubted if he'd understand. Not wanting to talk about the reasons behind why she never tried to tap into her inner werewolf, she turned and took a few pictures of the Eiffel Tower. Harley had to fight the urge to talk Sawyer into joining the ridiculously long line of people waiting to climb the steps to the top for a view of the city. But the wait was probably two or three hours. They didn't have the time.

Reluctantly turning away from one of the places she'd wanted to visit her whole life, she fell into step beside Sawyer as they began walking again.

"How far is it to the Pont Alexandre?" she asked, praying Sawyer didn't start asking questions she wasn't ready to answer as they made their way to the bridge. She might trust Sawyer with her life, but she wasn't ready to share all her secrets. Not when she refused to even discuss most of them with herself.

"About a mile," he murmured. "Probably less than twenty minutes."

Harley wasn't so sure about that, considering how much stuff there'd be to look at along the way, but she didn't bother pointing that out. She followed the sidewalk as it began to veer to the right, figuring she'd walk faster when there wasn't as much to see in this area. That would give her extra time for the good stuff.

They mostly talked about the sights as they walked and it quickly became apparent Sawyer knew a lot more about Paris than she did. That only made sense considering he lived across the channel. When they weren't discussing the buildings, scenery, or passing people, the main topic of interest was Adriana and her story about the supernatural auction. No matter how many times Harley thought they were done with the subject, she found her mind coming back to it. She couldn't understand why a group of supernaturals would do something like this to others of their kind. Wasn't it bad enough they had to worry about being grabbed up by the torch and pitchfork crowd? To have to look over their shoulders for other supernaturals coming after them was all kinds of wrong.

"Do you think there's any chance the kidnappers could have gotten their hands on a werewolf?" she asked.

She wasn't sure why that thought terrified her more than the idea of someone like Adriana being grabbed. But for some reason, it did.

"I'd like to think it'd be impossible to catch a werewolf by surprise," he said as they made their way across the ornate Pont Alexandre that spanned the Seine River, to the Champs-Élysées beyond it. "But considering they have other supernaturals working for them, like that guy who can disappear and reappear at will, it'd be silly to think we wouldn't be as vulnerable as anyone else."

That wasn't very reassuring.

It was dark by the time they reached the heart of the shopping and entertainment area along the crowded street. The beautiful store windows helped distract her from thoughts of the supernatural auction and the people who ran it. She and Sawyer wandered into several of the stores, and although everything was way too expensive for her to afford, it was fun anyway. Thankfully, Sawyer didn't look at her like she'd lost her mind when she spent a crazy amount of time *oohing* and *aahing* over a particular pair of Jimmy Choo strappy sandals so gorgeous she almost cried. In fact, he seemed to enjoy how happy something as simple as a pair of shoes made her.

When the thrill of window-shopping started to wear off, they found a quaint restaurant that was perfect for an early evening dinner. But then she got a look at the prices on the leather-bound menu displayed on a stand outside the place and thought maybe they should go to the McDonald's down the street. A salad cost as much as she normally paid for an entire dinner at the places she usually went.

"Look at these prices," she said.

Sawyer chuckled. "Come on. How often are you going to get a chance to eat at a fancy French restaurant in Paris? Besides, I'm paying, so you don't have to feel bad about spending so much money."

Harley opened her mouth to say he didn't have to do that, but Sawyer was already holding open the door for her. Deciding she could tell him after they were seated, she walked into the restaurant. And stared. Between the elegant tables with their fancy, folded cloth napkins, satin curtains on the picture-perfect windows, and the delicate chandeliers, Harley felt like they'd stepped into a fairy tale.

The hostess led them to one of the small dining rooms that made up the building's first floor. Only big enough to accommodate six intimate tables, the walls were covered in rich wood wainscoting and paintings straight out of the Renaissance. Best of all, there were no other people seated in there. Knowing she'd have Sawyer all to herself was inexplicably satisfying.

Harley was surprised when Sawyer pulled her chair out for her as they sat down. She definitely didn't have a problem with chivalry but didn't have a lot of experience with it. She hadn't gone on a lot of dates since becoming a werewolf.

Not that this was a date, she reminded herself. They were simply two werewolves having dinner. At the same table. Together. That's all.

Their server, a tall, thin guy with dark hair, appeared at the table the moment they were seated to describe some of his favorite dishes on the menu. Everything he recommended sounded delicious, but truthfully, as an alpha werewolf who hadn't eaten anything substantial in the past twenty-four hours, she yearned for something with lots and lots of protein. Sawyer must have felt the same because they both ended up ordering the same thing—beef fillet with pepper sauce, thin-cut french fries, spinach with cheesy Mornay sauce, a Caesar salad on the side, and crème brûlée for dessert. Harley refused to do the math to figure out how much all of that was going to cost. Like Sawyer had said, it was a once-in-a-lifetime thing.

When the server told them he'd bring back the perfect red wine to accompany their meal, Harley decided she'd have to take his word for that, since she knew less about wine than she did about being a werewolf. After the man poured it into their glasses and waited while they tasted it, she had to admit the fruity wine was delicious.

"I'm sorry about your friend," she said to Sawyer as the server left. At his questioning look, she added, "I overheard Weatherford talking to you and your team before we left the hotel."

She hadn't been eavesdropping, but she was a werewolf, so hearing other people's conversations without meaning to came with the territory. Sawyer's boss had been outside the conference room with the rest of the team when they'd walked out and said he needed to speak to Sawyer, so she'd wandered down to the far end of the hallway to wait for him.

Sawyer nodded, his blue eyes clouding. "Thanks. Silas was a good man."

According to Weatherford, Sawyer's former teammate, Silas Thompson, was killed early that morning while on a mission. MI6 didn't have many details yet and sounded like they were still trying to figure out what happened. All they knew for sure was that someone slit his throat. Sawyer and his team had all seemed to take the news hard.

"Something tells me this isn't the first time work has brought you to Paris," she said, partly because she was genuinely curious, but also because she felt badly for reminding Sawyer about his fallen teammate.

As Sawyer shook his head, Harley couldn't help but notice once again how handsome he was. Who knew she had a thing for British guys? Or was she so attracted to him because he was a werewolf?

"I've been here half a dozen times or more with my team, but this is the first time I've ever gone out to see the sights," he said. "The missions we go on are all about getting in and getting out. I've traveled all around the world and seen almost none of it."

Harley grimaced. "That sounds downright depressing."

Sawyer shrugged his broad shoulders. "Can't disagree with you there. I love my job and being with my team makes everything worthwhile, but sometimes, it seems like I'm missing something."

She understood that. The need to find whatever was missing from her life was the reason she'd taken McKay up on his offer to join STAT after she'd spent most of her time avoiding hanging around anyone for more than a couple weeks.

"Maybe you simply need a vacation," she suggested.

"Vacation?" He let out a husky laugh. "What's that?"

She smiled at him over the rim of her wineglass. "I hear ya. I haven't worked for STAT long enough to even earn any vacation time yet. Check back when I do and I'll let you know if I'm the vacation type."

Their server showed up to prepare their Caesar salad table side, then left, but not before placing a basket of crunchy, freshly baked bread. Harley had to fight the urge to moan at the first taste of tangy dressing that covered the assortment of greens. She'd had Caesar salad many times, but this was the best she'd ever eaten.

"You've only worked for STAT a little while, yet you've been a werewolf for eight years?" Sawyer asked after most of his salad was gone and he'd slowed his pace a little. "How did that happen?"

Harley tried to keep her fork moving so Sawyer wouldn't realize she was floundering for something to say. Well, something to say that wouldn't reveal how totally screwed up her life had been the past eight years.

"It's…complicated."

"Complicated stories are the best kind." The corners of his mouth tipped up a little before he sipped his wine. "But for the sake of conversation, let's start with something simple. How did you become a werewolf?"

Every trace of air left her lungs and she felt a tingle in her gums and fingertips as her aforementioned inner werewolf tried to make an appearance. But that was silly. That stuff didn't happen to her. She'd never been able to shift into her wolf form, partially or otherwise.

Thankfully, their server interrupted before she could say anything. He smiled when he saw they'd both demolished their salads and the basket of bread. Taking the plates away, he used one of those fancy metal spatula things to scrape up the crumbs from the linen tablecloth, then two assistants swooped in with their main course, the steaks still sizzling and the aromas savory enough to make even Harley's nose sit up and beg. The slim fries looked mouthwatering and she barely stopped herself from asking for a bottle of ketchup before their server left. They probably didn't have ketchup in a place like this.

Harley focused on her dinner, hoping Sawyer would forget what they'd been talking about. Perfectly cooked, the spicy beef melted in her mouth. When she finally glanced up, it was to see him regarding her with a raised eyebrow, and she knew she was out of luck.

"Well?" he prompted when she still didn't say anything.

"Isn't asking how I became a werewolf kind of personal?" She speared another piece of beef with her fork. "It's like asking a woman how old she is."

"It can't be that personal since you had no problem revealing your age at the drop of a hat earlier," Sawyer countered in that devastating accent of his, humor filling his tone.

She picked up a well-seasoned french fry and nibbled on it. *Mmm.* French fries in France really did taste better. "If it isn't a big deal, why don't you go first and tell me how you became a werewolf?"

He chuckled. "Seriously? That's how this is going to go? You'll show me yours if I show you mine?"

She laughed, unable to help herself. Just like that, she relaxed.

"I'd already been working covert operations with the British SAS for six years when MI6 approached me." He cut into his fillet and casually chewed the first bite. Werewolves had sharp teeth, even in fully human form, and the morsel disappeared quickly. "It wasn't that big of a career change, and who wouldn't want to be an agent for MI6? I jumped at the offer."

"How long did you work for them before going through your change?" she asked, taking a bite of her own steak.

Going through the change was the safe phrase werewolves used to describe going through the incredibly horrible event that would kill a normal person, but in their cases, it flipped the switch on a gene and turned them into something totally different.

His mouth edged up. "If you don't count the training, barely two months. I was with my team in Odessa on what was supposed to be a minor surveillance job. We thought there'd be a low probability of hostile contact because our intel said they were a group of wannabe terrorists, led by some Ukrainian oil magnate named Yegor Shevchenko. This guy and his brother were pissed off about something and were looking to buy weapons to stage their first attack.

"Erin, Rory, and Elliott had all been with the team for a year or two and Weatherford was the team leader. I was the new guy," Sawyer continued. "Our job was simply to monitor the situation and determine how serious the threat might become in the future. We weren't even there to stop the weapon exchange—just observe and report. It should have been a cakewalk."

"I'm guessing things didn't go as planned?" Harley asked.

Sawyer shoved a few fries into his mouth and shook his head. "Do they ever? But you're right. It went wrong—fast. Somehow, Shevchenko figured out we were onto him and turned the tables on us. They hit us the moment we walked into the compound outside our safe house. There were eight of us, but most weren't armed at the time. Let's just say it was…bad."

"You were shot?" Harley murmured softly, her stomach strangely tense at the thought of Sawyer being hurt. Which was crazy, considering she'd seen half her STAT teammates shot up already and barely noticed it. Hell, Jake had a tree branch shoved through his chest and she hadn't batted an eye.

"Shot?" The question earned her a soft snort from him. "That's an understatement. I was the first one hit by automatic weapon fire coming from the walkway overlooking the courtyard of the safe house. I probably should have died on the spot."

Harley stopped even trying to go through the motions of

eating, her whole body frozen solid as she pictured Sawyer lying broken and bleeding on the ground. The image made it hard to breathe.

"I was in so much pain, I could barely comprehend what was happening around me," he said quietly. "All I knew for sure was that I was going to die and my team was going to be wiped out. I'd only been with them for two months, but they were important to me. And while I probably should have been completely freaked out about dying, I was more worried about them."

She sat there silently, waiting for him to continue, part of her wanting to beg him not to even as the other part needed to know the rest.

"I had no idea what I was hoping to accomplish," he said, the distant expression on his face making her think he was reliving every moment of that time. "I shoved myself off the ground and ran toward the nearest target, figuring if I could take down even one of them, it might give the other members of my team a chance to survive."

He paused to take another bite of steak and though she didn't have much of an appetite anymore, Harley forced herself to do the same.

"I ended up taking down Yegor and caught another round in the hip for my trouble," Sawyer said, focusing on his plate. "I ignored the pain and headed for the next terrorist. I knew I was a goner, so I might as well go out swinging."

More silence followed and Harley wished she'd never asked Sawyer anything like this.

"Everything is sort of a blur after that," he added. "I remember getting the one on the walkway with the machine gun who'd shot me at the start of the ambush—it was Yegor's brother, Illya—then kept going until I took out all of them."

Harley held her breath, hoping the story had a good ending buried in there somewhere.

Sawyer speared another piece of steak. "Well, Yegor ended up surviving, at least long enough to get shipped off to a Turkish prison. The rest of them, including Illya, all died."

"And you became a werewolf."

He nodded. "I didn't know that at the time, of course. I laid there on the ground, trying to figure out how the hell I was still alive after all that. It wasn't until about a month or so later when I started going crazy with the change that I realized what had happened. But you know all about that part of it."

Yeah, Harley definitely remembered that part. Remembered how her body seemed constantly out of control, claws and fangs showing up at random times, anger bubbling out of control, senses going haywire. At the time, she'd been sure she was going insane, that she was hallucinating everything. And that was without having to deal with the trauma of getting shot like Sawyer had.

"How did you keep everything secret from your team and the rest of MI6?" she asked, forcing herself to go back to eating, trying to catch up to Sawyer, who was almost finished. "I mean, aren't spies supposed to be suspicious by nature? Didn't anyone think it was strange you survived getting shot that many times? Not to mention running around fighting in that condition?"

He gave her a small smile. "In the bedlam of the ambush, no one noticed how badly I'd been shot. They knew I'd been hit, but they were too busy trying to stay alive themselves to look too closely."

She was about to ask how that was even possible but stopped at the look on his face. He was lost in his memories of those moments once again.

"Silas Thompson was the one who picked me up and got me to the nearest hospital," he said slowly, his tone anguished. "He didn't want to leave me there on my own, but he didn't have a choice. It's MI6 protocol in a situation like that. Less chance of the team being compromised if they scatter. I stayed there while Weatherford got the rest of the team out of the country, so none of them were there to see all the damage when the doctors got around to stripping my clothes off."

Harley couldn't imagine what that must have been like for him. To go through something like that alone was beyond awful.

"I still can't believe they left you," she said.

If something like that happened to her or anyone else in STAT, there was no way she or her teammates would ever bail on each other. But maybe that was because they were more than a team. They were a pack. And that included the humans.

"It's not that they wanted to," he said. "But if they'd stayed, there's a good chance local law enforcement—or worse, some foreign covert organization—would have picked them up. It was safer for me to be a John Doe than to have my teammates hanging around."

Harley wasn't sure she believed that. She'd want to be with her teammate if one of them was badly hurt. "Didn't the doctors realize there was something strange going on once they saw how badly you'd been wounded? The extent of the injuries and the amount of blood you lost must have made it into your medical records."

He shrugged. "I suppose so. When the extraction team came a few days later to get me, they snagged my medical records too, and by then, my injuries didn't look nearly as bad. I was still beat up when I got back to London, but it wasn't bad enough to suggest how close I'd come to dying. And it wasn't like I was going to bring it up. MI6 put me on six weeks of medical leave to heal up, so there wasn't anyone around to see me going through the worst of the change. By the time I went back to work, I was in control of my abilities. I almost died ten times over and got turned into a werewolf because I have the gene and no one even noticed."

She frowned at that. "No one on your team noticed you saved their lives in Odessa?"

"I wouldn't go that far," he said with a soft laugh. Harley was amazed at how the sound lightened the weight that had been bearing down on her chest. "In between ducking and diving, they noticed my heroics. By the time I got back from medical leave, I had a reputation of sorts thanks to the stories Erin, Rory, and Elliott told. According to them, I was fearless, driven, selfless, etc. Most of it was complete rubbish, but Weatherford insisted the entire team would have been wiped out if not for me. It ended his field career but got me noticed by upper levels of management. They offered me my own team and anyone in MI6 I wanted. Silas was senior enough to get his own team, and Sarah Parker and Cedric Abbot got out of MI6. I heard though the grapevine that they'd ended up with new identities and got married. The rest, as they say, is history." His mouth curved into a sexy smile. "And now here I am having dinner with a beautiful werewolf in Paris and waiting to hear her story."

Harley was saved from having to reply right away by their server's arrival once again. This time, he had their crème brûlée and coffee. She immediately dug into the rich custard with its expertly caramelized top, thinking about what Sawyer had told her. The events that had led to his change had been drastically different than her own, but what struck her the most was how different his life had been after going through the change compared to hers. Other than the fact that he had to hide his werewolf identity from his teammates, he'd clearly embraced his animal nature. Harley couldn't help but compare that to her own situation. While she didn't have to hide what she was from her team, she didn't feel comfortable embracing her talents at all.

Harley could feel Sawyer's gaze on her as they ate dessert and she knew he was giving her time to tell her story. The only problem was, she didn't have any idea how to start. While her change hadn't been nearly as traumatic as Sawyer's, it was still difficult to talk about it. Hell, thinking about it made her stomach churn. But when her spoon scrapped the bottom of the ramekin and she still didn't know what to say, she accepted she was in trouble.

Then her phone rang. She was so happy to be interrupted.

"It's Jake," her alpha said when she answered. "You and Sawyer need to get back to the hotel ASAP. We leave Paris in an hour."

On the other side of the table, Sawyer caught the server's attention and motioned for the check. Obviously, the British werewolf had easily heard what Jake said.

"Where are we going?" she asked Jake.

"Morocco. Our analysts spent the past few hours going over every second of Adriana's captivity and believe there's another holding cell in Casablanca. They aren't sure if that's where the auction is supposed to take place or if the kidnappers took the captives they were holding here in Paris, but it's all we have right now."

Sawyer was signing the bill as Harley hung up. A quick glance at the bottom line of the receipt showed her that dinner for the two of them had cost about as much as a week of groceries. Yikes!

"I hope you don't think I'm letting you off the hook when it comes to telling me your story," Sawyer said, coming over to slide her chair out. "You know that, right?"

Harley didn't say anything at first, too floored by the gentlemanly gesture to get anything out. By the time she got her act together, they were already passing the hostess stand and heading for the door.

"Yeah, I know," she said, her stomach clenching once again at the thought of spilling her secrets. "Maybe by the time we find a place where I can repay you for that delicious meal by buying you dinner, I'll have gotten the courage."

"Works for me." Sawyer flashed her a devastating smile. "I'm a patient man."

"So, are we really gonna do this?" Caleb asked, dropping his overnight bag on the floor of Jake's hotel room and flopping back on the couch.

Harley sighed as she set her bag down beside Caleb's. She'd only finished packing a few minutes ago and had met up with him in the hall on the way to Jake's room, so they could wait with the rest of her team for the van that would take them to the airport. It was a carbon copy of hers, right down to the huge bed, period furniture, and ornate crown molding.

She and Sawyer had to practically jog back to the hotel from the restaurant to make it in time. The moment they'd gotten there, she'd immediately run up to her room, where she'd packed in record time. Thanks to spending the past eight years constantly on the move, that wasn't much of a problem. She'd learned long ago to travel light.

"Do what?" Jes asked from where she sat on the bed beside Jake.

Caleb scowled. "Work with MI6."

No one said anything. While the atmosphere in the room wasn't exactly tense, it wasn't the usual chill feel she'd become used to. They might only have started working together a few months ago, but she and her teammates were already as close as family. Harley supposed almost dying on their first mission could do that. But now, McKay was shaking up the whole dynamic by having them work with Sawyer and his team. After hanging out with Sawyer for a few hours, she was okay with that—and not simply because he was devastatingly handsome and easy to talk to. But it was obvious the rest of her friends weren't necessarily on board with the idea yet.

"It's either that or end up working against them," Jake said. "McKay feels these traffickers are a serious threat and wants us to stop them. And while I'm not crazy about working with people who don't think much of werewolves, it'll be easier if we team up with MI6 on this, since we're both on the same side."

"People who don't think much of werewolves?" From where he sat at the small table with Misty, Forrest snorted in obvious disgust.

"Their first instinct was to pull a gun on you guys the moment they saw you shift. I'm with Caleb. I'd rather go after the traffickers on our own than work with people we can't trust to have our backs."

"For what it's worth, I had dinner with Sawyer after the briefing and I feel comfortable saying we can trust him," Harley offered.

Caleb rested the edge of his boot on the coffee table. "That doesn't make me feel all warm and fuzzy considering he doesn't even trust his own team enough to tell them he's a werewolf."

"Can you blame him?" Harley countered. "Admitting you're a werewolf isn't easy, you know."

Caleb only grunted.

"Hiding what he is from his teammates has to suck," Misty said.

Jes looked thoughtful as she considered that. "How do you even hide something like that in our line of work and not slip up?"

Since Harley hadn't ever been in this line of work before, she wasn't sure how to answer that. Keeping her inner werewolf hidden had been challenging enough in the world she'd come from.

"I spent years as a cop in Santa Fe before joining STAT, and none of my beat partners ever had a clue." Jake shrugged. "If you try hard, it can be easy to keep people in the dark. Especially when most of them will ignore what they see because it seems too crazy to believe. It's easier to assume they didn't see what they thought they did than entertain the possibility that the world is a lot more complicated than they realized."

Or you simply did what Harley did. She didn't bother to point out it was a lot easier to hide in plain sight if you never used any of your more obvious werewolf attributes.

"Well, if we're going to work with MI6, I guess that means we're going to have to keep Sawyer's werewolf side a secret," Forrest said. "Question is, do we tell McKay about him?"

Even though Harley had just met him, she felt an incredibly crazy urge to stand up for Sawyer. But before she could say anything, Jake spoke.

"We aren't outing another werewolf. If Sawyer wants to keep his inner werewolf hidden, that's his business, meaning we're not mentioning it to McKay and I'm not putting it in any of the reports unless it becomes impossible to hide."

Harley sagged in relief. STAT and MI6 were only working together on this one mission, and then they'd probably never come across each other again, but at least Sawyer's secret would be safe.

Jake's phone dinged and he pulled it from his pocket. "Our ride to the airport is downstairs. The MI6 team is already in the van waiting for us."

As everyone grabbed their bags and headed for the door, Caleb caught Harley's arm, motioning for her to wait.

"I know you said you trust Sawyer and that's your call," he said softly after their teammates had moved down the hallway. "But this is me reminding you to be careful."

She barely had a chance to look baffled before Caleb continued.

"Look, I'm not trying to say there's some reason to distrust the guy. It's just that I don't want you, or any of our pack, getting hurt because Sawyer is more worried about protecting his secret than watching our backs. Okay?"

Caleb was out the door before she could say anything, calling for the others to hold the elevator and leaving Harley with no choice but to hitch her bag higher over her shoulder and hurry after him.

Was Caleb right? If push came to shove, would Sawyer go that extra step to protect Harley and her teammates even if it meant revealing he was a werewolf? She wanted to believe he would, but could she honestly say she knew him well enough to know the answer to that question?

CHAPTER 5

Morocco

"I COULDN'T HELP BUT NOTICE YOU AND THAT FEMALE werewolf seem to have gotten pretty chummy," Erin said from behind Sawyer, the barest hint of something suspicious and disapproving in the words.

Sawyer looked up from the photos he'd been scanning on and off for the past two days. They were shots taken from all over the city of buildings, vehicles, and people he and everyone else had pored over with agonizing intensity in the hopes of finding anything that might tip them off to the location of the supernatural trafficking ring in Casablanca. It was mind-numbing work, but it had to be done. Adriana had led them there. It was up to the joint MI6/STAT team to do the rest.

He swiveled his chair around to see Erin standing less than a meter away with her arms folded, even though she didn't need to be that close. The ground floor of the office space the MI6 and STAT operation had taken over was big enough to easily hold all the field agents and their combined support teams. Yet here was Erin, standing in his personal space with an accusing look in her eyes because she thought he'd betrayed her and the team somehow by hanging out with Harley.

On the far side of the room, Rory and Elliott were going through the motions of looking at computer screens where they were supposed to be combing through the manifests of all flights coming into both of the city's airports, looking for known traffickers. In reality, they were much more interested in eavesdropping on the conversation Erin apparently wanted to have with him. The support personnel were all out scouring the city for leads along with Harley and the other STAT agents, so there wasn't anyone else in the room right now. Which was probably why Erin had chosen this particular moment to confront him.

"Well?" she prompted when he didn't answer fast enough for her taste. "Nothing to say, or is it that you don't want to admit you've developed a taste for walking on the wild side?"

Sawyer's fingertips and gums started to tingle, a growl building in the back of his throat. He fought to gain control of his inner wolf at the same time he pushed back against the urge to tell Erin to mind her own sodding business. This crap had been coming to a head since the two teams had left Paris and Sawyer had spent the whole flight talking to Harley. He'd picked up on his teammates' confusion and anger almost immediately, the former coming mostly from Rory and Elliott, the latter from Erin. Since then, it had only gotten worse. His teammates didn't approve, and they'd apparently decided it was time for an intervention.

Sawyer never was the kind to appreciate an intervention.

"You're right," he said softly, eyes locking on Erin's, his voice sounding a whole hell of a lot calmer than he felt. "I don't have anything to say. Not if you're going to accuse me of doing something wrong when all I'm doing is talking to an agent from the other intel organization we're working with."

"An agent?" Erin cursed. "Are you bloody kidding me? She's not even human. She's a sodding monster, Sawyer."

And there it was. What Erin—and probably Rory and Elliott, too—really thought about Harley and the other STAT werewolves.

His gut twisted, thinking of all the times he'd come close to confessing his secret to his teammates, believing they'd gotten close enough to accept it. Now, he was glad he'd never worked up the courage to do it. He wasn't sure he could handle them looking at him the way they eyed Harley, Caleb, and Jake. The distrust didn't end there, either. They regarded the rest of the STAT team like there was something wrong with them for willingly working with what they considered monsters.

Sawyer stood up fast enough to send his chair sliding backward across the floor. Erin definitely hadn't seen it coming, and there was some part of him—his inner wolf maybe—that took a perverse pleasure in seeing her eyes widen in alarm. But at the same time, there was a larger part that couldn't help but wonder how she'd react if his fangs and claws were out.

Out of the corner of his eye, he saw Rory and Elliott slowly get up and move closer, their hearts beating a little faster. Like they'd picked up on the fact that the team dynamic had shifted drastically. He wasn't sure what, but he needed to say something because there was no way he was going to let things devolve into an *us versus them* game. There was too much at stake.

"Grow the hell up, Erin," he said, a little surprised when the hint of a growl slipped out along with the words. While it wasn't animalistic enough to make her jump to any conclusions, it was still out of character for him. But the idea of her calling Harley a monster bothered the hell out of him more than if she'd called him that.

"I'm sorry you're having a hard time handling the new reality we've found ourselves in," he added, getting his growl under control and throwing a look at Rory and Elliott to include them in the conversation. "And I'm sorry the world you thought you knew is a lie. But you need to grow up and get beyond the childish monster crap. Sometime in the next few days, we're going to be dealing with some serious shit, and if the three of you aren't fully on board and committed, then people are going to die. I won't let that happen. If you can't handle working with STAT, fine. Tell me now and I'll have Weatherford reassign you to new teams. You can be out of Casablanca tonight."

Erin, Rory, and Elliott all stared at him, seemingly stunned by his words. They searched his face as if trying to figure out if he was shitting them.

"You can't be serious," Erin said. "They have fangs for heaven's sake."

"Yeah, they have fangs. So does that vampire I shot half a dozen times," he pointed out calmly. "The difference is that the vampire will use his fangs to rip out your throat while Harley, Caleb, and Jake will be using theirs to make sure that wanker doesn't get the chance."

Erin didn't look convinced but didn't say anything.

"Do you really think we can trust them?" Rory asked.

"I wouldn't be working with them if I didn't," Sawyer said. "At the end of the day, it doesn't matter what I think. The three of you are going to have to decide for yourselves. But do it soon. I don't know when we're going to get the word to move, but when we do, I don't want to go charging into a firefight worrying you won't be there when I turn around."

His teammates looked shocked he'd even suggest they wouldn't be there for him. Sawyer supposed his ultimatum was a little harsh, but he couldn't find it in him to care. He, Erin, Rory, and Elliott had been together for nearly four years, fighting, sweating, and bleeding for each other, but there wasn't a doubt in his mind they'd abandon his ass in a fast second if they knew he was a werewolf. Knowing that made it difficult to care about their feelings, even if he was judging them for something they hadn't actually done yet.

Elliott opened his mouth to say something, but was cut off by the sound of the footsteps outside. Harley came in first, followed by the other five members of her team and Adriana. They looked tired, but also excited. In fact, little ripples of blue static danced along the pulse points of Adriana's neck and wrists.

Harley gave him a curious look in between throwing covert glances at his teammates. It wasn't hard to believe she'd picked up on the tension in the room, even if she claimed not to have much faith in her werewolf senses.

"Did you find out anything?" Sawyer asked as Misty sat down at one of the computers and stuck in a flash drive.

"We think so," Forrest said.

Sawyer grabbed the chair beside Harley's at the big table in the center of the room, appreciatively inhaling the sweet vanilla custard scent that always surrounded her. Around the table, his MI6 teammates sat down, too, and he breathed a sigh of relief. There was a part of him that truly thought they were going to walk away.

Caleb took a seat next to Erin, sliding a little closer and giving her a grin that displayed the slightest hint of fangs. The big omega seemed to know she didn't like werewolves and took great pleasure in rubbing what he was in her face.

Erin got up and moved to the other side of the table, refusing to look at Caleb. The American werewolf made a show of sniffing his shirt, as if checking to see if he smelled. Sawyer snorted. Even Rory and Elliott must have thought it was funny because they were definitely trying not to laugh.

Within seconds, Misty started displaying the photos on the monitor, flipping through them so fast all Sawyer saw was a blur. She stopped on a picture of a narrow street lined on either side with shops simply exploding with color. Sawyer had spent several hours walking through the large open-air bazaar with Harley their first morning in Casablanca but didn't recognize that particular section of the market. Then again, the place was a veritable maze of shops, many of them selling similar stuff.

"Jes and I checked out the Central Market near the marina again this morning," Jake said. "The place has been packed with people every day since we got here, so I wasn't holding out much hope of finding anything. But then I picked up the scent of blood belonging to that guy with the leather jacket Harley shot."

Sawyer lifted a skeptical brow. The smell of blood was everywhere in that market, most of it from the fresh animal carcasses hanging up in the various shops, but some from the butchers who accidentally cut themselves while working. Then there were the random splashes of blood here and there on the street from the various fights people got into. If Jake had been able to pick up and recognize one specific smell, Sawyer had to admit he was impressed. His nose was good, but it wasn't that good.

"You're sure it was his blood you smelled?" Adriana asked, face tense.

There was obviously something about the guy that bothered her. It made Sawyer wonder if the a-hole had mistreated her while she was a prisoner. He hoped not.

"I'm sure," Jake said. "I tracked the scent to a local man heading to his office carrying one of those old-fashioned-looking doctor's bags."

"You think he just came from treating the guy I shot?" Harley asked.

"Looks that way," Jake replied.

"The Central Market would make a good place to hide the kidnap victims," Rory said. "The place is a warren of interconnected buildings barely a mile from the marina. It'd be easy to get them in and out of the country from there."

"You said you saw the doctor this morning," Erin said, her voice dripping with suspicion. "What have you been doing since? If your nose is as good as you claim, you would have found the guy in the leather jacket already."

Caleb rolled his eyes, but Jake didn't get offended. "I radioed the rest of my team and we went back to where I first picked up the scent outside the market along Boulevard Ben Abdellah."

Another picture popped up on the monitor of yet more shops fit so tightly together it was hard to believe people could move between them. But the street out front was broader, and the camera had captured several vehicles zipping past.

"The scent dissipated by then, so we spread out and spent the morning canvassing the area, pretending to be tourists and taking as many photos and videos as we could without looking too obvious. That's how Harley caught sight of this."

A video replaced the latest still picture on the screen. It was of a crowd of people milling around some shops while merchants hawked their wares and customers looked through the mishmash collection of leather goods and metal wall art. The sounds of people haggling over prices and city noises filled the air. The clip played for a good thirty seconds before coming to an end.

"Focus on the background," Harley murmured as Misty played the video again. "Behind the racks of carpets."

Sawyer did as she suggested, looking more closely this time. That was when he saw the guy in a dark jacket and jeans with long, perfectly straight hair. Right before disappearing through an open doorway behind the racks of carpets, he briefly turned to survey the crowd, like he was looking for a tail. If the hair hadn't been a dead giveaway, the face was. It was the man from the nightclub. The one who could disappear whenever he wanted to. The one who'd nearly killed Harley.

"We pulled back the moment Harley IDed him, so they wouldn't spot us," Jake said as the video played one more time. "I've got half our support team sitting on the place and the other half digging up floor plans for that building and the ones on either side. They're also going over satellite footage so they can tell us how long the bad guys have spent there, how many people there are, and whether there's any indication the kidnapping victims are in there. We should have something useful in a few hours."

Sawyer tried to remember the last time his team had gotten access to satellite footage. Oh yeah, that would be never. Americans always got the cool toys.

"When do we go in?" he asked.

"Tonight, as the shops are closing up," Jake said. "There'll be enough people around to cover our movements, but the area should be mostly empty, which is good if it ends up being a gun battle."

They talked about tactics for a little while, discussing how MI6 and STAT would work together during the raid before deciding which half of the joint team would focus on getting the weapons and transportation while the other half went over whatever intel the support team was lucky enough to gather.

Before Harley followed her team out, she threw a curious look his way, like she sensed the tension between him and his teammates. A moment later, Sawyer found himself alone with Erin, Rory, and Elliott. They were all looking at him expectantly.

He was tempted to say the hell with it and shift right there in front of his friends, so he could get it over with and they could walk out the door.

He wasn't quite that stupid.

Or brave.

"So, the Americans are running this operation, I guess?" Erin asked, looking at him from where she sat on the other side of the table.

Sawyer's inner wolf didn't like the idea of letting someone else call the shots for his team, but he was smart enough to admit Jake had more experience with this supernatural crap and he was willing to let the American werewolf take the lead.

"Looks that way," he said bluntly. "As for what we talked about before, I'm going to need that answer sooner than I thought. We'll have to come up with a new plan for the raid if the three of you aren't in."

Without waiting for a reply, he got to his feet and headed for the door, keenly aware of their gazes on his back. The urge to turn around was difficult to resist, but he didn't give in. Looking sure as hell wouldn't make this whole thing any easier.

CHAPTER 6

SAWYER CASUALLY MADE HIS WAY THROUGH THE DARKENED streets, moving like he had somewhere to be, but not so fast he'd draw anyone's attention. Not that it mattered since there were few people out at this time of night to notice him. To the rest, he was one more foreigner in a city full of them. In some ways, it was almost like he was invisible.

He'd spent a little time in Tangier and Marrakesh, but his job had never brought him to Casablanca. The city was a unique mix of old and new, with five-hundred-year-old buildings beside towering skyscrapers. Inhaling slowly through his nose, his senses were flooded by the scents of dust, spices, gas fumes, and sweaty humanity. It should have been a nauseating mix, but somehow this place made it work. Suddenly, Sawyer found himself wishing he had time to sightsee with Harley, like they'd done in Paris. He got the feeling she'd find this city fascinating.

Sawyer pulled his duster a little tighter around him as a man walked past, instinct urging him to make sure his tactical vest and weapons were completely covered. Fortunately, it hadn't been especially hot today, and now that the sun had gone down and the ocean breeze was sweeping ashore, it had cooled drastically. His long coat didn't garner a second look even with the excessive amounts of gear he had strapped to his body. Going into this raid with all of it might have been a little overkill for a normal MI6 mission, but after the debacle in Paris, he wasn't taking chances. If they were walking into a shootout with supernaturals, he was going to be ready.

As he got closer to the building, familiar scents reached his nose. Harley's was the most obvious, but he could pick up Erin's as well. Rory and Elliott were somewhere nearby, too. It felt good knowing his team was out there. That they stuck with him.

Outside the office they were using as an operations center, his teammates had caught up to him before he'd made it halfway to the line of rental vehicles on the far side of the parking lot. They'd told him there was no way in hell they were letting him walk into a dangerous situation on his own. They weren't thrilled to be working with werewolves, but they'd put up with it for him.

It wasn't the ringing endorsement he'd hoped for and he doubted they'd be nearly as willing if they knew he was a werewolf, but it was enough for now. He only prayed they got more comfortable with fangs and claws soon because he couldn't imagine making it through this situation without his secret slipping out.

Sawyer slowed a block from the building the guy with the long hair had disappeared into earlier that day, making a production of checking his cell for a message.

"I'm in position," he murmured into his throat mic as he glanced around, looking for anything that might make him think the traffickers were aware of his presence. "We're all clear here."

"Copy that." Jake's voice came back slow and steady. "Stand by until everyone else is ready to move."

While he waited, Sawyer played with his phone like he was sending a text. But really, he was mentally shuffling through the floor plans of the building the STAT support team had come up with. It turned out the shop Long Hair had gone into was an entry point to a complex rabbit warren of interconnected rooms, tunnels, and storage spaces. While there'd only been one sublevel shown on the city drawings, the analysts were quick to point out there could be more that no one had ever bothered adding to the drawings.

The satellite footage they'd gotten hadn't made him feel any better. There weren't any images of the bad guys dragging their captives off any of the numerous ships that had docked recently or leading them through back alleys. In fact, there'd been nothing interesting to see around this particular part of the city.

Either Adriana had been completely wrong about Casablanca being one of the stops along the human trafficking railroad, or the traffickers hadn't brought the captives from Paris here. Of course, it was also a possibility that Adriana had been right and that they were holding the captives here but were so good at hiding them, they'd never left a trace.

Sawyer wasn't sure which of those possibilities worried him more.

When Jake finally gave him the go-ahead, Sawyer started moving again. As he approached the same door Long Hair had entered, he noticed there were a handful of merchants in the nearby shops, some putting away the last of their wares, others merely chatting. Sawyer ignored them as he slipped behind the now-empty carpet racks and made his way toward the doorway. It said a lot that none of the merchants even glanced at him. In fact, they seemed to go out of their way to look in the other direction. That meant they were used to seeing foreigners coming and going from the place and that they were leery enough of those same foreigners to look the other way.

The first room he entered was unoccupied, and a quick scan of the place didn't reveal any cameras or other security equipment that might alert anyone to his presence.

"I'm in," he said softly.

The only lights in the room came from those inside the glass display cases along the walls as well as a single naked bulb near the main counter. The cases held what looked like cheap costume jewelry, while the racks that filled the remainder of the shop were filled with boring dresses and simple robes. Nothing in the place was as high quality as the stuff sold in the surrounding shops, which meant it was almost certainly a front. He was surprised there wasn't someone guarding the place. Even if the locals were smart enough to avoid the shop, surely the traffickers would have put someone there to keep people out.

He heard Erin's footsteps before she walked through the door. She was quickly followed by Harley, then Caleb. Jake's plan had the four of them acting as shock troops coming in through the main entry, where they were most likely to be noticed. They would be the distraction while Jake and everyone else slipped in through one of the back tunnels and rescued the captives.

Strangely, Erin seemed to be rather pleased with the assignment. From her perspective, being sent in the front door with two of STAT's werewolves put her on par with them—at least in the ability to commit mayhem. Jake had just met Erin and had already figured out how to work her. Of course, while Erin might be thrilled to be selected to go in first, she didn't appear as warm on the idea of being partnered up with Caleb while Sawyer covered Harley. Sawyer would have laughed if the situation they were walking into wasn't so dangerous.

Caleb slipped a large frame gun from the holster on his hip and jacked a round into the chamber. "Well, if they don't know we're here by now, they will soon."

Sawyer dropped his duster to the floor and pulled out his own handgun, a Browning Hi-Power, the weapon he'd been carrying since his days in the regiment. It felt comforting and natural in his hand, familiar—like a friend. After chambering a round in the 9mm handgun, he slipped it back into the holster low on his right thigh, turning his attention to the shortened MP5 submachine gun strapped across his lower back. By the time he'd slid in a magazine and chambered the first round, everyone else was ready and looking in his direction.

"Okay," he said with a nod. "Let's go be a distraction."

It wasn't difficult to find the set of stairs behind the main counter, even though they were hidden behind a set of linen curtains. Dozens of scents hit him in the face as they descended. Of all the people who'd taken this stairwell in the past week, Long Hair's was definitely the strongest by a long shot. Sawyer wished he could say for sure he was picking up one of their trafficking victims, but other than Adriana, he'd never gotten close enough to any of them to memorize what they smelled like. At least he didn't smell the vamp, either. That had to be a good thing, right?

Sawyer led the way into the dimly lit corridor when they got to the bottom of the steps. The only light came from the old fixtures hanging every twenty feet or so. Why did there have to be more dark, dank tunnels? Hadn't he reached his yearly quota in Paris?

He turned right, following the path on the map that he'd committed to memory and that he knew led to the larger rooms in the maze, since they assumed that's where the bad guys and their captives would likely be. He braced himself, expecting to run into one or more of those aforementioned bad guys at any moment, but after not seeing anyone—or even picking up a fresh scent—in a few minutes, Sawyer knew something was wrong. It was too quiet. Too easy.

On the radio, Jake announced his group was in the tunnels now, coming in from the entrance to the north. They didn't run into any immediate resistance, either.

Three rooms and a long corridor later, Sawyer finally picked up a familiar scent. He started to announce it when he realized he couldn't, not with Erin there. He threw a quick glance over his shoulder at Harley and Caleb, assuming they'd smelled the same thing he had, but apparently not, as neither of them said anything.

"Vamp ahead," he whispered softly after slowing at one of the intersections in the hallway to let Erin pass him. He gave Harley a pointed look, tapping his nose. Fortunately, she seemed to get what he was saying, giving him a nod before turning to sniff the air. A moment later, she announced that the vampire was somewhere ahead of them.

"What does the thing smell like?" Erin asked, glancing over her shoulder at Harley, the question coming out as a mixture of curiosity and embarrassment.

Harley took another sniff before making a face. "Mud and blood. But old blood. Like it's drying out and starting to go rancid."

"Okay," Erin said before looking away. "Probably a little more than I needed to know, so thanks for that."

They'd barely made it a few more steps before Erin turned and gave Caleb a suspicious look. "Why didn't you say anything about smelling the vampire? You trying to hold out on us?"

Caleb kept walking, not even bothering to look back. "I'm an omega werewolf. I didn't say anything about smelling the thing because I didn't. My nose doesn't work as well as Harley's."

Erin looked baffled at that. Sawyer had to admit he was, too. The truth was, he didn't know a whole hell of a lot about werewolves, even though he was one. Sawyer knew he was an alpha, but that was because the only other werewolf he'd ever met—a beta—had told him so. The guy had only talked to him for a few minutes and had never mentioned anything about omegas.

"What the hell does that mean?" Erin asked. "Are you telling me you're some kind of junior version of the real thing? Like the B-team werewolf or something?"

Sawyer cursed under his breath. They didn't have time for this right now, but Erin never could pass up an opportunity to insult someone. It was like her superpower. Sarcasm and snark at the worst possible time.

But it didn't seem as if the jab got through to Caleb, at least not based on the grin he gave her.

"Wow. You're good." He stopped and turned to face Erin. "You got it right off the bat. Omegas are definitely second-class citizens when compared to alphas like Harley…and other werewolves."

Caleb glanced at Sawyer as he said that last part, then turned his attention back to Erin, eyes glowing with the slightest hint of blue instead of the usual gold.

"My nose isn't that good compared to theirs," Caleb continued. "My hearing isn't so great, either. Same with eyesight. I definitely can't see as far. Claws and fangs are a bit lacking, too, I guess. But of course, the big difference is control. Alphas are all over that control shit, while omegas like me have absolutely none."

As he spoke, Caleb moved closer to Erin until he was only a foot away and gazing down at her with an expression that had suddenly lost all its humor.

"You might want to think about that the next time you decide to rag on me like we're friends or something. I've been known to bite during my less-lucid moments." Turning, Caleb strode down the hallway. "We aren't gonna find that vampire by standing around talking, so let's go. I feel like shooting something."

Sawyer let his gaze travel back and forth between Harley and Erin before heading after Caleb. "Well, that could have gone better. Pissing off the guy you hope will be watching your back in the next few minutes isn't the way I would have approached the situation, but whatever."

Erin didn't say anything as she and Harley caught up to him, but he hadn't expected her to. Erin was good at burning bridges. She wasn't so good at building them. Hopefully, her lack of social talent wouldn't come back to bite them all in the arse.

As they moved through several more rooms and connecting corridors, the vampire's scent didn't get any stronger, which worried Sawyer. They should have encountered someone by now. But other than Long Hair and the vamp, it didn't seem like anyone had been here in a few days. That made his inner wolf wary. There was definitely something wrong.

"Sawyer, do you have something on your side yet?" Jake asked over the radio. "We can't be more than a few blocks from your location and haven't seen anything."

Before Sawyer could answer, he was interrupted by Adriana's panicked voice.

"What's wrong?" she demanded. "Do you think Kristoff is okay? If he was hurt, they wouldn't kill him, would they?"

Sawyer tried to tune the girl out, happy to let Jake deal with this one. Adriana had wanted to come on the raid with them, insisting she could help. While it'd be nice to have her supernatural abilities the next time they ran into the vampire, he and Jake had vetoed that, refusing to back down no matter how much the girl had begged. Jake told her she could listen in on the radio along with the members of both support teams. Based on the current outburst over the radio, she'd also gotten her hands on a microphone. Hopefully, she hadn't zapped all of the support agents.

"I heard something up ahead," Harley said suddenly, jerking Sawyer away from the radio drama.

He listened, trying to pick up on whatever she'd heard. "It sounds like someone moaning."

"I agree," Harley said softly, her eyes intent on the far end of the hallway, like she was afraid she'd lose track of the sound.

They moved forward slowly, Sawyer interrupting the conversation between Adriana and Jake, telling them to stand by, they may have found something. The whimpering got louder as they approached an arched doorway up ahead on the right. The room beyond was as poorly lit as the rest of the maze. Sawyer caught Harley's eye, covertly holding out two fingers before tapping his nose again.

She nodded. "I smell two people, but I don't know if they're bad guys or not, so watch yourselves. This feels really funny."

Sawyer agreed. They'd been wandering around down here for nearly twenty minutes without coming across anything. Now, out of the blue, whimpering draws them toward a specific room. If Sawyer had been trying to set up an ambush, this was exactly how he'd do it.

They approached the room carefully, Harley and Erin in the lead, Caleb covering the rear, while Sawyer stayed focused on the corridor ahead of them. If someone was going to attack them, it could come from anywhere.

Harley gasped as she stepped through the doorway. Sawyer quickly followed her and Erin in to find a long narrow room lined with a series of holding cells along both walls. Thick bars ran from floor to ceiling of each, more than twice what you'd expect to find in a normal prison. The lock plate on each door looked equally strong.

The place was intended to hold some extremely powerful prisoners.

Harley ran past the cells that were empty, stopping when she reached the very last one at the far end of the room. Sawyer kept his attention focused on the pitch-black hallway beyond the cell as Erin followed, more leery of an ambush than ever. Caleb was still out there keeping watch as well.

"Bollocks," Erin muttered, looking through the bars of a cell across the way from the one Harley stood in front of, eyes wide. "There's a little kid in here. She barely looks alive."

Another pitiful groan filled the room.

"There's a boy in this one who can't be more then twelve years old," Harley said, not taking her eyes off the cell. "He's hurt."

Shit.

Sawyer's heart thumped even faster as he sniffed the air urgently. Two kids left behind in locked cells, injured, weak, and in pain. They were bait.

This was a trap.

It had to be.

"Jake, we have two injured captives on our end—both kids," he said into the radio as Harley, Caleb, and Erin frantically searched the room for keys to the cell doors. "It's possible they were too much trouble to deal with and were left behind, but I don't think so."

Sawyer was waiting for a reply when the floor and walls started shaking around them, almost knocking him off his feet. He hadn't even recovered from that when a low rumbling sound echoed in the air, the scent of smoke and dust filling his nose.

"What the bloody hell was that?" Erin shouted, her handgun out and swinging in different directions as she tried to figure out where the threat was coming from.

Sawyer didn't answer. He was too busy trying to interpret the shouts and loud noises coming through his earbud.

"They blew a section of the ceiling!" Jake shouted, only to be interrupted by the sounds of gunfire. "They damn near brought it down on our heads, then opened up on us with automatic weapons before we even knew what was happening. Another second or two and we would have been under the rubble instead of trapped on this side of it. We'll deal with them and find another way to get to you. I think they dropped the ceiling to separate us, so watch yourselves."

Sawyer bit his tongue to keep from asking Jake how that was possible. There wasn't time for talk right now, but the American werewolf had to know the only way the bad guys could have gotten the explosive charges in the ceiling placed properly for something like this was if they'd known exactly when MI6 and STAT were coming and which route they'd be taking. And for those bad guys to purposely split up the teams meant they would have had to know there'd be two groups to start with. The only way they could have gotten that kind of information was if they'd sat through the joint MI6 and STAT mission briefing a couple of hours ago.

The implications of that were so stunning, Sawyer nearly missed it when Erin spoke. "Jake's right, Sawyer."

She was frantically digging through a desk by the wall, searching for keys she almost certainly wasn't going to find. If these two kids had been left behind as bait, there'd be no reason to make it easy to get them out. And those bars looked thick enough to need explosives to get through.

Explosives they didn't have.

"We need to get the hell out of here," she added. "This room is a completely crappy place to try and defend."

He opened his mouth to agree when he picked up the combined scents of a large group of people heading their way, along with one he couldn't identify. Jake was right. The shit had hit the fan.

"Company's coming," Sawyer shouted, turning to head back toward the door, both so he could deal with the bad guys *and* avoid the questioning look he'd be sure to find in Erin's eyes as she wondered how the hell he knew someone was coming. "Get those kids out of there. Now!"

"There aren't any keys," Erin snapped, ripping a drawer out of the filing cabinet near the desk and emptying the contents on the floor. "How are we supposed to get them out?"

Sawyer would have suggested trying to pick the locks, but right then a group of heavily armed men came around the corner into the hallway from the direction they'd just come and started shooting. Cursing, Sawyer ducked back into the room, then quickly leaned out to lay down suppressive fire with his MP5. He wasn't as concerned with hitting them as he was with making them reconsider an all-out assault.

Harley was at his side in a moment, dropping to one knee and peeking around the door with her handgun to start picking off whoever was dumb enough to expose themselves. But there were a lot more bad guys behind those who went down. Definitely way more than he wanted to deal with.

"Anytime you get those kids out of there would be good," he called over his shoulder. "We need to leave."

But instead of a snarky answer from his teammate, all he got was a loud growl in return.

Sawyer snapped a quick look over his shoulder to see Caleb striding toward the little girl's cell, claws and fangs fully extended, eyes glowing so blue they nearly lit up the darkness around them, muscles twisting and spasming along his arms and shoulders. With another growl, he grabbed the bars of the cell door and yanked like a man possessed.

Erin stood there, eyes wide in disbelief as Caleb lost it, snarling so loud it echoed off the concrete walls. Sawyer couldn't imagine what the werewolf thought he could accomplish until he saw the bars start to bend. A split second later, the concrete along the ceiling and floor began to crack and crumble.

"We got trouble!" Harley shouted, drawing his attention back to the crowd of trigger pullers in the hallway.

Sawyer didn't even have to ask what kind of trouble. There was no way to miss the mountain of a man coming their way. Well over seven feet tall, he had to be as wide as a sodding doorway. But it wasn't the size and muscles that worried Sawyer. Or even the earthy, reptile scent coming off him. It was the fact that the guy had brownish-green, scaly skin, which the bullets from Harley's handgun were bouncing off at the moment.

"Bloody hell," he muttered.

Stepping out from the doorway, he unloaded the remainder of the magazine from his MP5 straight into the thing's chest. While the hail of gunfire shoved the creature back at least ten feet, it mostly seemed to piss him off.

Sawyer heard Harley shouting into the radio as he reloaded, saying they'd run into another supernatural—a shifter maybe—who was big, green, mean, and apparently impervious to gunfire.

Sawyer barely got his MP5 reloaded and ready before the shifter came at them again. He fired slower this time, aiming at different weak points—or at least what he hoped were weak points. It was hard to tell when all the thing did was grunt occasionally.

Harley joined in with her handgun, sometimes aiming for the shifter, other times focusing on the human attackers who weren't as bulletproof. But even after seeing men go down and not get up and forcing the shifter back across the floor again and again,

Sawyer knew they couldn't keep this up forever. He'd brought a lot of ammo, but not that much.

"We need help here!" he shouted over his shoulder in time to see Caleb rip the second cell door completely off its hinges, chunks of the lock plate bouncing off the walls.

Before Sawyer could even rationalize how that was possible, Caleb charged past him, one of the twisted bars from the cell door in his clawed hands, snarls reverberating from his throat. The omega werewolf didn't slow as he rounded the corner of the doorway Sawyer and Harley were taking cover behind, but ran straight into the middle of the group of bad guys like a runaway truck, the metal bar swinging left and right like an oversized mace.

The scaly shifter went down under the onslaught—along with several other men—but Caleb continued to smash anyone within reach. When the bar got embedded in one of the bodies and dragged out of his grip, the omega didn't slow. He simply scooped up an abandoned assault rifle from the floor and used it like a club.

The big shifter got back on his feet and crashed into Caleb, almost crushing him through the concrete wall, but the omega shoved right back, trying to rip the thing's throat out with his claws.

Sawyer had never seen anything like it. The two supernaturals were fighting without hesitation or thought, like feral animals. The shifter was insanely strong, but Caleb was like a berserker.

Sawyer stepped out into the hallway, closer to the fight, ready to shoot. Harley was right there with him, trying to get an angle that would help Caleb, but he and the shifter were moving too fast. An errant shot was as likely to hit Caleb as the creature. The best he and Harley could do was keep the human bad guys from getting involved.

Caleb and the creature were bleeding heavily now. Bullets might not penetrate that brownish-green skin, but werewolf claws obviously did. It was hard to watch as they continued to slash and punch at each other, but harder to look away. Sawyer was about to say the hell with it, launch himself into the middle of the battle, and hope for the best when Erin appeared at his side.

She grabbed his shoulder. "You and Harley get the kids out of here. I'll take care of Wacko Wolf and slow these guys down until you get away." When Sawyer looked at her doubtfully, she gave him a shove. "Go. You know I'm not good with kids. I've got this."

Before Sawyer could point out that she was full of crap, Erin was running toward the fight. Screaming like a banshee, she threw herself on the creature's back. Sawyer had enough time to see her shove the barrel of her pistol in the thing's ear hole before Harley yanked him away.

"Let's go!" she shouted, disappearing back into the room with the cells and the kids he knew wouldn't survive if they didn't get them out of there fast.

CHAPTER 7

HARLEY HOLSTERED HER GLOCK AND RAN INTO THE CELL ON the left, bending down to scoop up the blond girl from the ratty mattress she lay on. She stifled a cry of dismay when she realized the little girl couldn't be more than fifty pounds. Her arms were thin and pale, spotted here and there with bruises and scratches from rough treatment. She didn't even stir as Harley picked her up, and if it wasn't for the slight fluttering pulse along the girl's throat and the unsteady heartbeat at the threshold of her werewolf hearing, Harley would have thought the child was dead.

Forcing those macabre thoughts aside, Harley focused on moving as fast as she could out of the cell without jostling the girl more than necessary.

Sawyer had slung his submachine gun over his back and was carrying the young boy in his arms, heading away from the battle still going on in the corridor behind them. Harley quickly followed. She had no idea where they were going, but she hoped this direction would get them somewhere safe. She didn't want to leave Caleb and Erin behind and couldn't help but feel like they were playing right into the hands of the traffickers by splitting up like this, but they didn't have a choice. They had to get the kids out of there and couldn't do that with that green creature and his buddies on their tail.

At every intersection, Sawyer stopped and sniffed the air. Harley prayed he had some clue where they were heading because no matter how well she'd studied the floor plan of the building before coming on this mission, she'd still managed to get completely turned around down here in this semidark maze.

Over the radio in her ear, everyone called out warnings and

instructions to each other over the constant sound of gunfire. The support teams offered suggestions, too, but their voices were hard to hear as they tried to give Jake a route to get him and the others past the collapsed ceiling. Nothing they recommended seemed to work, though.

On the bright side, Harley was certain she heard everyone who was with Jake say something at least once, convincing her that they were all still alive. That was the best she could hope for. Unfortunately, she hadn't heard a single peep from Caleb or Erin since they'd gotten separated. She refused to think about what that meant.

Harley was so focused on making sure no one slipped up behind them that she almost slammed into Sawyer's back when he suddenly slid to a halt. The tension in his shoulders told her something was wrong.

"What is it?" she asked, trying to get her gun out while keeping her grip on the girl.

The movement jostled her anyway and the girl let out a tiny squeak of pain. Her eyes fluttered open and Harley found herself gazing into the palest silver-gray eyes she'd ever seen. How could someone kidnap, starve, and abuse a child this precious?

"It's okay," Harley said gently when those beautiful eyes filled with fear. "You're safe now. I won't let anyone hurt you. I promise."

It occurred to her then that the girl might not speak English, but the words calmed her down regardless. She looked like she was about to say something in return, but Sawyer interrupted them, his voice low and urgent.

"I smell the vampire." He transferred the boy to one arm, so he could draw his handgun, his head moving left and right rapidly, testing the air currents through the corridors. "The thing is some-where close and getting closer. There are other people with him, too. Eight or ten of them."

Harley cursed. Lifting her nose, she sniffed the air, straining to pick up the scents. Out of the corner of her eye, she saw the girl regarding her curiously. She was probably trying to figure out why Harley was sniffing the air like a bloodhound. Harley considered telling her she was a werewolf, but there was no time. Later, they'd talk.

She inhaled deeply again, finally smelling the vampire. It was so nasty that once she had it, she wondered how she could have missed it. Her stomach clenched at the thought of the vampire catching up to them with the kids in their arms. How were they supposed to fight like this?

Sawyer must have come to the same conclusion because he took the first right they came to, heading away from the vampire's scent and breaking into a run. Harley didn't have trouble keeping up, but it was rough on the girl in her arms. She didn't complain, though. Instead, she latched her tiny fingers into the straps of Harley's tactical vest and held on for dear life.

When they reached another right turn, Harley picked up what she thought might be the smell of fresh air coming from somewhere up ahead. That meant they had to be close to one of the exits to the maze of underground passages. But before they'd gone more than a dozen strides in that direction, she was hit full in the face by a stench so overwhelming it made her stumble and almost drop the girl.

Rancid blood and foul, rotting mud, like something from the bottom of a swamp.

Sawyer shouted a warning, but Harley was already racing back the way they'd come, hunching over to protect the girl in her arms. She glanced over her shoulder to see the vampire and a handful of his goons coming into view, weapons coming up as they blocked the path between them, fresh air, and freedom.

Multiple rounds slammed into the back of Harley's tactical vest and the girl in her arms screamed as she and Sawyer ducked back down a side corridor and the protection it offered. Harley leaned against the wall for a second, evaluating if her vest had held up as she gathered herself for a sprint back the way they'd come.

Beside her, Sawyer's head snapped up. From the way his nose was working, this situation was about to get worse.

"Bad guys coming this way," he shouted over the hail of automatic gunfire the vampire and his friends sent skipping along the concrete floor near where they were hiding. "We're going to be pinned down in the crossfire with nowhere to go."

Harley's stomach plummeted. They'd been played from the moment they'd started this operation. The ceiling dropping to split everyone up, two weak and injured kids left in locked cells, the big, green shifter creature drawing Caleb and Erin away while they herded her and Sawyer down this path into ambush. They were being divided into smaller, easier-to-handle pieces by a group of international traffickers who seemed to know everything they were going to do before they did it.

Sawyer set the still-unconscious boy on the floor against the wall as gently as he could. Harley did the same with the little girl. She clutched at Harley's arms, terror in her eyes.

"No, baby," she said softly, carefully extricating herself from the girl's tiny grasp. "You have to stay here. I have to fight and can't do that with you in my arms."

Harley had no idea if the girl understood her, but at least she didn't try and grab on to Harley again as she stood up.

"I'll take the ones coming this way," she said, moving to face the direction Sawyer had smelled the bad guys approaching from. "You keep the vampire and his crew busy."

Sawyer gave her a nod, then pulled his MP5 off his back and darted around the corner to send a spray of bullets down the hallway they'd just escaped. Harley heard the thud of bullets impacting flesh, screams, and then the sound of boots scuffling on concrete.

"They're charging us," Sawyer said calmly, like he was commenting on the weather.

A moment later, four men came at Harley from the end of her side of the corridor. She barely had time to put herself between the shooters and the kids before bullets began to thud into her tactical vest…and other unprotected areas of her body. Pain tore through her and she screamed.

Not pausing to think about anything other than the need to protect Sawyer and the two children, Harley ran forward, going for head shots. She closed the distance between her and the four men, seeing their eyes grow round as she let out a growl that would have made Caleb proud. She would have loved to flash her fangs right then and really make them piss their pants, but while she could definitely feel a tingle in her gums and fingertips, that was as far as her wolf would go, even in the middle of a gun battle that had her bleeding like a stuck pig.

She shot two of the attackers in the face. The upper receiver of her Glock locked back on an empty magazine, but rather than bother with reloading, Harley dropped the weapon and reached out to grab the arm of the nearest man who was still breathing, yanking him to her body to use as a shield as she advanced on the fourth gunman.

Harley felt the man jump and twitch as the other guy shot him multiple times, but she kept charging forward until she was right on top of the last gunman. Dropping the body of the guy she was holding, she reached out to jerk the gunman's rifle out of his hand, then used the butt to smash in his throat.

She'd ended up getting hit two more times in the short fight, once in the left thigh and the other through the muscle along the outside of her right shoulder, but the four bad guys were down, and they weren't going to get back up.

Harley hefted the AK-47 assault rifle she'd taken from the last man and spun around. The sounds farther down the corridor told her the fighting was still going on, and she was terrified of what she'd find when she got there.

Bodies were strewn about the corridor and the two kids were wedged tightly up against the wall, the boy awake now, his stick-thin arms wrapped around the girl to protect her from all the violence around them.

Even though there were handguns and assault rifles lying on the floor, Sawyer and the vampire seemed to have no interest in them. Instead, they tore into each other with claws and punches, slashes and bruises crisscrossing both their faces. Seeing Sawyer bleeding like that broke something loose in her chest and anger rippled through her, finally making her fangs come out.

But her anger evaporated in an instant as the vampire back-handed Sawyer across the face so hard she heard bone break. Sawyer flew backward through the air, slamming into the far wall with a cracking sound, making a dent in the concrete. The vampire took a step forward, almost assuredly intending to finish Sawyer while he was stunned senseless.

Harley wouldn't let that happen.

"Hey!" she shouted, pulling the trigger on the large caliber assault rifle even as she tried to assess the damage to Sawyer from the corner of her eye.

The bullet hit the vampire in the neck and slammed him sideways across the corridor, thick, red blood so dark it was almost black streaming from the wound. The hiss the creature let out as it turned its dead eyes toward her was enough to send shivers up and down her spine.

Harley pulled the trigger again and again, stepping closer and closer as she continued aiming for the junction of the creature's head and shoulder. She remembered clearly what Jake had said about how to kill a vampire. *Behead it or rip out its heart.* Ripping out this thing's heart didn't seem like an option, but blowing his head off his shoulders? That seemed like a reasonable possibility.

She was three feet away from the vampire when she fired the

next round straight into the center of the thing's neck, hoping the large bullets coming out of the weapon would snap its spine. The mess it made was horrendous, but the vampire barely seemed to notice the damage.

The next round from the AK sent the thing stumbling back another few steps and tore away enough flesh from its throat, Harley could easily make out part of its cracked and chipped spine. Another couple shots and this thing would be dead. Then they'd be safe.

But when she pulled the trigger again, nothing happened.

Harley only had half a second to realize the weapon was empty before the vampire backhanded her across the corridor.

She hit the floor so hard she bounced, coming to a painful halt against the concrete a few feet away. Pain throbbed through her face and neck from the slap, through her back and head from hitting the floor, and from every part of her still dealing with the previous gunshot wounds. Her vision wavered, black specks floating in front of her, and in the few seconds it took for that to clear, she completely missed the vampire scooping up a handgun and advancing on her. By the time she was functional again, the thing was pointing the weapon at Harley. There was a smile on its face even as blood continued to pour out of its neck, deep and dark. A bullet through the head wouldn't do a thing to a vampire, but it would kill her for sure.

Behind the vampire, Sawyer scrambled to his knees and reached for one of the AK's lying on the ground. But his movements were clumsy and uncoordinated, and she knew he'd never get the weapon up in time.

Harley tried to push herself to her feet even as she heard the vampire's finger tighten on the trigger. She lifted her head in time to see the little girl on the floor reaching up one lone, timid finger toward the vampire.

Crap.

Harley opened her mouth even though she had no idea what to say. She couldn't let the little girl get involved in this. But before she could get a word out, that tiny finger touched the vampire's left hand.

There was a thud that Harley felt more than heard, like a rumble of thunder vibrating through the air and into her chest. At the same time the nearly inaudible sound washed over her, a pulse of light filled the corridor, and Harley couldn't help but notice that the silvery-gray light was the exact same color as the girl's eyes.

Time seemed to stop, then the weapon fell from the vampire's hand as the creature slowly crumpled to the floor. A second later, the little girl collapsed limply back into the boy's arms.

Harley was up and running for the girl at the same time Sawyer staggered to the vampire's side. She breathed a sigh of relief when she discovered the girl was still breathing and had a strong pulse. The little boy was holding her close, looking at Harley curiously.

"I think she's going to be okay," Harley told him.

The boy nodded and held the girl closer, his gaze filling with hatred as he looked at the vampire stretched out on the floor.

Harley stood and moved to Sawyer's side as he knelt beside the vampire, checking to see if the thing was still alive. Sawyer had a bad gash on the back of his head, but otherwise he seemed okay. It was impossible to put into words how good that made her feel.

"Um," Sawyer started slowly, taking his fingers away from the thing's neck after a long delay. "I think I felt a pulse, but it's really slow...like two beats a minute. I don't know if that's normal for a vampire or if it means it's dying."

Harley was about to tell him to check for breathing, then remembered reading something in the STAT files that said while vampires breathe, they breathe extremely slowly, so that probably wouldn't help. Before she could say that, the little boy spoke.

"It's as alive as it ever was," the boy said in a voice barely above a whisper. "Maya doesn't kill people when she touches them. She just makes them sleep."

Without another word, the boy went back to holding Maya, no longer interested in what the rest of them were doing.

Sawyer stood a little unsteadily and gazed down at the creature on the floor. "Any idea what we do with an unconscious vampire?"

Harley didn't have a clue, but as the vampire's neck began to heal itself, she wondered if it would be wrong to rip the thing's head off.

CHAPTER 8

SAWYER SAT ACROSS THE TABLE FROM THE UNCONSCIOUS vampire, counting the creature's insanely slow heartbeats. It was freaky to think that something could be alive when its heart only beat once or twice a minute. Then again, he'd always assumed that if vampires were real, they'd have no heartbeat at all. So really, was one beat a minute any freakier than no beats a minute?

A quick glance at his watch confirmed that they were approaching six hours since the fight had ended down in the depths of that underground maze, and there were no signs of the creature even thinking about waking up. He had to hand it to that little girl with the silver-gray eyes. When that kid put someone down for a nap, they bloody well stayed down.

When asked how long her touch usually put people under, Maya shrugged and went back to the grilled cheese sandwich Harley had made her. Sawyer wasn't sure if that noncommittal response was because the girl truly didn't know the answer or because she had no clue what Sawyer was saying. He was leaning toward the latter, considering the fact that the girl hadn't said a word since they'd found her. The theory was that she was Norwegian, and nobody on either team spoke the language.

When Sawyer had finally gotten a good look at Harley after the fight with the vampire, he'd freaked out at the sight of the blood all over her clothes. Because she was a werewolf, the wounds she'd sustained wouldn't be fatal, but the part of him that wasn't nearly as logical saw her bleeding and started to hyperventilate. Knowing how close she'd come to being shot in the head by that damn vampire hadn't helped.

Before he had time to get too lost in that moment, Caleb and

Erin had shown up, both looking like they'd gone ten rounds with a T. rex. The green, scaly creature had gotten away, but neither of them seemed too upset about that. From the grins on their faces, it was like they'd enjoyed the fight and were looking forward to doing it again. All Sawyer could do was shake his head. Erin had always been weird that way. Apparently, Caleb was no different.

Caleb and Sawyer had dragged the vampire with them on a hunt through the tunnels to find the rest of their combined teams, Harley and Erin carrying the kids. It had taken a while, but they'd finally found Jake and the others, who were as battered and bruised as they were. From there, they'd linked up with the support team and slipped out of the underground maze, using the cover of darkness to get past the local authorities who'd shown up to investigate all the shooting.

Sawyer looked up as the door opened and Jake and Caleb came in, the latter carrying a black gym bag. Both of them glanced at the vampire before giving Sawyer a questioning look.

"The thing is still out cold," Sawyer said, then winced. "No pun intended."

Caleb snorted as he moved over to check the ungodly amount of steel cables they'd used to tie up the vampire and keep him strapped down to the chair. They didn't know how strong the thing was, so maybe they'd gone a little overboard, but better safe than sorry. It was good vampires didn't have to breathe that often because if they did, this one probably wouldn't be able to.

Their lack of knowledge on vamps was also the reason Sawyer and the other two werewolves were the only people in the room at the moment. Since they'd found absolutely nothing down in those tunnels to suggest where the other prisoners from Paris had been taken or where this auction was being held, Sawyer and Jake had come to the conclusion the only option they had was to interrogate the vampire. But while the need to question the creature might be obvious, neither of them were naive when it came to how badly this could go if the thing got loose. Which was why there wasn't anyone in the room the vampire could easily hurt.

Harley would have been in there, too, but Jake wanted her to stay with Maya and the boy. Considering how the little blond girl was the only person who could put a vampire on his arse with a single touch, Sawyer thought keeping her safe was a good idea. Besides, the farther away Harley stayed from the asshole, the better.

Jake and Caleb had just sat down when Sawyer heard a slight change in the vampire's blood flow. A moment later, the steel cables around the creature's chest creaked and the thing's eyes snapped open, flat black and full of rage as it struggled against the restraints.

Sawyer was more than ready to let the creature flail for a while, figuring it would tire the thing out—assuming vampires got tired—but Caleb wasn't as patient.

"You might want to ask yourself if trying to get loose is really in your best interest," the omega werewolf said casually from his chair as he leaned over and dug around in the bag he'd brought with him. Coming up with a bloody big machete, he calmly placed it on the table in front of the vampire. "Because if I think you're getting anywhere close to being a problem, I'm going to separate your head from your shoulders."

The vampire struggled against the cables again, hissing and showing off a mouthful of teeth as it glared at Caleb. "I'm going to enjoy sinking my fangs into your flesh and hearing your screams as I rip out your throat."

Sawyer tensed at the heavily accented words, waiting for Caleb to lose control and lop off the vampire's head. After seeing the way the omega behaved earlier in the tunnels, it wouldn't be surprising. But when Sawyer glanced at Jake, the other alpha didn't seem too worried.

But instead of going all berserker again, Caleb merely leaned over and pulled something else out of the bag, dropping it on the table with a thud. The vampire was naturally pale to start with, but it got even pastier as it warily eyed the large pair of locking pliers beside the machete.

"I'm guessing here, but something tells me you'd find it difficult to rip anyone's throat out without your fangs," Caleb said.

That was pretty much the end of the struggling and hissing.

"Now that we have that out of the way, there are a few questions we'd like to ask you," Sawyer said.

The vampire's lips curled in a sneer. "Why should I tell you anything? You're going to kill me when we're done."

"Not necessarily." Jake leaned back in his chair, resting his ankle on the opposite knee. "If you tell us what we need to know, there are other alternatives."

Sawyer wondered if it would be that easy. But as the vampire's mouth tightened in scorn, he didn't think it would be. He looked at Caleb. "Did you find that thing we talked about earlier?"

Caleb reached into the bag once more, taking out a large syringe, needle still covered with a long orange cap. "The medics were a little concerned about why I wanted this and made me promise I wouldn't do anything illegal with it."

Sawyer chuckled. Taking the syringe from Caleb, he pulled the cap off the syringe and slipped the needle into the underside of his forearm and pulled back on the plunger, slowly filling the barrel with his blood. He kept going until he'd nearly filled the 10cc syringe, watching out of the corner of his eye as the vampire looked at him nervously…suspiciously.

"What's that for?" it demanded.

"This?" Sawyer held up the syringe, gently pushing the plunger until a tiny bead of blood bubbled from the tip of the needle, red and glistening. "I guess you could call it an experiment of sorts. I heard this crazy story about how werewolf blood is like acid to a vampire. That sounded a little far-fetched to me, but I thought since you're here, we'd find out one way or another."

If vampires could sweat, this one would have been as it stared at the blood on the needle tip, obviously doing its best not to let its fear show.

Sawyer hoped the vampire talked, because the truth was, he wasn't a fan of torture. Of course, all he had to think about was Maya and that young boy being left to starve in those locked cells or the dead tourists found in the Seine in Paris with their blood drained, and his hesitation faded drastically.

Knowing he had to show the vampire he meant business, he leaned across the table and pushed harder on the plunger until a few drops of blood dribbled out and fell on the back of the thing's hand where it was strapped to the arm of the chair. When the droplets hit the vampire's skin, hissing and bubbling exactly like acid, Sawyer realized the American werewolf hadn't been exaggerating.

The vampire screamed, teeth extending to fill its mouth beyond the point of reason, arms and legs yanking on the steel cables. Out the corner of his eye, Sawyer saw Caleb's hand inch toward the machete just in case, but the cables held. Within seconds, the thing's skin stopped bubbling and hissing, the blood doing as much damage as that tiny amount could do. Gasping for air, the vampire eyed the damage—three dime-sized burns that sunk at least a quarter inch into the creature's flesh. Since vampires didn't have to breathe regularly, Sawyer wasn't sure why it was suddenly short of breath. Maybe it was muscle memory or something like that when breathing used to be normal and necessary.

"I guess that answers that question." Sawyer sat back, still holding on to the syringe. "Now, back to business. Let's start with something simple. What's your name?"

The vampire hesitated, glancing back and forth between the syringe and his damaged hand. "Kajus Rebane."

"See how easy that was?" Jake commented. "How long have you been kidnapping and trafficking supernaturals?"

Kajus flicked a glance at the needle still poised in Sawyer's hand, then looked at Jake. "Not long. Maybe six months. My nest in Los Angeles was destroyed a while ago and I had to flee. I wandered around for a while before the man running the operation found me. He offered me money and safety. I couldn't turn them down. I had nowhere else to go."

Sawyer exchanged looks with Jake and Caleb, sure that neither of them had missed the similarities between the way the vampire and Adriana had been approached. No doubt, the traffickers wanted Adriana to do the same kind of work as Kajus—kidnapping supernaturals.

"If you've been collecting supernaturals for that long, you must have quite a collection by now," Sawyer observed.

"Twenty or so," the vampire admitted.

Jake looked skeptical. "That's all?"

Kajus stared down at the skin on his arm as it rapidly continued to heal. "That may not sound like much for six months' worth of work, but it's hard to find some of these things. Capturing them can be even harder. Then we still have to make arrangement to transport them. It can be very time-consuming."

"Must be a real bitch having to work so hard," Caleb said, his tone so flat you had to work to pick up the sarcasm.

The vampire glowered at Caleb but didn't respond.

"I have to wonder," Sawyer said, wanting to keep the vampire talking. "How do you decide which supernaturals get a job offer and which ones get sent straight to the auction?"

For a creature who was basically dead, it was surprisingly easy to read the shock on the vampire's face at the realization of how much the three of them already knew. Kajus was clearly reassessing whatever lies he'd been planning to tell now that he knew he could get caught in one.

"Someone else made that call," Kajus said slowly. "I don't know how the boss made the decision, but in most cases, we knew before we reached the target whether it was a bag and drag or a recruitment effort."

Sawyer was tempted to ask how Kajus and his crew identified the supernaturals in the first place, but something else the vampire said caught his attention.

"Your boss," Sawyer murmured, seeing Jake and Caleb perk up immediately. "What's his name?"

The vampire shook his head, mouth tight, obviously not wanting to answer that. Was Kajus afraid of the guy he worked for?

Kajus opened his mouth to say something, but before he could get the words out, Caleb was up and moving so fast he was practically a blur. Plucking the syringe out of Sawyer's hand, he buried it in the vampire's carotid artery before Sawyer even realized what he was doing. Thumb resting lightly on the end of the plunger, Caleb regarded the creature with absolutely no expression on his face.

The vampire froze.

"I know you don't want to answer those questions because you feel a sense of loyalty to the organization that took you in and the man who hired you," Caleb said. "Trust me, I completely understand that more than you'll ever know." He wiggled the syringe a little, making the vampire wince. "Which is why I've taken the necessary steps to help resolve the ethical dilemma you find yourself in. Now, you don't have to feel bad about answering our questions because you know you had no option. If I push this plunger, the results will be extremely unpleasant."

Sawyer wondered if Caleb would push the plunger and dump the entire syringe's worth of blood straight into the creature's neck. If the disinterested expression on Jake's face was any indication, then the answer to that was yes.

He was getting the feeling Caleb had a screw loose somewhere.

"I don't know his real name," Kajus said a few moments later, swallowing hard as Caleb jiggled the needle in his neck again.

"No one ever told me, and I never asked. Everyone calls him Boc."

Sawyer remembered hearing the term years ago when he'd been in Odessa. It loosely translated to *boss* in Ukrainian. Kind of literal, but he supposed it made sense. At least it was something to start with. If nothing else, they could dig into known traffickers with a Ukrainian background.

"He has a lot of people working for him, both humans and supernaturals," Kajus added. "I get the feeling trafficking is a side business for him, but I have no idea what else he's involved in."

"Where's he based?" Jake asked.

The vampire tried to shake his head, but then thought better of it. "I don't know. He shows up to talk to us whenever he wants, then leaves again."

"Is he a supernatural?" Sawyer said.

"Not that I can tell," Kajus said.

"Is anyone else ever with him?" Caleb asked. "Like a lieutenant?"

"There's a woman," Kajus said. "Dark hair, dark eyes. Pretty, French. I think her name is Brielle. I don't know her last name, but she's always with him when she's not out with the tracking teams. She doesn't talk much, but somehow she always seems to know where to look for the freaks we're after."

Sawyer got the feeling Kajus had been hired for his muscle because he obviously wasn't very observant. Sawyer wouldn't be surprised if the vampire didn't know the full names of any of the people he worked with. He probably considered them takeaway meals he wasn't allowed to eat.

"You knew exactly when we were going to be down in those tunnels below the Central Market, didn't you?" Sawyer asked.

When Kajus hesitated, Caleb moved the needle back and forth, grinning at the creature.

"Yes," Kajus said. "We knew when you'd be there, what your entry points would be, and your route through the tunnels. The kids were bait, and our job was to split you up and take out as many of you as we could."

"How did you get this information?" Jake asked.

"I don't know where Boc got it. He just called and told us where to be and what to do."

Caleb shoved the syringe deeper. "You don't know much of anything, do you?"

"I know where the auction is!" Kajus shouted, as if he knew that Caleb was getting tired of his lack of useful information. "I can tell you if you let me go."

Sawyer glanced at Jake. There was absolutely no way in bloody hell they could let the vampire walk out of there. Every person the creature attacked and drained from this point forward would be on them. There was no way Sawyer could live with that and he doubted the other werewolves could either.

"We aren't letting you go," Jake said. "But if you tell us something worthwhile, we'll make sure you go someplace where you'll be allowed to live and provided with the blood you need."

Sawyer frowned. What kind of place was Jake talking about? Sure, the Americans obviously had a head start on this supernatural stuff, but were they so far along they had a place that not only held vampires but provided them with blood? That was kind of creepy.

Kajus hesitated. "The auction is being held in the Meteora in Greece. Boc has arranged for access to one of those old cliff-top monasteries. They film a lot of movies there, so he told them that's what he was doing, figuring no one would be suspicious when they see a lot of people coming and going."

Sawyer could already envision the kind of place Kajus was talking about. He'd seen pictures of the monasteries on those mountains before. The thought of trying to sneak into a place that remote and difficult to access made his gut tighten. "When is the auction?"

"In three days," Kajus said. "Collectors from all over the world will be there."

"Like who?" Sawyer prompted.

"I don't know," the vampire said. "I'm not important enough to have access to that stuff. That's all I know. I swear!"

Sawyer threw a look at Jake, then Caleb. Both of the other werewolves nodded, probably thinking the same thing he was. The vampire honestly didn't have any more information to give them. Caleb yanked the needle out of the vamp's throat without another word.

Kajus was starting to relax when Harley walked in, the little girl, Maya, holding fiercely on to her hand as they approached the table and the restrained creature sitting there.

The thing's black eyes went wide and he strained against his bonds. "You never said anything about knocking me out! Keep that freak away from me!"

Harley led Maya around the table to the creature's side. At an encouraging nod from Harley, the girl reached out and touched the vampire's hand. There was that barely felt thud through the air, followed by the pulse of silver light, then Kajus was out cold, sagging against his restraints. Thankfully, Maya didn't pass out this time, but she still looked exhausted. Harley bent down to pick her up and snuggle her close. Something in Sawyer's chest twinged at the sight. Harley was a natural when it came to nurturing children. She'd be a great mother someday.

"Now what?" Harley asked as Maya sleepily rested her head on her shoulder.

"First we get the vampire packaged up and headed back to the States," Jake said, pointing at Kajus. "Then we head to Greece."

Sawyer stood. "Without either of our support teams."

Harley looked shocked, but Jake interrupted before she could say anything. "We have a leak somewhere in either STAT or MI6. That's how we walked into that ambush last night."

"And since it wasn't anyone in that maze with us, it has to be someone on the support teams," Sawyer added. "It will make our jobs a lot more difficult, but we're going to have to do the rest of this mission on our own. At least until we figure out who the leak is."

Harley sighed, but didn't look comfortable with the idea. "Okay. McKay has transportation home for the kids, so I need to get them ready."

Sawyer watched her leave before trading glances with both of the other werewolves. "I hate to even think about what I'm going to say, but I have to call my branch chief and somehow explain why my MI6 team is going off the radar."

Weatherford wasn't going to like it when he found out that MI6 might have someone dirty in their organization...or that STAT did.

CHAPTER 9

Greece

HARLEY SAT IN THE DARKENED VILLA ON THE NORTHEAST edge of Kalambaka, eyeing Sawyer covertly, wondering how a guy could possibly look so unbelievably handsome. The scratches across his face he'd gotten in the scuffle with the vampire had completely healed, and she swore he was even better looking now than he'd been when they'd left the hotel to start their shift.

Reluctantly dragging her gaze away from his perfect face, she turned her attention to the big plate-glass window and the row of monitors lined up in front of it. The view outside the window was the front of the mountain on which the Monastery of the Holy Trinity sat, while the monitors displayed different video feeds from the various cameras they'd spent the day setting up around the perimeter of the place. Even at night, lit only by a series of work lights, the cliff-top collection of red sandstone buildings was breathtaking. Looking at something that had been around since before Columbus had taken a wrong turn and stumbled over the New World made Harley want to stare at it for hours on end. Or run up to explore for a while.

Then again, since the place was more than a mile away and towered hundreds of feet above the already-mountainous ground in addition to being currently occupied by an army of workers and security guards, maybe that might not be such a good idea. Which was a definite pity because the monastery looked like a fascinating place to visit. So instead, she'd sit here with Sawyer and watch the monitors to see if anything interesting happened. If they got lucky, maybe they'd catch sight of the bad guys delivering the kidnapped supernaturals for the upcoming auction.

She and Sawyer had flown into Athens yesterday along with the rest of their teammates, doing so in four small groups and staggering their arrival over a period of several hours. They'd all taken rental cars from different companies for the drive to the Meteora area and spread out over three different hotels scattered through Kalambaka and the smaller village of Kastraki, all in the hope of avoiding notice. Without being too obvious about it, Harley had made sure she was on the same flight and staying in the same hotel as Sawyer. The villa they'd selected as their surveillance outpost and operations center was one of the closest available homes to the Holy Trinity Monastery, positioned on an isolated back road with little traffic, so there'd be no one to see them come and go.

It hadn't been that difficult to figure out which of the six active monasteries Boc and his crew were planning to use for the auction. The whole city of Kalambaka was buzzing with rumors about a production company—which was fake, of course—that had taken over the entirety of the huge Holy Trinity site to film a movie. Some people claimed it was for the follow-up *Game of Thrones* series, while others insisted it was for the next James Bond movie. There was word that hundreds of actors would be coming in over the next two days to film an extravagant party scene.

The monastery seemed like an over-the-top kind of place to hold an illegal auction, but Harley had to admit it was also brilliant. Boc and his traffickers could be seen hauling nearly anything up that mountain, and the locals would assume it was part of the movie set.

She glanced at one of the monitors on the backside of the mountain, watching a crane lift huge metal framework into position before a crew of workers clambered all over it.

"I can't believe Boc is constructing an aerial tram to get the buyers to the top of the cliff," she said. "That's got to be ungodly expensive for a one-time use."

Sawyer gazed out the window at the mountain and the buildings at its summit. "I guess if you expect people to come to your exotic supernatural auction and spend millions of dollars, it wouldn't be a good idea to ask them to climb up the side of a mountain."

"I suppose." Harley frowned. "It still seems like a lot of money simply to put his buyers in the right mood."

"I doubt he had to spend that much," Sawyer said with a snort. "The locals are so thrilled with the idea of having a tram to the top of one of their monasteries, they're probably paying for most of the construction cost themselves. The tourism boost the thing will bring will more than cover the cost."

Harley prayed the locals who'd been part of this deal didn't know the kind of people they were getting involved with or what Boc intended to do up there on top of that mountain.

"I read on the flight that there are a few monks in residence up there," she said, glancing once again toward the monitors and all the people scurrying around up there. "Do you think they're still alive?"

Sawyer considered that. "Probably, if only to maintain the facade for as long as possible. But after the auction is over? That, I don't feel so good about."

"That's what I was thinking."

Which meant when they finally got up there, they were going to need to save not only the kidnapped supernaturals, but also a handful of monks. Without any backup.

Beside her, Sawyer went back to staring at the monitors, but from the expression on his face, it was obvious his mind was a million miles away. Considering the call Sawyer had gotten when they'd landed in Athens, she supposed he had good reason to be distracted.

"How did your teammates take the news when you told them what happened?" she asked quietly.

Sawyer leaned back in his chair, crossing his arms over his broad chest, a frown creasing his brow. "About as well as you'd expect.

Erin is ready to say the hell with everything and head straight back to London. Rory agrees with her. And Elliott thinks we don't have enough information to decide anything one way or the other. It doesn't help that the local police still have no leads on who killed Sarah and Cedric."

Weatherford had called while they were standing at the airport rental-car counter and even though Harley hadn't been trying to listen in on their conversation, it was impossible to miss the man telling Sawyer that his former teammates, Sarah Parker and Cedric Abbot, were dead. Harley immediately recognized the names, even if it had taken a few seconds to remember them from the conversation they'd had back in Paris, when Sawyer had told her about the mission in Odessa and the two agents who'd decided to get out of the covert-ops world for good.

The former MI6 agents had been found dead in their home in Alberta, Canada, with their throats slit late last night. There'd been no signs of forced entry, much less a struggle or even defensive wounds. Weatherford said the attack had been so sudden, the couple didn't even have time to realize what was happening.

"I knew Sarah and Cedric were a thing the moment I met them," Sawyer said softly, not looking at her. "Even though they kept their relationship secret, everyone knew they were involved, so no one was surprised when they both decided to leave MI6. Everyone knew they had to quit if they truly wanted to be together. They got four years. I guess that counts for something."

Harley hurt for the couple even though she'd never met them. To leave the danger behind and be murdered in their own home was beyond terrible.

"Is MI6 going to get involved in the investigation?" she asked. "I know it happened in Canada, but they can still do something, right?"

Sawyer shrugged. "Weatherford says MI6 refuses to jump to conclusions and connect Sarah's and Cedric's deaths to Silas's yet, even though all three died from knife wounds. As far as they know, Silas was killed on a mission, and until someone proves differently, Sarah and Cedric lost their lives in a home invasion."

It was Harley's turn to frown. "But you aren't buying that?"

"No. Neither is anyone else on my team," Sawyer said. "And with three of his former teammates dead, Weatherford has to realize he could be next. It might have been years since he's been in the field, but he's still smart enough to recognize someone is settling old scores. He's already digging through every mission the team worked before I joined them, looking for likely suspects."

"What about after you joined them?" she asked.

The thought of whoever murdered his teammates coming after him made it suddenly hard to breathe and she had to force herself to calm down.

He shook his head. "Everyone we took down in Odessa is either dead or locked away in a Turkish prison, which is the next worst thing to being dead. Hell, for all I know, Yegor Shevchenko might *be* dead."

She let out a sigh of relief. "Do you think the person who killed them might be behind the ambush in Morocco? To get to Erin, Rory, and Elliott?"

Sawyer looked at her in surprise. "That'd be a hell of a coincidence. Besides, that doesn't explain how Boc's crew knew our every move."

No, it didn't.

Unfortunately.

She'd hoped that theory might help defuse the tension that had been growing between STAT and MI6 since that damn vampire had revealed the mission in Morocco had been compromised before it started. That there would be an obvious bad guy they could point to instead of blaming each other's support teams for leaking the plans for the raid. Whatever little goodwill there'd been between them was essentially shot to hell by the knowledge of a traitor among them.

For a while there, Harley'd been sure McKay was going to shut down the whole thing and tell her and her teammates to come home. He'd understood why Jake wanted to leave the support team behind and also why he was so intent on keeping a close hold on the information they'd gotten from the vampire, but their boss hadn't been comfortable with the idea of continuing to work with an MI6 team they might not be able to trust or going on a rescue mission without backup. Jake had barely managed to talk their boss off the ledge, swearing he still felt comfortable working with MI6. Even with that assurance, McKay had been quick to tell them if there was one more screwup that even suggested MI6 couldn't be trusted, he was going to pull the team back and cancel the joint operation for good.

For some reason, that thought terrified Harley more than she wanted to admit. Because that would mean never seeing Sawyer again.

"How hard would it be for someone to get their hands on Sarah's and Cedric's new identities and the location of the mission Silas was on?" she asked, changing the subject before her mind could go too far down that particular path. "Who would have access to info like that?"

Sawyer scanned the monitors. "Anyone with a high enough clearance would be able to get details on an active mission like Silas was on—supervisors, branch chiefs, senior support personnel. But Sarah's and Cedric's identities would be more difficult to dig up. Few people, even at the highest levels, would have access to that information."

Harley thought that was what he'd say. "What if someone had access to the MI6 records repository? Would they be able to find everything there?"

Sawyer swiveled his chair toward her with a sigh. "I know you're trying to find a connection between their murders and the guy we followed to Mexico City, but like I said before, it's a huge leap to think someone who has a grudge against my old team just happens to work for Boc."

"Maybe," she replied. "But coincidence or not, we can't ignore the fact that a man associated with Boc broke into the MI6 records repository where all kinds of personnel and agency records are kept, then a couple weeks later, your old teammates start showing up dead."

Harley thought Sawyer would argue that point, but after a long silent pause, he nodded. "Okay, I'll admit you might be onto something, but there isn't a lot we can do to prove your theory. Even if we trusted our support teams, what would we have them look for? The guy who broke into the records repository died in Mexico City and we don't know enough about Boc to connect the two of them. The best I can do is tell Weatherford our suspicions and see what he can dig up."

Harley appreciated Sawyer said *our suspicions*, instead of hanging her out to dry on her own. It was a little thing, but it still meant a lot to her.

They both fell quiet as they turned their attention back to the monitor. The silence should have been uncomfortable, but sitting there with him watching the construction team working on the mountain was relaxing.

"You hungry?" Sawyer asked a little while later. "It's been hours since we had dinner at the hotel restaurant."

"I could eat," she said.

Getting up, he walked into the kitchen and turned on the small lights underneath the upper cabinets, bathing yellow walls and a colorful tile backsplash in a soft glow. Opening the fridge, he took out two bottles of orange-flavored soda, then set them on the counter so he could rummage through the paper grocery bags there. Without the support people to set everything up, Caleb had volunteered to stock the villa with food. Knowing her teammate as well as she did, Harley wasn't holding out much hope for quality snacks.

"We have bags of something called Drakulinia, which look like cheese puffs," he said, holding it up so she could see before reaching in for another. "Next we have Tsakiris Chips with oregano flavoring." He grimaced. "I was good until I saw that. I am definitely not a fan of oregano."

She didn't mind oregano but wasn't sure she wanted potato chips doused in it. "Anything chocolate in there?"

He dug around in another paper bag and pulled out a small red cylinder. "Chocolate wafers filled with chocolate cream. That work for you?"

Her mouth was already watering. "Definitely."

Coming back into the living room, he handed her the cardboard canister of cookies and a bottle of soda. Harley eagerly pulled the plastic lid off the canister, then popped the metal lid underneath. The delightful scent of chocolate immediately reached her nose, along with something that smelled a little like a waffle cone. She couldn't resist holding the container up close to her face to take an extra deep sniff.

"Mmm," she breathed.

Sawyer chuckled. "Should I leave you two alone for a while? I could step outside for a bit. Maybe go for a walk around the block."

Unable to resist the urge, Harley stuck out her tongue at Sawyer, who snorted and made a teasing comment about her maturity before ripping open the top of his bag of Drakulinia snacks. While he attempted to figure out what the twisted cheese-puff shape had to do with Dracula, Harley tried one of the chocolate-filled rolls from the can. The cream inside the rolled-up tube wasn't as sweet as she expected, but it was delicious anyway. Something told her she'd eat the whole can before their shift was over.

"How're those things working for you?" she asked as he crunched on a handful of the strangely shaped cheese puffs.

"They taste like Cheetos with a hint of tomato soup mixed in. I could definitely get addicted."

She reached over and shoved her hand in the bag trying to grab a few.

"Hey," he laughed, pulling his bag away with one hand while making a shooing gesture with the other. "These are mine."

She held out the canister of Caprice cookies and flashed him a smile. "I'll share if you will."

"Deal," he said, offering access to his bag at the same time he reached out and took one of the chocolate-filled wafer rolls out of the can.

Reaching for more of the powdery orange snacks, she popped them into her mouth, then bit into a cookie. "Cheese puffs and chocolate…who knew?"

He chuckled as they both went back to eating, sharing from their packages and occasionally taking a sip of the soda that tasted like orange soda and lemonade mixed together.

"So, is now a good time to talk?"

Sawyer's voice was so casual, Harley barely took note of the question until she looked up and realized he was regarding her expectantly.

"Talk about what?" she asked, taking out another chocolate cookie and biting into it as she tried to figure out what Sawyer meant by that. She thought they *had* been talking.

"About how you became a werewolf?" he prompted. "You didn't think I'd forget you promised to tell me your story, did you?"

Her heart suddenly beat faster. "I thought the deal was that I'd tell you the next time I found a place to repay you with dinner."

Sawyer held up his bag of cheese puffs with a grin. "We have dinner, and since I saw you give Caleb a handful of euros before he headed out for food, you therefore paid for dinner. So, start talking."

Harley opened her mouth to argue but then gave up. What else would they do for the rest of their shift if they didn't talk? And she *had* promised him her story.

She only wished it weren't so hard to talk about it.

Sawyer rolled his chair closer, tossing his bag of cheese puffs on the table with the monitors and taking her hand. "Hey, calm down. Your heart is thumping out of control. You don't need to tell me anything if you don't want to, okay?"

While she appreciated the offer, she still shook her head. "I want to tell you my story." She took a deep breath, trying to get her heart rate back under control. "I just need a second."

"Take all the time you need." Relieving her of the canister of cookies, he set it on the table so he could take both of her hands in his and give them a squeeze. "We have all night if you need it."

That wasn't quite true. Their shift here at the villa finished in a few hours. But she knew what he was trying to say. They had time. She could do this.

"I was home on winter break from the University of Colorado Boulder," she said slowly, figuring she'd start with the easy stuff and work her way into the more difficult part later. "I wanted to make some extra money, so I joined the ski patrol at Silverton Mountain. It was close to my home in Montrose, so it was a perfect setup for me."

"What did you study in uni?"

She smiled at the question, knowing he was asking simply to help her relax. "I was working on my education degree. I was going to be a middle school teacher like my mom."

"Nice." His mouth curved. "Mum always wanted me to go to uni. She tried to talk me into it even after I got out of the army. She's pretty much given it up as a lost cause these days."

She tried to picture him in a classroom environment, a big alpha werewolf surrounded by hipsters and the party crowd. "What kind of classes did she want you to take?"

He gave her an embarrassed look. "She always wanted me to be a dentist like my dad. And before you ask, no, I'm not kidding."

Harley tried not to laugh, but the thought of him sitting on a stool, fingers shoved in someone's mouth while he talked about the importance of proper flossing was an image she simply couldn't resist. It didn't help when he pretended to be offended, telling her he'd looked good in a white coat and rubber gloves.

"Okay, I know absolutely nothing about Colorado," he said when she finally stopped giggling. "I know it's somewhere in the middle of the United States and it has mountains, but that's about all. What's it like?"

Harley smiled. In actuality, she didn't know much more about the UK. Yeah, she knew about London and all its major iconic buildings, even some of its history—mostly the stuff on wars, since that was all her history classes ever seemed to care about—but that was it. She definitely couldn't hold his lack of knowledge of Colorado against him.

"It's beautiful," she told him, glancing down at their clasped hands as she thought about the last time she'd been there. "Montrose is in the western part of the state, close to the border with Utah. It's surrounded by mountains and national forests, which makes it a wonderful place to live, especially if you love skiing. Heck, I learned to ski before I even learned to ride a bike."

"That explains the job on the ski patrol." Sawyer absently rubbed his thumb back and forth over the back of her hand. "Were you skiing when you became a werewolf?"

She nodded, a little distracted by the memory. "Silverton Mountain has a few traditional runs, but mostly specializes in backcountry excursions that take skiers in by helicopter and drops them at the top of some of the toughest slopes in the country. The chance to shred fresh snow in places few people have even seen, much less skied, is a lure that draws a certain kind of person."

"Sounds dangerous," Sawyer murmured.

"It can be," she admitted. "The slopes are steep and rugged, and with no marked trails, there's always the chance of skiers getting lost or going over a cliff. Avalanches are always a concern, too. They try to make sure the people they take there know what they're doing and that they stay to routes they suggest, but some-times…well, a few bad decisions and it's easy for people to quickly get in over their heads."

"Is that what happened in your case?" he asked, prompting her when she fell silent.

She nodded, remembering how that day at the mountain had started, how bitterly cold it had been when the call came in.

"They dropped off a group of four college kids on one of the tamer backcountry slopes at sunrise. It should have taken them about four hours to get down the slope to the pickup location, but they didn't make it back. Before we lost radio contact, dispatch was able to confirm they'd left the planned route looking for adventure and gotten lost. By the time we pinned down the general area they ended up in, the sun was going down, temperature was dropping, and wet, heavy snow was falling."

"That doesn't sound good."

"It isn't," she replied. "Heavy snow on a steep slope is a recipe for an avalanche, especially if there's already a lot of snow there to begin with. Some of the slopes in the area they ventured into had as much as fifteen feet of buildup, which is about as bad a situation as you could come up with."

He didn't say anything, this time waiting patiently for her to continue. It was hard to explain—or understand why—but it was easier talking to him about this than anyone else in the world.

"They dropped six of us into the area with survival gear and satellite phones, hoping we could find the skiers before it got too cold. It was so windy the snow was coming down sideways and I could barely see a few feet in front of me." She took a deep breath. "By the time I stumbled across them, they'd been trying to ski down the slope in the dark and two of them had crashed out, lost their equipment, and twisted themselves up pretty good. The group was trying to walk down the slope while all four of them were in the first stages of hypothermia. I was calling in the rescue helicopter when a deep rumbling sound from higher up the slope told me I'd run out of time. I couldn't see a damn thing, but I knew what was coming."

Harley opened her mouth to tell him the rest but paused as she realized he'd tightened his grip on her hands, almost like he was in pain. His breathing was faster than normal and his heart was beating so hard she could actually hear it.

"Um," she began, trying to focus on what she was saying instead of the obvious effect her words were having on Sawyer. "I knew we didn't have a lot of time, so I shoved the four of them toward the first outcropping of rocks I saw, praying there'd be a crevice for us to hide in. I found one, but unfortunately, it was only big enough for the four of them. I tried to make myself fit in there with them, but it wasn't enough."

"Shit," Sawyer said, his voice so low she could barely make out the word. "The avalanche hit you?"

"Like a freight train." She swallowed hard. "I tried to stay on the top of the flow like they teach you in the survival classes, but it was impossible. I got scooped up and tossed around like a rag doll, hitting every rock and tree on the mountain on the way down the slope. I never imagined there could be so much pain. Every time I hit something, another bone broke."

Glancing down again, she noticed Sawyer's claws had extended, his fingers flexing like he was fighting to regain control. She remembered how upset she'd been as Sawyer had told her about the trauma he'd gone through. It seemed like the same for him now. Maybe it was a werewolf thing. Maybe werewolves were affected by the trauma and pain another of their kind had experienced when they turned.

"It felt like hours before I stop tumbling," she whispered. "I was wearing an avalanche airbag pack, but it got ripped off at some point during the fall, so I was trapped there under the snow with no idea how far under I was or even which way was up. Not that it really mattered, since I was too busted up to try to dig my way out. So I laid there in the snow, not sure what would kill me first—the trauma from the impact or the lack of oxygen. I should have been freaking out, but truthfully, I was in too much pain to care."

"How long were you buried under there?" he asked, though from the expression on his face, it didn't seem as if he truly wanted to know.

"Five hours," she said, replaying the few glimpses of that horrible time she remembered. "The rest of the ski patrol arrived minutes after the avalanche stopped, but even with the people I rescued pointing them in the right direction, it took them forever to find me. The debris field was over a thousand feet long and nearly as wide. Later, my friends on the patrol admitted that after the first hour, they thought they were looking for my body because I should have suffocated by then. They couldn't believe it when they dug me up and found out I was still breathing. They didn't think I'd even make it to the hospital."

Sawyer's breathing was more regular now that they were past the traumatic part of the story. "How long was it before you realized something strange was happening to you?"

Harley considered that. She'd never spent a lot of time thinking about those weeks and months right after the avalanche. In fact, she'd done everything she could to forget it.

"The doctors had me drugged to the gills for a few weeks after the accident on the mountain, assuming I was in pain from all those broken bones," she said. "Even though my inner werewolf burned through the narcotics as fast as they gave them to me, they kept me loopy enough to miss most of what happened. It wasn't until eight weeks later, after I was out of the hospital and back at home, that I started having nightmares about what happened. By the time my fangs, claws, and anger management issues showed up, I was sure there was something horribly wrong with me. I thought maybe the pain and trauma of falling down that mountain had driven me insane."

"Did your family figure out what was happening?"

Harley hesitated. This was the one thing she'd worked the hardest to forget.

"I tried so hard to keep it from them," she said, not surprised when the words came out as little more than a whisper. "I loved my family more than anything, but I knew this wasn't something they could handle. If they saw the claws and fangs and glowing eyes, they would have thought I was a monster." Tears stung her eyes and she blinked them back. "It turned out I was right."

When she didn't say anything more, Sawyer moved his chair so close his thighs were touching hers and she could feel his warmth through both of their jeans.

"It started with an argument with my brother," she said, focusing all her attention on the thumb rubbing little circles on the back of her hand again. "He was nagging at me about showering too long and using all the hot water. Before I knew it, we went from arguing to shouting so loud the whole house heard us. My emotions had been all over the place for the past few days, the pressure building as I tried everything I could to hide the changes from everyone, and for some reason, I lost it."

"Did you shift?"

She nodded glumly. "Further than I ever had before. When my brother freaked out, my parents and sister all ran upstairs. My dad grabbed me and shoved me away, I slashed him with my claws, tearing open his shoulder. Seeing all that blood pulled me back from the edge, but it didn't matter by then. My whole family had seen what I was and the look of horror on their faces is something I'll never forget. The worst was my little sister, Jenna. She'd always idolized me, but seeing her look at me like that crushed me. My mom told me to get out and never come back. I did and haven't let myself shift that far since."

Harley promised herself she wasn't going to cry, but when

Sawyer gently pulled her onto his lap, she did just that, the tears she'd never let fall back then coming after all these years. She waited for the embarrassment to come, but it didn't happen. Instead, as Sawyer's big hand came around to rub her back, she felt like a weight had been lifted from her shoulders.

He let her cry for a long time before tenderly wiping the tears away from her face with his fingers. The intimate touch felt like the most natural thing in the world.

"Did you go back to uni after you left home?" he asked.

She should probably climb off his lap, but being in his arms felt too good.

She shook her head. "The idea of going back to school and becoming a teacher was out. All I could imagine was losing control in the middle of a classroom and slashing up a bunch of kids."

"You'd never do anything like that," he said firmly.

"Now I wouldn't, but back then, when I was fighting the change with everything I had in me, I wasn't so sure. Regardless, I took every penny I had left in my bank account and disappeared."

"Where did you go?" he asked, his face so close to hers she could feel his warm breath on her skin, the scent of cinnamon coffee cake surrounding her, and it was all she could do to keep from shoving her nose into his neck so she could inhale even more of it. How had she not realized the delicious scent was coming from him the first time she'd experienced it?

Harley took another breath, letting it out in a long sigh before shaking her head to clear her senses. "A better question would be where didn't I go? I was so scared of being found out again, I never stayed in any one place for too long. Before joining STAT, I spent time in nearly every state in the continental U.S. Except Colorado. I never went back there."

As she relaxed against Sawyer's muscular chest, she realized it'd been an exceedingly long time since she'd been in a man's arms. It was amazing how comforting it was.

"Speaking of STAT, how did you end up working for them?" he asked. "Did they find you, or did you find them?"

She laughed a little at that. "It was definitely the latter. While I got very good at hiding the more obvious aspects of my werewolf nature, I constantly found myself in situations where someone needed help, and the next thing I knew, I'd toss someone through a window, or get shot at or run over by a car. It's like I was a magnet for trouble."

"That's your innate alpha instincts," Sawyer murmured, rubbing soothing circles along her back. "Your inner wolf sees someone who needs your help and you can't help but get involved."

She snorted. "I guess. Regardless, that's how STAT found me. I was waitressing at a diner in Omaha when McKay sat down at a table and offered me a job. They heard about all the situations I'd gotten myself into and figured out I was a werewolf. I was terrified when he told me, but in the end, knowing there were other people like me out there who'd accept me for what I am was too good an opportunity to pass up."

"Have you talked to your family since you left?" Sawyer asked.

Harley felt tears fill her eyes again and Sawyer's big hand moved up and down her back until she relaxed. Damn, he had really good hands.

"Jenna is the only one I've kept in contact with." She wiped away a stray tear. "I text her a few times a week and talked to her twice. She was eight when I left, and while she saw what happened, she doesn't get why I can't go home. She thinks it's as simple as apologizing to Mom and Dad. I'd do it in a heartbeat if I thought they'd forgive me, but I'm nothing but a monster to them now."

Even though she knew how they'd felt about her for years, there was something about saying it out loud that made her feel more hollow and wrung out than ever. She was on the verge of losing it again, fighting the tears that threatened to overwhelm her, when she felt Sawyer's hands on her hips, lifting and repositioning her on his lap until she was sitting astride him. It was an intimate position, there was no denying that, but as she rested her hands on the hard planes of his chest, she decided it was exactly where she wanted to be right then.

"You aren't a monster," he said. "After the run-ins we've had with the traffickers and the supernaturals who fight with them, I know a monster when I see one, and you aren't even close. I'm not going to apologize for your parents' behavior. They turned their backs on you and that's on them. But what they believe doesn't matter. You're a werewolf—a beautiful, perfect werewolf."

His words made her—and her inner wolf—feel warm all over. She wasn't sure how it happened, but one moment she was gazing at Sawyer, wondering if it was magic that had caused her to stumble across the most amazing man in the world, and the next, she was kissing him.

It was merely a gentle brush of the lips at first, like he was giving her the chance to pull back if this wasn't what she wanted. If that was the case, he'd be waiting a long damn time.

She slipped both hands into his hair, weaving her fingers into it as she opened her mouth to his teasing tongue with a moan. He tasted even better than the cinnamon coffee cake he smelled so reminiscent of.

Harley was so into him, she didn't even realize his fangs were out until they grazed her tongue. The sensation sent sparks of arousal through her body, making heat pool between her legs. She moaned as his burning hot lips traced their way along her jaw and down her neck. And when his fangs grazed the sensitive skin there, she growled a little—something she never ever did.

It wasn't until his big hands slipped under the hem of her shirt, the warmth of his fingertips gliding along the sides of her ribs, that she felt her gums and fingertips begin to tingle like her fangs and claws were trying to make an appearance. She had a sudden vision of herself tearing Sawyer's shirt open and latching on to the muscles at the junction of his neck and shoulder and biting him. Excitement pulsed between her legs at the image.

Okay, where the hell did that come from?

She didn't have a lot of time to figure it out because her hands were too interested in the front of his button-down, preparing to tear it open. Her inner wolf knew what it wanted and at least a part of that involved getting Sawyer naked.

Harley was more than ready to give in to the werewolf inside when she heard a noise outside the villa.

She was off Sawyer's lap in a second, pulling her gun and spinning around to face the door even as Sawyer did the same. That was when she picked up a handful of familiar scents drifting into the room. She wasn't sure what was more surprising—that her nose was working so well it could ID people through a closed door, or that she'd smelled their scents even before Sawyer had.

Both she and Sawyer had put their weapons away by the time Caleb, Erin, and Forrest walked in. Harley thought they did a good job hiding what they'd just been doing, but if the look on Caleb's face was any indication, he'd realized they'd been up to something. She prayed his crappy omega nose wouldn't tell him that she and Sawyer had been making out. Beside her, Sawyer looked like he was wondering the same thing.

"Anything interesting happen?" Caleb asked, eyeing her and Sawyer curiously as he walked over to the monitors.

As Erin moved over to stand beside him, Harley couldn't help but look twice at the odd pair. Ever since the fight in the tunnels below the Central Market in Morocco, Caleb and the abrasive MI6 agent had been acting differently toward each other. They definitely weren't friends or anything, but the open animosity wasn't there anymore. Maybe getting tossed around by a scaly-skinned lizard shifter had made the two of them able to see past their differences.

Or maybe they'd declared a detente until the next wrong word screwed everything up.

"Just a lot of construction," Sawyer said, gesturing to the mountaintop still bright with lights. "No sign of any of the traffickers, but from the looks of it, they'll definitely have the tram built and ready in time for the auction."

"Speaking of the auction," Harley said, hoping to distract Caleb, who was still looking back and forth between her and Sawyer with an all-too-knowing expression. "Has Jake come up with a plan on how we're going to get up there? It's not like we can just sneak on the tram when no one is looking."

"Misty is doing her magic on the computer, sifting through the international arrivals from both air and sea," Forrest said, checking each monitor to double-check the cameras and recording connections. "Luckily, the people rich enough—and twisted enough—to attend an event like this aren't worried about hiding their movements. Jake wants her to find some of them who are fairly similar in appearance to us, then Jes will do the makeup thing to make sure we can pass for them."

In another life, Jes had been into theatrical makeup and special effects. The things she could do with a little polyurethane, latex, and contact lenses were almost scary. But the chances of finding clones for all of them wasn't going to be easy.

"What about those of us who won't pass for attendees?" she asked, worried she already knew the answer.

Forrest glanced out at the mountain before looking at them. "We have to hope they aren't afraid of heights because they'll be climbing up the monastery."

Harley groaned. That was exactly what she'd been afraid of.

CHAPTER 10

DON'T LOOK DOWN.

Sawyer wedged the inside edge of his right boot against a slim ledge of rock, carefully testing it before putting his full weight on it. Reaching up with his right hand, he shoved his fingers into a crevice wide enough for them to fit, then with a heave of his shoulder and arm, he pulled himself higher up the mountain in the darkness.

Just a few hundred meters more to go.

It was an agonizingly slow way to climb, but he didn't have a choice. The face of the cliff was made mostly of sandstone. One wrong move and he was looking at one long drop to the base. While the fall probably wouldn't kill him—unless he smashed in his head—it wasn't something he wanted to experience.

Boots scraped against stone and he glanced to his right to see Jake a dozen meters away, climbing as carefully as he was. On Sawyer's left, Caleb was at least a hundred meters ahead of them and moving absurdly fast. Sawyer had already come to the conclusion that reckless and out of control were defining characteristics of the omega werewolf.

"Hold your position." Caleb's voice was soft in his radio earpiece. "Patrol moving past up top."

Shit.

Sawyer hugged the cliff face, holding his breath and trying to make himself disappear into a crack not nearly big enough to hide in. Somewhere above him, he heard the tread of heavy boots as guards walked along the perimeter of the monastery. The aforementioned guards were the reason Sawyer, Jake, and Caleb decided to climb the mountain free solo. Going without anchors, ropes, or gear of any kind increased the chances one of them would fall, but all it would take was one metal carabiner smacking against a rock when one of those guards was nearby and they'd have a dozen automatic weapons pointed in their direction. Exposed as they were on the side of the mountain, they'd be dead for sure.

Sawyer was still hugging the rocks when Harley whispered over the radio that she and Misty were in the line to board the aerial tram and about to get their invitations checked. While he was worried about Harley's makeup and fake ID holding up, he was glad she wasn't on the mountainside with him. The thought of her dangling by her fingers from a rock ledge the way he was at the moment made him want to throw up.

Thankfully, she'd been able to pass as one of the buyers attending the auction. Forrest, too. Jes had been able to use prosthetics, wigs, and makeup to make them look exactly like the real people they were pretending to be. Sawyer had watched the whole transformation and been seriously impressed with the STAT agent's work. He hadn't even recognized Harley afterward.

Misty and Erin were accompanying Harley and Forrest as their personal assistants. They didn't look nearly as close in appearance to the real people even with Jes's makeup magic, but hopefully whoever was checking the invitations wouldn't pay much attention to them.

Since he, Jake, and Caleb were too big to consider getting into the auction as prospective buyers, they'd slip in with the security guards once they made it to the mountain top. With the makeup Jes had done to hide their features, hopefully none of the bad guys would recognize them from their previous encounters in Paris and Morocco. That said, Sawyer wasn't thrilled with wearing the latex appliances on his face that changed the shape of his jaw and chin. They made his skin itch.

Unfortunately, Jes, Elliott, and Rory hadn't been able to match the rest of the team up with any of the auction attendees, and because none of them was comfortable climbing the mountain, the plan had been for them to stay down at the base of the mountain and rescue each of the supernaturals purchased at the auction as they were brought down on the tram if things went sideways. Then, a few hours ago, they'd learned Boc was bringing in known criminals from the Athens area to do some work for the night. Sawyer had no idea what the work entailed, but it had been incredibly easy to slip Rory, Jes, Elliot, and Adriana, of all people, in that way. Thanks to a little makeup, no one would recognize them, either.

"The guard is gone," Caleb said over the radio. "The coast is clear."

Sawyer started climbing again, moving a little faster now. He didn't want to get caught out here.

Makeup or no makeup, it was probably crazy to allow Adriana to come with them. But she'd insisted she could help them with the rescue by using her powers to take out the monastery's power grid, shut down the tram, or even zap a few guards if that's what they wanted her to do.

"I need to be there for Kristoff. If he dies up there and I did nothing to stop it, I'll never be able to live with myself," she said tearfully. "He saved my life. I have to help save his."

It was that heartfelt plea that had finally made Sawyer and Jake agree to let her come with them. Who could say no to someone when all they wanted to do was save their boyfriend's life? Besides, how could they go wrong having someone with them who could electrocute anyone who pissed her off?

Harley came on the radio again, letting them know she, Misty, Forrest, and Erin were boarding the tram and that there hadn't been any problems with the invitations. Someone had simply checked names off a list.

Sawyer breathed a sigh of relief at that.

He grinned as he thought of the past two days he and Harley

had spent together. After years of trying to make relationships work, he'd finally met a woman who completely got him. They clicked without any effort at all, even if all they'd had time to do was sit around in their hotel rooms or pull shifts at the surveillance villa and talk while eating souvlaki and gyros.

Sure, they'd kissed some more, and damn, it'd been amazing. He would have liked to do more than kiss, but they'd been too busy getting ready for the raid on the mountaintop monastery to do more than steal a few moments together here and there. So, he'd settled for what he could get…and taken a lot of cold showers.

But even if they mostly spent their time talking, that was fine, too. She'd been surprised when he told her that his mum and dad knew he was a werewolf, but also happy to know they still loved him anyway. It made him want to fly to Colorado right then and lambaste her family for turning their backs on her. He was glad she'd at least found a new family in her pack. He hadn't ever thought about werewolves being part of a pack, mostly because he didn't realize there were that many of them around. He had to admit, his inner wolf was curious about what it would be like to be part of one.

While he'd definitely enjoyed getting to know Harley better, there'd been one glaring reality that overshadowed every moment they spent together. As soon as this mission was done—very likely in a few hours from now—he and Harley would go their separate ways. They could keep in contact with each other, of course, but with their jobs, there was little chance of that working out. Sawyer rarely stayed in one place for long and never had a clue where he'd be the next day, much less the next week. He couldn't imagine making something with Harley work long distance, even if admitting it hurt more than he would ever have thought possible.

Sawyer was so wrapped up in thoughts of Harley and the disappointment over how he knew this thing with her was going to end, he only realized he was getting to the top of the mountain when

Caleb whispered over the radio for him and Jake to freeze again, that there was another guard walking right above them who was close enough to the parapet to see over the side.

The warning caught him out in the open again, this time barely ten feet from the top of the mountain, reaching for the next handhold, tips of his boots barely finding purchase on the tiny ledge beneath him. He looked left and right, desperate to find someplace to hide—because where he was now, they'd see him for sure—but there was nothing, not above him or to either side. So he did the only thing he could.

He let go.

It seemed like he fell forever in a single heartbeat, scrabbling for anything that would save his life. When his fingers finally caught on a ledge of rock, his shoulders almost tore out of their sockets.

Cursing, he hung there, his heart beating fast at the realization of how close he'd come to buying it.

Boots thudded across rough stone somewhere above him, reminding him that dying on this mountain was still a distinct possibility. Holding on to the narrow ledge with a single hand, he slowly inched the other toward the pistol strapped to his right thigh.

"Don't move," Jake warned over the radio, his voice urgent. "The guard must have heard you falling and is leaning over to take a look. I don't think he can see you from where he is, but don't move anyway."

"I don't think"?

That didn't exactly fill Sawyer with confidence. Especially when the boots came to a stop directly above where he was dangling.

"The guy is right on top of me," he murmured into his mic, reaching for his pistol again. "If he sees me, it's over."

Hand on his weapon, Sawyer glanced up to see the guard looking right back at him with wide eyes.

Shit.

He pulled his pistol at the same time the guard leaned out over the parapet, angling his own weapon to line up for a shot. Then, out of nowhere, a big hand reached around from behind the guy and grabbed his chin, giving it a twist. The snap it made was loud enough to echo off the rock walls around him.

A moment later, Caleb leaned over, eyeing him curiously, like he was wondering what the hell Sawyer was doing down there. Then again, maybe the omega was waiting for him to fall. Something told Sawyer that Caleb wouldn't be too upset about that.

"You done screwing around down there?" Caleb demanded.

Sawyer had the distinct sensation the omega didn't like him much. Maybe Caleb knew about him and Harley and, for some reason, didn't approve of it.

Shoving his pistol back in its holster, Sawyer quickly climbed the rest of the way to the top of the mountain. When he got there, Caleb watched him pull himself over the parapet, then turned and walked away, muttering something about checking for other guards. Sawyer shook his head. Oh yeah. Caleb definitely knew there was something going on between him and Harley and didn't like it one bit.

Looking around, Sawyer took in the tall hedges and flowering plants. They'd picked this side of the mountain as their entry point because it was behind the monastery and directly opposite where the tram dropped off the guests. From where he stood, Sawyer could see the tile-covered rooftops of five different buildings and while he could hear people moving around the property, none of them were close to him and the other werewolves.

"We all made it to the top," Jake reported over the radio as he crouched down beside the guard Caleb had killed.

Sawyer moved over to help him check the dead man's uniform, pulling off the radio and earpiece. Jake listened in on the bad guys' communications while Sawyer took a quick look at the guard's tactical gear, confirming it was an exact match for the stuff the three of them were wearing, right down to the MP5 submachine gun they'd brought with them. That would help them blend in.

Sawyer could hear chatter coming through the guard's earpiece. It sounded like someone doing a security check-in. That was definitely a problem. As soon as whoever was on the other end didn't get a response from the guard, they'd know he was out of commission.

"The dead guy's call sign is kilo-one-one," Caleb said, coming over to join them. "I heard him say it before I snapped his neck."

Jake slipped the radio in his tactical vest and the bud in his left ear, since the one for their own team radio was already in his right. "I'll listen for it and respond if necessary."

"Where are we going to hide the body?" Sawyer asked.

Maybe they could get away with shoving it under a hedge. There was a chance another guard could find it while on patrol, but it was either that or drag the dead man into one of the nearby buildings that was unoccupied.

Caleb snorted and picked up the man's body without a word, then slung it over the wall. It made a thud as it hit the ground far, far below.

"There. The body has been hidden." Turning, Caleb headed toward the monastery buildings. "You ready to do this?"

Sawyer glanced at Jake, who shrugged and keyed his mic, telling the rest of the team that they were moving into position.

Harley moved to the front of the fancy aerial tram, gazing through the spotless glass window as they slowly approached the well-lit monastery atop the mountain. In the glass, she could see her face reflected back at her, the long, flowing black wig; brown contacts; and tan foundation making her unrecognizable.

Misty stood slightly behind her, while Forrest and Erin were on the far side of the crowded tram chatting with some of the other hopeful buyers, all smiles and fake laughs like they were attending an evening social and not an auction were they intended to buy another living, breathing creature.

Out the corner of her eye, Harley could see Misty casually tapping on an iPad, making a show of scanning the currency figures listed under a number of international banks. Every once in a while, she'd move closer to Harley to point at something as if going over the status of available funds so she'd know exactly how much money she had for tonight's auction. The funny part was that the overflowing bank accounts Misty was busy skimming through were real and so was all the wealth they contained. The not-so-funny part was that the real Abella Herrera, the Spanish socialite Harley was impersonating, would have used that money to purchase a supernatural.

Abella had anchored her yacht off the nearby coastal village of Alexandrini late last night, planning to make the short two-hour drive into Kalambaka for the auction. But the real Abella and her assistant wouldn't be going anywhere. Thanks to Jake and Jes, both of them—along with the ship's entire crew—were passed out cold in their staterooms and would remain that way until sometime tomorrow. If Abella called the police, it would seem like they'd all been victims of a small carbon monoxide leak from the yacht's engine compartment.

As they neared the top of the mountain, Harley heard Caleb saying something over the radio about holding their position because a guard was walking past their part of the cliff face. Her heart clenched in her chest.

Harley hated the entire idea of Sawyer being on the side of the damn mountain with Jake and Caleb from the get-go. The thought of him out there on that smooth rock, risking a fall that could kill or seriously injure him, had nearly given her an anxiety attack. She wanted to say she had no idea why it was making her feel this way, but that'd be a lie.

She had a serious thing for Sawyer.

Since that night they'd kissed in the villa, they'd spent every free minute taking surveillance shifts together, then slipping away for meals on their own, even going for walks around town in the middle of the night.

And in between, they kissed and then kissed some more.

Harley had no idea what was going on, but it was impossible to ignore the chemistry between the two of them. When his lips were on hers, it was like getting zapped by Adriana, but in the best possible way. If they weren't in the middle of a covert operation, where their entire focus needed to be on stopping this auction, Harley would have jumped him three or four times already. That wasn't something she'd normally do. While she'd slept with a few guys since becoming a werewolf, and obviously some before, none of them had generated the same intense desire that Sawyer did by simply kissing her. In the darkest hours of the morning, when she was all by herself in bed, Harley could admit she was falling hard for him.

And the reality of their situation scared the hell out of her. If this mission went well tonight, Sawyer would almost certainly go back to the UK with the rest of his MI6 team and they'd probably never see each other again. The thought was enough to make her feel physically ill.

To make matters worse, she was pretty sure Caleb knew there was something going on. She'd caught him eyeing her and Sawyer more than a few times over the past two days. Jumping up and running out of the room during the mission briefing after Sawyer and Jake had overruled her objections to climbing the mountain hadn't helped. The expression on Caleb's face made her think he knew exactly what the deal was, which wasn't only crazy, but also impossible since she didn't know what the deal was herself.

Harley was still wondering what she was going to do about Sawyer—and Caleb—when she heard Jake urgently saying something on the radio about a guard coming to take a look. Had he said Sawyer fell?

She gripped the railing around the inside of the tram, swaying a little on her feet.

The tram shuddered a bit as they reached the topside station, but Harley ignored it as she strained to hear something that would tell her Sawyer was okay. She didn't realize her claws had extended and embedded themselves in the polished hardwood of the handrail until Misty reached out and put a gentle hand on her forearm. Her claws weren't out more than a quarter inch, but considering they hadn't made an appearance in eight years, she was a little stunned.

On the radio, Caleb was sarcastically asking if someone was done screwing around. That someone had to be Sawyer, which meant he was still around to rag on. But she refused to breathe easier until she heard Jake announcing they'd all made it to the top. Finally prying her claws out of the wooden railing, she turned to see if anyone had noticed. No one was looking at her curiously. Except Misty, of course. Harley nodded, silently letting her teammate know she was okay. Good thing, too, because the door of the tram slid back with a pneumatic hiss.

Showtime.

"This way, please," a man in an expensive suit said in a slightly accented voice from where he stood outside the door.

Harley almost froze as she recognized Long Hair, the guy who could appear and disappear at will. The one who'd stabbed her. She tried not to flinch when the man's dark gaze swept the tram, but if he recognized her and Misty, he gave no sign of it.

"If you'll form a line right out here, we can do a security check and scan your invitations, then get you on your way," he said.

The first person who stepped out of the tram, a distinguished-looking man in his midsixties with perfectly styled hair and neatly trimmed salt-and-pepper beard, frowned like he'd sucked a lemon. "We already presented our invitation down below."

"And now you're showing them to me," Long Hair said coldly. "Or you can turn and get back on the tram. Your choice."

The older man reached into an inside jacket pocket for his invitation and held it out with a disdainful expression. "Do you know who I am?"

Long Hair didn't say anything as he scanned the matrix bar code on the back of the card with an iPad. Harley couldn't see what it displayed, but Long Hair scrolled down and back up, studying whatever it was as a burly guard ran a handheld metal detector over the older man.

"I do now, Mr. Caron." Long Hair gave him a cool smile. "As well as everything else I'd ever want to know about you. Have a nice evening."

Caron looked like he was tempted to say something, but then appeared to think better of it and stepped past Long Hair. Harley applauded his common sense.

She tried to stay relaxed as she and Misty moved forward through the line. Jestina's makeup was top notch. There was nothing to worry about. That didn't keep her heart from thudding extra fast when she finally stood in front of Long Hair. The scar on her chest from where the bastard had stabbed her started to tingle.

When Long Hair scanned her invitation, she peeked over the edge of the iPad to see what was on the screen. Crap—not only did it show Abella's photo, but where she was from, what schools she'd attended, even her blood type. It was the picture that worried Harley the most. At the bottom of the mountain, they'd simply crossed her assumed name off a list, but this was an entirely different situation. What if her makeup wasn't good enough and this a-hole realized she wasn't who she was supposed to be? They'd kill her and Misty for sure.

Long Hair looked up from his iPad to study her closely while the guard ran the metal detector over her entire body. Harley tried to project an air of calm, entitled confidence as Long Hair scrolled through the info on the screen. Thank goodness she and her teammates hadn't attempted to bring weapons up here. That would have gotten them in trouble regardless of how good their makeup was.

"Ms. Herrera," he said slowly, drawing out each syllable much more than necessary before glancing at Misty. "And your plus one."

His gaze snapped back to Harley, his expression verging on suspicious. The scar on her chest burned even more, and she tensed, knowing things were about to go to hell in a handbag in another minute. She tensed, ready to take the guy down before he could say a word—or disappear.

"Have a nice evening," he said suddenly, offering her the card, then holding on to it longer than necessary before letting go, his eyes still locked with hers.

She resisted the urge to shudder.

Creepy much?

"Seamus," a woman's voice said from Harley's right. "Stop torturing the potential buyers. Boc wants them inside so we can start the auction as soon as possible."

Harley turned to see a pretty woman in her late twenties or early thirties, with long, silky, dark hair, walking toward them with a smile, a man at her side who looked so much like her that he had to be her brother.

"Oh, come on, Brielle," Seamus said with a laugh, motioning Harley and Misty through. "Can't a man have any fun?"

"When it holds up the boss's profits, then no. Nothing gets in the way of business. You should know that better than anyone."

Several other men arrived with iPads in hand, presumably to help Seamus check in the other guests. Harley quickly hurried past, Misty at her side. As they did, Harley glanced over her shoulder at the tall, slender woman. So, that was the woman who knew how to find supernaturals. Harley sniffed the air, trying to see if Brielle smelled supernatural. If she was, she didn't have a distinct scent Harley could pick up. Maybe Brielle was human. Either that or Harley's nose had decided to stop working again. It seemed the only thing she could consistently smell was Sawyer. Which, while very pleasant, wasn't so helpful right now.

Harley and Misty followed a red carpet toward the main building, bright lights illuminating the stacked-stone construction, terracotta roof tiles, and stone archways over the windows and door. But as breathtaking as the Holy Trinity Monastery was, it was the well-armed men positioned around the area that captured her attention. Most were facing outward, alert for exterior threats, but it was hard to miss the ones focused on the people arriving on the tram. If things suddenly went to crap, the men would probably fire at anything that moved, including the potential buyers.

"We need to get our hands on one of those iPads if we can," Misty whispered. "With all that information on there, it's almost a certainty they're connected to a central server of some kind. If I can get in there, I could get everything we need on these people."

Harley nodded. She'd watched Misty merge with a computer before and while it was amazing to see, it was also more than a little disconcerting.

"Misty and I made it through another checkpoint up top," Harley said softly into her radio, then quickly explained about Seamus and Brielle before telling them about Misty's idea.

"Sounds like a plan," Jake replied. "But be careful. And stay away from Brielle. We have no reason to think she knows you're both supernaturals, but let's not give her a reason to suspect you."

"We'll be searching for where the captives and the monks are being held," Sawyer added. "I'll also find a place to stash your weapons."

Harley didn't respond to his comment about the weapons, mostly because she was too focused on how good it felt to hear his voice. A weight she hadn't known was there lifted off her chest, making breathing a bit easier now.

The large room she and Misty stepped into was the quintessential image of what Harley expected a medieval monastery to look like, right down to the beautiful wall murals, soaring ceilings, and rough flagstone floors. She supposed it was the main chapel, though it was difficult to tell for sure since there wasn't any sign of all the usual religious items that'd almost certainly been there before Boc took over. All that remained now was a large rectangular space with a raised dais at one end along with several dozen tall-boy cocktail tables draped in black fabric here and there. Longer banquet tables on either side of the room held a buffet of assorted food and beverages that smelled delicious. And expensive.

The murmur of conversation grew louder in the room as more people began to fill the space. Harley glanced around to see Forrest and Erin casually chatting with Mr. Caron and several other well-dressed excuses for human beings. Everyone knew what was about to happen in here in a few minutes and no one seemed to care. They merely drank their expensive champagne and ate their dainty hors d'oeuvres.

"I'm going to see if I can find one of those iPads," Misty whispered, drifting away to disappear down a side corridor.

Harley pasted a smile on her face as two middle-aged women dripping in jewelry came over to chat. Her Spanish accent wasn't the best, so she had to be careful not to slip up. It was hard making nice with a group of people who got enjoyment from purchasing a supernatural creature. She couldn't help wondering what they'd say if they knew she was a werewolf. Would they scream and run away or demand to be allowed to bid on her?

"We found the captives and the monks," Sawyer announced softly over the radio in her ear. "They're being held in the dormitory area, but there are too many guards around for us to free them without starting a major firefight. We're going to have to stick with the plan and try to rescue them as they're being moved off the mountain."

Crap.

"Adriana and I are topside now," Elliot reported, interrupting whatever else Sawyer might have been about to say. "They're calling for some of the guards to help move the captives, so I think the auction is about to start."

A few minutes later, Harley saw several guards, including Sawyer, slip into the room and take up positions along the outer perimeter of the space. A tremor of concern slid down her back at the sight of all the tactical gear they wore and their expressionless demeanor. While the buyers in the room obviously assumed the men were here for their protection, something told her, once the shooting started, the guards would gladly shoot every rich snob in the place to stop her and her teammates.

She casually glanced at Sawyer, noticing he kept to the farthest, darkest corner of the room. To anyone else, it would seem like he was completely focused on the area he was guarding, but Harley knew he was taking everything in—marking the location of each threat, the number of windows and doors, and the complete lack of cover the room provided if this turned into a firefight. Which it almost certainly would at some point.

"Weapons are in the bottom of an empty trash can in the storage room near the restrooms," Sawyer murmured over the radio.

He was good. She didn't even see his lips move.

Harley wandered over to the buffet to help herself to some hors d'oeuvres. Tiny plate in hand, she nibbled on a canapé as she strolled around the room admiring the murals on the wall. When she reached the corridor near where Sawyer stood guard, she casually set the empty plate on a nearby serving tray, then headed down the hall toward the restrooms. Slipping into the storage closet, she quickly grabbed her small-frame Glock and backup magazine, tucking them into the holsters attached to the waistband at the back of her tailored pantsuit. Unlike at the club in Paris, she and Misty—along with Erin—had opted for slacks on this rescue mission, instead of dresses and high heels. When things got crazy tonight, they wanted to able to move quickly.

Peeking out the door to make sure no one had seen her, Harley walked back into the main room, taking a glass of champagne from the tray a nearby server offered as Erin passed by and walked down the same hallway to get her weapon. A few moments later, Forrest did the same. Harley would feel a lot better after all of them were armed.

The black velvet drapes at the back of the dais rustled, catching her attention, and Harley watched as a big man wheeled a large, cloth-covered box out from behind it. She frowned when she heard something sloshing around and realized it was full of some kind of liquid. To say she was curious was an understatement.

She was a little surprised one man was strong enough to handle the box. Then again, that guy was at least seven feet tall and muscular as hell. Harley did a double take. The guy's skin might not be green right now, but she was sure he was the scaly shifter they'd fought in Morocco.

Harley was relaying that information over the radio when Seamus stepped out from behind the curtain with someone else she recognized, this time from Paris—the guy she'd shot as he tried to escape with Adriana. She'd recognize that beat-up leather jacket anywhere.

"The guy in the leather jacket I shot in Paris is here, too," she added softly into her mic.

The guests fell silent as the large crate was finally positioned in the middle of the dais and the big man who'd been pushing it moved aside. It was like they all knew they were about to see something no one else had probably ever seen and were holding their breath in anticipation.

Stepping up to the box, Seamus pulled the satin cloth covering it away with a dramatic flourish. All around the room, gasps of surprise filled the air.

Harley blinked. What she'd assumed was a box turned out to be a glass tank filled to the very top with seawater and inside floated a girl who couldn't be any more than sixteen or seventeen at most, long, pale hair as fine as corn silk swirling around her. Naked from the waist up, she tried to find purchase on the inside of the slippery tank with one arm while attempting to hide her breasts with the other. Her pale green eyes were filled with so much fear and anguish, Harley wanted to cry.

Dragging her gaze away from the girl's, she saw the girl's lower body was covered in blue and green iridescent scales like a fish, ending in a webbed tail twice as wide as her shoulders.

Crap. The girl was a mermaid.

"I don't think I need to tell anyone what you're looking at," a deeply accented voice said.

Harley turned her attention away from the poor creature in the tank to see a man stepping onto the dais. In his midforties, with curly, brown hair and a beard, he had gray eyes the color of steel.

There was a sharp intake of breath over the radio, but Harley ignored it as the man stopped beside the mermaid's tank. The young girl darted to the opposite side, like she'd do anything to put space between her and the man.

While the man didn't introduce himself, Harley instinctively knew he had to be Boc. One look at him convinced her the guy was soulless. You had to be to kidnap a mermaid from her ocean home and sell her like a piece of meat.

"The tank will be made available to the winning bidder," Boc continued, reaching over to rap his knuckles loudly on the glass and smiling when the mermaid winced in pain. "If you'd rather not transport it, however, we'll gladly drag her out. Her human legs will reform as soon as she dries off. Though I feel obliged to tell you now, the transformation is extremely painful for her. The screams she lets out during the process are unlike anything you've ever heard in your lives." He chuckled. "Which, in my opinion, are well worth the purchase price alone."

It took everything Harley had not to pull her gun and shoot Boc then and there, even as everyone around her beamed. These people were sick.

"Since this is our first item tonight, let's start the bidding on the low side just for the sake of fun," Boc continued. "Say…five hundred thousand euros?"

Harley only got more disgusted as the people around her eagerly began to outbid each other. If she hadn't already been willing to risk her life to save the captives, one look at these sickos would have changed her mind.

Movement out the corner of her eye caught her attention, and she turned her head to see that Sawyer had stepped out of the shadows. He seemed visibly stunned as he stared at the dais, his face paler than she'd ever seen it.

She weaved through the crowd toward the buffet, feigning disinterest in the bidding as it quickly climbed over eight million euros and pretending to focus on the plates of fancy food and glasses of champagne. The move took her closer to Sawyer and allowed her to talk to him without anyone noticing.

"What's wrong?" she asked quietly. "I know that what they're doing to that poor mermaid is disgusting, but you look like you've seen a ghost."

"Almost." He looked around as if scanning the room for threats, then whispered, "Boc is Yegor Shevchenko, the Ukrainian terrorist I put away four years ago. The one who's supposed to be in a Turkish prison."

CHAPTER 11

SAWYER'S HEAD SPUN. HOW THE HELL COULD YEGOR Shevchenko be standing here in a room full of morally bankrupt bastards auctioning off supernatural creatures? The man had been sentenced to twenty years in Diyarbakir, the worst hellhole of a prison on the planet. The thought of him surviving long enough to even attempt an escape was laughable. The fact that he'd obviously done it—without MI6 ever knowing—was terrifying.

Or did his bosses at MI6 know and simply never bothered to tell him?

A few feet away, Harley did a double take. "Are you sure?"

"He's right," Erin's voice came over the radio before he could say anything. "I've been standing here telling myself it couldn't possibly be that son of a bitch, but Sawyer's right. It's Yegor."

Harley locked eyes with Sawyer's, the look in them reminding him of their conversation the other night in the villa. The realization that she'd been right about the murders of his former teammates being tied to the traffickers was like another kick to the bollocks. Yegor was tracking down and killing everyone he blamed for his imprisonment and the death of his brother.

Was kidnapping supernaturals and auctioning them off to the highest bidder a complex scheme to lure Sawyer and his team here, so Yegor could kill them all in one place? It seemed impossible to fathom, but how else could Sawyer explain nearly all of the remaining members of that original MI6 team being hand delivered to the man who wanted them dead?

Shouts of excitement from the front of the room snapped Sawyer out of his musings. Damn, he must have zoned out for a while. The mermaid and her water-filled tank were gone from the dais to be replaced by a despondent young man in his twenties. Naked from the waist up, he had a pair of feathered wings hanging down his back all the way to the floor.

Bloody frigging wings!

The winged supernatural fetched even more than the mermaid and was quickly led away even as another captive took his place. This one was an older man who looked so completely ordinary in comparison to the previous supernaturals, it defied logic to think he was one. Within seconds, ice began to form on the palms of the man's hands, filling his palms. A minute later, the bidding on the old man was over, happening so fast it made Sawyer wonder how many other bids he'd missed while he'd been trying to figure out how the hell Yegor was free.

"I have to get back and make it look like I'm interested in bidding," Harley said softly.

He gave her a nod, watching as she slipped into the crowd of people gathered around the dais.

Sawyer stayed where he was, watching as one supernatural after another was auctioned off. He didn't catch what most of their abilities were because he was listening to Jake and Caleb on the radio saying the supernaturals already purchased were being taken back to the dorms instead of to the tram. Jes chimed in, saying she and Rory were topside now as well, letting them know Rory had slipped away to check on the monks. At the same time, he heard Harley trying to get into contact with Misty, who hadn't responded to a radio check since she'd walked out of the room fifteen minutes ago.

Okay, that was serious reason for concern. Especially when Forrest said something about Misty getting *lost* in the networks when she melded with them. He wasn't surprised when Jake and Forrest said they'd go find her. With Jake's nose, it shouldn't take too long.

Sawyer looked at the dais, expecting them to drag out another supernatural for bidding, but instead servers appeared carrying trays of champagne and hors d'oeuvres, moving through the crowd of guests. At the same time, several men walked around with iPads, providing money transfer confirmation to the buyers. This crap was so efficient it make him sick.

On the dais, Yegor was talking to several of his goons, including the big guy Harley thought might be the scaly green shifter. Looking at the size of the guy, Sawyer couldn't say she was wrong. As the conversation continued, he strained to hear what was being said, but between the distance, the murmuring of the crowd, and how quietly Yegor spoke, he could only make out about every fifth word or so. Something about changing the order of the auction and making sure everyone was in place for the surprise.

He didn't like the sound of that, even if he had no idea what they were talking about. He caught Harley's eye, then Erin's. Yeah, they realized something was off, too.

Sawyer checked in with everyone else over the radio, but no one knew what was going on. Jake and Forrest were still tracking Misty, following her scent all the way across the monastery and were on their way back. Unfortunately, they hadn't found her yet. Jake hadn't heard anything suspicious over the radio he'd taken from that guard, so there was nothing to make him think Yegor was onto their presence.

Caleb was still keeping an eye on the captives in the dormitories, both those awaiting their turn on the auction block and those already sold. Elliot, Adriana, and Jes, along with most of the muscle brought in from Athens, had all been told to take a break in the monastery's kitchen until the auction started again. Jes was a little concerned about being so far away from the rest of the team but hadn't gotten the feeling there was anything to worry about. Though she was antsy about Rory being out of contact for so long.

But as normal as everything seemed—if you could call anything about this normal—Sawyer couldn't ignore the instincts telling him something was off. He threw another look Harley's way, those same instincts urging him to move closer to her, insisting he put his body between her and some unknown threat. Of course, that was kind of hard to do when he had no idea where the danger was coming from. Not to mention the fact that it might look a little odd for a guard like him to take a sudden interest in any one particular buyer.

"I apologize for the delay," Yegor said, turning to face the crowd, a broad smile on his face as the guy they thought was the scaly shifter rolled out another large, fabric-covered crate. "But I think you will all agree the next creature up for bid is certainly something worth waiting for. This one is truly unique."

Sawyer tensed as Seamus and several other men he recognized from Paris, including the guy in the leather jacket joined Yegor on the dais. When half a dozen more guards strode into the room, he knew things were about to get ugly.

"Things are about to go sideways," Sawyer murmured into his mic. "I don't know how, but I think we've been made."

"This particular creature possesses an unparalleled talent." Yegor casually rested a hand on the fabric draped over the crate. "She can meld her consciousness with any complex electronic device. This allows her to bypass any existing security features, then extract and memorize megabytes of information. In fact, I found her a few minutes ago in the process of stealing secrets from my own network."

Sawyer cursed. "That asshole has Misty."

Over the radio, he heard Forrest let out an anguished "*No!*" accompanied by boots on stone as he and Jake ran toward the main room.

The sound was still echoing in Sawyer's earpiece when Yegor yanked the fabric away from the cage to reveal an unconscious Misty. The auburn wig she'd been wearing was gone and her long, purple hair cascaded over her slim shoulders. Beside the cage,

Seamus flicked open his switchblade, casually holding it down at his side.

Eyes locked on Sawyer from across the room, Yegor's mouth twisted in an evil smile.

Gunfire suddenly erupted from somewhere off the main room and Sawyer heard Jes shouting over the radio that Yegor's men had found them even as she, Rory, and Elliot returned fire.

Shit.

From the corner of his eye, Sawyer saw the guards lining the perimeter of the room close in, guns coming up as the people with their iPads and serving trays hurriedly left the room. The guests looked around in confusion, realizing something was happening but not knowing what.

Sawyer had to admire the way Yegor had manipulated this entire evening. He'd gotten them all on the mountaintop, separated from any backup support, and then split them up into smaller groups, making it easier to take them down. Now, he was using Misty to control the situation. If Sawyer, Harley, or Erin made the first move, Seamus would kill Misty. If they didn't make the first move, the guards would put a bullet through all of their heads. And Misty would die anyway—if she wasn't sold off to this disgusting collection of morally corrupt assholes.

Cursing, Erin pulled the handgun from the holster hidden under the jacket of her pantsuit, aimed it at Seamus, and pulled the trigger. The guy immediately disappeared, but not before Sawyer saw a splatter of blood exit his right shoulder, staining the black curtain behind him.

Harley ran for Misty's cage as the entire room erupted into gunfire. A hail of bullets zipped past Sawyer as he brought his own weapon up to cover Harley. He fired a burst of automatic weapon fire from his MP5, aiming for Yegor and the other men near Misty's cage, driving most of them back. The huge shifter didn't seem to care at all about being shot at, even when one of the 9mm rounds from Sawyer's submachine gun hit him in the thigh. With a guttural growl that would have been right at home in a swamp, the shifter charged off the dais, skin thickening and turning more greenish brown with every stride.

Sawyer felt multiple rounds slam into the back of his tactical vest, but he ignored it as the shifter charged him. He aimed for the guy's knees, remembering how little effect bullets had on the thing the first time around but hoping he could at least slow the creature down a little.

Then out of nowhere, Erin came running in, throwing herself on the shifter's back and shoving her weapon against the side of his head, squeezing off round after round as the creature spun around, trying to throw her off.

Sawyer moved to help her, his fingertips and gums already tingling from the adrenaline pouring through him. But before he could take more than two steps toward them, a blur of movement near the cage caught his attention. He spun in time to see Seamus popping into existence behind Harley as she knelt by the door of the cage, frantically working at the lock with a pick set. Murder in his eyes, Seamus lifted the knife, ready to plunge it into her back.

Keeping his inner wolf in check wasn't an option anymore. Sawyer's claws and fangs fully extended as rage filled him. But the partial shift didn't keep him from bringing his MP5 up and firing a three-round burst at Seamus. None of the 9mm's bullets hit the supernatural, but it made the a-hole jump back. It also alerted Harley to the danger. Throwing herself to the side, she brought up her gun to put a round through Seamus's head, but the bastard disappeared again.

A scream of pain pierced the air and Sawyer snapped his head around in time to see the big, green shifter toss Erin across the room like a rag doll. Growling in frustration, Sawyer looked around wildly, trying to figure out where that damn disappearing psycho Seamus would show up next while at the same time attempting to avoid the bullets Yegor and the guards were sending his way.

Sawyer fired the remainder of his magazines at the guards and Yegor, hitting some and making the rest of them duck. Then he dropped his MP5 and launched himself at the big shifter, knocking the huge creature to the ground and pulling his handgun from the holster low on his thigh. Knowing the scaly monster was as close to bulletproof as any living thing could get, Sawyer didn't waste time going for the usual targets like the stomach, chest, or head. Instead, he shoved the barrel of the large caliber weapon right against the shifter's crotch and emptied half a magazine into his private parts. The creature immediately yanked himself into a fetal position, screaming like Sawyer had dumped acid on him.

Maybe the thing wasn't covered in armored scales everywhere.

Sawyer didn't pause to enjoy the moment. Jumping to his feet with a snarl, he sprinted toward Harley, arriving just as Seamus popped back into view. Sawyer didn't even slow as he wrapped one clawed hand in the man's long hair and shoved him backward into Misty's cage. He shoved the man's head into the steel bars, fully intending to crush his miserable frigging skull to pieces for even thinking about stabbing Harley again. Unfortunately, the fucker disappeared before Sawyer could do any serious damage to him, making him growl so loudly in frustration it echoed off the walls.

Harley had Misty out of the cage before Sawyer turned around, the automatic in her hand firing steadily at the crazy number of guards pouring into the auction room. She shielded her unconscious teammate as she killed one guard after another.

All around them, the room was total bedlam, bullets tearing up the beautiful wall murals and bouncing off the floors as the rich buyers in their fancy clothes screamed, pushed, shoved, and climbed over one another in an attempt to get to the exits. Some tried to hide in the corners and alcoves, but it didn't help. The guards might not be aiming for them but didn't seem to care if one or two guests went down in the crossfire as they tried to kill Sawyer, Harley, and Erin.

Sawyer looked around for Yegor, finding him rallying his troops—including the one with the leather jacket from Paris and the woman Harley said was the supernatural hunter, Brielle. Neither of them seemed to be very interested in shooting at anyone, but Yegor's other goons blazed away at anything that moved.

"The werewolves!" Yegor shouted. "Kill the two werewolves!"

Sawyer's blood ran cold as the implication of the words hit him. He glanced at Harley to see that she'd heard it, too—and looked as shocked as he was. Sawyer didn't know how it was possible, but Yegor somehow knew they were werewolves.

He threw himself to the stone floor to avoid an incoming hail of gunfire from the guards but couldn't keep from sliding his eyes in Erin's direction, wondering if she'd heard what Yegor said. It turned out Erin wasn't in a position to hear anything because the shifter had a hand around her neck and was holding her three meters off the floor while she tried to punch and kick at him.

Cursing, Sawyer jumped to his feet, the muscles of his back and legs twisting and spasming to give him more speed as he ran to help her. Multiple bullets tore through his body, and it was the worst pain he'd felt since Odessa. But he pushed all that aside, running faster even as a voice in the back of his head told him he'd never get there before the big shifter either crushed Erin's throat or snapped her neck.

He was still twenty meters away from his teammate when a snarling blur crossed in front of him, slamming into the gigantic shifter so hard Erin was pitched ten feet through the air. The impact of her body as she hit the stone flooring was hard enough to make Sawyer feel it.

Then Caleb was on top of the creature, attempting to smash in his face with a boot he'd picked up somewhere—a boot that seemed to have part of a leg and a foot still in it. Sawyer found himself absently wondering where the rest of the man's body might be at the moment.

Praying the omega could handle the shifter, Sawyer skidded to a stop long enough to make sure Erin was still alive, then turned and headed back to Harley. Every instinct he had screamed to get to her side and protect her. And even though it was obvious she could take care of herself, those instincts couldn't be denied.

Sawyer got to Harley's side and helped her get a better grip on Misty.

"Stay behind me," he said. "We need to get her out of here."

He ignored what he was sure was a complaint about being able to take care of herself. Instead he turned and charged straight at Yegor and the cluster of guards with him, emptying the rest of his handgun magazine into the middle of them as he cut loose with a snarl that shook dust from the ceiling. Some of the men went down from the gunfire, while the others froze, eyes widening as he came at them with fully extended claws and fangs.

The first guy he got to went down under his claws, something Sawyer had never done before. Refusing to dwell on that fact, he scooped up the submachine gun the guy had been holding and started blazing away at full auto.

He wasn't sure when Forrest showed up, but out of the corner of his eye, Sawyer saw him take Misty from Harley, cradling her protectively and freeing up Harley so she could fight. Sawyer would have preferred if she stayed behind him, but that was never going to happen. While her claws and fangs might not be out, there was little doubt that Harley was an alpha werewolf to her core. She snarled and fought with an anger and intensity that had people stumbling back to get away from her.

When Jake and Elliot arrived, Yegor must have realized the numbers were against him because he started to retreat, edging toward the main doors. There was no way in hell Sawyer was letting that son of a bitch get away.

Reloading the MP5 he'd taken away from the guard, he swung it around, aiming straight for Yegor's head. Before he could pull the trigger, Yegor grabbed Brielle, dragging her in front of him like a shield and putting a gun to her head, forcing Sawyer to ease up on the trigger.

Brielle immediately struggled to get lose, but Yegor kept her in front of him, one arm wrapped around her neck as he backed toward the door. A younger guy who looked a lot like Brielle ran over to help her, but Seamus appeared out of nowhere to plunge his knife into the man's shoulder.

Brielle screamed, her dark eyes going wide with terror, and she fought Yegor harder than before. But Yegor merely backpedaled until they were both out of the room along with a handful of his men. Seamus and the rest stayed behind to cover their boss's retreat.

"Yegor's getting away!" Sawyer shouted over the radio.

He had no doubt Yegor would head straight for the aerial tram and probably kill Brielle along the way. She might work for Yegor, but apparently, she wasn't that valuable anymore.

Over the gunfire going on around him, Sawyer heard Adriana screaming for Kristoff to get down and vaguely remembered that was the name of her boyfriend. He assumed that meant some of the captives had gotten free and had come into the room. Somewhere in the midst of the fighting, Erin shouted over the radio for Rory again and again, wanting to know why their teammate wasn't responding. Sawyer hated like hell to go there, but he knew it was probably because Rory had already been killed. They hadn't heard a word from him since the shit hit the fan.

Over by the doors, Seamus suddenly disappeared. Sawyer barely had a chance to wonder where the hell he'd gone when the damn guy popped back into existence next to the big green shifter, where the creature was still brawling with Caleb. Sawyer cursed, expecting Seamus to go after Caleb with the knife, but instead he slapped a hand against the creature's shoulder. A split second later, both Seamus and the shifter disappeared into thin air, leaving Caleb standing there in shock.

Sawyer stared in disbelief. He hadn't realized Seamus could do that.

It took less than thirty seconds for the last of the guards to realize the fight was over. They dropped their weapons and lifted their hands in the air, giving up. Jake shouted something about tying them up as Sawyer shoved his way through them to get to the doors. He sprinted for the aerial tram, Harley and Erin right behind him.

Yegor and the green shifter were already on the tram, Brielle lying on the ground, unconscious. Seamus must have gone back to grab Adriana because he was dragging her into the car. Surely, he knew how close he was to getting fried right then.

But right as blue sparks began to dance over Adriana's skin, the guy in the leather jacket burst out a side door and raced over to them. Punching Seamus, he shoved him into the tram just as it pulled away from the station. Wrapping an arm around Adriana, he urged her off to the side.

The moment Adriana was clear of their line of fire, Sawyer, Harley, and Erin started shooting, scattering the few goons who'd been left behind by their boss. Sawyer didn't blame them for bailing when it was obvious the Ukrainian didn't care if they lived or died. But whether they realized it or not, even the few seconds they'd held their ground were enough to allow the tram to slide a few hundred meters down the cable.

Sawyer brought his submachine gun up to his shoulder, slowing his breathing and sighting in on the glass-enclosed car carefully. There was nothing but glass between him and Yegor, and that wasn't going to be enough to keep that bastard alive this time. But he had to make the shot before the car was out of range.

Ignoring the tingles he suddenly felt all over his body, he started to squeeze the trigger when a blur of movement appeared in front of him, blocking his view. Sawyer only had a fraction of a second to realize it was Seamus, popping into existence centimeters away from him, before a searing pain erupted in his chest.

Harley's scream echoed in Sawyer's ears as he stumbled back. Confused, he looked down and saw the knife sticking out of the center of his chest. Bloody hell, that hurt like a son of a bitch. Seamus had shown up long enough to shove a knife through his chest before popping back into the moving tram. The bloody fucking bastard waved at them as the car continued to descend, already too far away for the rounds Erin was busy firing at it to do any damage.

Then Harley was there, yanking the knife out of his chest even as Erin turned and stared at him in complete horror. Out of the corner of his eye, he saw Adriana throwing herself in front of the guy with the leather jacket, purposely putting her body between him and the rest of the team that had shown up.

"Don't shoot!" she shouted, sparkles of electricity covering her skin, making her hair float up around her like it had when she'd zapped Harley. "He's my boyfriend!"

Sawyer didn't have a second to wonder how the hell that was even possible because Erin's face was suddenly in his, eyes furious. He didn't understand why until he realized she was looking at his fangs and claws.

"You're one of them," she accused, her expression rolling through a dozen different emotions before finally settling on anger. "You're a frigging werewolf!"

Bloody hell.

There was no way he was going to be able to talk himself out of this one.

CHAPTER 12

HARLEY SLOWLY WALKED DOWN THE STEPS OF THE SAFE house, absently following her nose toward the wonderful smell of fresh coffee coming from the first floor. She'd gotten a grand total of an hour and fifteen minutes of sleep before the sound of her teammates' voices woke her up. While she'd like nothing more than to turn around and crawl back in bed for a few more hours, she couldn't.

She'd expected everything to boil over at some point, but she'd been hoping everyone would wait until after breakfast. Or brunch, she supposed, considering it had already been after eight in the morning by the time they'd all arrived at the safe house the support team had set up for them on the southern outskirts of Athens. But apparently, that was too much to ask.

As she walked down the hall to the kitchen, Harley wondered if there was any chance they could put their differences aside and focus on the reason STAT and MI6 were still in Greece this morning instead of on a flight back to their respective homes. Namely, Yegor Shevchenko and the millions upon millions of euros he'd gotten away with from the auction. Both STAT and MI6 wanted to know where the man and his millions had gone, as well as what he planned to do with all that money. Actually, MI6 wanted to know a whole lot more than that. Like how the hell the man had gotten out of that prison cell in Turkey without them knowing about it. Unfortunately, while all those issues were definitely important to management, there were a few other problems that were pretty high up on the priority list for each team as well. Problems they were going to have to deal with before doing anything else.

It was hard to figure out which one of those concerns would be the most contentious this morning—that Sawyer was a werewolf, that Adriana's *boyfriend* was actually one of the traffickers, or that Rory had been the one feeding Yegor information since the morning after what happened in Paris.

Harley hoped it was the latter. She and everyone else had been stunned when they'd found Rory fifteen minutes after the fight was over, holding a young girl who'd been...tortured...for lack of a better word. The girl was Rory's younger sister, Tilly. His *supernatural* younger sister. Rory hadn't been too forthcoming, but from what he'd been willing to tell them last night, they'd learned Yegor had been holding the girl and using threats of violence against her to force Rory to keep him informed on STAT/MI6's plans.

Maybe the most shocking part of that particular confession was when Sawyer, Erin, and Elliott had decided to keep the information from Weatherford. At least for now. Maybe that meant everything else would work out okay, too.

That hope was dashed when Harley stepped into the immense white kitchen with its stucco walls and blue accents and picked up on the tangible tension in the room. She noticed she was the last one down. Well, except for Adriana, who was nowhere in sight. Then again, Adriana was almost certainly still with Kristoff. He was being held on the far side of the city at an abandoned clinic the support team had set up to serve as a makeshift hospital/jail. Not only had they needed a place to keep all the supernaturals until they could get them home, but they also needed somewhere to hold the bad guys they'd arrested. Harley had no idea how she and her teammates would have managed without the combined support teams' help.

When Jake called McKay to give him a report, they'd fully expected to have to deal with everyone themselves until the support teams could get there from Morocco, which was nearly a full day away by plane. Luckily, McKay knew better than to listen to them, because he and Weatherford had already moved both backup teams to the airport in Albania, where they'd been waiting on a plane that was fueled up and ready to fly. Two hours later, the support teams showed up to handle transportation and accommodations for everyone on the mountain, including one very happy mermaid in a seriously heavy water-filled tank.

And since they now knew where the information leak had come from, living without backup was no longer a requirement.

Harley glanced around as she moved over to the granite island that separated the kitchen from the adjoining living/dining area. As she filled a plate with scrambled eggs, a custard-filled pastry, cheese, yogurt, toast slathered in orange marmalade, and fresh fruits, she noticed her STAT teammates had chosen to grab seats on the far side of the living room while the MI6 agents were at the dining room table on the other side of the room, with Rory sitting at the far end away from the others. Yeah, that particular dynamic was going to take a while to work out. Almost as long as it'd take for them to reconcile with the fact that Sawyer was a werewolf.

She looked over at Sawyer, noting that he'd moved a chair closer to the coffee table, sitting halfway between the two teams while he ate. He met her gaze, his blue eyes full of hurt, but also resolve. Like he already knew his teammates had rejected him. From the way they were acting, maybe he was right.

Erin looked so angry she seemed like she might burst into flames—or shoot someone. Elliott kept his eyes on his plate the whole time, even though it was empty, refusing to acknowledge anyone. Rory appeared to be lost in thought for the most part, ignoring his plate of food. No doubt, he was thinking about his sister. Or maybe how the hell he was going to salvage what was left of his career. Assuming MI6 didn't simply fire him on the spot when they found out.

Harley's STAT teammates weren't quite as tense. As they sipped their coffee, Jes and Forrest darted curious glances back and forth between Sawyer and his friends like they were wondering when someone would light the first match and blow this whole thing to pieces. Jake ate in silence, maybe willing to simply let the MI6 team tear themselves apart if that's what they wanted to do. Caleb was too busy making roll-ups from cold cuts and cheese and eating them like Twizzlers to pay attention to what anyone else was doing. And Misty looked too exhausted to care about any of this crap. Harley didn't blame her. Misty had only come out of her coma an hour before sunrise—the coma Yegor had put her in when he'd found her buried in one of his iPads and forcibly ripped her out. To say that yanking Misty out of a network connection was brutal on her consciousness was putting it mildly. Harley and everyone else in STAT worried that one of these days, they'd lose Misty forever.

Plate in one hand and mug of coffee in the other, Harley moved a kitchen chair over to sit beside Sawyer. That earned her a self-satisfied snort from Erin, as if where she sat confirmed something she already knew, although Harley wasn't sure what.

"How's your chest feeling this morning?" Harley asked, resting her plate on her lap and loading her fork with scrambled eggs. They were mixed with spinach, tomatoes, and feta cheese and simply delicious. She could kiss every member of the support teams for getting all this food delivered.

Sawyer lifted his hand, his fingers lightly grazing his chest through the button-down he wore, wincing a little. "It's healed for the most part but still a little tender to the touch and hurts when I cough. Your medics confirmed there weren't any metal fragments in there, so it should be completely good to go by tonight."

"That's a relief."

Harley used a slice of cantaloupe to scoop up some of the yogurt, chewing slowly. Werewolves could heal quickly from nearly any wound as long as there wasn't any foreign debris in it. When Seamus had stabbed Sawyer, that had been the least of her worries. She'd been sure the blade had gone right through his heart, a wound that would kill even a werewolf.

At that moment, Harley had thought Sawyer was going to die right in front of her and it had been the most horrible moment of her life. Worse than getting hit by that avalanche. Worse than getting buried alive in freezing snow. Worse even than when her family had looked at her like she was a monster and turned their backs on her. At that moment, her chest had constricted so tightly that breathing was impossible and she knew she was going to die right along with him.

But then she'd pulled out the knife, Sawyer hadn't died, Adriana had thrown herself on top of her criminal boyfriend, and Erin had lost her ever-loving mind. Somewhere buried in the middle of all that drama, Harley's heart had started to beat again. With it, came a serious realization that the British MI6 agent meant more to her than she could ever have possibly imagined.

"You bit him, didn't you?" Erin demanded, yanking Harley out of the confusing thoughts swirling around in her head. "You turned him into a bloody werewolf!"

Harley looked up to see Erin, glaring at her and Sawyer. Well, actually, glaring mostly at her. On the other hand, Elliott *was* staring straight at Sawyer. But his expression involved less anger and a lot more pity. Maybe he felt badly Sawyer had been turned into a monster by another monster.

Rory glanced up for a second, his face harder to read, but he didn't seem nearly as upset as the other two. That was probably because he had a lot more experience with the supernatural world than his teammates. Unlike them, he didn't look mad or even filled with pity. It was more like he was disappointed in some way.

"It doesn't work that way, Erin," Harley said, nibbling on the sweet custard pastry, hoping the other woman would listen to reason. "People can't be turned into a werewolf from a bite."

Erin stood so fast she nearly flipped over her chair. "Yeah right!

You expect us to believe it's a coincidence that within a few days of running into a team with three werewolves, Sawyer became one by accident? If you didn't bite him, it's only because the werewolf curse is sexually transmitted."

Caleb snorted so hard Harley was shocked he didn't choke on his food. When he fixed Erin with a hard look, Harley could tell he definitely wasn't amused.

"I thought you were smarter than this," he scoffed. "If becoming a werewolf was as simple as having sex with one, don't you think we'd be up to our ears in them by now? Even if it were a bite, there'd still be thousands of us by now. Instead, you're sitting in the room with the only five werewolves you're probably ever going to see for the rest of your life."

Erin shook her head, her expression making it obvious she was ready to deny everything Caleb said, but Sawyer cut her off.

"Erin, stop," he said, his voice firm and impossible to ignore. "Harley didn't turn me. I was a werewolf long before we ever ran into STAT."

Erin and Elliot looked stunned, like they'd been punched in the gut. Rory still seemed more hurt than anything else. Was he more upset Sawyer was a werewolf or that he hadn't told them?

"That's pure rubbish," Erin insisted. "We're your teammates. I'd think we'd know if you were a sodding monster."

Sawyer went completely still, and for a moment, Harley wasn't sure if he'd get up and walk out. She wouldn't blame him if he did.

"I've been a werewolf for more than four years," he finally said, his voice so soft even Harley had to strain to hear it. "I turned during the shootout in Odessa. After the rest of you dumped me in that hospital and bailed, I coded out three times on the operating room table. I would have died if I hadn't gone through the change. Being a werewolf was in my blood all along, simply waiting for the right event to bring it out."

Harley hated that Sawyer's teammates were forcing him to

admit all of this. But even more, she hated that he had to relive the pain of that night all over again. It was clear now he'd been lying when he said being left behind by his teammates hadn't bothered him. The agony in his eyes made her want to cry—or tear something apart.

"What do you mean, it was in your blood?" Erin asked.

"We call it the werewolf gene," Harley said, trying to keep her voice calm as she filled the silence. "If we go through something painful and traumatic, we turn. It doesn't have anything to do with getting bitten or being a monster. It's genetic."

Elliott frowned. "None of that explains why you never told us. You should have come to us and explained what happened."

It was Sawyer's turn to let out a snort. "I tend to remember someone drawing a weapon on the first werewolf she ever met." He pinned Erin with a look. "And based on how you've treated me since last night, it doesn't seem like my greeting has been that much different. You can't even stand to be within ten feet of me. So, you tell me, why would I have told you anything? Why would I open myself up to your rejection when I knew that's all I'd get?"

Erin crossed her arms over her chest, mouth tight. "We wouldn't have acted that way if you would have come out and told us right after it happened, instead of waiting to spring it on us like this."

Beside her, Harley could see how hard Sawyer was fighting back the hurt and disappointment.

"Right." Sawyer got to his feet, facing off against teammates. "You expect me to believe that any of you would have reacted better four years ago if I'd told you I was a werewolf? That I was waking up in the middle of the night with a mouth full of fangs and thought I was going mad most of the time? Please. You think I'm a monster now even after all the time we've spent together, the parties we've had, holidays we've spent together, all the times I've saved your lives. If I came to you back then, can any of you look me in the eye and honestly say you wouldn't have turned your back on me? Or would you have simply turned me over to MI6 headquarters and let them deal with me?"

Elliott had the decency to look at least somewhat chagrined at Sawyer's words, but Erin didn't seem fazed at all.

"I guess you'll never know how we would have reacted," she snapped. "You never gave us the chance to show you one way or the other. Instead, you decided not to trust us. You lied to us!"

"Trust? Lies?" Harley was so frustrated on Sawyer's behalf that her fangs started coming out. She stood and walked over to stand beside him, something insisting they present a united front as she glared at Erin. "Are you kidding me? How can you talk about any of that crap after Sawyer saved your butt last night? Hell, if it wasn't for him, all three of you would have died in Odessa and probably a dozen times since. But all you can do is whine about the secrets he kept from you because he knew you'd never understand or accept him."

Harley braced herself for another cutting comment from Erin, but it was Rory who spoke.

"Is that why you were willing to ditch us before the mission in Morocco?" he asked, eyeing Sawyer. "Because you'd already decided you'd rather work with a team that would be able to accept your secret than stay with us?"

Harley looked sharply at Sawyer. She didn't know what Rory was talking about, but it was obvious from the expression on his face that something had happened before they left Paris.

Sawyer opened his mouth to answer, but Erin interrupted before he could.

"Don't bother," she said, all her anger gone now to be replaced by what appeared to be resignation. "It's clear you made your decision a long time ago. You trust your new team more than you trust us, and that's fine. You do what you have to do and we'll do the same."

Harley stared in shock as Erin and Elliott walked out of the room and up the stairs. She glanced at Sawyer to see the muscle in his jaw flex. She wanted to say something—anything—but she was too filled with anguish over what he must be feeling to come up with the words. Not that it mattered because anything she said would have gotten interrupted by Erin and Elliot stomping down the steps and out the front door, overnight bags slung over their shoulders.

For a minute, Harley expected Sawyer to go after them, but he didn't. Instead, he stood there, face expressionless, and she couldn't help but think about the day her family turned their backs on her and remember how much it had torn her insides out. She wished like anything he'd never had to experience that.

Sawyer slanted Rory a look. "What about you? Are you walking out, too?"

Rory gave him a rueful smile. "I think I should be the last person on the planet throwing around words like *trust* and *lies*. I don't know where the hell I'm going to be tomorrow, but for now, until I figure out what I'm doing next, I'll stay."

Harley suspected that had more to do with whether MI6 found out what Rory had done than if he hated the idea of Sawyer being a werewolf.

Sawyer gave him a nod, then looked at Jake. "We should go talk to Brielle and Adriana's boyfriend. See what they can tell us about Yegor."

Harley would have preferred to talk to Sawyer alone before they did anything, but one look at him told her that wasn't going to happen. He was in full-on alpha-male mode right now.

Jake nodded. "Agreed. If we're lucky, maybe they know where to find him."

"I'm in," Caleb said. "But first we all need to finish breakfast. That fight last night took a lot out of all of us. And for heaven's sake, Harley, could you skip the fruit and yogurt and eat some protein? You're a werewolf, not a wererabbit."

Everyone laughed at that—even Sawyer—and for the first time, Harley realized Caleb was a lot more astute than she gave him credit for. As she and Sawyer headed into the kitchen to grab more food, a smile on her face, she turned and mouthed *Thank you* to her teammate for helping Sawyer forget people he thought were his friends had abandoned him.

Caleb acted like he didn't see it, but a smile tugged at the corners of his mouth all the same.

CHAPTER 13

"I DIDN'T EVEN KNOW TILLY WAS MISSING UNTIL I RECEIVED a message at my hotel room in Paris," Rory said softly, leaning against the doorjamb of his sister's room, watching grimly as one of the medical support team members carefully tucked a blanket around the girl. "They sent me photos of Tilly in their captivity." He swallowed hard, clearly reliving the memory. "I was just leaving the room to tell you about it when Yegor called my cell saying he had Tilly and that if I ever wanted to see her again, I had to do exactly as he instructed." Rory gave Sawyer an apologetic look. "I didn't want to betray you, but Yegor told me he'd kill Tilly if I didn't. I couldn't take the chance he was bluffing. Not when it came to my baby sister. I'd do anything in the world to keep her safe, no matter what. I hope you can understand that."

Sawyer glanced at the bed. Rory's sister was eighteen, but she was so damn pale and looked so fragile lying there sleeping that she seemed much younger. The STAT support team doctor assured them the girl would be okay physically, but Sawyer wasn't so sure of her mental and emotional health after this.

Looking at the frail girl on the bed and seeing Rory torturing himself for what happened to her, any residual anger and resentment Sawyer might still have felt disappeared in that moment.

"I can," Sawyer told him. "I don't want to imagine ever being put in your position, but if I were, I probably would have done the same thing."

Rory gave him a grateful nod.

"What kind of supernatural is your sister?" Harley asked from beside Sawyer, gazing sadly at the girl in the bed.

"She can start fires with her mind. All she has to do is think about doing it and poof…flames." Rory's mouth curved into a small smile. "It freaked the hell out of my parents, brothers, and me when she was little. But we've gotten so used to it, we don't even think about it anymore. And Tilly is much better at controlling it now than she was when she was a kid."

Harley looked at Rory in surprise. "Your parents and brothers are okay with her being different?"

"Yeah, of course," he said, his smile broadening. "We're family."

Harley nodded, but Sawyer knew how much Rory's answer hurt. Here was another family completely fine with one of its own being different when she'd been cast aside. Sawyer ached for her all over again and if they'd been alone right then, he would have taken her in his arms.

Even though he'd known it would be bad when his teammates finally learned his secret, he'd still been gutted when they'd walked out on him. He'd never be able to forget the way they'd looked at him. He didn't want to try to equate his pain with Harley's, but after what happened this morning with Erin and Elliott, he knew what she was feeling. He now knew why she'd hidden herself away from the world for so long, going so far as turning her back on her inner werewolf. If the crap with Erin and Elliott had happened right after his first change, there was a good chance he would have done the exact same thing.

Hell, for a few seconds there, right after his teammates had left the safe house, he'd almost buried his own wolf. He wasn't sure what had stopped him from walking out until he saw Harley standing there, silently supporting him. He couldn't leave because this was where Harley was.

He only wondered if Erin knew how close she'd been when she said he trusted his new teammates more than his old ones. In fact, she'd been spot-on. And while the entire STAT team made him feel accepted, Harley made him feel a lot more than that.

"I need to call my mum and dad and tell them about Tilly,"

Rory said, pulling out his cell. "As far as they know, she's at uni right now. I don't know how I'm going to explain any of this."

Sawyer didn't envy the guy. As Rory walked away to have that conversation in private, Sawyer turned to ask Harley if she wanted to find the rest of her teammates when her phone rang. Thumbing the green button, she held it to her ear.

"That was Jake," she said when she hung up. "They're about to talk to Brielle and figured we'd want to join in."

It was a quick ride up in the elevator to the fourth floor, where they found the rest of Harley's STAT team gathered in the hallway talking to Tessa, the agent from the support staff, who was filling them in on everything that had transpired overnight. There'd been a lot of logistics involved when it came to getting the supernaturals who'd been kidnapped home, as well as finding holding areas for Yegor's goons and the people who'd attended the auction that they'd taken into custody. STAT was a whole lot better at the behind-the-scenes stuff than MI6, that was for sure. He counted eight armed guards as well as security cameras positioned at various places. Harley's organization definitely knew what they were doing.

"Getting the low-level trigger pullers into a local jail wasn't a problem," Tessa said. "The buyers, on the other hand, are a different matter. McKay has been working with Europol all night to figure out what to do with them, but honestly, with the money these people have, there's a good chance most of them will walk. They're too well-known to hide them away in a backwater prison somewhere, and it's not like we can put the supernaturals they purchased on the witness stand for a trial."

Sawyer had a sudden vision of lawyers trying to wheel the mermaid's tank into a courtroom. Yeah, he didn't see that going over very well.

"So, these rich assholes try to buy a bunch of supernaturals for fun and they're going to just get away with it?" Caleb said. "Doesn't that seem kind of fucked up?"

"It is," Tessa replied. "But unfortunately, there isn't much we can do about it."

Caleb shrugged. "We could just kill them."

That got a laugh from Tessa. "Yeah right. I wish." When Caleb didn't so much as crack a smile, her eyes went wide. "You're kidding, right?"

"Do you see anyone else laughing?" Caleb said.

Sawyer almost chuckled at the nervous look Tessa threw the omega's way. Caleb was out there, but Sawyer had to admit, the guy was growing on him.

"Okay, then," Tessa said, looking at the rest of them. "I assumed you'd want to talk to Adriana and Kristoff as well, so I had them brought in with Brielle. Her brother, Julian, on the other hand, is still recovering from the knife wound he sustained in the fight. Before we go in, I should probably tell you that McKay is eager to get Brielle and her brother back to DC ASAP, so don't even think about offering her any kind of deal."

Caleb frowned. "She isn't going to tell us anything if she's looking at prison time. Trust me, once you know that, you don't have any desire to tell anyone anything."

Sawyer wondered if Caleb was speaking from experience.

Giving them a nod, Tessa opened the door and led the way into the room. Since the place had once been a hospital, Sawyer expected a small office with barely enough space for all of them. Instead, it was a conference room with a table big enough for twenty people.

At Tessa's nod, the two agents guarding the room walked out without a word, leaving them alone with Brielle, Adriana, and her boyfriend, Kristoff.

Sawyer and Harley took seats opposite Adriana and Kristoff while Tessa and the rest of the STAT team spread out around the table. Adriana was clearly nervous, but she also seemed excited at the same time. He wasn't sure which of those emotions was responsible for the little blue sparks running across her skin every few seconds as she sat there holding her boyfriend's hand where it rested on top of the table.

As for Kristoff, the blond man was carefully composed, his face an unreadable mask as he assessed each of them in turn. But while he might appear calm, his elevated heart rate gave him away. The guy was worried about how this was going to go, and with good cause. The only reason he was sitting here right now and not in one of the local jails along with the other people they'd arrested was because Adriana swore up and down to anyone who'd listen that he was a good man who'd gotten caught up in a bad situation.

But while Kristoff might look relaxed, Brielle seemed like she truly was. She was still wearing the vivid blue dress she had on last night and was sitting back in her chair, legs crossed, her dark eyes taking them in one at a time. She spent a few extra moments sizing up Caleb, and Sawyer wondered what that was about. Did she recognize that he was an omega? Or had she heard his comment outside the door earlier and was trying to figure out what made him tick?

Sawyer opened his mouth to ask Brielle how she'd gotten involved with Yegor—considering how quick he'd been to use her as a human shield when things went bad, the man couldn't be that fond of her—but Adriana interrupted before he could get the words out.

"I know I should have told you the truth from the beginning, but I knew how it would sound if I admitted Kristoff was one of the guards, so I left out that detail," she said quickly, like she'd been rehearsing exactly what she wanted to say and had to get it out before she forgot it. "But Kristoff isn't like those other jerks. He protected me and kept me safe. It was only after you rescued me in Paris that I realized I'd fallen in love with him." She leaned forward to cover their clasped hands with her free one, her dark eyes pleading. "Please don't send Kristoff to prison. He doesn't belong there."

Sawyer exchanged looks with Harley to see that she looked as conflicted as he felt. Adriana's kidnapping and imprisonment had been traumatizing for sure, and Stockholm syndrome was definitely a real thing. On the other hand, maybe that wasn't what this was at all. Maybe they truly were simply two people who'd fallen in love.

"How did you get involved with Yegor, Kristoff?" Jake asked. "If we know how you ended up working for him, we might be able to put in a good word for you."

Kristoff glanced at Adriana, giving her a small, reassuring smile before turning back to Jake. "I started working for Yegor over a year ago," he said with a slight German accent. "I took the job knowing he was a criminal, but things hadn't been going so well lately and I needed the money. I thought he'd hired me to steal stuff or sell drugs, maybe rough up some people who owed him money. When he had that first auction a few months ago, I couldn't believe what I was seeing. I had no idea I was getting involved in trafficking people. That isn't what I'm about."

He gave Brielle an accusing glare as he spoke but didn't directly address her. The Frenchwoman had the good grace to look chagrined. It was still mind-boggling to think how a supernatural like her—if she *was* supernatural—could work for a piece of crap like Yegor who sold people just like her to the highest bidder.

"Wait a minute," Jestina interrupted, leaning forward, dark eyes intent. "You said *first auction*, implying there have been others. How many auctions has Yegor held?"

"Last night was the third." His eyes filled with regret. "The first two were smaller, like only five or six people to bid on each time. But after Yegor realized how much money he could make, he expanded the operation, hiring more men and setting up the entire transport network."

Sawyer cursed. This was way worse than they'd thought. The idea that there were other supernaturals out there who'd been sold off to the highest bidder made him want to rip Yegor apart with his claws.

"I was going to leave after the second auction," Kristoff continued. "I wanted no part of the kidnapping and the abuse and the terror those poor people endured. Yegor isn't the kind of man who lets people who work for him walk away, but I didn't care. I couldn't be involved anymore."

"What changed?" Harley asked softly.

Kristoff looked at Adriana again, smiling at her again. "They brought Adriana in. She was unconscious and weak…vulnerable. I couldn't leave her. I just couldn't."

"He made sure I always had enough to eat and drink," Adriana added, her expression earnest. "He kept the other guards from messing with me and the other prisoners as much as he could. He even brought us aspirin to help with the headaches some of us got from the sedatives they gave us."

"I wanted to do more," Kristoff said. "But there were never less than three or four guards watching the captives. And that's not counting that damn vampire who was always hanging around, trying to get a taste of any of the prisoners he thought might not be missed. I knew I had to get Adriana out of there, but I didn't know how. I was getting desperate when you showed up in that club in Paris. Making sure you rescued Adriana was the best I could do."

Adriana squeezed Kristoff's hand, tears glistening in her eyes. "You almost got yourself killed in the process."

"I didn't care," he said. "I'd do anything to keep you safe."

"Why didn't you bail after Paris?" Misty asked, regarding Kristoff thoughtfully. "Adriana was safe. Why stay with Yegor?"

Kristoff glanced at Adriana. "I realized that if I stayed, I might be able to help the other captives get away, too. Unfortunately, that was harder than I thought and I didn't free any of them. I was never so glad as when I saw you show up at the auction."

Nothing made Sawyer think Kristoff was lying. After becoming a werewolf, he'd gotten extremely good at knowing when someone wasn't being forthright, and he'd never been wrong. But this wasn't his call, at least not entirely. He glanced at Jake, trying to figure out if they were on the same page, when Adriana spoke.

"I know this is a lot to take in." Blue sparks covered her skin, making her dark hair lift up at the ends. "But Kristoff honestly didn't know what he was getting into. When he realized how bad it was, he did the best he could to make it right. You have to see that."

Kristoff took both of Adriana's hands in his, uncaring that she was so emotional right now that she could zap him at any moment. "It's okay, *schatzi*. Calm down."

Adriana looked around the table desperately, squeezing Kristoff's hands so hard he winced. Or maybe that was from the electricity running back and forth across her fingers.

"Please," she begged, tears welling in her eyes. "Kristoff isn't the first man to get involved with the wrong people and then regret it. There has to be some way he can walk out of here, right? I mean, he's willing to tell you anything and everything he knows about Yegor's operation. Please give him another chance."

Sawyer knew what he'd do if he were running the show, but once again, he wasn't in charge of what STAT did with the people they'd arrested last night.

"I can't truthfully say I've ever regretted any of my life choices because that requires introspection, which really isn't my thing," Caleb said, casually leaning back in his chair. "But I know what it's like when those choices end up getting you involved with some bad people, so I vote for giving Kristoff a second chance."

Across from Sawyer, Adriana gave Caleb a tremulous smile, then looked at Sawyer and the STAT agents hopefully. Sawyer saw Jake exchange looks with his mate, Jes, before giving Adriana a nod.

"As long as Kristoff is willing to tell us everything he knows about Yegor and anything he remembers about the supernaturals who were sold at the previous auctions, he'll be free to go," Jake said.

Adriana threw her arms around her boyfriend, insisting she knew it would be okay all along. Kristoff grinned and hugged her back.

"What do you want to know first?" Kristoff asked Jake a few moments later.

Jake didn't even have to think about it. "Were the previous two auctions like the one last night?"

Kristoff nodded. "Yeah. Except the supernaturals at those were all adults. No one was under twenty-five years old. But for the one last night, Yegor specifically wanted kids, too." He glared at Brielle. "Anyone she could find."

Brielle flinched at that. Almost like she genuinely felt badly for her part in the whole thing.

"Going after kids was never my idea," she said. "Hell, finding people for these auctions was never part of the deal, either. I did what I had to do to protect my brother."

"How exactly do you find supernaturals?" Tessa asked, intense curiosity clear on her face. "Do they smell different? Look different?"

Brielle turned her gaze on Tessa, a glint in her dark eyes that made Sawyer wonder if she'd overheard them talking out in the hallway earlier. If she had, that meant her ears were as good as a werewolf's.

"I think I'll hold on to that tidbit of information for the time being," Brielle said with a cool smile. "Until it's in my best interest to share."

Tessa's mouth tightened and she looked ready to argue, something Sawyer knew would make Brielle shut down completely. They had a lot more questions they needed answers to before that happened.

"Don't worry about that," he said, throwing a hard look in Tessa's direction. "I'd much rather hear about how you and your brother got involved with Yegor in the first place."

Brielle met his gaze but didn't answer right away. Sawyer could practically see the gears turning behind those dark eyes. No doubt, she was wondering if this was something she should offer up for free or demand some kind of compensation for as well. Yeah, she'd definitely heard the stuff Tessa had said about not making a deal. They'd be lucky to get anything useful out of Brielle thanks to her.

"Julian's life has been an ongoing series of poor choices," Brielle finally said. "In this case, he thought selling heroin on the streets of Ankara, Turkey, was a good idea. He got arrested and shipped off to Diyarbakir on a twenty-year sentence before word even reached me in Lyon that he was in trouble. I tried to get someone from the French embassy in Ankara to help, but they couldn't get in to see Julian because my brother said something stupid to the wrong person within a few days of getting to Diyarbakir and ended up in the prison hospital."

Brielle paused to take a deep breath, obviously upset by the memory. From the corner of his eye, Sawyer saw Caleb lean forward in his chair, gazing at her intently, caught up in her story.

"But that's my brother for you," she continued with a sigh. "Letting his mouth get him into trouble he can't possibly handle. I knew that if I didn't get him out of there, he'd be dead in a month, if not sooner. Unfortunately, while I have many talents, getting a person out of prison isn't one of them. That meant I needed someone to protect my idiot brother and keep him safe until I could come up with a plan."

"Yegor Shevchenko," Sawyer said simply.

She nodded. "It didn't take long to figure out Yegor was the most powerful man in the prison. I knew if I could find a way to put Julian under his protection, he'd be okay until I got him out."

"Why would Yegor do something like that for you and your brother?" Jake asked. "He doesn't strike me as the altruistic type."

"Beyond the fact that I agreed to break him out along with my brother, I was also able to give him something he desperately wanted."

"And what was that?" Sawyer asked.

"You," Brielle said simply, meeting his gaze. "Once I identified Yegor as someone who could help me, I did some digging and learned you were one of the people responsible for putting him in prison—and that you're a werewolf. I went to visit Yegor and offered him that information, telling him all about the supernatural world. In return for protecting my brother, I offered to break him out and put him into contact with supernaturals who could help him track down you and the rest of your MI6 team. As you can imagine, he quickly agreed."

Sawyer bit back a growl, angry as hell at her, but also pissed at himself. While he hated Brielle for the part she'd played in his friends' deaths, was it really any different than what Rory had done? They'd both helped Yegor to save people they loved.

"Hold up there a second," Caleb said, regarding her with what could only be called amusement. "You expect us to believe you waltzed into a Turkish prison, dropped a supernatural bomb on Yegor—along with a promise to break him out of a place that people simply don't break out of—and he agreed just like that?"

Brielle smiled. "Yes, just like that. When I'm properly motivated, I can be extremely persuasive."

Caleb sat back in his seat with a chuckle. "I bet you are."

Sawyer replayed everything Brielle had told them and, just as importantly, everything she'd left out. Because it was obvious she was purposely leaving out a shitload of details. Considering she had the ability to find supernaturals, he wasn't shocked she'd figured out he was a werewolf. The fact that she could apparently do it all the way from Lyon, France, was a bit scary, though. And that part about knowing he'd been responsible for Yegor going to prison was disconcerting as hell, too.

"When did you break Yegor and your brother out of Diyarbakir?" Sawyer asked. "And more importantly, how?"

"Fifteen months ago," Brielle said, looking his way again.

Sawyer cursed. And according to Weatherford, whom he'd spoken to last night, MI6 had no idea Yegor had escaped.

"As far as how I got them out of prison, I think that's another piece of information I'll hold on to for now," she added with a smile. "A woman doesn't want to reveal all her secrets at once."

That provoked another huff of complaint from Tessa.

"Do either of you know where Yegor and the rest of the people who work for him are now?" Jake asked, throwing another warning look Tessa's way. "We know Seamus and that big green shifter are with him, along with at least three or four others. Conservatively, we're guessing he got away with at least twenty million euros from the auction. With that kind of money, he's almost certainly going underground for a while, so it'd help if you could tell us where they might hide out."

Kristoff frowned. "I don't think going underground is something Yegor would do. It's not his style. And he has a lot more than three or four men still working for him. The crew he had here in Greece for the auction represents only a fraction of his total operation. He has an army of people at his disposal."

Sawyer got a sinking feeling in his gut at that announcement. He'd thought this thing with Yegor was almost over and that there'd be nothing left to do but the cleanup. Apparently, he was wrong.

"Where do you think he's heading then?" Harley asked. "Does he have a place he normally goes when he needs to fall back and regroup?"

"Yegor falls back and regroups about as well as he goes underground," Kristoff said with a snort. "More likely, he's moving on with the next phase of his plan."

Sawyer didn't like the sound of that. "What plan?"

"The auctions were a means to an end. Yegor used them to make money and recruit people for his main objective."

Sawyer looked at Harley and her STAT teammates. They looked as worried as he was.

"And what's his *main objective*?"

Kristoff shrugged. "You're asking the wrong person. I was one of the grunts. I guarded the prisoners. If you want to know what it is, you'll need to ask someone from his inner circle."

Sawyer looked at Brielle, along with everyone else in the room.

A small smile tugged up the corners of her lips. "Before you ask: Yes, I know where Yegor is. Yes, I know what his main objective is. And no, I'm not telling you anything." Smile disappearing, she pinned Tessa with a look that could melt steel. "Not until I get assurances that my brother and I go free with no charges. Because regardless of what you seem to think, I have no intention of working for STAT."

Yup, she'd definitely overheard their conversation.

Pushing back her rolling chair, she stood. "I'd like to see my brother now. If you want to think over my proposal, you might want to do it quickly, because trust me, the fallout from the thing Yegor has planned will be much worse than the auction you put a stop to last night."

The echo of the door closing behind Brielle filled the room for what seemed like forever before an uncomfortable silence took its place.

"Well," Caleb said. "That could have gone better."

CHAPTER 14

"Do you think Erin and Elliott have already gone back to London?" Harley asked from where she sat on the couch gazing out the window at the cars moving past in the darkness.

Instead of an answer, all she heard was the clinking of glasses in the kitchen as Sawyer got them something to drink. Everyone else had left after dinner to go back over to the clinic, Rory to be with his sister and her teammates to have a teleconference with McKay. Harley had been all ready to go with them, but Caleb had pulled her aside and suggested she might want to stay there with Sawyer.

"The guy just got abandoned by most of his team," Caleb said, his voice full of concern she hadn't known he possessed. "He could probably use someone to talk to."

So Harley had agreed to stay, even if she was sure it was all a setup. It was a foregone conclusion that Caleb knew there was something going on between her and Sawyer, and if she had to guess, she'd say he was actually trying to give them some alone time together. She genuinely didn't understand men. Or at least omega werewolves. One second it seemed like Caleb wanted to tear out Sawyer's throat, the next it was as if he was purposely trying to get them together. Not that she minded staying here with Sawyer, of course. In fact, she'd been hoping to be able to spend some time with him after all the crap that had happened with his teammates. He'd been doing a good job of hiding it, but she knew he had to be hurting.

"Probably," Sawyer finally answered with a heavy sigh as he sat down beside her, holding out a glass of white wine. "Neither one of them are the type to stop and think anything through. If they aren't already back at MI6 headquarters, they soon will be."

Sawyer's glass was filled halfway with what Harley thought

was whiskey. She didn't know very much about hard liquor and probably wouldn't be able to identify it even if she took a sip, but Sawyer struck her as a whiskey kind of man. The funny thing was that alcohol didn't have the same effect on them, now that they were werewolves, as it had when they were human. Werewolves couldn't get drunk.

Taking the glass, Harley kicked off her sandals and tucked her legs under her, turning toward him as she did so. This close, the scent of cinnamon coffee cake washed over her in waves, making her want to bury her face in the curve of his neck and take a big, long sniff.

She controlled herself.

Barely.

"What do you think they'll do then?" She took a small sip of wine, figuring the strong taste on her tongue would distract her nose. Light and delicious, it was kind of fruity. "I mean, will they tell anyone that you're a werewolf?"

Sawyer sipped his whiskey, turning toward her a little so his knee was touching hers. "I wish I could say Erin and Elliott would never do anything like that to me. That they still have enough loyalty to a former teammate to protect me."

He took another slow sip of his drink, the scent of the alcohol wafting up and tickling her nose to intertwine with the scent of cinnamon. The combination was intoxicating.

"But…?" she prompted.

"You saw the way they looked at me when they left. I think it's almost a given they'll go straight to Weatherford and tell him everything. Hell, they probably would have told him over the phone before now if they weren't worried about their conversation getting intercepted by the wrong people."

The hurt and disappointment in his voice made Harley ache inside. She wanted to tell him that his friends wouldn't betray him, but he knew them better than she did.

"Okay," she said softly. "Let's assume you're right and Erin and

Elliott tell your boss you're a werewolf. What do you think MI6 will do with that information?"

Sawyer winced, uncertainty, along with a serious amount of concern, in his eyes. It tore at her to see him like that.

"I have no bloody idea," he said. "I can't honestly see Weatherford—or any of the people in charge—ever being open to the idea of having a werewolf on an MI6 team."

She opened her mouth, on the verge of asking him if he'd ever consider bailing on MI6 and moving to the U.S. to work for STAT with her, but then stopped herself when she realized how insane that sounded. England was Sawyer's home. He had family there. Why would he ditch his whole life over a woman he'd just met? It wasn't anywhere close to rational and Harley didn't know why the thought had popped into her head in the first place. Maybe she'd been wrong about werewolves not being able to get drunk. Because she was feeling pretty light-headed right now.

"MI6 might surprise you," she said instead. "I doubt STAT even considered working with supernaturals until they met people like Jake and Misty and realized we aren't all monsters."

He snorted. "Maybe you didn't notice, but I'm almost certain Erin and Elliott consider me a monster. And that's how they're going to describe me to Weatherford and everyone else at MI6."

"Yeah, I noticed." She sighed, wondering if she should have put the offer to join STAT out there anyway and feeling like an important opportunity had passed her by. "As long as you know that simply because other people see you as a monster, it doesn't mean you are one. That's Erin's and Elliott's baggage, not yours."

Sawyer gave her a warm smile. "Says the werewolf who hasn't shifted since the day her family called her a monster and threw her out of the house."

Harley couldn't argue with that.

"Haven't you ever heard the old adage, *do as I say, not as I do*?" she quipped.

He laughed and so did she, right up until she realized it wasn't funny at all. Sawyer was right. While they'd both been rejected by people they cared about, it seemed as if he was already dealing with it and moving on, whereas her entire life—right down to her ability to control her inner werewolf and keep that part of her hidden away—was still tied to that one painful moment eight years ago. It was more than sad. It was pathetic.

Harley didn't realize there were tears in her eyes until Sawyer took the wineglass from her and placed it on the coffee table. A moment later, he gently pulled her onto his lap, his strong arms cradling her as he soothingly caressed her back with his hand. If she wasn't trying so hard not to cry, she probably would have laughed. She'd thought she needed to spend the evening being a rock for Sawyer and here he was having to comfort her.

"Hey, I'm sorry," he whispered, the soft words rumbling up through his chest as his cinnamon scent completely enveloped her. "I didn't mean to upset you with that crack about shifting. You'll get there in your own time."

She shook her head, taking the opportunity to blink her eyes a few times to clear the tears before they could fall and embarrass the hell out of her. "It's not that," she said softly, draping one arm around his neck to rest on his broad shoulders and placing the other hand against his chest. His skin was warm and solid beneath the button-down he wore. "At least, it wasn't what you said. Not really."

He dipped his head to catch her eyes, the expression on his face making her think he didn't believe her. Not that she blamed him, since she wasn't sure she believed it herself.

"Sometimes, it feels like I'm stuck," she explained, the words coming slowly as she struggled to find the right ones. "Jake talks about using his werewolf abilities like it's as natural as breathing. Hell, even Caleb, who can't smell anything unless he steps in it, can wolf out at the drop of a hat—even faster if he's pissed. But me…" She shrugged. "I've never known what any of that is like.

Sometimes, I worry I've hidden from myself for so long that there's no way to ever get back what I gave up all those years ago."

Harley hadn't known it until this moment, but as she admitted it out loud, she realizing that genuinely *was* it. She was terrified of what she was now, terrified she'd always be a werewolf stuck in a person's body, terrified that was all she'd ever be. That didn't seem like enough anymore.

Sawyer slipped a finger under her chin, gently lifting her face until she met his gaze. The warmth in those beautiful blue eyes of his was enough to take her breath away.

"So stop hiding."

"That's easy to say," she murmured, liking the way he slowly slid his fingers along her jaw until his palm rested against her cheek. She leaned into his warmth, closing her eyes. "But I'm not even sure how to start."

"Maybe start by finding someone you can be yourself with." He leaned closer, his breath warm on her skin. "Someone who can make you feel things without having to think so much. Someone who sees you as you truly are—beautiful and perfect."

She opened her eyes to see that his lips were only inches from hers, his eyes rimmed with the slightest hint of yellow gold. "Someone like you maybe?"

"Someone exactly like me," he said simply, his mouth coming down to meet hers.

This wasn't the first time they'd kissed, but Harley continued to be amazed at the thrill that shot through her every time they did. She tingled all over, her heart racing. Her hand found its way into his silky, dark hair, weaving in and holding tight as she melted into him, their tongues teasing each other, his taste so overwhelming, it made her dizzy. She was the last woman on earth to think in cliché terms, but it really did seem like she saw fireworks explode behind her lids when she closed her eyes again.

When Sawyer's hands dropped to her hips, urging her to move,

Harley did so without thinking, instinctively knowing where he wanted her. A moment later, she was straddling him, her knees pressing into the couch on each side of his hips, the junction between her thighs pressing firmly against Sawyer's rapidly hardening cock.

She shivered when he slid his hands underneath her shirt, his warm fingers tracing lines of fire along her lower back and around to the bottommost ribs. His touch had her letting out soft little moans of pleasure even as she kept kissing him like a woman possessed. She surrendered to the moment, following Sawyer's advice to stop thinking so much. She realized that with him, that wasn't very hard to do at all.

As they continued to kiss and caress each other, the whole concept of time started getting a little fuzzy. In fact, Harley honestly couldn't say how long they'd made out. But it must have been a little while because when she finally came up for air, she noticed that at some point, both she and Sawyer had lost their shirts and one of her bra straps was hanging loose down her shoulder.

She took a moment to enjoy the view of all that exposed skin, having a hard time deciding what she liked more when it came to Sawyer's half-naked body—the broad shoulders, bulging biceps, sculpted pecs, or ripped abs. In the end, she decided getting her mouth on all those yummy muscles was a distinct moral imperative.

It was while she was busy nibbling on a bare shoulder that could have been sculpted from bronze it was so perfect, that she abruptly realized she and Sawyer were sitting there with their clothes halfway off, going at each other like they'd overdosed on lust. If their teammates walked in, this would be beyond awkward. Or maybe plain mortifying. Harley had no doubt Caleb in particular would rub it in for as long as they both lived.

"Sawyer, we have to stop," she said breathlessly, forcing herself to stop kissing the tasty collection of muscles at the junction of his shoulder and neck and sitting back on his thighs.

She didn't miss the startled expression in his eyes, immediately followed by one of confusion and then something more… Pain? He recovered quickly, hiding it all away, but she'd seen it there… the longing for more.

The same longing she was feeling herself.

"I don't mean stop like that," she corrected, leaning forward with a smile, placing her hands on those magnificent pecs. "I meant I think we need to move this somewhere besides the middle of the living room. I don't think either of us want to be interrupted when everyone comes home."

Sawyer stared at her for all of a second, then his eyes flared brighter gold. A heartbeat later he was on his feet, both hands cupping her butt and holding her tightly against him as he headed for the stairs.

"Our shirts," she shrieked, laughing as she wrapped her arms and legs around him like a koala bear. "We can't leave them on the floor. They'll know what we were up to."

Sawyer turned around with a growl, then stomped back into the living room, letting Harley hang upside down from his waist long enough to snag their two shirts. Then he strode toward the stairs, taking them two at a time, making her laugh again.

The sound was abruptly cut off when Sawyer pushed her up against the wall in his bedroom, kissing her senseless at the same time he kicked his door closed. The sensation of him grinding between her thighs as he pressed her forcefully against the wall, his mouth driving her crazy, was about the sexiest thing she'd ever experienced. His erection was so hard in his jeans she could feel it throbbing against her core.

His mouth moved from her lips to her jaw, tracing hot kisses along it and then down her neck. When she felt the scrape of sharp fangs on the sensitive skin there, she almost lost her mind. Would it be too much if she asked him to bite her…just a little?

Getting her fingers into Sawyer's hair, Harley got a good grip and shoved him far enough away so she could look him directly in the eyes.

"I definitely love what you're doing," she said, her voice rough with arousal, "but you need to get me naked and in bed—now."

The demand earned her a growl and his eyes swirled deeper gold. A split second later, he tugged her away from the wall and up into his arms, then tossed her on the big bed. She was wrestling with the buttons on her jeans before she'd even stopped bouncing.

Sawyer worked feverishly at his jeans right along with her, a task made more difficult by the hard-on he was dealing with and the fact that his claws were partially extended. Knowing she was causing both reactions had Harley feeling pretty proud of herself.

She won—who knew it was a competition?—getting undressed first. Then she leaned back on the plump pillows, enjoying the show as he finally managed to get his jeans off. The wait to see him completely naked had certainly been worth it.

Sawyer was perfect.

Actually, now that she thought about it, he put the term *perfect* to shame.

Those scrumptious abs she'd seen before continued below the belt line, combining with the muscles of his hips in a V shape that naturally led her eyes downward to the rest of his angelic form. His legs were long, lean, and muscular and his shaft was so thick and hard she didn't know whether to weep with joy or sigh in amazement. Both seemed appropriate.

Sliding off the king-size bed, she dropped to her knees in front of him. He started to open his mouth to say something, but Harley hushed him by reaching out to wrap her fingers around his hard shaft and tugging him a little closer.

They both moaned in unison as her mouth came down to engulf the head of his cock. She tried to keep the smile off her face as he let out a string of very British curse words. Marveling at how good he tasted, she moved her mouth up and down his shaft.

Harley took her time, alternating between taking him deep and teasing the tip with her tongue. She paid attention to the way he reacted to what she was doing, remembering all the places and ways he liked to be touched, praying she'd have a chance to do this again.

She sighed in pleasure as he weaved his fingers in her long hair, the tips of his claws surprisingly soothing against her scalp. What he was doing felt so good, she could do this for the rest of the night.

Sawyer didn't give her the chance, taking her hand and pulling her to her feet just when it seemed like things were getting interesting. She was about to complain, but the kiss he laid on her then made all rational thoughts slip away before they could form properly. His big hands came up to cup her breasts, massaging lightly as he tweaked her nipples. She gasped against his mouth, those wonderful, little sparks running from where he was touching her straight down to the center of her core.

Between his kisses and the attention he was paying to her breasts, Harley barely noticed when one of his hands glided lower, his long fingers gently urging her legs apart.

"Yes, right there," she breathed as those fingers slid along her wetness, grazing her clit and then the opening of her pussy. She wasn't sure which one she wanted him to pay more attention to right then. It had been a while since she'd been touched like this, and if he spent more than a few seconds on her clit, she'd explode right where she stood.

Not that there was anything wrong with exploding. She enjoyed it immensely and would be thrilled if Sawyer had her doing it a few times tonight. And as for orgasming while standing up…well… there was a first time for everything.

Fortunately—and unfortunately—he avoided the sensitive, little bundle of nerves, instead sliding two fingers into her wetness, teasing her and then backing off.

Torn between kissing him and wanting to watch, she finally— reluctantly—dragged her mouth away from his to watch Sawyer's face as he fingered her, loving the expressions he made every time she gasped with pleasure. His eyes glowed brighter than ever, giving her the impression he liked making her feel good. Or at least hearing her make sexy, little whimpers of ecstasy.

Sawyer moved a little to the side, slipping his free arm down and around her. When the two fingers inside her curled up slightly to caress that perfect place, she was glad he was holding on to her. If not, she probably would have collapsed when her knees started to go weak.

The tingles began deep inside her, building quickly, and Harley knew she was going to come. But when Sawyer began grinding the heel of his palm against her clit at the same time, the pressure deep in her core became intense and even breathing was difficult.

"Oh, Sawyer," she whispered, leaning into him, letting him hold her up completely as she buried her face in his shoulder, losing herself in his scent and giving herself up to him. "Don't ever stop, I'm begging you."

"I got you." His warm voice rumbled in her ear, as arousing as his touch. "Just let go and fall."

She did, screaming as the orgasm rushed up so fast it took what little breath she had left right out of her lungs. Waves that were more like electrical currents than water washed over her, making every inch of her body tingle and spasm, white light filling her vision. Some distant part of her mind knew she'd never come this hard before, that it was Sawyer's perfect touch making it possible.

Then she stopped thinking completely and simply melted as Sawyer continued to caress that place inside her, the hand making rhythmic circles against her clit drawing out the tremors until insanity seemed likely. Orgasms this good had to be illegal. Or at least only offered via a prescription. This kind of pleasure available over the counter would become addicting.

Harley was a complete weak-kneed noodle by the time Sawyer was done with her. She would have been doing her best imitation of a puddle on the floor if his arm hadn't been around her. She was equally grateful when he slipped the other one behind her knees and scooped her up to place her on the bed. Then he leaned over her, kissing her neck and nibbling on her ear in a lazy fashion as she attempted to regain control of her arms and legs.

In all honestly, if she *could* move at the moment, she'd almost certainly be climbing on top of Sawyer and riding him like an attraction at Disney World. Though maybe it was just as well she was too wiped out right now. She wasn't sure if she could handle another orgasm right away.

Okay, that was probably a lie. She was always up for more orgasms. They were like pizza. Good anytime of the day or night and impossible to have enough of.

"As much as I'd love to be inside of you right now," Sawyer whispered in her ear, making her shiver, "I think we might have a problem."

She opened her eyes and gave him a lazy look, praying he was messing with her. "What's wrong?"

Sawyer's breath was warm on her slightly sweat-slicked skin. "I don't have any condoms with me, so unless you do—or you're on some kind of long-term birth control—I think we'll have to skip that particular activity. There are still a lot of other things we can do."

Harley pushed herself upright on the bed. "Crap. I don't have any condoms, either. And I'm not on any long-term birth control." She grinned as a solution occurred to her. "But I can go steal some condoms out of Forrest and Misty's stash." She could have pilfered some from Jake and Jes, too, but she wasn't sure where they kept them and it would take too long to find them. "I'll be right back."

Giving him a quick kiss on the lips, she hopped off the bed. Her first few steps were a little unsteady as she practically ran for the door, but she covered it well, throwing a little extra sway in her hips so Sawyer wouldn't notice how much he'd rattled her.

It only took a minute to grab a handful of condoms from the night table beside Misty and Forrest's bed, but somewhat longer to write a quick note on the pad there, explaining she'd borrowed some and would pay them back later. It probably didn't help that her hands were shaking so much she had a hard time writing. But Harley hadn't slept with a guy in damn near forever, and in truth, she'd never wanted a man as much as she wanted Sawyer. It was actually making her nervous.

The second she was out of Misty's room, she ran as fast as she could down the hallway, refusing to think about the fact that she was as naked as the day she was born. She only prayed she didn't find Sawyer crashed out on the bed asleep because it had taken her too long.

Thankfully, he wasn't. In fact, he was still standing there beside the bed, his cock as hard as it had been when she'd left. And if the golden glow in his eyes was any indication, he wanted her as much as she wanted him. It was hard to explain how amazing that made her feel.

Harley slowed as she entered the doorway, not wanting to give away how excited she was at the prospect of sleeping with him. The two of them were perfect for each other. She had never felt so sure about something in her life.

She tossed four of the condoms on the nightstand beside the bed, then moved toward Sawyer with the last one in her hand. He reached for it, but she waved him off, tearing open the foil packet and pulling the piece of latex out, reaching down to roll it onto his hard shaft.

Sawyer slipped a finger beneath her chin, tilting her mouth up for another kiss. Only when they were both breathless did he gently nudge her onto the bed. She rolled onto her hands and knees to crawl toward the pillows, wondering what position they should make love in first. All it took was one look over her shoulder to see Sawyer was gazing at her butt like he'd suddenly found the meaning of life to make up her mind.

Stopping where she was, she stayed on her hands and knees, flashing him a sultry smile. "This work for you?"

That earned her a long, deep growl as he climbed on the bed behind her, his hands tracing their way up her thighs to her hips and then across her bottom. His claws lightly teased her skin, pulling another shiver from her before he slowly moved his hands to get a grip on her hips.

Harley arched her back, resting her face on the bed as she felt Sawyer position the head of his cock at her opening, moaning as he slowly slid in. The sensation as he filled her was unreal, stealing her breath away. The part where he tightened his grip on her hips wasn't bad, either.

Sawyer stayed buried deep inside her for what seemed like forever before slowly pulling out, then plunging back in equally slowly. And with the grip Sawyer had on her hips, there was nothing Harley could do about it.

"Are you trying to drive me insane?" she murmured.

"Yes" was all he said, the amusement clear in his voice.

Thankfully, Sawyer took pity on her a little while after that, his pace picking up more and more until her whole body was shaking with the force of his pounding. As his hips repeatedly smacked into her butt, Harley slid a hand down between her legs to touch herself, making little circles directly over her clit in time with his thrusts. At the same time, her other hand fisted in the blankets, holding on for dear life.

It was about then that Harley realized she was muttering a nonstop plea for Sawyer to go faster and harder. He must have heard her, if the way he started slamming her was any indication. When he started to growl in time with his thrusts, Harley lost it. Between his shaft inside her, his hands hard on her hips, and her own fingers on her clit, she climaxed again.

Harley cried out so hard as the pleasure hit her that she thought her throat would tear, but she couldn't stop it. It was like this time was even better than the first, which shouldn't have been possible, since the first time had nearly turned her into mush.

The climax was just beginning to ebb when Sawyer flipped her over, her back hitting the soft bed before she even realized he'd slid out. She was too addled at first to understand what was happening until he climbed between her legs and slid back in, his forearms coming down on either side of her shoulders and his mouth capturing hers. Harley automatically wrapped her legs around his waist, locking her ankles together and squeezing tight. Her arms followed, draping over his muscular shoulders, fingers threading into his hair to keep him where she wanted. She kissed him so hard that breathing—even thinking—was nearly impossible.

After the intensity of her last orgasm, the intimacy of this position, with Sawyer's strong arms caging her in and his heart thumping hard against her own, was almost more than she could take. And when he started moving this time, the head of his cock touched a completely different place inside her, his muscular body pressing her firmly into the mattress. That was when it got even better.

She broke the kiss, wanting—needing—to look at him. The sight of his eyes glowing yellow gold, his fangs extended slightly over his lower lip, had to be the most beautiful thing she'd ever seen.

Harley moved with him, squeezing her legs and digging her heels into his back to force him deeper with every thrust. But in comparison to the sex they'd had before, this time was slow and languid. But she wasn't complaining. After the night they'd already had, she could do with some lazy lovemaking.

Every once in a while, Sawyer ducked his head to kiss her again or nip at her neck and shoulders, his fangs on her skin making her shiver. When she happened to find that particular collection of shoulder muscles she loved so much in the vicinity of her mouth, she naturally returned the favor, biting down on him in a way she'd never considered doing with another man. And when she felt the tingling in her gums, felt him jerk a little as the tips of her fangs pierced skin, she didn't let herself overthink it.

As the third orgasm of the night hit her, she locked eyes with Sawyer, fighting to maintain contact even as the pleasure made it hard to even think, much less see. The climax continued to grow more intense, lightning burning bright in the bottle of her soul.

Then it all changed and Harley wasn't sure if she wanted to scream or cry as something more powerful than an orgasm settled in her chest. The sensation didn't crest and then ebb. Instead, it simply blossomed inside her and stayed there. Suddenly, the urge to hold on to Sawyer and never let go was overwhelming in its intensity.

Their gazes stayed locked until Sawyer growled his release. Only then did Harley close her eyes when he bent his head to kiss her again, his warm lips moving slowly over one of her ears.

"You have the most beautiful green glow to your eyes when you let yourself go," he whispered. "And your fangs are the sexiest thing I've ever seen."

She was too exhausted to truly register what any of that even meant, simply lying there in Sawyer's bed, breathing in his scent from the pillow she somehow found under her head. It struck her as a little odd that her nose seemed to be working so well at the moment. Picking up a scent on something as simple as a pillow was usually beyond her. But she dismissed that as unimportant as she watched Sawyer move to turn out the light, then slip back into bed and under the blanket with her.

How she'd gotten under those covers remained a mystery, but as Harley felt Sawyer's warm body spoon up behind her, she decided it was unimportant as well. Instead, she wiggled back into him, latched on to the arm he'd wrapped around her, and dropped off into the most relaxing sleep of her life.

CHAPTER 15

"So, I guess you and Harley are a thing now?" Rory said from where he sat on the other side of the table, the words deceptively casual.

Sawyer snapped his head up, sure he'd heard wrong. Which could be true. Admittedly, he hadn't been paying attention to his teammate. He and Rory were in the support team's makeshift safe house/hospital conference room waiting for Weatherford to call in from London for what was bound to be a horribly painful video teleconference. He fully expected his boss to fire him this morning. Or order him back to headquarters for interrogation. He wasn't sure which would be worse. And when his head hadn't been spiraling with those thoughts, it had been filled with ones involving a certain female werewolf and a night like he'd never experienced. Leaving a naked, beautiful Harley in bed to come over here with Rory so they could talk to their boss had been one of the hardest things he'd ever done.

Bloody hell. It was like Rory had read his damn mind.

"Harley and me?" he murmured, figuring if he repeated the question, it would give him time to think of something better to say.

"Yeah, you and Harley." The corner of Rory's mouth tilted up in a smile. "You know, the woman you slept with last night?"

Sawyer stared, fumbling to collect his thoughts. "I don't know what you're talking about. Harley and I—"

"Seriously, mate?" Rory lifted a brow. "I saw Harley coming out of the bathroom last night. She was wearing one of your shirts and walked straight into your room. It's not hard to figure out what's going on."

For a moment, Sawyer considered trying to come up with something that would explain everything Rory had seen but decided against it. It wasn't like he had anything to hide. He supposed he was so used to covering up his secrets that lying to his teammates had become instinctive.

"I'm not sure if we're a thing, but yeah, Harley and I slept together," he admitted. "Is that a problem for you?"

Rory chuckled. "It's not a problem for me. Though I get the feeling if you and Harley are sleeping together, it's definitely a thing."

"What makes you so sure?"

"Because she doesn't strike me as someone who does this kind of thing lightly," Rory said. "Now that I think about it, you've never been one to jump into bed with a woman on a whim, either. I'm guessing this means something to both of you."

That wasn't the response Sawyer had expected. Of all his teammates, Rory was the one most likely to shag a girl he'd met whenever they had some downtime on a mission, so he expected his friend to rag on him, not come at him with something this real.

Sawyer rested an ankle on the opposite knee, swiveling back and forth in his chair a little. "It means something to me at least. But I know how complicated the situation is, so I'm trying not to read more into it than might be possible."

Rory seemed to consider that for a moment, eyes appraising. "Do you want there to be more to it? If things weren't complicated, would you want a long-term relationship with Harley?"

Sawyer felt like he was looking at his teammate through a new lens. Had Rory always been this perceptive? If so, why hadn't Sawyer ever noticed?

Then again, Rory had hidden that his sister was a supernatural, so maybe his friend was even better at hiding his true self than Sawyer was.

Back to Rory's question. It was the same one Sawyer had asked himself that morning as he lay in bed with Harley draped across his chest, fast asleep. Sliding a finger through her hair to gently brush it away from her face, he'd daydreamed about what it would be like to wake up with her in his arms every morning. The notion made something well up in his chest in a sensation so powerful and overwhelming it scared him a little. The only thing that scared him more was the idea of such a future never coming to pass at all.

"If Harley and I were simply two normal people in a normal world, then yes, I'd want to take things with her as far as they'd take us," he said slowly. "But you and I both know we aren't two normal people and that the world we live in is about as far from normal as you can get. She's STAT and I'm MI6. There's no way a relationship could ever work."

Sawyer's inner wolf howled at the thought.

Rory shrugged. "Coming from someone whose sister can melt a car when she gets angry, I can say without a doubt that normal is overrated. Stop worrying about the details and focus on the fact that you and Harley are perfect together. Don't mess that up because the logistics seem too hard to deal with."

His friend was right, and his inner wolf knew it. His human side—while on board with the idea of seeing Harley wherever and whenever he had to—wasn't sure how to make it happen. Damn, why couldn't things ever be simple?

"At the risk of sounding like a complete prat, any idea how to make it work when we won't even be in the same part of the world most of the time?"

Rory's mouth twitched. "I'm no werewolf, so I don't know exactly how a werewolf should handle it, but I'd start by telling Harley how you feel and see if she's as open to the idea of seeing each other after this mission is over as you are."

That sounded incredibly reasonable—and more than a little terrifying. They'd slept together for the first time last night, and now he was supposed to ask her if she thought there might be a future for them? She'd probably think he was off his trolley. He was about to tell Rory as much when a flicker from the big computer monitor STAT's support team had set up on a rolling cart caught his attention.

A lead weight settled in the pit of Sawyer's stomach as Weatherford came on-screen. The branch chief was seated at his desk in his office and Sawyer could see part of a tapestry on the wall behind the branch chief. Sawyer half expected to see Erin and Elliott standing to either side of Weatherford, but they were nowhere in sight. That didn't mean they weren't in the room and hadn't already told MI6 about him.

Sawyer glanced at Rory to see that he looked just as nervous. That was when Sawyer realized that he wasn't the only one worrying about what secrets Erin and Elliott had spilled. When Sawyer had briefed Weatherford after they'd stopped the auction on the mountain and subsequent fight with Yegor, he hadn't mentioned anything about Tilly or that Rory had been the one who leaked the details about the mission. But would Erin and Elliott cover for Rory, too? He'd sent texts to their phones several times asking that very question, but neither had replied. Given Tilly's abilities and the fact that Erin and Elliott didn't think much of supernaturals, Sawyer didn't see them having Rory's back.

"Sawyer. Rory. Good to see you again," Weatherford said, then looked around the table with a frown. "Where are Erin and Elliott? I expected everyone to sit in on this call. We have a lot to cover."

Sawyer did a double take. Erin and Elliott should have been back in London by now. He exchanged glances with Rory, who looked as baffled as he was. A dozen different possibilities shuffled through his head, including the notion that Yegor and his goons had intercepted their teammates and killed them.

Knowing he had to say something fast—before Weatherford became suspicious—he decided to play it safe with his answer. "I know you wanted to see all of us, but Erin and Elliott are out doing some other stuff. I'll give them a full rundown after we talk."

Weatherford was silent as he chewed on that and Sawyer braced himself, waiting for his boss to ask for more details. But he seemed to decide he could live with Sawyer's answer because he nodded.

"That's fine. Just make sure to catch them up on what we talk about."

Before Sawyer had a chance to comment, Weatherford began explaining what information MI6 had come up with since their call the previous day.

"Brielle wasn't lying," Weatherford admitted. "I have no idea how she got him out, but Yegor and Julian have been missing from Diyarbakir for at least fourteen months. As far as we can tell, they walked right out of there without anyone trying to stop them."

That seemed too improbable to even consider. Then again, there was a lot about Brielle that they didn't know, including how she could locate supernaturals anywhere in the world. Maybe she had some kind of unique skill that allowed her to break her brother and Yegor out of prison unnoticed.

"If Yegor escaped over a year ago, why didn't we know about it?" Rory asked. "Isn't this something MI6 should have been keeping an eye on?"

Weatherford bristled visibly at the question, his mouth tightening, like Rory was attacking him personally. But just as quickly, their boss's demeanor changed and his shoulders slumped a little.

"I'm still digging into the details, but it seems someone at the prison *did* report Yegor missing. The word simply hadn't filtered down to us yet."

That was scary.

"Unfortunately, the bad news doesn't stop there," Weatherford continued. "Based on what you said about Yegor possibly being involved in the murders of your former teammates, we did some digging and found video footage of Seamus arriving at Calgary International Airport in Alberta an hour before Sarah and Cedric were killed. We found no direct link to Silas's death yet, but considering all three of them had their throats slit, I think Seamus killed him, too. He's obviously getting revenge for Yegor."

Sawyer's gums and fingertips ached, his fangs and claws trying to get out. He'd already hated Seamus before, but now he flat-out wanted to kill the bloody bastard—preferably by ripping his throat out with his bare hands.

"It goes without saying that MI6 wants to get Yegor back in our custody—badly." Weatherford scowled. "It's an embarrass-ment that the man escaped without us knowing it. The fact that he's responsible for the deaths of three of our agents only makes it more imperative we find him quickly and before he goes after anyone else on your team. Unfortunately, while we were able to collect a lot of information on Yegor's actions prior to the auction in Greece, we have no idea where he is at the moment."

Sawyer couldn't help but notice Weatherford didn't mention the fact that he was likely on Yegor's list, too.

"Finding Yegor would be easier if we knew what he might be up to next," Rory pointed out. "It's possible he's trying to arrange another auction, but since he doesn't have Brielle to find more supernaturals for him, that seems unlikely."

"We've had our analysts working on it nonstop since talking to you the other night and have even been working directly with the Americans in STAT, but we still don't have anything concrete on what Yegor's up to," Weatherford said. "Our best bet is that he might be looking to pick up where he left off with his original plans."

Sawyer had to actually think awhile to dredge up the mem-ories of what Yegor had been up to four years ago. Most of the details escaped him, but all he could say for sure was that Yegor and his brother had been pissed about the Russians encroaching into areas historically accepted to be Ukrainian territory. When the European members of NATO, especially France and the UK, had refused to get involved, the two brothers had lost their entire family oil business, something that made them furious.

"Do you think Yegor might be planning a major terrorist attack against the Russians?" Rory asked, his dubious tone giving away the fact that he wasn't buying that.

Weatherford made a face. "I agree it seems like a stretch, but right now, it's all we have. We're working on this around the clock. Once we find something, I'll pass it on to you and the STAT team."

"The easiest way to figure out what Yegor is up to is to talk to Brielle," Sawyer pointed out. "She was part of his inner circle from the very beginning and implied she knows what he's up to. She's willing to tell us if we let her and her brother go, but STAT is more interested in getting their hands on her for her ability to detect supernaturals than in stopping Yegor. Any chance MI6 can put some pressure on them to let her walk in return for information?"

Weatherford thought about that a moment before letting out a heavy sigh. "We're well aware of her abilities and the Americans' interest in her. I'll talk to McKay, but honestly, I'm not holding out a lot of hope."

The virtual meeting broke up shortly after that, with Sawyer's team stuck in a holding pattern until they knew more.

"Erin and Elliott never made it back to headquarters," Rory said the moment the teleconference connection was off. "Do you think Yegor got to them?"

Sawyer frowned. "I don't think so. If Yegor killed them, he'd want us to know they were dead. There's no payoff for him otherwise. I'm hoping they're just having second thoughts about walking on us and are at some hotel figuring things out."

"Considering you're a werewolf and probably have better instincts than I do, I'm willing to go along with that," Rory said. "So what's the plan?"

"I'll keep trying to contact Erin and Elliott, but since they haven't answered my calls or replied to my texts yet, I doubt they're going to." And Sawyer would be lying if he said that still didn't sting. "In the meantime, we keep working with STAT to figure out what Yegor is up to."

Rory nodded. "Okay. What about Harley? Are you going to talk to her?"

Sawyer didn't have to think about it. "Yeah. I just have to find the right time."

"Bollocks," Rory said. "Something I learned from experience is that if you wait for the right time, you'll be waiting a long time. Take my advice and talk to her. Or you're going to end up regretting it."

Harley heard her teammates talking softly in the kitchen at the same time she picked up the delicious aroma coming from that direction. She smiled as she hurried down the last few steps, touched her new family was keeping the noise down so they wouldn't wake her up. She hadn't meant to sleep in, but after Sawyer left this morning, she couldn't help snuggling his pillow and breathing in his scent. When she opened her eyes again and looked at the clock on the night table, it was well past noon.

She'd hoped Sawyer was back from his teleconference with MI6, but he was nowhere to be found. She supposed the reality of both their jobs had to intrude on the fairy tale that had been last night at some point...no matter how perfect that fairy tale might be. Her teammates, on the other hand, were all gathered around the big table having lunch.

"Hey," she said, giving them a smile as she walked over to the counter where everything was set up buffet style. She was half afraid there wouldn't be much food left, considering Caleb ate more than the rest of the team combined, so she was pleasantly surprised to find a nice selection of pita sandwiches, kabobs, salad, and baklava.

"Late night, huh?" Caleb asked.

She shrugged as she took two pita sandwiches from the tray and put them on a plate, then filled a bowl with salad, adding as many tomatoes and cucumbers as she could find, burying the whole thing under a mountain of feta cheese and dressing.

"A little bit," she admitted.

Setting the plate and bowl on the table, she went back for iced tea and a slice of baklava, then sat down beside Misty.

Harley was just biting into the pita sandwich, savoring the combination of grilled chicken, tomatoes, cucumbers, tzatziki sauce, and feta cheese when she realized everyone was staring at her. Had she dribbled sauce on her chin?

"What?" she asked.

Instead of answering, her teammates only grinned, each of them looking like that proverbial cat who ate the canary.

That's when it hit her. *Well…crap.*

"You know about Sawyer and me, don't you?" she asked softly.

On the other side of the table, Jake tapped his nose. "I knew the moment we walked in the house last night. Obviously, I had to tell Jes."

"Obviously," Harley muttered, then glanced at Misty. "Let me guess. You saw my note and couldn't resist the urge to share, right?"

Misty laughed. "Actually, Forrest saw the note but had no idea what you were referring to, so I had to translate."

Across from Harley, Caleb let out a snort. "Damn. For a bunch of secret agents, you guys aren't very observant." He looked at her. "I figured out you and Sawyer were a thing since that night Erin, Forrest, and I relieved you guys at the villa when I saw the bite marks on your neck. Never knew you were into the kinky stuff. It's always the quiet ones."

Caleb waggled his brows at her, making Harley roll her eyes.

She vaguely remembered Sawyer nibbling on her neck that night they'd been pulling surveillance duty at the house in

Kalambaka. She hadn't considered Sawyer might have broken the skin. There certainly hadn't been any marks on her by the time she'd gotten back to her hotel room that night. Then again, she was a werewolf. A little nip like that would have healed up in minutes.

She speared a juicy tomato and popped it into her mouth. No doubt, her teammates had spent the entire morning talking about her and Sawyer. She definitely wasn't embarrassed they were sleeping together, but having everyone know about it made her feel a little off-balance. She guessed she'd been on her own for so long, she'd forgotten what it meant to be part of a family where everyone knew everything about each other.

"So," Jes said, leaning forward with an eager smile. "Is it serious? Are you guys going to keep seeing each other after this mission?"

Harley didn't even have to think about the answer to that question because she'd already thought about it while she'd laid in bed after Sawyer left, blissed out beyond belief.

"It's serious for me," she admitted, sipping her iced tea. "I wouldn't have slept with him if it wasn't. And while I'd love to keep seeing him, I'm not dumb enough to think it'll be easy to do that. I'm STAT and Sawyer is MI6—at least for the moment—so seeing each other is going to be difficult."

"Forget about that stuff for now," Jake said before she could continue with the whole list of obstacles—the list she'd compiled while showering this morning and having a minor panic attack over the depth of her feelings for a man she'd slept with once. "Would you want to make a relationship work with Sawyer if you had the chance?"

Harley looked at Jake to see him studying her with an earnest expression. "Sawyer and I haven't talked about anything like that yet."

"Too busy doing other things with your mouth, huh?" Caleb teased with a chuckle that earned him a smack on the shoulder from Jes, a glare from Harley, and a laugh from everyone else.

"Never change, Caleb. Never change." Shaking his head, Jake turned back to Harley, dark eyes intent. "You didn't answer the question. I asked you what *you* wanted, not if you and Sawyer have talked about your future yet—although you should. So what do *you* want out of this relationship?"

She took another bite of the chicken pita and chewed thoughtfully, aware of her teammates looking at her. How had she gotten so lucky to have friends like them?

"I want to find a way for us to stay together," she admitted quietly. "I know this is going to sound insane since I've barely known Sawyer for a week and we've only slept together one time, but I'm already falling for him. He's the most amazing, sweetest, most perfect man I've ever met."

Harley held her breath, waiting for them to tell her she was losing her mind. That no one could possibly fall for a guy this fast. But instead, her teammates all looked thoughtful, as if her bizarre proclamation was the most normal thing in the world.

"I get it," Caleb said, sliding the chicken and vegetables off a skewer with his fingers and onto his plate. "I mean, I don't necessarily see the attraction to Sawyer. He doesn't do a damn thing for me at all. But I can see why you might like him."

Harley laughed along with everyone else this time, relaxing in her chair as she realized her friends were okay with her and Sawyer. "So you guys don't think it's kind of crazy for me to feel like this about a guy I just met?"

"Werewolves fall fast when they meet *The One*," Caleb said. "It only took Jake and Jes a few days to crash and burn. They could fight it all they wanted, but in the end, it was going to happen. I saw the same thing go down with these two werewolves I knew when I was back in Dallas—and they were on opposite sides of the law at the time. But when a werewolf meets their soul mate, it's kind of a done deal."

"Wait. What?" Harley looked around the table to see if everyone heard the same thing she had. "*Soul mate?*"

Caleb opened his mouth to answer, but Jake's phone rang, interrupting him. Jake pulled it out, grimacing when he saw the screen.

"It's McKay. Hopefully, he'll have more info for us on Yegor than he did last night," he said, pushing back his chair. "Let me know what I miss."

Caleb speared a piece of chicken, then added a tomato to the fork, shoving both in his mouth. "There's something incredibly ironic about the fact that out of the three werewolves on our team, I'm the only one who knows anything about soul mates. You guys realize I'm an omega, right? The antisocial one with poor pack instincts. Yet I'm the one who had to tell Jake about *The One* when he met Jes, and now, I'm gonna have to tell you."

"*The One?*" she repeated, a little dazed.

She'd thought when he said those words before that it was in a casual way, but considering the rest of her friends were grinning like idiots, she realized there might be more significance to them.

"Yeah—*The One*," Caleb said in exasperation. "As in *The One*-in-a-billion person you're meant to be with for the rest of your life. Your soul mate. Our inner werewolves instinctively know who we're supposed to spend the rest of our lives with the moment we meet them, even if it sometimes takes our human side a lot longer to figure out."

"How is that possible?" she asked.

"Beats the hell out of me. Who knows how our inner werewolves know half the crap they do?" He shrugged. "Look, I'm not saying for sure that Sawyer is *The One* for you—only you know the answer to that question—but it definitely explains why you're falling for him so fast."

The idea that she might have to rely on her inner werewolf for something so important scared the hell out of her. She hadn't exactly been on the best of terms with her furry side. Could she truly trust it?

"What if my inner werewolf is wrong and Sawyer isn't *The One* for me?" she asked. "Worse, what if Sawyer *is The One* for me, but not the other way around? Is that even possible?"

The idea suddenly made it hard to breathe and she gasped for air. If she didn't calm down, she'd be hyperventilating in a minute.

"You need to stop freaking out before you pass out," Caleb said, devouring another kabob. "You've found someone who's perfect for you. Stop thinking so damn much and enjoy it."

Jes nodded. "He's right."

On Harley's side of the table, Misty and Forrest nodded, too.

"Okay." Harley took a deep breath. "So if Sawyer is *The One*, then making a long-distance relationship work shouldn't be that difficult, right?"

Then why did the thought of not being in the same zip code as Sawyer make her want to freak out again?

Caleb shrugged and started in on a chicken pita. "Hell if I know. But if he's *The One*, you'll figure it out. You might want to start by telling Sawyer how you feel about him." He grinned. "Then again, I'm an antisocial omega, so what the hell do I know about talking and feelings?"

Harley would have laughed, but just then, the scent of cinnamon coffee cake hit her nose. A split second later, the front door opened and Sawyer walked in. His blue eyes immediately locked on her and he grinned. Heart doing a somersault, she smiled back. Suddenly, every doubt she had a few minutes ago disappeared and everything felt right in her world again.

"Hey," he said, giving her friends a nod in greeting as he made his way over to the counter to fill a plate with food.

"How was your call with Weatherford?" Harley asked.

He helped himself to three pitas and four kabobs, skipping the salad but grabbing some baklava. "Better than I expected."

She exchanged looks with her teammates to see that they looked as surprised as she was. "MI6 is okay with you being a werewolf?"

"They don't know." He carried his plate over to the table and sat down beside her. "Erin and Elliott didn't go back to headquarters. I'm hoping that means they're having second thoughts about leaving."

Harley hoped so, too.

As she started on her salad and Sawyer dug into his own lunch, everyone debated why people had started calling "kabobs" by the more recent and now widely accepted "skewers." It was a silly conversation for sure, but also fun, and Harley was struck by how well Sawyer got along with her pack and vice versa. It was ridiculous how happy that made her. If he liked her friends and they liked him in return, that had to be a good start, right?

They were talking about British versus American English when Jake walked into the kitchen. The scowl on his face made Harley think his conversation with McKay hadn't gone well. Everyone else must have thought the same thing because they all fell silent.

"What's up?" Jes asked as Jake sat down beside her.

"McKay still won't sign off on letting Brielle and her brother go free in exchange for information." Jake glanced at Sawyer. "He wasn't too happy with MI6 trying to pressure STAT into giving her a deal. He was even less thrilled when I pushed him to do the same thing. As far as the brass is concerned, having someone like Brielle at their beck and call is more important than anything Yegor has planned."

Sawyer frowned but didn't say anything, and Harley wondered what he was thinking.

"According to McKay, a transport team is coming in from DC tonight to escort Brielle and her brother back there," Jake added, then quickly brought them up to speed on what else their boss said, which wasn't much since they still had no leads on Yegor. When he was done, he looked at Sawyer. "How'd Weatherford handle finding out you're a werewolf?"

Sawyer told Jake the same thing he'd told the rest of them—that

MI6 didn't know—then shrugged. "They're bound to find out at some point, and something tells me that when they do, I can kiss my job there goodbye."

Jake glanced at Harley before looking at Sawyer again, his face thoughtful. "You know, if that ever happens, you're always welcome at STAT."

Out of the corner of her eye, Harley saw her teammates smiling as discreetly as they could. She tried to hide how giddy she was at the idea, but the moment Sawyer's gaze met hers, she couldn't help grinning. The prospect of working with Sawyer was too perfect for words.

Sawyer opened his mouth to say something, but Jake's cell rang. A split second later, Sawyer's rang as well. Harley heard Tessa shouting something about Yegor's crew attacking the abandoned hospital to Jake even as Rory did the same to Sawyer before gunfire drowned out both of them and the phone connections went dead.

Muttering a curse, Jake relayed what Tessa said for their non-werewolf teammates who didn't have ears keen enough to hear what she said, then they were all heading for the door. Unfortunately, whatever Sawyer had been going to say would have to wait until later. Harley only prayed they got to the hospital before the assholes who worked for Yegor killed everyone in it.

CHAPTER 16

It took them eight bloody minutes to get to the abandoned hospital. Sawyer knew for a certainty because he'd kept one eye on the digital clock in the dashboard as he drove. He'd sped like a madman the entire way, and it had still taken too long.

He was shocked there wasn't any local law enforcement in the parking lot of the converted hospital when he slid to a stop against the curb, Jake right behind him in the other SUV. Sawyer had no idea how Tessa had managed to keep the Athens police away from there in a situation like this, but he was glad she had. Regular humans getting involved in a situation they couldn't possibly understand would only end up in grave danger or dead.

Putting the SUV in park, Sawyer jumped out of the vehicle. From the passenger side, Harley and Caleb did the same. He pulled out his gun, forcing himself to approach the building slowly. They had no idea what was happening inside and running headlong into whatever was going on could get them—and everyone in there—killed. Harley had tried calling both Rory and Tessa the whole way over, but neither of them answered. That scared him. Almost as much as the fact that he couldn't hear anything coming from inside the building. Not even gunfire. Did that mean the fight was over?

The concrete in front of the entrance was covered with thousands of pieces of glittering, reflective glass, along with a sizable pool of blood smack in the middle of it all. It took a second to realize the glass had come from one of the big windows on the fourth floor. Someone had either jumped out or been pushed. A curious part of his mind wondered where the body was.

"Watch yourselves," Jake murmured as they all approached the double doors. "Identify your targets before you shoot. There are a lot of innocent people in there."

That was true enough. Luckily, that morning, STAT had moved out all the buyers who'd been at the auction the other night, as well as the supernaturals they'd been there to bid on. Well, all except the people who'd been injured, like Rory's sister.

The acrid odors of smokeless powder and a recent fire were heavy in the enclosed space of the lobby, along with the sickening stench of blood. Sawyer tried to analyze the different scents, hoping to pick up Rory's and anyone else's he might know, but it was no use. There were simply too many competing smells.

They found four bodies a few meters into the entryway—two bad guys and two STAT support agents. Misty and Forrest immediately crouched down to check them for a pulse. Sawyer could have told them it wasn't necessary. He would have heard a heartbeat if either of them was still alive. They got to their feet with a shake of their heads, confirming he was right.

Jake pointed at Sawyer, Harley, and Caleb, then gestured toward the stairs, indicating he wanted them to check the upper floors. Sawyer gave him a nod, heading toward the stairwell with Harley and Caleb, while Jake, Jes, Misty, and Forrest spread out to clear the smoke-filled first floor. Sawyer fought the urge to stay downstairs and search for Rory. There was no way Rory would willingly have left his sister alone, and her room was on the ground floor along with every other injured person who was still recovering. Sawyer had to trust Jake and his STAT teammates would find him.

They found two more bodies on the steps leading up to the second floor, a STAT agent and one of Yegor's goons. Since the second and third floors were where the buyers and supernaturals had been, clearing them was quick.

"Thank goodness Tessa got all of the supernaturals out of here before Yegor's goons showed up," Harley whispered as they continued up to the topmost floor. "Do you think that's why he was here?"

"Maybe. But I think it's more likely he was here for Brielle." Sawyer glanced over his shoulder as they neared the fourth-floor landing. "She knows too much about Yegor's operation."

When they got to the top of the stairs, Sawyer opened the door carefully. Three dead bad guys were lying on the floor, the front of their tactical uniforms stained with blood from gunshot wounds. Sawyer picked up the murmur of voices coming from down the hall and he took a careful peek around the doorjamb only to duck back inside as a bullet slammed into the wall near his head.

"Don't shoot!" he shouted. "We're the good guys!"

He heard Tessa mutter something that sounded like, "About damn time," then shouted for everyone to hold their fire.

Sawyer darted a quick look out into the hall again to see Tessa and three other STAT agents using the old nurses station and pieces of furniture as protection so they could cover both the stairwell and the elevators. Tessa and another guy were holding STAT-issued handguns, but the other two had MP5 submachine guns like the guy at the bottom of the stairs. They must have picked the weapons up from some bad guys they'd taken out.

He, Harley, and Caleb stepped around the bodies on the floor and into a combat zone. The nurses station, along with the surrounding walls and floor had been shredded by small arms fire, what looked like hand-grenade blasts, and scorch marks that could only have come from Adriana's lightning. Most of the ceiling tiles had been blown out and were either hanging loose by their metal framing or lying in a smoldering mess on the floor. Half a dozen additional bodies were strewn along the floor, both Yegor's men and STAT agents.

The air held a burnt-ozone smell, again probably courtesy of Adriana, making Sawyer's nose sting. The damage wasn't limited to the area around the nurses station, either. Several sections of the wall along the corridor seemed like they'd been smashed by a charging rhino. Some of the holes were so big he could see into the rooms beyond, where wounded agents scrambled around trying to help others who were hurt even worse.

Harley swept around him, hurrying to Tessa's side to help steady her. "It's okay. I've got you. It's over."

But Tessa—dazed and looking like she was having a hell of a time staying upright—shook her head. "It isn't over. Seamus was here. He got away with Adriana and that boyfriend of hers. They were both fighting right beside me, and he showed up out of thin air and took them."

"Not that anyone was asking for confirmation," Rory said, slowly walking into the conference room and sitting down at the table across from Sawyer with a groan. "But Caleb and I searched the whole building again and Adriana and Kristoff are nowhere to be found."

Everyone had filtered into the conference room a little while ago and, after righting chairs and moving broken ceiling tiles out of the way, took seats at the table. Sawyer knew it was a long shot to hope Adriana and her boyfriend had gotten away from Seamus and were hiding somewhere, but they'd wanted to check anyway.

"How's Tilly?" Misty asked as Caleb joined her and Forest at the other end of the table.

"She's exhausted, but okay," Rory said. "She's back in her room, sleeping again if you can believe it. I wanted her to go to the hospital with everyone else who was injured in the fight, but she didn't want to be that far away from me."

According to Rory, Tilly was a big reason none of the supernaturals who'd still been there recovering had been killed. She'd managed to get out of bed and set fire to four or five of Yegor's men. The rest hadn't wanted to get anywhere near her after that. But the fighting had cost the teen girl a lot and she'd been nearly unconscious by the time Yegor's goons had taken off.

Sawyer was wondering if Yegor's men had intended to kill all of the supernaturals on the first floor or recapture them when footsteps outside the door caught his attention. He looked that way to see Tessa coming in. She still looked as dazed and battered as she had when they'd first gotten there and probably should have been taken to the local hospital along with the other wounded agents from the support team, but instead, she was here.

"I just got off the phone with the admission staff at the Central Clinic," she said, dropping heavily into the chair beside Jes. "Everyone who made it to the hospital is alive, but will be out of commission for a few weeks."

"How many did we lose?" Forrest asked quietly in a voice that implied he didn't want to know the answer.

"Eight dead. Eleven wounded," Tessa said in a worn-out tone.

"To be honest, when we first got up here and saw all the damage, I was surprised to find anyone alive," Caleb admitted.

"We got lucky." Tessa rested her head back on her chair with a sigh. "If it wasn't for Brielle, that big, scaly shifter would have killed us all for sure. Bullets didn't seem to do more than piss him off, and she was the only one who stood a chance against him hand-to-hand."

Sawyer did a double take, not sure if he heard right. Around the table, everyone else looked just as confused.

"Wait a minute—back up." Caleb sat up straight in his chair and held up a hand. "That shifter outweighs Brielle by two hundred pounds. You're saying she fought him in hand-to-hand combat?"

"She didn't merely fight him," Tessa clarified. "She pretty much kicked his ass. One second that shifter was ripping through the door into her brother's room and attacking him, and the next Brielle was on top of him, throwing him right back out the door.

The two of them went at it like animals, punching and smashing each other through walls. That's where all those gigantic holes came from. Until Brielle picked him up and tossed him out the window."

Caleb looked stunned. "How is that possible? I could barely handle him and I'm a werewolf."

"Maybe I'm something stronger than a werewolf," a lightly accented voice said from the doorway and Sawyer looked over to see Brielle standing there. "Batu was here to kill my brother and me. I refused to let him do it."

Walking into the room, Brielle took a seat beside Tessa, wincing a little as she sat down. Sawyer didn't see any injuries, but she was clearly in pain.

"Batu?" Harley prompted from where she sat beside Sawyer.

"The big green shifter," Brielle murmured softly. "Seamus was here specifically for Adriana, while Batu was here for my brother and me. Mostly me, but I imagine Yegor would have gotten an inordinate amount of pleasure from knowing I'd been forced to watch my brother die first."

Caleb pinned her with a look. "While I'm thrilled that we now have a name for big and scaly, I'm more interested in knowing how you were able to fight him."

Brielle met his gaze, giving him a small smile. "I bet you would. Sorry to disappoint you, but that's another secret you're not getting your hands on. Not for free."

Caleb looked like he wanted to keep pressing her for an answer, but Jake cut him off. "You said Seamus was here for Adriana. If so, why take Kristoff? And more importantly, are they still alive?"

Brielle flipped her long, dark hair over her shoulder with a tired hand. "They're alive. Well, Adriana is alive at least. Kristoff probably is, too, but only as long as he has some value as leverage to make her fall in line and do exactly what Yegor needs her to do. After that, he'll almost assuredly kill both of them."

"Since you seem to know a hell of a lot about what Yegor is planning, did you know he'd send people here to attack everyone?"

Brielle leveled her gaze at him. "I knew Adriana was critical to his plan, so I assumed he'd try to get her back at some point. But to answer your question, no, I didn't know exactly when he'd try it."

Tessa slammed her hand down on the table, fury on her face. "Why the hell didn't you warn us? Eight of my friends are dead because of you!"

Brielle glared at her coldly. "Their deaths are on you, not me! I offered to make a deal for everything I knew. You're the one who decided that keeping me locked up for life and forcing me to find supernaturals for you was the only thing you were interested in. Tell me, what will STAT do with all the supernaturals they collect? Do you think the people in charge will ask nicely if they want to work for you? Or will they force them to be part of the organization like you're doing to me?" She let out a delicate snort. "Now that I think about it, it's funny how much you people and Yegor have in common. You're even holding my brother's life and freedom over my head just like he did."

Tessa jumped to her feet, hand going for the gun holstered at her hip. Jes quickly stood, putting a hand on the woman's arm. "Tessa, she's right. She may have said it more harshly than she had to, but Brielle is telling the truth. Right now, STAT *is* more interested in getting their hands on Brielle than they are in finding out what she knows."

The STAT agent hesitated—like she was torn on whether to shoot Brielle or not—but then she slowly shoved the weapon back in its holster. Giving Jes a nod, she sat down.

Brielle looked around the table at all of them, her expression more earnest than Sawyer had ever seen on her. "This thing Yegor is planning is so much worse than you could ever imagine, and I don't want it to happen any more than you do. But I'm not letting you imprison my brother and me for the rest of our lives. I can't."

Bloody hell, this was getting old.

Sawyer exchanged looks with Jake. Nodding, the other were-wolf pulled out his phone and punched a number on his contact list.

"McKay, it's Jake," he said, dark eyes locked on the Frenchwoman. "You aren't going to like this, but we're making that deal with Brielle. If STAT doesn't like it, that's too damn bad. You can fire me after this mission. She and her brother go free in exchange for everything she knows about Yegor."

CHAPTER 17

France

WHEN HARLEY JOINED STAT, SHE'D TRIED TO IMAGINE ALL THE different places her new job might take her. Since she didn't have much experience with the world outside the United States—and none at all with covert operations—she hadn't come up with a very realistic list of possibilities. But if there was one thing she could say with certainty, it was that she'd never expected to find herself at a microbrewery overlooking endless rolling hills of hops trellises on a tract of farmland right outside Calais, France. Probably because she didn't know that there *were* microbreweries in France. Though in her defense, when Harley drank beer, she didn't think too much about where it came from.

But as she stood on the back loading dock of the brewery, looking out over the tall trellises covered in thick, green vines as the late-day sun slowly set behind it, Harley decided it was one of the most beautiful and tranquil places she'd ever seen. She hoped she and Sawyer could come back here someday so they could look around at their leisure.

It seemed almost sinful that this tranquil locale was positioned smack-dab in the middle of where Yegor was going to strike…and soon, if Brielle was right about everything she'd told them. Not that there was any reason to think she'd lied to them. As soon as Jake had agreed to the deal, the woman started talking so fast it was hard to keep up with it all.

Unfortunately, the more she'd told them, the more terrified Harley and everyone else had become. It was official—Yegor Shevchenko was a psychopath. Basically, the whack job was planning to nuke the entirety of northern France, along with southern Britain and parts of Belgium and Germany. No doubt he considered the last two countries a bonus.

Harley breathed in the wholesome aromas rolling off the hops field, wondering how Tessa had been able to arrange the use of this place so quickly. They'd flown out of Athens late yesterday, and by the time they arrived in Calais, she'd already taken care of the paperwork to rent the brewery that had previously been up for sale. It made Harley wonder if STAT had simply bought the place outright. She was sure Caleb would approve. He liked beer. A lot.

Harley picked up Sawyer's scent before he stepped out of the building and onto the loading dock. She turned, giving him a smile.

"There you are," he said with a grin, his deep voice making her feel like she'd been wrapped in a soft, fuzzy blanket. "Everyone's here. Jake and Forrest are about to start the briefing."

As they walked inside, he rested his hand lightly against her lower back, his palm warm through the T-shirt she wore. It was difficult to describe how much that little bit of contact affected her. They'd been moving nonstop since Yegor's crew had attacked the hospital, and opportunities to talk, much less touch each other, had been nonexistent. She leaned into his hand, her body coming to life under his fingers.

If they weren't on their way to the mission briefing, she would have suggested finding a quiet, out-of-the-way place so they could talk. And yeah, make out, too.

Not that there were many places in the brewery to find that kind of privacy. The place was more warehouse than bed and breakfast, with big, open rooms full of cots in place of separate bedrooms. While the microbrewery was large enough to hold everyone from STAT and MI6 combined, along with their respective support teams, it didn't make it easy to spend a few moments alone with Sawyer.

She glanced at him as they passed a collection of large stainless steel mixing and brewing kettles. "If there's time after the briefing, do you want to get out of here for a little while? Maybe take a walk?"

Sawyer reached out and took her hand, giving it a little squeeze, mouth curving into a smile again. "I'd like that."

As they stepped into a big room that had been used for tastings when the microbrewery was operational, Harley noticed all the new support people STAT had brought in. There had to be at least twenty agents. Maps and briefing charts were pinned to every available surface along the walls, and analysts were busy clicking away on computers set up on one of the larger tables.

Brielle stood off to one side, looking tense and uncomfortable. Thanks to some convincing from Caleb of all people, she'd agreed to come help them in return for Julian's immediate release and a promise STAT would let her go as soon as they took down Yegor. Was she concerned they wouldn't be able to stop him? Or worried they'd go back on the agreement now that she'd told them everything she knew?

McKay was standing near the map board with Weatherford, Jake, Jestina, and some other guy Harley didn't recognize dressed in a suit and tie. About McKay's age, with a mustache, he gestured wildly at several points on the map. From listening in on their conversation, it sounded like he was worried about how close their current location was to the Channel Tunnel and London. Based on the map they were looking at, the city was less than a hundred miles as the crow flies. Any other time she'd consider that far away, but not in this case.

"Weatherford and McKay arrived together from the airport a few minutes ago," Sawyer said in a low voice as they grabbed seats in between Rory and Caleb. "MI6 and STAT must be nervous as hell if they've sent both of them here."

All Harley had time to do was nod as Jake spoke. "Now that everyone is here, let's get started."

"Wait a moment." Weatherford looked around the room with a frown. "Where the bloody hell are Erin and Elliott? I haven't seen them since I walked in."

Beside her, Sawyer tensed. Harley knew without asking this was the moment he'd been dreading. Harley had no idea why Erin and Elliott had yet to return to MI6 headquarters or even call Weatherford and tell him about Sawyer. But for some reason, they hadn't, and now it was on Sawyer to explain everything.

He took a deep breath and opened his mouth to answer when movement by the door interrupted him.

"Sorry we're late," Erin said, walking casually into the room.

Elliott followed, scanning the room until he saw Sawyer. Their eyes locked, and Harley couldn't help but hold her breath.

"We were dealing with some stuff," Elliott said as he and Erin slipped into seats that allowed them to keep an eye on Sawyer as well as the briefing maps. "It took a little while to work through all of it, but we're good now."

Silence filled the space, and from the corner of her eye, Harley could see the confused expressions on both Weatherford's and McKay's faces. But no one said a word as Sawyer and his teammates continued to study each other.

"Are you sure you're good?" Sawyer asked quietly. "This isn't something you can do halfway. You're either in or you're out."

"We're in all the way," Erin said firmly. "It took a while to figure it out, but in the end, it wasn't as complicated as we thought when we remembered what was important."

Weatherford looked even more baffled than he had before, but thankfully, Jake spoke first.

"Everyone, I'd like to introduce Dr. Tristan Jones," he said, gesturing toward the blond man in the suit and tie. "He's a nuclear physicist from the Office for Nuclear Regulation in London. He's here to help us figure out how we're going to stop Yegor."

The man nodded awkwardly and moved a little off to the side, like he had no interest in being involved in this any more than necessary.

"And this is Brielle," Jake added, motioning toward the Frenchwoman.

McKay and Weatherford both regarded her sharply.

"It seems we have you to thank for the information on Yegor," Weatherford said thoughtfully, then looked at McKay. "Though I understand you had to give up a lot to procure that information."

McKay nodded, mouth tight. Even though he hadn't fought Jake on agreeing to a deal with Brielle, he wasn't happy with letting her get away. Who knew? Maybe if STAT approached Brielle in the future with an offer that didn't involve giving up her freedom, the woman might reconsider working for them.

"Indeed," McKay said. "But I think you'll agree it was worth the price when you hear what Brielle has to tell us."

"Based on everything Brielle and her brother said, these are Yegor's most likely targets," Jake said, moving over to the map. "Gravelines Nuclear Power Station is in Nord, about twelve miles northeast of here. Penly Station is near Dieppe, about ninety miles from here." As he spoke, he pointed out each of them. "Gravelines is the largest nuclear power plant in western Europe with six reactors. Penly is smaller, with two reactors, but is likely an easier target. Not that the number of reactors really matters. All it takes is one reactor going into meltdown to give Yegor exactly what he needs."

Weatherford looked at Brielle again. "You claim to have been part of Yegor's inner circle, and yet you don't know which target he's going to hit?"

"Yegor started planning this attack within days of me breaking him out of that Turkish prison. It's all he ever talked about," Brielle replied calmly, as if Weatherford hadn't implied she was lying to them. "He originally started with a dozen possible sites, then constantly rearranged them based on perceived vulnerabilities, proximity to large cities, size of the reactors, when the fuel rods had been changed out last, wind patterns, safety systems, security forces, even local response capabilities. The list changed constantly. These two plants were at the top of his list right before the auction in Greece, which makes me think one of them is the target."

McKay crossed his arms over his chest. "How was he able to gather so much information? Some of that has to be classified."

Brielle shrugged. "He's rich. Offer someone enough money and they'll give you whatever you want. It probably didn't hurt that Yegor is also very good at threatening people."

"I get why he's going after England," Caleb said. "MI6 killed his brother. What I don't understand is why he's targeting France. What the hell did they ever do to him?"

Brielle met his gaze, hers assessing. "In early 2014, pro-Russia separatists took over the Donetsk and Luhansk regions in eastern Ukraine with direct support from the Russian military. Yegor and his brother lost control of the family's oil business that was based in that area. He immediately turned to the pro-Ukrainian forces and NATO, begging them for help. France and the UK played politics while Russian forces murdered every member of Yegor's family except his brother. I'm sure France and the UK had good reasons to stand back and watch, but in the end, Yegor blamed them for everything that happened."

"That's kind of crazy," Misty murmured.

"I won't argue with that," Brielle responded. "Losing his family twisted Yegor into something barely even human anymore. Everything he's done since that war has been about getting revenge. The supernatural auctions were nothing more than a means of raising money so he could hire the right experts, buy the right equipment, and pay people to look the other way. He's determined to destroy everyone he blames for his family's death. He's going to force a nuclear power plant into meltdown, then he's going to blow everything to pieces, scattering catastrophic levels of radiation from Paris to London and beyond, if he can manage it."

"Is it possible for radiation to travel that far?" Jes asked.

Dr. Jones nodded. "Radiation from Chernobyl was detected in Sweden, which is almost a thousand miles away. That's how the rest of the world found out about it when Russia was doing everything it could to hide the incident."

Weatherford scowled at Brielle. "How do we know you're not making all this up so you can gain your freedom? Asking us to trust you on something like this is a big leap."

Brielle gave him a cool look and a shrug. "Don't believe me then. You'll find out soon enough, one way or the other. I can live with the knowledge that I did what I could." She lifted a brow. "Can you live with the knowledge that you did nothing with the information?"

McKay cleared his throat. "Let's assume Brielle is telling the truth." He regarded her thoughtfully. "You said Adriana is integral to Yegor's plan? How?"

"From what he said, it's actually difficult to get a modern nuclear power plant to go into meltdown," Brielle said. "Too many automated safety features, I guess. That's where Adriana will come in. They're going to pull all the control rods, then make her fry the computer system running the reactor, so none of the safety systems will work. That will cause the meltdown."

Dr. Jones seemed vexed at that.

"That won't work," he said firmly. "I don't know how you expect this woman to fry the control computer system for the reactor, but even if she did, the loss of power would drop all the control rods. That's how they work. A loss of power releases the rods without need for any safety action. It would shut down the reactor completely."

It was Brielle's turn to frown. "I heard Yegor say something about bringing in electromagnets. I don't know what he's going to do with them, but they're big and expensive, and he has a lot of them."

The doctor stiffened. "How many does he have? More importantly, how big are they?"

That earned him another shrug from Brielle. "I don't know for sure—twenty-five, thirty, maybe. The one I saw was the size of a petrol drum."

Harley definitely didn't like the expression on Dr. Jones's face after that. "What are control rods? Would the magnets do what Yegor needs?"

"Control rods do exactly what their name implies," he said. "They're inserted into the core of a nuclear reactor and move up and down to control the rate of the nuclear chain reaction. If they're all the way in, there's no reaction. If they're all the way out, there's too much reaction. Modern reactors use electromagnets to pull the rods and hold them in place. If power is lost, the magnets don't work and the rods drop automatically. But if Yegor has his own magnets, he might be able to use them to pull the rods regardless of what the main electromagnets are doing. Frying the computer at that point will ensure that none of the other safety features, like cooling spray, boron dumps, and water circulation will work."

"He *might* be able to use them?" McKay pressed.

It was the doctor's turn to shrug. "He'd have to know exactly where to put them and when to turn them on."

"Yegor has a dozen physicists on his payroll," Brielle said softly. "Including some from the French Nuclear Safety Authority."

Dr. Jones paled at that, unmistakable terror evident on his face.

"We don't honestly think Adriana would do what Yegor wants, right?" Jes asked. "She has to know what's at risk."

"If Yegor puts a gun to Kristoff's head, she'll do it," Harley said. "She'd do anything for her boyfriend. She's head over heels for him."

"Is there any chance Kristoff and Yegor know that and are playing her?" Tessa asked. "I mean, I hate to think that, but it sounds like something Yegor would do. And someone gave up the details of the hospital we were using in Athens."

Crap. Harley hadn't even thought about where Yegor had gotten his information on the hospital. She hoped Tessa was wrong. "I'm going to go with my instincts on this and pray that, for Adriana's sake, Kristoff isn't involved. Which means when we go into that nuke plant, we're going to need to rescue him along with her."

"Speaking of which," Tessa interjected. "Why don't we call in the French army and have them put a couple thousand troops around each of these sites? That's got to be less risky than waiting for them to attack and then hoping we get there in time."

"There are fifty-eight nuclear plants in France alone," Jones said with a tired sigh. "And fifteen more in the UK. If we scare Yegor off from his original plan, what's to say he can't just as easily hit one of those? At least now we have some idea where the threat is coming from."

Beside Harley, Caleb leaned forward to rest his forearms on the table. "There's a good chance he might not hit either Gravelines or Penry. Yegor must have assumed Brielle would rat him out, right?"

But Brielle shook her head. "Yegor will assume I'm too terrified to talk. Especially after he had Batu try to kill Julian and me. He has a low opinion of people like you and me, even the ones who work for him. His opinion of women is even lower."

The Q&A session continued for another fifteen minutes, but in the end, all they could do was wait. They had support team personnel running surveillance on both Gravelines and Penry, praying Brielle hadn't steered them wrong. Hopefully they'd know the second anything started to happen. Then Harley and everyone else would go in, with McKay and Weatherford staying back to coordinate for local support, and Dr. Jones on the line to provide technical help.

"You coming in with us, Brielle?" Caleb asked as they all got to their feet. "After the way you fought Batu in Greece, we could use the extra firepower."

Brielle gave him a smile that seemed genuinely rueful. "That was a one-time thing, I'm afraid. But I'll be back here with the support team, in case you have any questions."

Harley was surprised to see Caleb look disappointed.

"When you go into whatever nuke plant Yegor attacks, stay on your toes," McKay said. "We can't afford to make a mistake. If Yegor pulls this off, radiation will spread across half of Europe."

And on that cheery note, Jake told everyone to try to get some rest. "We have no idea when this is going to kick off, and we've all been going nonstop for days."

As everyone slowly filtered out of the room, Erin and Elliot wandered over to where Harley stood with Sawyer.

"Sorry we walked out on you the other day," Erin said. "Finding out that you're a werewolf threw us for loop."

Sawyer nodded. "Where were you the whole time? When we realized you didn't go back to London, Rory and I were worried Yegor had killed you, and we just hadn't found the bodies yet."

"We never left Athens," Elliott admitted sheepishly. "We got rooms at a hotel, then found a bar and drank for pretty much two straight days while we tried to figure out what we were going to do. It wasn't until we got a text from Rory telling us about the attack on the hospital and explaining you were heading to Calais that we realized we'd been gone long enough."

Sawyer's mouth edged up. "Well, I can't tell you how glad I am that you came back. The team needs you. But more importantly, I need you. When you two walked away like that, I... Well...it was hard."

Harley felt tears come to her eyes at the heartfelt words. She'd known getting rejected by his teammates had been difficult and seeing how happy Sawyer was because they'd come back made her inordinately happy, too.

Erin gave Sawyer a sisterly hug. "You might be different than the Sawyer we thought we knew, but you're still the same teammate we've always had. It simply took us a while to remember that. There was no way we could let you face Yegor alone."

Harley was pretty sure Erin was close to tearing up, too, but Sawyer was smart enough to make their exit at that point, saying he and Harley needed to talk about some stuff before trying to catch some sleep.

Once outside, she and Sawyer strolled toward the hops fields behind the brewery, their hands finding each other's as they walked. The sun had already gone down, but the moon provided more than enough light. Not that she needed the extra glow. Her night vision—which usually wasn't any better than a regular person's—had suddenly decided to work for her, so she could see as perfectly as if it were daytime. Surrounded by all the trellises, the earthy scent of hops swirled around them, reminding her a little of a pine forest.

They walked in comfortable silence for a little while before Harley finally gathered her courage enough to say what had been on her mind since long before they'd even slept together.

"After tonight, our respective teams will go their separate ways," she said softly. "You'll be back in London, or wherever MI6 sends you, and I'll be back in DC, or wherever STAT sends me."

When Sawyer didn't say anything, she wondered if he'd heard her. Or perhaps he *had* heard but didn't know what to say. Maybe the reason he was taking so long to reply was because he was trying to figure out how to let her down gently. Maybe bringing up whatever this was between them had been a bad idea. But if they didn't talk about it now, there might not be time later and she couldn't imagine walking away from him after the mission and never seeing him again. The mere thought made her heart shrivel up.

"While that's true," he finally said, his voice equally soft in the darkness, "it doesn't mean we can't keep seeing each other."

Harley felt like the sun had just risen somewhere in her chest, and her heart basked in its warmth. She smiled. "I was hoping you'd say that."

"Did you ever doubt it? I mean, I don't know how we're going to make it work with our schedules, but we'll figure it out." He gave her a sidelong glance, his mouth edging up. "This is probably going to sound crazy, especially since we just met, but I've never felt this way about anyone else."

"Me, either," she admitted.

Should she tell him why they were falling for each other so fast? What if it scared him off? Then again, maybe he already knew about the legend of *The One*. And if he didn't know about the legend, it was better he learn about it from her rather than someone else in her pack. She didn't want him thinking she'd kept something so important from him.

Taking a deep breath, she gave his hand a tug, pulling him to a stop.

"There's a reason we're both feeling this way," she said when he turned to face her.

Sawyer studied her in the moonlight, blue eyes curious. Like he thought she was going to suddenly profess her love for him. Crap, *was* she in love with him? Or was it the soul-mate thing making it seem that way?

"What's wrong?" he asked when she didn't say anything.

"There's nothing wrong." The night breeze played with her hair, brushing it against her face, and she reached up with her free hand to tuck it behind her ear. "It's just that there's this werewolf thing you should probably know about. It's not really a thing, I guess. It's more of a legend or a folktale. I wasn't sure I believed it the first time I heard about it, but it kind of makes sense."

Harley knew she was babbling, but she couldn't seem to stop. Hell, she was on the verge of hyperventilating.

Sawyer took her other hand in his, holding on to them both. "Harley, what are you trying to say?"

She swallowed hard. "I'm saying there's a connection that's supposed to exist between a werewolf and the person they're meant to be with. They call it finding *The One*. As in *The One* you're supposed to spend your life with. Like soul mates."

Sawyer gazed at her for a long time, and for the life of her, she couldn't read his expression.

"Soul mates?" he echoed. "Like we're destined to be together?"

She cringed, not sure she liked the way he said it. "I don't know about the whole destiny thing. I just know that some werewolves are lucky enough to find the person who's perfect for them. Like Jake and Jes. Caleb told me he's seen it happen with other werewolves back in Dallas."

Sawyer didn't say anything. Crap, she'd screwed up. This was exactly what she'd feared. He might be her soul mate, but she wasn't his. Maybe he didn't care for her at all. Maybe his idea of seeing each other was getting together for sex every so often.

"Is it that you don't like the idea of soul mates or that you don't think I'm yours?" Harley asked softly, barely able to get the words out.

Sawyer stared at her for a second, then his eyes widened. "No, it's nothing like that! It's just that until five seconds ago, I thought soul mates were make-believe. Like something in books and movies. It's a lot to take in. As far as you and me being soul mates? How the bloody hell am I supposed to know?"

Her heart sank even deeper. Sawyer must have seen it reflected in her eyes because he sighed.

"I'm making a mess of this," he muttered. "Look, I don't know anything about soul mates or being *The One*. But I do know that I don't want to lose what we have. I've never felt like this with anyone before and I don't even want to think about it ending."

"So, you think maybe we could be…?" She trailed off, desperately wanting to finish with *soul mates* but terrified of scaring him off.

"I don't think either of us knows yet what we can be." He wrapped his arms around her, pulling her close. "But we'll only find out if we stay together long enough to figure it out. And I promise I'm not going anywhere until we know."

Harley went up on her toes to kiss him. He weaved his hands in her hair and kissed her back, the touching of their lips becoming more urgent with every passing second.

"Before we get around to figuring out what comes next, we have to get through this mission," Sawyer said, cupping her face in his hand. "I want you to promise you'll be careful. No crazy stuff. After we save the world, we'll have that serious conversation on exactly what we are to each other and how we'll make this work, okay?"

Harley smiled and nodded. "Promise."

She pulled him down for another kiss, about to ask what he thought of making out in a field of hops, when she heard Caleb calling them from the loading dock.

"Stop making out and get back in here. Yegor made his move on the Gravelines plant."

CHAPTER 18

SAWYER PICKED UP THE SCENT OF BLOOD LONG BEFORE HE LED the way around the corner and saw the three bodies lying twisted in the hallway of the Gravelines Nuclear Power Station. The large pools of blood near each told him everything he needed to know, even if his ears hadn't picked up any heartbeats. Rory must have realized the same thing because he didn't bother to check for a pulse. Misty couldn't stop herself from at least making an effort. Then again, she hadn't been doing this job long enough to recognize when it was too late for someone. If she was lucky, she'd never get to that point.

"These people were unarmed. There was no need to kill them," Misty whispered as they kept moving, stealthily heading in the direction Sawyer hoped would take them to the facility's main security office. "Yegor's men could have locked them up in a room."

Sawyer didn't say anything. They'd caught sight of some of the armed men herding whole groups of people into various room and locking them in, so he wasn't sure why the three they'd just passed had been killed while others hadn't. Maybe because people like Yegor didn't need a reason to kill. They did it simply because they could.

It had taken Sawyer and the rest of the joint STAT-MI6 team less than fifteen minutes to get to the plant after they'd gotten the call, but in that time, Yegor's crew had taken control of the power plant, including the two hundred or so people who normally worked the night shift. As far as Sawyer could tell, no one had been able to get away and no one had been able to get a call out for help. In this age of cell phones and smart watches, that was saying something.

They moved through the large complex quickly but carefully, avoiding both people and security cameras. It was actually harder to get past the people than the cameras, since it seemed like Yegor had brought a small army with him.

"We're almost at the security offices," Sawyer whispered over his radio. "The place is crawling with Yegor's men and they're all heavily armed."

He, Rory, and Misty had to duck into a supply closet to avoid a group of armed men—five of them moving fast toward the front of the building. As hard as it was to resist the urge to take them down, Sawyer wasn't there to engage. It was his job to get Misty to the facility's security offices without Yegor knowing they were here. Once there, they'd take control of all the facility's cameras, so Harley and the others could slip in more easily. After that, hopefully, Misty would be able to jump from the security computers to the system that controlled the reactors. If she could take all the reactors offline before Yegor got around to doing whatever the hell it was he had planned, they'd be halfway home. Then it would simply be a matter of taking down Yegor and his crew.

Sawyer hesitated as he reached the open door of the facility's security room, his nose picking up four distinct scents. He turned to Rory and Misty, holding up four fingers before motioning Rory to the right and Misty to the left. Then he pointed at himself and held up two fingers. Rory and Misty nodded, then stepped forward at the same time he did.

Misty might be a technopath, but she could pull the trigger when she had to. All four of the bad guys in the security room went down without a sound.

"The security room is clear," Sawyer said into his mic, taking in the twenty monitors covering the far wall, each showing a different part of the facility and flipping through scenes that changed every few seconds. "You're good to move."

"Roger that," Jake replied. "We see lots of movement outside one of the containment bunkers—reactor five, I think. Can you confirm that's where Yegor and his people are headed?"

"Give me a second to figure out what I'm seeing on all these monitors," Sawyer said. "There are a lot of them."

He scanned the images on the screens, noting the labels positioned to the lower left of each one. Unfortunately, they were meaningless words and numbers to him. It wasn't hard to understand what he was seeing when a large room full of nervous-looking people popped up on one of the monitors, though. There had to be sixty or seventy of them, some bleeding from cuts across their faces and heads, others bruised and battered.

As the monitors continued to flip through other cameras, he saw more captives locked away in other windowless rooms.

"Misty, can you get control of these monitors?" Sawyer asked. He was tired of watching the pics flip through so fast he couldn't understand what he was seeing. "Maybe figure out where Yegor and his crew are and what they're up to?"

"I'm already on it," she said.

Pulling out a chair by one of the desks in front of the monitors, she quickly sat down. But instead of clicking on the keyboard, she reached out and put her hand on the closest mouse. Then her eyes went white. Her face went completely still, too, like she simply wasn't there anymore. If Sawyer hadn't heard her heart beating, he'd swear Misty was dead.

It was beyond weird. And more than a little unsettling.

Within seconds, the camera views changed to scenes of armed men walking around and vehicles moving outside. One camera froze on what Sawyer knew had to be the reactor room. There was a number 5 on the lower left of the screen, meaning Jake had been right. The place didn't look nearly as menacing as Sawyer thought it would. There weren't any glowing pools of blue water or red strobe lights flashing to warn people of the proximity of dangerous radiation material. Instead, there were multiple levels full of pipes, gantries, railings, a few stainless steel tanks, and a floor full of black tiles with numbers and symbols all over them. The only thing that stood out were the men in tactical gear scrambling around the room, wheeling in fifty-five gallon drums with wires coming out of the tops. He didn't have a clue what an electromagnet looked like, but something told him that's what they were.

As bad as the scene on that monitor was, the one on the next was worse. A large cargo truck was parked outside the building, the back doors of the vehicle opened to reveal what had to be hundreds of cases of high explosives, the orange Class 1 hazard labels on the boxes clear as day. As he watched, men jumped in with wires and pry bars in their hands to open the crates, rigging them to blow. He remembered Brielle saying Yegor wanted to take down the walls of the containment structure around the reactor, so the radiation from a meltdown would spread even farther.

He started to fill Jake in on what he was seeing when another monitor lit up, freezing him. Yegor, Seamus, Batu, and about a dozen other men were standing in a room full of computers. Behind them was a wall of panels covered in buttons, dials, and LED displays. Adriana and Kristoff were off to one side, one of Yegor's goons holding a gun to the blond man's head. Adriana looked terrified and there were blue sparks already sparkling across her skin.

Shit.

"Jake, reactor five is definitely the target," Sawyer said. "But we need to move fast. They're already setting up the electromagnets atop the reactor core, rigging a truckload of explosives outside the containment bunker, and Yegor has Adriana starting to spark in the control room. Misty is inside the computer system, but I'm not sure if that's going to help now. By the way, both Seamus and Batu are in the control room with Yegor."

Jake cursed. "Erin, Caleb, Harley, and I will head for the control room. Forrest, Elliott, and Jes will take care of the truck. That leaves the reactor room for you, Rory, and Misty, if you can get her out of that damn computer. You need to make sure those magnets don't get turned on."

"Copy that," Sawyer said.

He glanced at Misty, who looked more like a zombie than ever. Something told him that getting her out of the computer wasn't going to be easy.

Harley had shot three men in black tactical gear before she, Erin, Caleb, and Jake made it into the building. And even though the others had done as much damage, it barely seemed like they were making a dent in the numbers they were facing. As the four of them charged through the main doors leading toward the control room for reactor five, they were slowed down by a handful of bad guys ahead of them and another group coming up from behind.

STAT had dealt with some tough situations before, but this time, they might be in over their heads.

As they moved through the hallways, the four of them covered each other like they'd been doing it for years. From the corner of her eye, she saw Erin watching Caleb's back. Man, she was so damn happy the woman had decided to come back. Harley had to admit she hadn't been so sure when Erin and Elliott had first walked into that microbrewery, but seeing Erin fight to protect Caleb now, she knew it had been the right thing.

She prayed Jake knew where the hell they were going because she simply went into point-and-shoot mode, the MP5 she was carrying firing out regular and rhythmic three-round bursts as targets appeared around her like she was in a video game. Some part of her wondered how a wannabe-school-teacher-turned-werewolf had gotten so natural at pulling a trigger, but then more bullets came her way, and she stopped thinking completely.

As they continued through one corridor after another, Harley heard voices coming through her earpiece—Jes shouting they were encountering stiff resistance in their efforts to reach the explosive-laden vehicle along the backside of the complex and Rory saying they were having problems getting Misty to disconnect from the computer system.

She strained to hear something from Sawyer, but nothing came. She told herself Rory would have said something if Sawyer had been hurt. Still, she couldn't help but worry a little, even if there was a little voice in the back of her head assuring her she'd know if he was in trouble. Sawyer was her soul mate, even if they hadn't gotten around to talking that much about it. She would always know if there was something wrong with him. Of that, she had no doubt.

Harley was still lost in thoughts of her soul mate, reloading and firing her weapon on automatic pilot, when the four of them rounded another corner and found themselves in front of a big glass wall, a room full of computers and control panels on the other side.

The reactor control room.

Harley took in the scene in the room. Yegor yelling, Seamus and Batu standing there expressionless, a man in black tactical gear shoving his weapons against the side of Kristoff's head, Adriana standing by herself near the wall of control panels, sparkling so bright it was like she was glowing from within even as lightning streaked between her and the control panels.

They were too late.

In the second it took for that thought to flicker though Harley's mind, it happened. Adriana seemed to…erupt. Jagged lines of raw, white electricity ripped through the air, hitting the wall full of computer equipment and one of Yegor's goons who'd decided to stand too close. Both the panels and the man exploded. Fire, sparks, and pieces went everywhere.

Time seemed to stop as Harley and everyone else froze.

When it started again, Adriana was tumbling to the floor, Kristoff diving forward to catch her. Emergency alarms started ringing throughout the facility, immediately followed by flashing red-and-blue lights mounted to the ceiling. Just when it seemed that it couldn't get any crazier, Caleb let loose a growl and dumped an entire magazine of 9mm rounds into the window in front of them, throwing shards of glass everywhere.

Then Seamus disappeared from inside the room, reappearing at almost the exact same moment, his knife coming at Harley's chest.

CHAPTER 19

MISTY WENT FROM TRANQUIL AND CATATONIC TO SCREAMING in the space of a single heartbeat, and it was the most blood-curdling sound Sawyer had ever heard in his life. Rory must have thought so, too, because he stumbled back with a wide-eyed expression of near panic on his face.

Sawyer had no idea what the bloody hell had happened, but he leaped forward all the same, catching Misty as she collapsed sideways out of her chair. He eased her to the floor as the sound of intense gunfire filled the air. Shouts over the radio confirmed the situation in the control room had gone completely pear-shaped. Adriana had apparently fried the computer system that controlled reactor number five.

While Misty had been in there.

He had no idea what that meant, but if the scream she let out was any indication, it couldn't be good.

Sawyer shook Misty's shoulder as Rory moved over to the door, keeping an eye on the corridor outside in case Misty's screams brought someone running. But from the chatter over the radio, the alarms, and the chaos of gunfire coming from multiple locations around the complex, Sawyer was confident worrying about screams was pretty low on the bad guys' priority list.

When shaking her shoulder didn't wake Misty up, Sawyer shouted her name as loud as he could. If the scream hadn't given them away, this probably wouldn't, either.

He called her name for the fifth time when Misty's eyes suddenly snapped open, confusion and pain reflected in violet irises that were no longer milky and glazed.

"Ugh. What the hell happened?" she asked, slowly sitting up

with a little help from him, shaking her head like she was trying to clear out some cobwebs.

"Adriana fried the computer system that controls reactor five," he said. "I was worried you'd gotten trapped in there."

Misty shook her head again, wincing in discomfort as she pushed herself up off the floor. "I almost was."

Helping Misty, he gently nudged her toward Rory. She still looked unstable, but they didn't have any more time to waste. He needed to get to the reactor room and those magnets. Rory got an arm around her shoulders to help her walk.

"Were you able to do anything to help the situation while you were in the computer?" Sawyer asked as he led the way out of the security room. He replayed the maps of the power plant through his head, trying to remember the shortest route to reactor five. It was going to take forever to get there with Misty in this condition.

"No," Misty said. "I'd just made it through the security firewalls and was about to put the reactor into emergency shutdown when a wall of electricity came racing toward me. I barely made it out before my brain melted."

Not even wanting to think about that, Sawyer stopped mid-stride, turning to her and Rory. "If we keep going at this pace, we'll never make it to reactor five in time to help."

Misty opened her mouth to say something stupid about leaving her behind, but Sawyer cut her off.

"No way. Rory's staying with you and that's final. The only thing you get to decide is whether the two of you are going to follow or head for the rooms holding all the plant employees. Those are closer, so that would be my choice."

Then, before either of them could argue, he turned and ran, the muscles of his legs and back twisting and spasming as he partially shifted to give him all the speed he could manage.

Even though it took him less than a minute to run from the security office to the corridor outside reactor five, it felt like forever. He reached the intersection that led to the reactor room, having every intention of heading that way, but then the incessant chatter on the radio broke through. Harley, Jake, and Erin were shouting back and forth as they tried to protect themselves from Seamus and all of Yegor's men, while Caleb contended with the big shifter, Batu.

Sawyer didn't consciously decide to turn and sprint toward them instead of going to the reactor room. Something inside him wouldn't give him a choice. After the conversation he and Harley had about *The One*, it wasn't difficult to figure out what instinct was guiding him. His soul mate was in danger and his inner wolf demanded he go after her.

The scene at the control room looked like something from a nightmare. Bodies covered in blood littered the floor, along with endless shards of broken glass as men in black tactical gear fired automatic weapons at everything and anything that moved. Kristoff was in one corner of the room, Adriana pale and unmoving in his lap. Caleb and Batu were smashing each other back and forth across the space, tearing each other to shreds. Yegor was yelling at his men to keep fighting as Seamus popped in and out of existence with his knife.

Jake, Erin, and Harley were all bleeding from multiple wounds. As he watched, Harley stepped in front of Erin, purposely taking a bullet meant for his MI6 teammate. A split second later, Harley snapped her head around until her beautiful, blue eyes met his, as if somehow, in all the madness, she'd known he was there.

Words couldn't convey all the emotion that passed between them in those few seconds of eye contact. All he knew was that when he got the chance, he was going to tell Harley how much he loved her. He couldn't believe he'd been so stupid not to admit it before, out in the middle of that field at the microbrewery.

Growling, Sawyer lifted his weapon and started shooting. Most of Yegor's goons had their back to him, but he didn't care.

He simply emptied the magazine from his MP5 into the center of them, then quickly reloaded and repeated the process. There was hardly anyone left standing by the time they even realized he was there.

Seamus popped up to his left, slicing open Sawyer's shoulder on that side before disappearing again. He cursed, knowing the bastard was likely going to come at him again any second. Sawyer forced himself to remain calm, reaching out with his ears and nose, praying he could somehow pick up something that would clue him in on which way the man was going to attack from.

Tingles ran across his body as Seamus came at him again, first from the right, then again from directly behind. Sawyer ignored the rapid strikes, his attention snagged by the little tingles he felt right before each attack. With a start, he realized this wasn't the first time he'd felt the sensation of pins and needles. He'd felt them back on that mountaintop in Greece, right before Seamus stabbed him in the chest.

Hoping he wasn't imagining things, Sawyer relaxed and let his inner wolf guide him, listening to whatever the tingles were trying to say to him. A second later, when a line of sensation zipped down his right side, he spun that way without thinking, squeezing the trigger on his submachine gun before he even saw anything.

He wasn't sure if he hit Seamus when the guy materialized on that side because the supernatural disappeared again too fast to be sure. But he'd definitely freaked the bastard out enough to make him think twice before charging at him again.

Taking advantage of the momentary reprieve, Sawyer fired a dozen or so rounds at the last of Yegor's men, then popped off a few at Yegor, wanting the wanker to know what it was like to duck and bleed like everyone else. When he was out of bullets, he dropped his submachine gun and took off running straight toward Caleb and Batu.

Based on the way all of their previous run-ins with the huge, green shifter had gone, it seemed obvious that bullets didn't bother him that much. Caleb's werewolf claws, on the other hand, definitely seemed to be capable of penetrating that thick, scaly hide. Knowing there was no way they'd get to Yegor without taking down his two lieutenants first, Sawyer decided to try something out of the box.

Caleb's eyes were glowing vivid omega blue, a clear sign he'd lost nearly every shred of self-control he possessed and was fighting on pure animal instinct. But when he caught sight of Sawyer, he seemed to still have enough presence of mind to keep Batu's attention focused on him long enough for Sawyer to get a shot at his exposed back.

Sawyer stiffened his fingers and rammed his claws straight into the shifter's lower back, aiming for the thing's kidney. Then he wrapped his free arm around the shifter's neck, yanking him backward as he continued to shove and twist with his claws.

The shifter howled in pain and rage as Caleb began to rip and tear at his exposed stomach and chest. The sound was loud, echoing off the walls and drowning out even the blare of the alarms. It was so deafening Sawyer almost missed the tingle running along his back.

Almost.

Trusting his instincts again, Sawyer heaved, twisting his body and dragging the shifter around to use him as a shield for the attack he knew was coming at him from behind.

Seamus popped into existence right there, knife already coming down. But this time, the supernatural didn't materialize a few feet away like he had all the other times. Instead, Seamus appeared right in front of him, like he didn't want to give Sawyer a chance to react.

But that space right in front of Sawyer wasn't clear any longer. And the look of horror on Seamus's face when he realized that he had materialized in the middle of Batu's body, was something Sawyer never wanted to see again.

Sawyer tried to hold up both of them, but when the supernaturals began to convulse violently, keeping them upright became impossible. Seamus and Batu were screaming in anguish as they crashed to the floor.

Just when it seemed there was no way the two supernaturals could survive another second, there was a concussive thump Sawyer felt through his whole body, and the two men were thrown violently apart, each flying ten feet through the air only to slide and roll another dozen feet across the floor before coming to a bone-cracking halt against either wall. Neither one moved. They barely breathed.

Movement from the corner of his eye caught Sawyer's attention, and he spun around, yanking the handgun from the holster on his thigh at the same time.

Sawyer expected to see Yegor pointing a gun at him or one of his teammates, but instead the man was aiming his automatic at Adriana, where she still lay in Kristoff's arms. But while the evil smile on Yegor's face was disconcerting, it was the cell phone in his left hand that really worried Sawyer.

"It's over Yegor," Sawyer said as Harley and the others spread out, each taking a different angle on the Ukrainian, lining up shots at his head and chest. "You're surrounded and all your men are dead or dying. I know you did all this to get revenge for your family, but it stops now. You can't win."

Everyone tensed as Yegor held up his phone, thumb moving over something on the screen Sawyer couldn't see even as the smile on his face grew wider. "I've already won. You're just too stupid to realize it."

Turning to Adriana, Yegor lifted the pistol a little, lining up for a shot at her head. Sawyer didn't hesitate, squeezing the trigger on his own gun at the same time that four other weapons went off all around him. Yegor slowly crumpled to the floor of the control room without ever getting a shot off at Adriana. Sawyer couldn't help but shake his head now that it was all over. The psychopath had committed suicide simply because he wanted to kill one more person.

Additional sirens suddenly went off and from the corner of his eye, he saw the few remaining dials and LEDs on the panel that were still working beep, click, and flash.

Cursing, Jake ran over and pulled the cell phone out of Yegor's hand, staring at the screen before looking at Sawyer. "Did you take care of the magnets in the reactor room?"

All Sawyer could do was shake his head as Jake turned the phone to show them the screen and some kind of app covered in words and symbols he didn't recognize. Not that it mattered. The wailing alarms told him more than he needed to know about what was happening.

"I think the app turned on the magnets to pull the control rods," Jake said. "With the automated safety systems destroyed, there's nothing to stop the reactor from going into meltdown. We need to shut down the magnets."

Sawyer cursed. This was on him. He should have ignored his inner wolf and headed to the reactor room. Now, thousands of innocent people were going to pay for that mistake.

"I'll do it," he said.

"We'll go with you," Erin announced, holstering her weapon and already stepping forward like she was ready to run straight to the reactor room.

"The hell you will!" Dr. Jones shouted over their earpieces. "If those rods have all been fully retracted, the radiation level in the reactor will already be at dangerous levels before you can reach it. It's a suicide mission for whoever goes in there."

"Which is why I'm going alone," Sawyer said firmly. "We all

know the only person who has a chance of surviving going in that room is a werewolf, and since it was my job to begin with, it might as well be me."

He turned and headed for the door, fully aware he'd just outed himself to everyone on the radio, including his branch chief and a nuclear physicist who almost certainly hadn't been aware of the supernatural world. In fact he could hear both men stumbling over their words as they tried to get clarification, but Sawyer didn't bother to answer them. It was too late to worry about crap like that.

"I'm going with you," Harley said, hurrying after him.

The spike of panic that ripped through Sawyer nearly took his breath away. He stopped in his tracks, spinning around to glare at her.

"No, you're not. It makes absolutely no sense to risk both our lives."

"If it's safe enough for one werewolf to be in there, it's safe enough for two," she insisted. "The longer we stand here and argue, the worse the radiation is going to get and the closer we'll be to meltdown. So I'm going. If you're coming with me, you'd better keep up."

Sawyer snarled in frustration, but Harley was already out the door and running down the hall.

Sawyer growled and ran faster, catching up with Harley as she turned down the corridor that would take them into the heavy-duty concrete bunker that housed reactor five. The sirens were even louder in this direction than they'd been in the control room, but the moment Harley looked over her shoulder at him, all of the background noise seemed to fade away. The strobing red-and-blue lights reflected off her skin, revealing a beauty that made breathing seem like a waste of time.

It was as if the soul bond chose that very second to click firmly into place for him. It was also the moment Sawyer knew there was no way in hell he could let Harley go into that reactor room with him. He'd just found her; he couldn't let her get hurt. No matter how much she would hate him for pushing her away.

His mind was moving at a hundred miles an hour as they approached the heavy steel door designed to seal off the concrete bunker. If Adriana hadn't destroyed the safety systems, the computers would have already slammed and locked down the door. He supposed the fact that the door was still open could be viewed as some kind of silver lining—if it hadn't meant Harley could walk through as easily as he could.

"We need to close the door behind us," he said, catching her arm and tugging her to a halt outside it. "If we can't stop the meltdown, it might give everyone else a few extra minutes to get away from here."

Sawyer could hear the way fear made Harley's heart pound faster. Far more than the running ever had. But she nodded, reaching out to grab the edge of the door. The thing had to be at least four inches thick and would look right at home in any bank vault.

"Crap," she said with a grunt as the door barely moved. "This thing is heavy."

"You push from the outside and I'll pull from the inside," he said. "Once we get it moving, slip through."

Harley didn't hesitate to follow his instructions, which only made Sawyer feel worse when he gave a savage yank and the door closed far quicker than she probably thought it would. She barely had time to realize what was happening before it clanked shut with a solid thud, the metal rasping as he ripped the bolt on the inside way past the point of no return.

"What are you doing?" she screamed, her voice muted by the thick metal of the door and the concrete surrounding it. There was a small glass port near the top of the door, the clear material as thick as the steel itself, and Sawyer's heart clenched in his chest at the sight of her starting to panic as she yanked on the handle outside, fighting to get the thing open again. "Sawyer, open the damn door!"

Maybe his imagination was messing with him, but being this close to the reactor, it seemed like the sirens were wailing even faster, as if they knew the radiation was getting out of control. Even if he was wrong about that, he couldn't stand there the rest of the night and stare at the woman he loved. He had to move.

"I love you!" he shouted, making sure to enunciate clearly so she could read his lips as he said the most important words he'd ever uttered. "Now, run!"

Turning, he raced toward the reactor. He heard Harley pounding on the door behind him and he prayed she'd do as he told her and get the hell out of there.

The reactor room looked no different than it had when he saw it on the monitor in the security office earlier. Well, except for the twenty or thirty large drums set up on the tiles in the center of the room, each with a thick cable coming out of the top and disappearing off into the far reaches of the room. A distinctly high-pitched humming came from each of the drums as they pulled the control rods out of the reactor buried under the tiles.

He charged forward, noting in passing that every loose piece of metal in the room had been dragged to the center—chairs, tools, pieces of lifting equipment, random bits of chain. Everything was frozen to the side of the drums. His weapon flew from his thigh holster, slamming into one of the drums so hard the clang filled the room like a gong, making his teeth ache.

Dr. Jones was in his ear, telling him to stop the magnets and shut down the power that made them work, but Sawyer was suddenly having a hard time thinking clearly. He knew there was no way he could feel radiation passing through him, but nevertheless, it felt like every cell in his body was vibrating, making movement next to impossible.

His original plan had been to disconnect the power cables from the top of each drum. Either that or trace the spidery collection of them to their origin point and pull the plug that way. But when his head started getting fuzzy, he gave up the complicated plan and, instead, swung his claws at every cable he could reach. Sparks and chunks of melting insulation flew everywhere, zapping the bloody hell out of him. He ignored the pain, flinging whole drums aside as he moved across the room.

Sawyer kept going long past the point when his vision blurred and faded, until he was kicking and slashing purely by feel. And when that became impossible—when he stumbled and fell to his knees and then onto his face—he still continued shoving drums aside as hard as he could.

Until he couldn't move at all. And everything around him faded to black.

CHAPTER 20

HARLEY COULDN'T BELIEVE IT WHEN SAWYER SLAMMED THE heavy door closed, with her on the wrong side. She thought for a second he'd simply pulled too hard by mistake. But when she heard him twist the handle until it would be useless, she realized he'd done it on purpose.

"What are you doing?" she screamed, pounding on the metal door and yanking on the handle, starting to panic as he gazed at her through the small glass portal. "Sawyer, open the damn door!"

But all he did was say *I love you*, then order her to run before turning to race down the corridor, leaving her behind.

Like hell he will!

She wouldn't let Sawyer do this alone. Thinking about him going into that room full of God knew how much radiation—by himself—made her heart beat so hard she thought it might jump out of her chest. The more she imagined the pain he might be in, the worse it got, until she swore she could feel his emotions washing over her. She didn't understand how it could be possible, but she could *feel* him getting weaker, *feel* everything starting to close in around him.

Harley yanked on the handle, but the door was so heavy it barely trembled. She attacked the steel door, pounding on it as snarls of rage echoed in the hallway. When the handle broke away, she tried to wedge her fingertips into the gap between the edge of the door and the frame, tearing her nails in the futile attempt. The frustration and fear continued to build, making her whole world spiral out of control as she pictured Sawyer dying in the reactor room all alone.

She didn't realize she was shifting until her claws sprang out. By then, the muscles of her arms and shoulders were already twisting and tearing, reshaping themselves in ways they hadn't since her last true change in what felt like a lifetime ago.

The metallic taste of blood was jarring as fangs filled her mouth, but the urgency to reach Sawyer only continued to grow, forcing her to keep pushing, smashing, and slashing at the door over and over. Her claws gouged deep grooves in the metal and the concrete around the edge of the jamb. She kept going, the muscles of her shoulders and arms singing in exhilaration at the strain. She refused to believe she might not make it in time.

She would save Sawyer.

He was the only thing that mattered.

He was her world.

Harley was so caught up in the repetitive motion of digging and tearing, she almost missed it when her claws exposed the edge of the doorframe where it was buried in the concrete wall. She focused her efforts on that area, ripping away concrete in fist-sized chunks. When she'd made a big enough gap, she shoved her hands in and got a firm grip on the doorframe.

Not letting herself dwell on how impossible it was, she tugged at the frame, snarling and growling, wondering if this was how Caleb felt when he lost control and became more animal than human. If so, there was a part of her that could see the attraction. It was freeing to give up control like this.

With a shriek of metal and a crack of concrete, one whole piece of the wall came out. That only drove her to pull harder, and a few heartbeats later, she was through the door. Ignoring the red and blue lights flashing overhead, she pushed even harder, running faster than she ever had in her life.

When bones cracked under her skin, Harley realized she might have pushed too far. She glanced down to see her arms elongating, her fingers merging as fur erupted through the skin. The sensation was painful, but surprisingly, not as terrifying as she thought it probably should be.

The popping and cracking as her head and back reshaped itself was unnerving for sure, but it didn't hurt any more than anywhere else. She shook her upper body violently, fighting to get out of her uniform top and tactical vest before she could become trapped. Amazingly, the worst part of the whole ordeal was trying to grow a tail while still wearing her pants. She swore the long, bushy appendage was being twisted into a knot in its efforts to break free.

Following her instincts, she lowered her head and tore at the web belt and pants hanging loosely around her middle, noting in the exhilaration of the moment that her teeth were incredibly sharp as they ripped right through the material. It was only after the fact that she wondered what the hell she was going to wear now that she'd destroyed her clothes.

She pushed that thought aside. *Save Sawyer first—worry about clothes later.*

Having only a general sense of her wolf form, the first few running strides she attempted once the change was finished were incredibly awkward. But within a few feet, she was running at full speed, all four legs moving in concert, the wind created by her passage ruffling her fur. Damn, she was fast!

From her lower perspective, it took a second to find Sawyer once she entered the reactor room. In that short time frame, she was nearly overwhelmed with grief and terror, fearing the worst. Then her nose took over, leading her to the center of a jumble of ripped-up drums. That's when she finally saw him slumped over on a bizarre-looking tile-covered floor.

She realized then the drums must be the electromagnets. Given the way they were toppled and tumbled around, the heavy cables coming out the top of each one sheared away, Sawyer must have been able to get them shut down. The fact that the klaxon alarms weren't ringing as loudly seemed to support that theory. Not that it mattered very much for Sawyer. His skin was pale and sweaty, his breathing slow and labored. Her big ears told her his heart was beating far too slowly.

Was she too late? Had he already absorbed more radiation than he could survive?

She forced herself to stop thinking and latched her teeth on the shoulder of his tactical harness, tugging violently as she started backing away. It was a cumbersome way to rescue someone, her paws slipping on first the tiles and then the slick concrete flooring. She fell over on top of Sawyer more times than she could count, but she kept pulling, dragging his body through the gap she'd made in the door until they somehow ended up outside the building entirely.

Harley collapsed on top of him on the damp grass, the cool evening air blowing through her fur, her large snout nuzzled against him, breathing in his scent while she prayed he'd be okay.

She had no idea how long they lay there. She absently heard Jake's voice coming through the earpiece Sawyer was still wearing, asking if the two of them were okay. The voices of their other teammates soon followed, words urgent and worried. There was nothing Harley could do. It wasn't like she could talk, and she sure as hell wasn't leaving Sawyer to find any of them.

She allowed the slow but steady beating of his heart to lull her into a state of relaxation. She guessed a person could only go for so long on pure adrenaline and fear. Even werewolves crashed at some point.

It was as Harley was lying there, draped across the chest of the man she loved, that the change occurred. Maybe shifting wasn't as painful in this direction or maybe she was simply too exhausted to care. Either way, one moment she was a four-legged furry creature with a long, bushy tail; the next she was naked and human, draped half on Sawyer's chest and half on the wet grass.

Sawyer's chest was much more comfortable, even considering all the tactical gear he was wearing. But Harley forgot all of that when she looked up and found him gazing at her, his beautiful eyes making her think he was fully aware, but also somewhat baffled.

"Was there a wolf sitting on my chest a minute ago?" he murmured, one of his hands coming up to caress her bare back, his touch making little sparks skitter across her skin.

"You're alive!" she squeaked, shoving herself upright to get a better look at him She knew how stupid that comment sounded, but she couldn't come up with anything better.

Sawyer's mouth edged up. "Yeah. I'm tired and it feels like I was hit by a truck, but I'm alive. I guess I was right about werewolves being able to recover from radiation exposure. But back to my question, why are you naked and did I really see you shift back from a full wolf?"

Harley stared at Sawyer for a moment, finding it impossible to explain how relieved she was he was okay. She should probably be worried about long-term effects of the exposure, but at that moment, all she cared about was that he was alive.

And that he'd scared the hell out of her!

Moving to straddle him, she smacked her fists against his chest in frustration. "Don't you ever do anything that stupid again for as long as you live! You selfish idiot! I love you and you could have died. And that would have killed me, too!" Tears blurred her vision and she was on the verge of hyperventilating. "You have to promise to never, ever, do that again."

Sawyer sat up and shucked his tactical vest, then his uniform top, leaving him in the T-shirt he wore underneath. Slipping it on her, he buttoned it up. The thing was so large it draped down to midthigh, and she imagined she looked ridiculous. But she couldn't care less as he caught her hands and pulled her against his chest. This was much better. No MP5 magazines poking into her breasts. Only nice, strong, muscular pecs.

"I won't ever apologize for loving you," he whispered, brushing his warm lips across her jaw all the way to her right earlobe. "And part of that means doing anything I have to when it comes to keeping you safe, even if that isn't what you want. With this soul mate thing, I get the idea that protecting you is hardwired into me now."

Harley pulled away, ready to tear into him as rage reared up inside her. "So, what? You think I don't feel the same way? That I don't love you just as much? That I won't risk my life for you without a second thought?"

He hugged her close again, his big, warm hands on her back calming her, and almost against her will, she turned to Jell-O and relaxed against him. "I'm sorry for scaring you, and for taking away your freedom to make your own decision about the risks you're willing to face for me and for your job."

"You can't ever do that again," she whispered, running her fingers through his hair and burying her face in the junction of his neck and shoulder. "I won't let this thing be one-sided. If we're going to do this together, you have to accept that."

There was silence for a time, the sounds of sirens in the distance and people murmuring in excitement somewhere on the far side of the complex, intruding on their moment.

"I know." He sighed. "I doubt it will be easy, but I promise I won't do anything like that again. But you'll have to keep me straight, okay? Having a soul mate—having you be *The One* for me—is all new. It might take me a little while to get it right."

She nodded against him, loving the way one hand slid lower to settle possessively on her hip. "We have all the time in the world to figure it out."

More silence followed, but the sound of sirens was getting closer, and Harley could smell several of her teammates moving closer to them. She guessed her nose was working better now that she and her inner wolf knew each other better. Or maybe it was finding her soul mate. Someone who would always accept her—fangs, claws, and all.

"So how is this going to work?" she asked. "Are you going to join STAT, or should I see if MI6 is hiring?"

Sawyer chuckled. "I think you already know the answer to that."

She waited for him to finish that thought but was interrupted by the sound of heavy boots treading on concrete, followed by a snort of laughter.

"Seriously?" Caleb said from behind her. "All of your teammates are out here searching for the two of you, worried both of you are either dead or glowing in the dark, and instead, you sneak out to get naked in the grass? What the hell has this British werewolf done to you, Harley? You were never this irresponsible before you met him. I think he's a bad influence."

Harley didn't turn around. Instead, she laughed and snuggled tighter against Sawyer's chest. "Yes, he's a bad influence, but he's my bad influence now. All mine."

CHAPTER 21

"And this is the mandatory selfie from the top of the Eiffel Tower," Harley said with a laugh, leaning over the granite island that separated Jake and Jestina's kitchen from the living room, turning her phone around so the beta werewolf twins, Zoe and Chloe, could see the photo of her and Sawyer. "If you look in the background, you can see the club in the Bastille District where Sawyer and I first met."

Tall and slim, with long, straight, platinum-blond hair and light-blue eyes, the eighteen-year-old identical twins shared a knowing look as they *oohed* and *aahed* over the picture in the same way they had all the others she and Sawyer had showed them as they waited for everyone else to show up for the team party. Chloe grabbed the phone and started flipping through the pics, pointing things out on the screen to her sister without ever saying a word out loud.

From the corner of her eye, Harley saw Sawyer fighting to keep a straight face. She could totally understand why. The twin were-wolves Jake had taken into his pack after their parents had been killed were unique. Though no one ever said as much, Harley was convinced Zoe and Chloe could actually talk to each other in their heads, like mental telepathy. And it was scary how fast they picked up on certain things most everyone else missed. Admittedly, it took a while to get used to them. Even Jes, who'd moved in with Jake after coming back from saving half the world from nuclear disaster, admitted the twins baffled her sometimes.

Sawyer was taking it all in stride, even if he was embarrassed with all the *oohing* and *aahing*. Even though the twins had met Sawyer about two weeks ago when he and Harley had first gotten back from their impromptu vacation, there hadn't been time to talk much. But the moment they'd gotten to the apartment, the girls had demanded to see every picture they'd taken on their getaway.

"How long did you get to stay in Paris?" Zoe asked, always the more practical one of the two. When it came to hearing about the little vacation Harley and Sawyer had taken right after the mission, she was the one asking where they'd stayed, how much it cost, whether they used public transportation or rented a car, and how the weather had been. Chloe, the more emotional twin, had asked about the experience, the smell of the Seine, whether the paintings in the Louvre were as beautiful in person, and if Paris was truly as romantic as it seemed. It was the Jimmy Choo shoes Sawyer had bought for her in Paris that both girls couldn't stop talking about, though. Harley hadn't realized he'd seen her drooling over them that first night they had dinner together in Paris, so she was completely wowed when he surprised her with the strappy shoes. They probably didn't go with the jeans and tee she was wearing, but who cared?

"We spent four days in France and then four days in London," Sawyer said, sipping his beer.

"We even got to spend a whole day with his family at their house outside Leeds," Harley added. "His mother was thrilled he was finally settling down with someone, although less thrilled he was doing it here in America."

"Oh please." Sawyer snorted. "She absolutely loved you. Dad, too. Of course, neither one of them can figure out how we ended up together." He gave the twins a grin. "I think they believe she's out of my league. I didn't bother telling them they're right."

Zoe and Chloe giggled, sharing another of those secretive glances.

"Did MI6 make it hard for you to leave?" Zoe asked, first to recover and get back to the practical questions.

"They didn't try to convince Harley to join MI6 instead, did they?" Chloe asked, her face betraying how nervous she was that might have been a possibility.

Sawyer slipped his arm around Harley. "After my boss there realized I'm a werewolf and that Harley and I are together, he fell all over himself trying to get both of us to stay. And while I wouldn't have minded continuing to work for MI6, I couldn't ask Harley to leave her pack."

"I'm glad you didn't." Chloe smiled. "Because she's part of the family. And now, so are you."

They all laughed at that, but it wasn't lost on Harley how important it was that her pack mates had welcomed Sawyer into the fold. And while she would have left to be with him, she was relieved he hadn't asked that of her. She'd longed to find a family for years and had found it in her pack. She was just glad McKay had been open to having Sawyer join STAT.

The doorbell rang shortly after that, Misty, Forrest, and Caleb coming in and immediately making their way straight across the living room over to where Sam and Dean, two adorable black lab mix puppies, were relaxing on the floor.

"Don't get them spun up, Caleb," Jes warned from the kitchen. "Jake took them both out for a long run this morning just so they'd be calm for the party. If you get them all crazy again, you'll be the one who takes them for a walk while we eat dinner."

Harley laughed as Caleb stood there with a pout on his face, looking like a kid told he wouldn't be able to open his Christmas presents if he didn't behave. It didn't stop him from crouching down beside the puppies, both of whom greeted him excitedly.

Jake came in from the small balcony where the grill was, plates piled high with cheeseburgers, hot dogs, and steak in his hands. "Okay, who's hungry?"

That had to be a rhetorical question, Harley thought, her stomach growling at the aroma of all that grilled perfection.

"Did you get all of your stuff moved into Harley's place?" Jake asked after they'd all filled their plates and spread out around the living room to eat.

"I did," Sawyer said after pausing to swallow the bite he'd taken from his burger. "Although I didn't have much to worry about. A couple of suitcases full of clothes we flew back with and a few boxes of stuff from my flat in London. Harley and I are thinking of getting a slightly larger place now that there are two of us."

Harley smiled, amazed at how happy the simple notion of getting a place together made her. Since they both loved to read, they wanted one with a room they could designate as a library, where they could showcase all the knickknacks and mementos they'd pick up on their future travels in addition to books. The idea of a home gym was also intriguing. Truthfully, though, it wasn't the particular details of what they were looking for in a home that interested her. It was living with Sawyer that had her excited.

Still, she nodded her head at all the right times as everyone gave suggestions on where they might look for a place and what price range might be best for them. Jake was focused on practicality, saying they should try to find a place close to STAT headquarters so they could get through DC traffic quickly when they got called in on a mission on short notice. Jes and the twins wanted them to move into their apartment building. Misty and Forrest suggested a brownstone near them in Mount Vernon Square. Caleb thought they should get an RV. Harley had no idea if he was serious or not.

They laughed and talked about anything and everything while they ate, and once again, Harley was struck by how easily Sawyer fit in with her pack.

"Did McKay ever tell you what happened with Adriana and Kristoff?" Forrest asked curiously as he reached for another burger. "I know he was trying to get Adriana to join STAT, but I haven't heard whether he was able to pull it off or not."

"Weatherford was working her pretty hard, too." Jake took a long sip of beer. "But I don't think Adriana was interested in either offer. She told me before we left Calais that she and Kristoff wanted to spend time together without worrying about people trying to kill them."

"What about those two supernaturals you told us about?" Zoe asked, nibbling on a Dorito. "Did they ever recover from being melded together?"

"As far as I know, Seamus and Batu were still unconscious when they transferred them to the STAT supermax in Colorado, so I'm not sure," Jake said.

Sawyer frowned. "Assuming he wakes up at some point, how the bloody hell do you keep someone like Seamus imprisoned? He'd only pop through the walls and bars of whatever cell they put him in."

"I don't know," Jake admitted. "But McKay mentioned that holding them, along with the vampire we captured, won't be a problem. For all I know, maybe they'll keep Seamus unconscious the whole time."

That idea didn't seem to sit too well with Zoe and Chloe, if the expressions on their faces were any indication. Harley had to admit, she wasn't thrilled with the concept, either. Both Seamus and Batu were horrible people, no doubt. But keeping someone drugged and unconscious came off a little bit too much like what Yegor had done to the supernaturals he'd captured to auction off, and he was one of the bad guys.

Caleb squeezed mustard onto a hot dog. "The person I'm curious about seeing again is Brielle. I never did get her to tell me how she was able to throw Batu out the window like she did. I tried to find her after we took down Yegor, but she'd already left."

"McKay talked to her before she took off," Jake said. "He wanted to make one more run at her, with a job offer this time instead of a prison sentence, but she turned him down. As far as I know, she and her brother have both fallen off the radar. I don't think we're ever going to see her again."

Caleb looked disappointed but didn't say anything.

Harley thought Jake was probably right. If it hadn't been for her dumb-ass brother, Brielle would never have shown up on the radar to begin with. Now that he was out of prison, with his record wiped clean, it would be easy for them to disappear.

"Any luck with trying a full shift again?" Caleb asked, catching Harley's eye from the other side of the coffee table where he sat on the floor.

She shook her head. Since the raid at Gravelines, she hadn't been able to make it back into her wolf form no matter how hard she tried. "I've been trying every night," she admitted. "But while I can get my claws and fangs to come out easily now, even get muscles to reshape so I can run faster, I can't get close to wolfing out. It's like I forgot how."

"I don't think it's so much forgetting as it is not being able to get back in the same headspace you were in during your first full shift," Caleb remarked. "You said you were riding on pure adrenaline and terror, worried that Sawyer was about to die. You're going to need to re-create some of those same feelings if you hope to be able to do it again. At least until you figure out a better way to make it work for you."

She shuddered. "Well, if it takes Sawyer almost dying to make me shift, I'll be fine of it never happens again."

Beside her, Sawyer leaned in close, his lips brushing her ear. "Giving up your full wolf if it means keeping me safe is the most romantic thing I've ever heard."

Harley turned her head to kiss him. "I think we both know that's not the only thing I'd give up to keep you safe. I love you like crazy."

Sawyer whispered that he loved her just as much. A declaration that had Caleb making gagging noises, which made everyone laugh, including Harley.

They were still teasing her and Sawyer when Jake's cell phone rang. He pulled it out of his pocket and got up to go into the kitchen. Harley forced herself not to eavesdrop on the call. Even before what happened in Calais, where her werewolf abilities had improved so much, she would have been able to hear most of the conversation, even from this far away. These days, she'd be able to hear the words being spoken on the TV in the background of the person making the call. She'd had to learn to control all of her senses much better since getting back from the mission, just to keep from being overwhelmed—or hearing something she shouldn't.

Jake walked into the living room a few minutes later. "Sorry to break up the party, but that was McKay. We have a situation in Turkey. We're all booked on a flight out of Reagan National in a little over four hours. Support team is already en route."

"What kind of situation?" Caleb asked, shoving what was left of his hot dog in his mouth.

"McKay didn't say. But it must be something big because he wouldn't even hint at it over an unsecured phone line."

Harley looked at Sawyer. "It looks like we have our first official mission with you on the team. You ready for this?"

He gave her a kiss. "I'm always ready."

The next SWAT (Special Wolf Alpha Team)
werewolf romance from *New York Times* bestselling
author Paige Tyler is sure to make you howl for more!

Read on for a sneak peek at

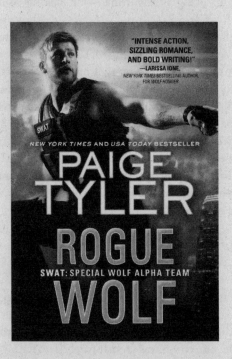

"INTENSE ACTION,
SIZZLING ROMANCE,
AND BOLD WRITING!"
—LARISSA IONE
NEW YORK TIMES BESTSELLING AUTHOR,
FOR *WOLF HUNGER*

NEW YORK TIMES AND *USA TODAY* BESTSELLER

PAIGE
TYLER

ROGUE
WOLF

SWAT: SPECIAL WOLF ALPHA TEAM

Coming August 2021 from Sourcebooks Casablanca

CHAPTER 1

Dallas, Texas

"MAN, I HOPE THEY'RE WRONG ABOUT SOMEONE DUMPING A body out here," Officer Connor Malone murmured as he moved through the heavily wooded area ten yards to Trey's left. Fellow SWAT teammates and werewolves Corporal Trevor McCall was another ten yards beyond Connor, while Officer Hale Delaney was a bit farther out, bringing up the end of the search line. "I mean, dumping a body anywhere is sick, but this place is way too beautiful for crap like that."

Trey agreed with his blond teammate. The Trinity River Audubon Center was part nature preserve, part public park along the southern side of the county. In the distance, he could hear the drone of vehicles speeding along the Interstate 20 belt loop, but for the moment at least, the area he and his pack mates were in was quiet and tranquil.

That would all change if they found anything. In a heartbeat, a place usually known only for its slow-moving streams and mist-shrouded walking trails would immediately be overrun with cops and crime scene technicians looking for clues to help them identify the person the local papers had tagged as "the Butcher."

While the name of the latest serial killer to terrorize Dallas might not be original, it was unfortunately devastatingly accurate. Four bodies had been found over the past week and a half. Or more precisely, *parts* of four bodies had been found. In each case, the corpses—all men—had been found dumped in wooded or remote locations missing their heads and both hands. The theory was that the killer was mutilating the bodies to make it harder to identify the victims. If that was the plan, it was working, because the Dallas Police Department had yet to put a name to a single one of them.

Four bodies found with hands and heads removed was morbid and depraved enough, but unfortunately, there was more. Each victim was also missing at least one other body part—the right arm in the first case, right leg in the second, both lungs in the third, and on the body found two nights ago, several whole sections of skin had been missing. The DPD had tried to keep those details secret until they had a suspect, but somehow, it'd leaked out and the media had been running the Butcher storyline nonstop ever since.

"Did you hear what happened to make them think there's a body out here?" Hale asked as he dropped to one knee to look under some thickets near the edge of the stream that served as the leftmost boundary for this part of the search grid. Tall and muscular, he had dark-blond hair and blue eyes.

Trey could have told him there weren't any remains to be found under there. If there were, they'd be able to easily pick up the odor. But even by normal human standards, Hale's nose was bad. Compared to the other members of the pack, their fellow werewolf couldn't smell anything at all. That's why he tended to trust his keen eyesight for everything.

"Something about an older couple out here walking their dog, I think," Trevor said as he waited patiently for Hale to finish looking under the brush. There was a time when everyone in the Pack used to rag on Hale about his nose, but now, they all felt bad for him.

"Yeah, that's it exactly." Hale stood and rejoined their line moving through the woods. "But you missed the best part. It turns out the couple's dog ran off while they were here, and when the poor guy finally came back a few hours later, he was covered in blood. They assumed he was hurt, so they took him to the vet.

When the vet figured out the dog was okay and the blood wasn't his, she ran a precipitin test, then called the PD first thing this morning when she confirmed it was human."

"No wonder Chief Leclair pushed to get so many volunteers out here searching." Trevor ran his hand through his dark hair. "If the dog was loose for hours, there's no telling where he was when he found the body. It could be miles from here."

Trey didn't comment and neither did his pack mates. They searched in silence for a while until Trevor spoke again.

"So, how'd your date go last night, Connor?"

If they had been close enough, Trey would have fist-bumped Trevor to thank him for coming up with something to talk about besides the mutilated remains they were out there looking for.

"In a word—disaster," Connor said, tilting his head back to sniff the morning air like he'd picked up a scent. But whatever it was must not have been all that interesting because he continued, "Seriously, it was the worst date ever."

Trey was fairly sure his pack mate was exaggerating. He'd seen Connor and the nurse talking a couple weeks ago after Connor had gotten roughed up during a confrontation with a drunk man on a bulldozer. Connor hadn't been hurt—he was a frigging werewolf after all—but a reporter had seen the blood, so a trip to the hospital had been mandatory. Which meant Trey had been forced to watch her and Connor flirt for nearly an hour as she'd taken her time cleaning his injuries. There'd definitely been a spark there.

"Come on," he scoffed. "It couldn't have been that bad."

Connor snorted. "Trust me, it was worse." He sighed. "I mean, dinner went fine and there was some chemistry—not any kind of serious connection, but we clicked well enough to see where it might lead—but it all went downhill once I took her back to my place and she met Kat."

"Ah," Trey said in understanding even as Hale and Trevor did the same.

In theory, Kat was the SWAT team's feline mascot, but honestly the cat put up with the SWAT Pack simply because that's who Connor hung out with. She was definitely his cat. Hell, she even followed him on their incident calls, regardless of the danger. And forget trying to keep her and Connor separated. Trevor had tried locking her in the armory to keep Kat from going out on a barricaded active-shooter situation, and the damn cat had shown up at the scene five minutes after the SWAT team, somehow having hitched a ride with a uniformed patrol officer who had no idea she was even in his car. No one had a clue how she'd done it. Suffice it to say, Trevor was her least favorite werewolf in the Pack. The look she gave him every time she saw him would melt the paint off a car. The only reason the creature hadn't come this morning was that it was o dark thirty. Kat never got out of bed this early unless it was to watch Connor and the rest of them shower after physical training.

"What happened?" Trey asked, though he was sure he already knew. Kat had a way of letting people know what she thought of them.

"Nothing at first," Connor said. "Kat was nowhere in sight when Michelle and I got back to my place after dinner, but the moment we sat down on the couch, she jumped up and shoved her way between us, deliberately knocked the glass of wine out of Michelle's hand, then clawed her dress."

Trevor snorted. "I guess Kat didn't approve of your date."

"You think?" Connor asked drily. "Suffice to say, the date was over. And before you ask, Michelle and I won't be going out again."

"It's not her fault she decided to date a werewolf with a possessive cat for a pet." Trey would have said more, but a familiar scent caught his attention. He stopped and looked left, out across the slow-moving stream.

Trevor and Connor must have smelled it, too, because they both paused and sniffed the air.

"What is it?" Hale asked.

"Blood," Trevor murmured.

Hale didn't bother to try to trace the scent, but simply followed them as they ran along the bank of the stream.

"How are we going to explain ending up on the other side of the stream and well outside our search grid?" Connor asked.

"Don't worry about it," Trey told him. "I'll come up with something believable if anyone asks. Right now, just focus on finding the source of that scent."

They followed the trail for another thousand yards or so before the stream narrowed enough for them to leap across. Not that a normal human would have been able to do it, but that was simply one more lie Trey would have to come up with once the questions started.

The scent led them to a low-lying area blanketed with thickets and brush, the kind of place Trey recognized as perfect for hiding a body—even if getting it here would have been a major pain in the ass for whoever dumped it.

He and his pack mates stopped the moment they saw the body, staying far enough away to hopefully not trample any forensic evidence that might have been left behind. It helped that there was no reason for them to move closer to check for a pulse. Even from fifteen feet away, Trey's hearing told him the victim didn't have one.

It was another one of the Butcher's victims. The man lying in the shallow grave had been partially dug up. Probably by the wandering dog. The head and hands were gone, along with another leg. It also looked like the stomach cavity had been ripped open, but that might have been the dog's doing, too. As a cop, and before that a soldier who'd seen more than his fair share of combat, he'd seen a lot of dead bodies, but this was as bad as anything he'd ever experienced. This killer was sadistic as hell.

"What am I smelling?" Trevor asked, sniffing the air.

Trey took a whiff and realized there were two separate scents competing—and neither of them were blood. The first one was sharp, like a cleanser or disinfectant, but with floral notes, like perfume. The other smelled almost human, but something wasn't quite right about it. He was still trying to figure out what it was when he picked up a burnt electrical odor. While the first two scents lingered on the body, the third hovered around it. As if it belonged to whoever had carried the body and dumped it here.

Trevor must have concluded the same thing because he gave Trey a worried look. "You think we're dealing with some kind of supernatural killer?"

Trey almost groaned. That was all they needed. Serial killers were bad enough. But if this one was indeed supernatural, there might be more to the Butcher than they'd thought.

"How exactly did you end up finding the body on this side of the stream when you and your teammates were assigned to a grid nearly a quarter mile away from here?"

Dark hair pulled back in a neat bun, Chief Leclair regarded Trey curiously where they stood several yards away from the organized chaos that was the crime scene.

"Pure luck," he said. "We finished clearing our assigned grid when we saw some buzzards circling this area, so we decided to check it out."

Leclair continued to study him as if she somehow knew he was lying through his teeth. Trey hoped not.

"I see," she finally said in a soft, noncommittal tone before glancing down at the bottom of his tactical uniform pants. "And how did you get across the stream without getting wet?"

Trey did a double take, completely caught off guard by the question. Which is probably why she'd asked it. Damn, he and his pack mates were going to have to be careful around the chief. She was cop through and through.

"The stream narrows quite a bit if you wander down that way," he said as casually as he could, jerking his thumb in the stream's direction. "We were able to jump across it."

Leclair didn't look like she believed that for a damn second, but at least she didn't continue grilling him about it. "I suppose we should be thankful you followed your instincts and searched this area. I doubt anyone else would have bothered to fight their way through so many thickets on a whim. Then again, it's starting to become the norm for me to find my SWAT team in places where they're not supposed to be. Fortunately, things always seem to go right when you and your teammates go off script."

With that, the chief walked away, heading toward the taped-off crime scene to talk to one of the detectives from the serial killer task force. Given that no one had approached the body yet, it was likely they were waiting for a medical examiner to arrive. Hopefully, they'd get here soon and Leclair would be too focused on that to worry about him and the other members of his pack. Because she definitely seemed suspicious right now.

"Everything okay?" Connor asked as he came up beside him. "You and the chief seemed to be having an intense conversation."

"I think we're good," Trey answered. "Though I'm pretty sure she knows I'm lying about how we found the body."

Connor blew out a breath. "I figured as much. We need to be careful around her. She's sharp."

Trey opened his mouth to agree, but the words got stuck in his throat as a woman carrying a heavy-looking bag with the Dallas County Medical Examiner's Office emblem on the side approached the crime scene tape and walked directly over to the chief. Between the bag that she had to lug half a mile through the woods in the mid-August heat and the navy blue coveralls she was wearing over her regular clothes, complete with high rubber boots, Dr. Samantha Mills was glistening with sweat, some of her long, blond hair escaping from her messy bun.

Damn, she was the most attractive woman he'd ever seen in his life.

"You ask her out yet?" Connor said casually.

Trey glanced at his buddy to see him wearing a knowing grin. It wasn't a secret that Trey had a thing for the assistant ME. He'd done nothing to hide it from the moment he'd first seen her at the site of the SWAT team's raid two years ago when half the Pack had fully shifted into wolves. After that, Samantha seemed to show up at every crime scene to collect forensic evidence all while looking at them sideways. Hell, just this past June, while helping them with a case, she'd openly admitted to knowing the team was playing fast and loose with the truth when it came to how they did their jobs. He and the rest of the Pack had been worried she might be onto their secret—that the DPD SWAT team was composed entirely of werewolves—but when she hadn't exposed them, they'd relaxed a little.

Now, if only Trey could figure out how to man up and ask her out when he couldn't even seem to talk to her without getting tongue-tied.

"I've been meaning to, but I haven't found the right time to approach her about it," he said.

Connor shrugged. "How about right now?"

Trey snorted. "Yeah right. She wants some guy to ask her out while she's leaning over a dead body."

"Dude, she deals with dead bodies every day, so you're going to need to come up with another excuse. You're a werewolf, not a werechicken. Just ask her to go out to dinner. What's the worst that could happen?"

Trey would have laughed at the werechicken comment if this thing he had for Samantha hadn't gone on for so long it had some-how taken on a life of its own. The thought of asking her out only to be turned down was something he didn't even want to think about. That was why he kept putting it off. He was waiting for some sign to light up and tell him to finally go for it.

But that was stupid. There wasn't going to be a sign, and if he kept waiting, the worst that could happen—*would happen*—was someone else would make a move on the beautiful, brilliant woman and he'd be left thinking about what could have been. The thought alone made Trey's gut clench.

Dammit. He was going to ask her out—today.

But as he watched her drop to a knee beside the body and lean over to study the headless corpse, he decided he'd wait until she wasn't leaning over a mutilated body.

CHAPTER 2

SAMANTHA UNLOCKED HER OFFICE AND WALKED IN, LETTING the quirkiness of the space soothe her aggravated mind and soul. With its light gray color scheme, the room was sleek and modern, like the rest of the Dallas Institute of Forensic Sciences. While the shelves filled with medical journals were fairly standard for a pathologist's office, it was the other shelving units on the far wall that defined the space. The display cases showcased her collection of antique medical devices and various other medical curiosities, including a human skull saved from a sanitarium where they'd practiced medicine that could only be labeled as barbaric. She kept it as a reminder that psychos could be found wearing all kinds of disguises...including doctor's garb.

Standing in the middle of her safe zone, she took a deep breath and let it out slowly, releasing the urge to throttle somebody.

"Briefing go that badly?"

Samantha turned to see her best friend, coworker, next-door neighbor, and all-around confidant Crystal Mullen in the doorway. Petite with brown eyes and her shoulder-length dark hair in its signature ponytail, Crystal was always there when Samantha needed to vent about something. These days, that was a lot.

When her boss, Louis Russo, said he was assigning her to the serial killer task force, Samantha had been thrilled. Okay, that sounded bad. For a nerd like her who was used to working miles behind the lines, where she barely had a clue what case she was involved in, the chance to team up with the police as they chased down a murderer, uncovering clues and questioning suspects, sounded exciting. Then she'd started going to meetings, and the shine had quickly worn off that particular apple. Now, after only a little more than a week, she dreaded every briefing she was forced to attend and their ability to frustrate her beyond all rational explanation.

"No worse than usual, which is to say horrible," Samantha admitted, moving over to her mini fridge to pull out a bottle of water. She held another up to her friend, but Crystal shook her head. Crystal was a die-hard caffeine addict. Seriously, her friend would wheel around her coffee in an IV stand if Louis had let her.

"Let me guess," Crystal said as she perched in the chair in front of Samantha's desk. Her friend never actually sat back in the comfortable club chair like a normal person. Probably because she had way too much caffeine in her system. "They're upset you haven't already solved the case for them."

Samantha sat down behind her desk with a sigh. "Pretty much. They didn't want to hear that I barely had time to do more than an initial assessment of the body found this morning." Opening the bottle, she took a long drink of water. "Never mind that I was able to establish an approximate time of death and confirm the amputations were accomplished with the same type of saw as the one used in the previous Butcher cases. Or that the cuts were made by the same person, based on the angle and technique involved. I even got samples collected and prepped for DNA profiling and checks against CODIS and NDIS, but that still wasn't enough for them."

"Sounds like a lot to me," Crystal said. "What else were they expecting?"

Samantha shrugged, relaxing back in her chair and lazily swiveling from side to side. "I think they're all waiting for the wow factor to kick in like all those *CSI* shows on TV. You know, where they collect and profile DNA, then a computer spits out a name before the first commercial break? They don't want to hear this killer chooses his victims specifically because they aren't in the system and that he's too meticulous to leave behind any hair, fiber, or blood evidence. And because I know the killer is a man from the size and depth of his boot prints, they think I should be able to track those boots to a specific store and found out who bought them. But I can't do that because it doesn't work that way." She sighed. "I know they're just trying to catch this guy, but so am I. But when there's no evidence, there's no evidence."

"Maybe I can find something to make the task force happy," Crystal said.

"Let's hope," Samantha agreed.

Crystal was a forensic technician at the lab, working on a little bit of everything, but concentrating mostly on latent prints and tool marks. Before coming to work at the institute, Samantha never would have thought there'd be a call for someone to do that full time, but Dallas was a busy city when it came to crime. Crystal could work overtime for the rest of her life and never catch up with the backlog of cases that needed her expertise.

Samantha was about to ask Crystal if she wanted to start going over the body together when footsteps outside her office interrupted her.

"Senior Corporal Duncan," she said with a smile even as Crystal snapped her head around to see who was at the door. "Come in."

Trey and the other three officers with him from the SWAT team exchanged looks before stepping inside. Her office wasn't small by any means, but with the four very large cops in there, it suddenly seemed much harder to breathe.

Or maybe that was simply a side effect of being so close to Trey.

Samantha would be the first to admit she and Trey had been bouncing around in each other's orbits ever since she'd responded to a crime scene involving the SWAT team and found a handful of dead criminals who'd supposedly been mauled by wild coyotes in the middle of the Dallas-Fort Worth International Airport. Her experiences with the team had only gotten stranger from there. To say that they weren't quite normal was an understatement.

Okay, so maybe her intellectual curiosity wasn't the only reason she'd spent most of the past year and a half stalking Trey. With that square jaw, intense blue eyes, and perfect amount of scruff, the man *was* extremely attractive. Not to mention the fact that he looked amazing in the dark-blue tactical uniform. But there was more to it than that. Simply put, there was something about him that mesmerized her every time she was around him. His presence at the Audubon center this morning had made it damn hard to focus on her work, that was for sure. Even with a headless corpse there to distract her.

The funny thing was, she wasn't surprised at all to see him and his teammates here in her office today. In fact, since hearing that it had been Trey and his fellow SWAT officers who'd actually found the body, she'd been pretty much expecting a visit from them. Just like back in mid-June, when they'd inserted themselves in the middle of that delirium drug thing…which really hadn't been a drug thing at all. When things got weird in Dallas, SWAT was going to be there.

Realizing she'd yet to make any introductions, Samantha quickly did so. Trey did the same, introducing Connor, Trevor, and Hale, though she could have easily introduced them herself since she had files on every member of the SWAT team. Crystal was well aware of Samantha's fascination with all things SWAT—and Trey in particular—so it was no surprise when her friend came up with an excuse to leave, saying she needed to start working on the body Samantha had brought in earlier.

"Normally, I'd ask what brought four of Dallas's finest down to my office," Samantha said as she moved around the side of the desk and sat on the edge to study the four men, "but since you showed up minutes after I got done briefing the task force—and you were also at the crime scene this morning—I'm assuming your visit is related to the Butcher."

Trey glanced at his teammates, who returned the look, as if saying *your call.*

"You're right. It is." Trey gave her a smile, flashing the most perfect dimples. "We're hoping you might be able to tell us a little about the case."

Samantha had to fight the urge to return his smile. Damn, when Trey put on the charm, it was scary how badly she wanted to walk over there, climb him like a sloth, and start coming up with names for their future children. But she fought off the desire. Besides, she didn't need to think about names. She had all four of them picked out a few days after meeting the hunky cop. No, she needed to play this cool and use the situation to get what she wanted.

"I really don't think I should be talking to you four about the Butcher case since none of you are on the task force," she said.

Trey smiled again, his eyes holding hers captive. "I know we're not on the task force, but we're asking anyway."

"And why is that?"

He crossed his arms over his broad chest, treating her to a pair of biceps she couldn't have gotten both hands around if she tried. And boy, would she like to try. "Do you remember what I said to you back in June to get you to help us with that delirium case?"

That had been two months ago, so Samantha had to really think about it to come up with what part of the conversation he was talking about. Most of her memories were of the stunningly attractive Trey Duncan practically begging for her help on that case and her feeling badly about not being able to offer up anything.

"I remember you said you needed my help because you and the rest of the SWAT team were the ones who had to deal with the people you thought were on some drug called delirium and that you needed to understand what you were up against."

Trey gave her another distracting smile. "Exactly."

"I don't understand," she said.

Samantha thought back to the delirium case. Was there some kind of connection to the current serial killer terrorizing the city?

She couldn't see how that was possible. The two men responsible for those crimes had something in their DNA that allowed them to turn people into puppets and control their minds simply by wiping their blood on their victims. Unfortunately, she hadn't been able to figure out exactly what was in their DNA, and while the Butcher might be scary as hell, she hadn't found anything to make her think he wasn't a regular human.

Unless…

"Wait a minute," she said, her mind starting to spin at a hundred miles an hour. What had she just said to herself only a few minutes ago? *When things got weird in Dallas, SWAT was going to be there.* "Are you saying the Butcher isn't a normal killer? That he's different like the men responsible for making all those people do things against their will are different?"

Another look passed between the big cops before Trevor, Connor, and Hale all seem to pass some kind of unspoken signal to Trey. Only then did he nod.

"We noticed something at the body dump this morning that makes us think the person who dragged the body there wasn't a normal human. Don't ask me to explain what that something was because I can't tell you, and you wouldn't believe me if I did. I simply need you to trust me."

Samantha almost said to hell with it. If they didn't want to tell her anything, why should she tell them anything? It was her butt on the line if her boss found out. But then she looked at Trey and realized there was no way she could say no to him. He was like her own personal brand of kryptonite.

"Okay." She leveled her gaze at Trey. "Same deal as before. I'll tell you everything I have on the Butcher, but you personally owe me a favor."

Trey's mouth edged up, the twinkle in his eyes making her a little weak in the knees. "You know, you still haven't collected on the first favor I owe you."

She smiled up at him. "Maybe I'll just keep collecting them so I can use them all at once."

He chuckled, the husky sound doing crazy things to her pulse. Beside him, she caught the smiles on his teammates' faces.

"Deal," Trey answered with a dip of his chin. "One favor for anything you have on the Butcher right now and anything you might find on him in the future."

It wasn't a shock he'd try to weasel a little extra information out of her, but she'd already made up her mind to tell him as much as she could. Partly because she had a thing for Trey and partly because she already believed there was something strange going on with this serial killer case. She had no idea what it might be, but it could explain why they had so many victims and still no serious clues about who the killer was or why he was mutilating them.

"I guess I should start by admitting we don't have a whole hell of a lot on the killer, even with all the emphasis the chief is putting on the task force," she said. "What I can tell you is that this guy is no random slasher. Most of the cuts on the bodies were professional and surgical in nature, without a single sign of hesitation or doubt. On top of that, I found signs of arteries and veins being tied off prior to some of the amputations, along with indications that some of the victims were still alive when the killer did it. Believe it or not, keeping someone alive while you dismember them is actually rather difficult."

"And sick," Trey muttered. "So what you're saying is that we're dealing with a doctor of some kind. Or at least someone who went through a good portion of medical school."

"Which means we're not talking about a small pool of potential suspects," Connor added with a frown. "Especially if we include everyone who was kicked out or dropped out of med school."

"It definitely isn't a short list," Samantha agreed. "Unfortunately, the situation is even more complicated than that. Like I said. *Most* of the cuts were clean and precise. But there were others, namely the ones at the neck and wrists, that were quite ragged. They were basically hack jobs."

That earned her a grimace or two from Trey and his friends.

"So what are you saying? That there are two killers working together?" Trevor asked, clearly surprised. "I never heard of serial killers teaming up."

Samantha shrugged. "Me, either. I wish I could say for sure there are two killers, but I can't. Some people on the task force think there are, while others insist it's one guy and that the less precise cuts are because he loses control and goes completely psychotic."

Trey grimaced. "Any connections between the victims yet? Or how the killer selects his targets?"

When she admitted the answer to both of those questions was no, Trey and his teammates were clearly surprised they hadn't identified any of the victims yet, much less establish a serious connection between the men.

"So far, the only thing we can say for sure about the victims is that they're all in their late twenties to midthirties, in good shape, over six feet tall, and weigh more than two hundred and thirty pounds," she said. "And before you ask, no we're not sure if this is significant in some way or simply a coincidence."

Trey and his teammates seemed more than ready to keep grilling her for information about the case, but just then, all four of them got odd looks on their faces, then turned as one to face the door. Samantha was just about to ask what the heck they were doing when she heard footsteps in the hallway. A few moments later, her boss walked in with two of her coworkers.

"Samantha." Her boss eyed Trey and his teammates curiously from behind his wire-rimmed glasses before looking at her. "We were walking by and heard you talking to someone. I didn't realize anyone from the task force was still here."

How many more people were going to try to squeeze into her

office? The room had been crowded before with the four large cops, but now it was nearly claustrophobic. "These officers aren't with the task force. They're here to tie up a few loose ends on a case from back in June." Before her boss could ask which case, she quickly made the introductions. "Officers, this is Louis Russo, the chief medical examiner. And this is Hugh Olsen and Nadia Payne, two of my fellow assistant MEs."

Her gray-haired boss immediately reached out to shake hands with Trey and his teammates as she continued with the introductions. Hugh merely nodded stiffly in greeting while Nadia offered them a cool smile. No surprise there.

While Samantha loved working with Louis, who was a brilliant pathologist, a willing mentor, and completely above the politics that sometimes made working in the ME's office a pain in the butt, she couldn't say the same about Hugh and Nadia. They were both smart and capable at their jobs, but spending so much time among the dead had made them cold and detached. Almost like they didn't know how to interact with the living anymore. The only time either of them pretended to care was when Louis was around to see it. To say they'd been pissed when Louis had assigned Samantha to the Butcher task force was putting it mildly. The way they saw it, this was the kind of case that could catapult their careers to the next level and put them directly in line for chief ME when Louis left. The fact that there were people actually dying out there thanks to this psychopath didn't seem to register with them at all. Hugh, in particular, had campaigned heavily for the assignment, and when Louis gave it to Samantha, he'd nearly exploded. Since then, he never let a chance to bash Samantha pass him by. Nadia was more circumspect about it but equally bitter. Luckily, Louis never listened to their crap.

The moment Hugh and Nadia figured out they weren't going to be able to undermine Samantha—or hear anything about the serial killer case—they both left her office, mumbling something about needing to catch up on paperwork. Louis left soon after they did, asking Samantha to stop by his office before she left for the day so they could go over whatever she had learned from the Butcher's latest victim.

Thirty seconds later, Connor, Hale, and Trevor headed for the door, too, saying they'd be waiting out by the truck. And just like that, Samantha found herself left alone with Trey. It occurred to her then that it was the first time that had ever happened.

"Not very subtle, are they?" Samantha asked with a soft laugh.

Getting to her feet, she moved closer, mesmerized by the way his presence still seemed to fill the room even with only the two of them in it. Samantha found it impossible not to stare up at him. To say he was the most gorgeous man she'd ever seen was an understatement.

"No, I guess they aren't," Trey murmured, gazing down at her, his low, sexy voice drawing her in even closer. "Sorry we chased off your coworkers like that."

"Did you hear me complaining?" she countered. "Anything that gets me out of talking to Hugh and Nadia is all good in my book."

Trey snorted, his lips curving into a smile. Samantha had an overwhelming urge to rub her face against his like a cat just so she could feel that scruff on his chiseled jaw against her skin.

"Yeah, I couldn't help but pick up on the bad vibe between you and those two," he said. "If you want to use up one of those favors, I happen to have a few friends in the federal government. I could have them sniff around their background, see if Hugh cheats on his taxes or Nadia hacks into their neighbor's Netflix account."

Samantha was too caught up in Trey's blue eyes to answer right away. Sometimes they seemed darker in color, like the sky at night. Other times, they reminded her of the sky on a sunny day. She wondered if it was possible for eyes to change color like that, to lighten and darken with one's mood. Maybe she should ask for permission to lay on his chest for a few hours to study them just to see if she was right.

But while lying atop Trey certainly sounded like fun, Samantha realized maybe she needed to start with something a little less familiar.

"If I'm going to use up one of my favors," she said softly, keenly aware of Trey leaning in even more, then closing his eyes and inhaling. Like he was trying to breathe in her scent. "It wouldn't be for snooping into either of their backgrounds."

"What would you use it on then?" he asked, lifting his gaze to hers. Oh yeah, his eyes definitely darkened a bit more, like the ocean in the middle of a storm.

Inspiration hit then, and Samantha didn't even pause to wonder if she should do it or not.

"I'd use it to have you take me out to dinner," she said before she could come to her senses and chicken out.

From the way Trey gaped, Samantha could tell she'd thrown the big cop for a loop. Fear and doubt immediately started creeping in, making her think she'd royally screwed up. Maybe Trey was one of those men who was more comfortable doing the asking instead of being asked. She didn't like to think someone who was clearly so strong and confident would be insecure over something like that. But maybe she'd read him all wrong.

"Are you asking me out on a date?" he said, and she was relieved when she saw a spark of interest there in those mesmerizing eyes. Like he suddenly found a game he unequivocally liked.

She stepped closer, smiling as his eyes darkened again. "Actually, I'm using one of my favors to have you ask me out. That way, I can be progressive and traditional at the same time. That doesn't bother you, does it?"

He grinned, his expression making her pulse skip a beat. "Definitely not. I'm a huge fan of progressive traditions. Dinner tomorrow night work for you?"

She had to force herself not to pump her fist in excitement. "It does."

"Good. Should I pick you up at your place? Say seven o'clock."

She nodded, then watched in disappointment as he turned and headed for the door. Not that seeing him from behind was a bad view or anything.

"Hey," she called before he disappeared into the hallway. "I didn't give you my address."

Trey paused long enough to give her another one of those smiles that turned her knees to Jell-O. "At the risk of sounding like a stalker, I already know where you live."

He was out the door before Samantha could say whether it made him seem like a stalker or not. But in all honesty, it wasn't like she could complain very much since she already knew where he lived, too.

CHAPTER 3

WHEN TREY GOT THE CALL FROM HIS COMMANDER/PACK ALPHA at five o'clock in the morning telling him to get to the McCommas Bluff Landfill, he'd assumed it was going to be another body dump. And when he'd pulled up the map on his phone and realized the landfill was only a couple miles from the Trinity River site where they'd found the body a few days ago, he'd been even more sure. So he was a little stunned when he reached the front gates of the landfill and didn't see a single member of the press or the normal collection of morbid gawkers who liked showing up at any scene that might belong to the Butcher. Trey found it hard to believe the DPD could have kept something like this quiet. No matter how hard they tried, word always seemed to get out.

He got another surprise when he reached the backside of the landfill and saw only four vehicles parked on the side of the road. Typically, there'd be a frigging parking lot full of city, county, and state emergency vehicles at a scene like this. But other than the bulldozer sitting in the muddy field across the road, this part of the landfill was essentially deserted.

Trey climbed out of his truck, immediately spotting Connor, Trevor, Hale, and their other pack mate, Zane Kendrick, standing a few yards away staring at something on the ground behind a big pile of construction scraps. He'd only taken a few steps in their direction when he caught sight of two other people he definitely hadn't expected to see here. For the first time, he began to think maybe there was something different going on.

"Corporal Duncan." Deputy Chief Hal Mason stepped forward in the dim morning light to shake Trey's hand. "I'm sorry for dragging you out of bed this early, but as you'll soon see, this isn't something that could wait." Mason oversaw the SWAT team, along with several other specialty units within the DPD. And while he was fully aware that the entire team was composed of alpha werewolves, it was rare to see him in the field. The man was high enough up on the food chain that he didn't go after bad guys himself, but low enough that he wasn't expected to show up at crime scenes purely for publicity's sake. "You already know Agent Carson," he added, motioning toward Zane and the tall, slim woman with blond hair pulled back in a neat ponytail standing beside him.

Yeah, Trey knew her. And Alyssa, on the other hand, had no business being at any normal DPD crime scene—publicity or not. She was Zane's mate and also an agent with STAT, aka Special Threat Assessment Team, the secretive joint FBI-CIA group that had the job of dealing with those things that went bump in the night. Things that very few humans ever had the opportunity to learn about until they were unfortunate enough to get eaten by one of them. If she was here, it couldn't be good.

Or normal.

"I'm guessing this isn't another Butcher body dump?" Trey asked as he and Mason moved over to join everyone else.

"No," the deputy chief said. "At least we don't think so."

That sounded ominous.

Trey walked around the shoulder-high pile of construction debris, slowing at the sight of a black cat sitting there all prim and proper atop a pile of bricks. The cat looked back at him, impatience clear on her furry face. If the creature could talk, Trey was pretty sure she'd be asking what took him so long to get there.

Trey threw a glance in Mason's direction to see what he thought about there being a pet at a crime scene. It said something about how jaded the deputy chief had become to the strange and unusual that he acted like the cat wasn't even there.

Pulling his attention away from the cat, Trey turned to look at whatever was on the ground that had everyone's attention, grunting when he finally caught sight of it.

"What the hell?" he murmured, stepping closer to the body lying among the rubble near a beat-up piece of plywood.

If Trey had to guess, the victim had to be in his nineties at least. Hell, for all Trey knew, the guy might even be a hundred years old. Then again, maybe the killer had left the body someplace really hot and really dry…like an oven. Because that was the only thing that might explain why the corpse looked like a mummy. The body was shirtless, the pants undone and shoved halfway down his legs to his knees. Other than being dried out and shriveled up like a raisin, the body appeared completely intact. Trey couldn't even see any visible wounds on the man.

He definitely had to agree with the deputy chief. This didn't seem like the Butcher's MO.

Pulling a pair of rubber gloves out of a cargo pocket, he slid them on, then knelt down by the body, his medic instincts demanding he figure out how this guy had ended up like this. The moment he picked up the man's wrist—and almost snapped off the hand—he realized the nearly weightless corpse wasn't just dry. It was desiccated. Peeling one eyelid back revealed nearly empty sockets. The eyes were nothing more than pea-sized kernels of hardened goo. And everything that was supposed to be behind the eyes was dried up to the point of being little more than gray dust. It was hard to even look at it without being sick.

Trey glanced at Alyssa as he straightened up and took off his gloves. "Do you think it's possible he was tortured? Like whoever did this took an old man from a retirement home and stuffed them in a ceramics kiln or something like that?"

Alyssa shook her head. "If this is like the last body we found this way, we're going to find out the victim is probably in his midtwenties or early thirties at the most."

Trey looked down at the body again, trying to understand how that could be possibly be true. He couldn't see it. "There have been others like this you said?"

"Two of them, killed about a week apart, both in Dallas," she said. "The first one was found in a garbage truck parked at the Fair Oaks Transfer Station and the second was found in the middle of the DFW landfill. Our working theory is that the killer murders them somewhere else, then uses the nearest convenient dumpster to get rid of the bodies. If that's the case, who knows how many others there are? We wouldn't have found this one if the truck hadn't accidentally dropped off this load of construction scraps in the wrong place and someone had to come out here to move it."

Trey exchanged looks with his teammates before turning his attention back to Alyssa. "If you're involved, I'm assuming you think whoever did this is some kind of supernatural."

She nodded. "Our medical examiners are still arguing over the actual cause of death. Some are going with heart failure due to rapid loss of fluids and electrolytes. Others are sticking with some vague concept that the killer sucked the life force out of these people, whatever the hell that means. Ultimately, it doesn't matter. We need to stop this thing."

"STAT has officially asked for our help on this one," Mason said.

"Unfortunately, San Antonio PD has some murders that look like ritual sacrifices that STAT wants me to take a look, and Zane is coming along for backup," Alyssa said. "Which means you'll be on your own for this."

Trey could understand why Zane would be her first and only choice for backup. If you were heading into a freaky, unknown situation, it never hurt to have a werewolf around to help. If that werewolf was your soul mate, even better.

"You sure you don't need a little more help?" Connor asked. "One of the other guys or I could go with you."

Kat didn't seem to think much of that idea if the way she

jumped off the pile of bricks and sank her claws into the leg of Connor's uniform pants was any indication. The glint in her green eyes suggested she'd shred him to pieces if he even considered going with Alyssa and Zane.

Muttering something under his breath, Connor scooped Kat up with one hand and stuck her in the SWAT SUV, where she sat on the dash, staring at him with a pissed-off look that only a cat could come up with.

There is something seriously wrong with that cat.

That thought earned Trey a long-distance glare from Kat…like she'd actually heard him thinking it.

"Thanks for the offer," Alyssa said. "But I think it'll go better with just the two of us. We'll draw less attention that way. Besides, there's a good chance this is nothing but a bunch of college students playing with some old books they dug up somewhere. If it turns into anything more, we'll call you guys."

They talked for a while longer about what kind of supernatural creature might be involved in murders that would leave a desiccated corpse until an unmarked SUV that belonged to STAT showed up. A moment later, a man and woman got out to collect the body, as well as take pictures and samples from the surrounding area.

"All my files from the previous murders are waiting for you at the SWAT compound," Alyssa said before she and Zane headed for their car. "You'll have access to STAT intel support and our medical examiners. If you need anything else, just ask and they'll get it for you."

"What about the Butcher investigation?" Trey asked Mason as his pack mate and fiancée drove off.

"I'm hoping you can work both cases," the deputy chief said. "Gage told me that you have an inside track with the medical examiner assigned to the Butcher task force. If she's willing to float you a few leads now and then, you should be able to sniff around and find something they might not recognize."

Trey scowled at Connor, having no doubt he was the pack mate who'd ratted him out to their SWAT commander/pack alpha, Gage Dixon. That was the only way the boss could have learned about the "inside track" he had with Samantha. The grin Connor gave him confirmed he was to blame.

Mason left a little while later, telling them he expected frequent updates. "And try not to do anything that attracts Chief Leclair's attention. She's already suspicious of your team."

Trey watched the deputy chief drive away, wondering how the hell the man expected them to track down what was possibly two supernatural killers when they knew next to nothing about these creatures. This was so far outside the SWAT job description it wasn't even funny.

"Okay, now that Mason's gone, tell us what happened with Samantha," Connor said, looking at him expectantly. "Did you finally ask her out or what?"

Connor and his other pack mates had been riding him nonstop about whether he'd asked her since they'd left the forensic institute yesterday. They all assumed he had, since he'd been grinning like an idiot when he came outside. After the way they'd ribbed him for the past two years, he figured he earned the right to mess with them.

"You know, it's okay if she turned you down," Hale said. "Rejection stings like a son of a bitch, especially when you're really into the person, but it happens to everyone. I've been there, so trust me, I know how you feel."

Trey snorted. "While I'd love to stand around this landfill and talk about it, in the interest of full disclosure, Samantha didn't turn me down. We're going out to dinner tonight."

Connor did a double take. "Damn. You actually asked her out?"

"What, I thought you were all about me going out with her?" Trey frowned. "In fact, you were the one pushing for me to do it the other morning. Over a dead body, no less."

Hale laughed. "Don't take this the wrong way, but we had a pool going at the compound over how long it would take before you two actually went out. Connor is pissed because he bet it'd be at least another two weeks."

Trey looked at Connor, not bothering to hide his disappointment. "Really? Two weeks?"

"Sorry." Connor shrugged. "But damn, dude. You've been dragging this out for months. At two weeks, I was actually one of the optimistic ones. Not as optimistic as Gage, who pegged you for this weekend. But at least I wasn't as bad as Trevor. He put twenty dollars on you never asking her out at all. He insisted you'd never get off your butt and do it and that Samantha would have to make the first move."

Trey didn't say anything. Because the truth was, he'd been shocked as hell when Samantha asked him out. He'd always thought he'd be doing the asking. The only reason he'd waited so long was because he genuinely *had* been worried she'd turn him down. He wasn't afraid of going up against bad guys with machine guns half as much as he was afraid of being rejected by the woman he'd been head over heels for, for going on two years.

"Wait a second," Connor said, looking at him sharply. "You did ask her out, right? Not the other way around."

Trey grinned as he opened the door of his pickup. "Actually, she asked me. Though technically, she collected on one of the favors I owe her by having me ask her to dinner, so I'm not sure how you guys are going to work that out."

Climbing into the truck, he started the engine and put the vehicle in gear, chuckling as Trevor insisted he should win the bet. Trey was tempted to hang around and see if his teammates won that argument but decided against it. If he stayed, they'd only end up ripping on him for not asking Samantha out in the first place.

CHAPTER 4

"So, does Trey know you've been stalking him?" Crystal asked as she watched Samantha try on yet another dress.

Samantha ignored her friend for the moment as she studied her reflection in the full-length mirror on the inside of the closet door, checking out the little black dress she was wearing. After going through nearly half her clothes, she'd ended up going back to her trusted LBD, throwing on a silver chain necklace and over-sized matching hoop earrings. It was the perfect blend of casual and elegant for a first date, and she probably should have simply picked it to begin with, but her head was spinning a bit.

"I have not been stalking him," Samantha insisted, most of her attention now focused on which shoes to wear. She was leaning toward the black sandals with the kitten heels, but she wanted to see if there was anything else that might work.

"Oh, right," Crystal murmured, pulling out a pair of black wedges with silver accents and handing them to her. "You've been *investigating* him. Following him around, taking pictures of him and his SWAT teammates, and snooping through his trash. Sounds more like stalking to me."

The urge to stick her tongue out at Crystal was hard to resist, but she did, because she was an adult. And sticking your tongue out at people—even if they deserved it—wasn't a very adult thing to do.

"I *have* been investigating him," she said firmly, deciding to go with Crystal's choice of shoes, then turning to check her makeup one more time in the mirror. "And don't act like you don't know why. Not after everything Trey and his teammates have been involved in."

Crystal shook her head in exasperation. "The coyote thing again?"

"It's more than that and you know it." Samantha caught her friend's eye in the mirror. "The list of unexplainable crap SWAT has been involved in boggles the mind. There was that crime boss who got all clawed up at the airport, then those Albanian mobsters who said some kind of creatures attacked them. And don't even get me started on that naked SWAT cop in the middle of a blood-spattered crime scene. Or that blood sample I thought was his. I still haven't figured out what happened to it."

Crystal rolled her eyes. "You mean the sample that came back contaminated with animal DNA?"

Samantha had been sure she'd get something useful from the sample she'd collected at the black market organ-harvesting operation, but the lab she'd sent it to claimed it was contaminated and had destroyed it. Crystal had ribbed her for months about it.

"Yes, that one," Samantha replied, ignoring the smirk on her friend's face. "Toss in the wolves people claim to have seen running around crime scenes where SWAT just so happens to also be, the city's former chief of police trying to assassinate them, and mysterious federal agents scooping up suspects after SWAT has arrested them, and you can't tell me all that doesn't make you the least bit curious."

Crystal's dark gaze was assessing. "Sure, I'm curious. But that doesn't mean I'm willing to play games with a guy I'm interested in on the off chance I might learn a few secrets. I don't mess with other people that way."

The accusation hit a little too close to home and Samantha saw herself blush in the mirror. Her conscience had already spent the past few days berating the hell out of her for what she was doing. "It's not like that. I'm not playing games with Trey."

"Really?" Crystal asked, her expression downright dubious. "Here's a simple question then: Is this thing tonight a date or part of your investigation?"

Samantha fussed with the big, bouncy curls she'd put in the ends of her long, blond hair. "Can't it be both?" she asked after delaying as long as she could.

"No, it can't." Crystal sighed. "Look, if you're going out with Trey Duncan because he's a sexy guy and you have the hots for him, that's one thing. But if you're going to dinner with him tonight because you think it'll help you dig up all his secrets, that's another. They're mutually exclusive and it's screwed up. Not to mention something the friend I thought I knew would ever do."

The air left her lungs all at once, and before she knew it, Samantha found herself sitting on the edge of her bed, Crystal down on her knees in front of her, asking if she was okay.

"Yeah." Samantha nodded even as she struggled to get over her minor panic attack. "It's just that…I don't have a clue what the hell I'm doing. Sometimes, I am so attracted to Trey that it's hard to breathe when he's around. But at the same time, I know he and the other members of his SWAT team are hiding something huge. I don't what or how coyotes and wolves play into all of it, but I know it's something big. And you know I don't deal well with secrets. So I'm stuck between wanting this thing with Trey to work out and wanting to figure out what they're hiding."

Crystal shook her head in exasperation. "And you're not worried that going for the latter will destroy any chance of the former?"

Samantha shrugged. "I'm hoping it doesn't come to that."

Frowning, Crystal opened her mouth to say something, but the ringing of the doorbell interrupted her. A glance at the clock showed that it was seven o'clock. Trey was right on time.

With a sigh, her friend stood, pulling Samantha up with her. "Well, I think you're crazy. If I had someone like Trey interested in me, I'd do everything I could to make sure he stayed that way. But if this is how you want to do things, I guess I'll just wish you luck. And hope you don't end up regretting this plan."

"I hope I don't, either," Samantha said.

"Wait a second. What do you mean, it was destroyed?" Samantha asked as the hostess at the grill and bar showed them to their booth. "Why would someone destroy your truck?"

The woman gave them a curious glance before telling them to enjoy their dinner, then leaving them to look over the menus. North of the city center in the Greenville area, the restaurant had lots of exposed wood and bare light bulbs strung along the ceiling in a way that surprisingly worked with the decor. Samantha had never eaten there, but Trey assured her they had the best burgers and cheese fries in town. If the aromas coming from the kitchen were any indication, he was right.

Admittedly, Samantha had been amazed at how relaxed she'd been on the drive across town. After her conversation with Crystal, she'd expected to be a little tense, but within minutes of getting into his new silver Jeep Gladiator and discovering they both loved that wonderful new-car smell, it felt like they'd known each other for years. Trey had totally floored her when he said he bought the pickup because his 1990 Ford Bronco had been destroyed. Samantha knew SWAT got involved in crazy stuff, but that was a story she simply had to hear.

"You remember when those guys attacked Diego in the parking lot outside the SWAT compound back in June?" Trey asked, glancing at the menu. "The ones we thought were high on delirium?"

Samantha remembered it very well. She'd gotten there less than thirty minutes after the shootout to find four dead assailants, their bodies still warm. There'd been a lot of confusion at the time about what had happened, but she definitely remembered it had seemed like a war zone to her inexperienced eyes. In fact, one of the vehicles in the parking lot had been ripped to shreds from all the gunfire.

"Crap." She gasped, suddenly realizing the implications. "That shot-up vehicle in the lot was yours?"

Trey nodded sadly. "Yup. Diego swore he didn't pick my vehicle to hide behind on purpose, but I think he's being less than honest since he's been hounding me forever to get a new truck. Regardless, he did, and it was totally destroyed. Every window was broken, all the tires were flat, and the engine block got turned into swiss cheese. My insurance payoff barely covered the cost of towing it to the junkyard. But on the bright side, it finally got me off my butt and into a vehicle made in this century."

Samantha couldn't help laughing. How anyone could find a silver lining in having their car shot up was beyond her, but the fact that Trey could was another indication of how amazing he was. Even if he failed to mention at least one of those men who'd attacked Diego Martinez back in June had somehow ended up with their throats torn out by some kind of claws.

"Since you've eaten here before, what do you recommend?" she asked, turning her attention to the menu.

"You can't go wrong with anything they serve. It's all basic comfort food that tastes like it's homemade," he said with a smile Samantha decided she was becoming dangerously addicted to. "We definitely have to get the cheddar fries to start with because it would be criminal not to. After that, I usually go for one of their cheeseburgers, but their chicken strips and chili dogs are good, too. Sometimes I can't decide, so I end up just getting all three."

Samantha stared at him, sure he was kidding. But from the sincere expression on his face, it seemed he wasn't. "Mind giving me your secret? If I ate that much, I would be in serious trouble."

The smile on his face slipped for a second as he glanced down at the menu in his hands. "I've always had a fast metabolism."

Trey might have been wearing an untucked button-down, but Samantha had seen him in his tight uniform T-shirt more than once, so she had a pretty good idea of the kind of shape he was in, and it sure as hell had nothing to do with a fast metabolism. "Okay. I'll share some of your cheddar fries, but I think I'll limit myself to one entrée."

When their server came over to take their order, Samantha got the classic burger with cheese and a side of guacamole along with an iced tea. She had to bite her tongue to keep from laughing as Trey ordered the chili cheddar burger with double beef patties and a full-sized bowl of chili on the side. And if that wasn't enough, he also got a large order of cheddar fries with a double serving of bacon.

"Fast metabolism, huh?" she teased after the server left.

He shrugged, his gaze locked on hers, the warmth in his eyes enough to make it feel like someone had turned up the temperature. "I'm lucky that way, I guess."

Resisting the urge to fan herself with her hand, she picked up the iced tea the server brought and took a sip. "How'd you find this place? I've driven past it at least a dozen times and never seen it."

Trey sipped his beer before answering. "SWAT got called out to a barricaded suspect near here a few years ago. We ended up spending over twelve hours waiting for our negotiator to talk the guy out of the house and this was the first restaurant we saw after packing up. We all fell in love with the burgers—and the prices. We stop by to eat anytime there's a call in this part of town."

She pictured all of those big cops in here, eating their weight in burgers and hot dogs. "I get the feeling you and your teammates spend a lot of time together outside of work."

His mouth edged up. "Yeah. Our team is like a big family. We get together at least once or twice a week in addition to the weekends. And even when we're not getting together as a pack, smaller groups of us hang out together all the time."

Samantha stared at him, wondering if she'd heard right. She opened her mouth to ask but was interrupted by the server showing up with a ridiculous plate of fries buried in melted cheese and crumbled bacon. Her mouth watered at the sight and she eagerly reached for a fry, moaning as the combination of cheddar, fried potato, and crispy bacon hit her tongue.

She was helping herself to another when she remembered what she'd been going to say before. "When you were talking about your teammates, you called them a pack."

Trey paused, a handful of cheesy fries halfway to his mouth. "I did?" he asked, the words coming out light and casual.

She nodded. "You did."

"It's just a nickname we have for the team." He shoved the fries in his mouth, then wiped his hands on his napkin before undoing a few buttons on his shirt and tugging it to the side to reveal a tattoo of a wolf head on one side of his muscular chest. As far tattoos went, it was amazing. And as far as chests went, it was spectacular. "We all have this same tattoo, so we call ourselves a pack. Goofy, I know."

Samantha laughed, telling herself that made complete sense. But if that was the case, why did she still think it was total BS?

They ate in comfortable silence for a while before curiosity got the better of her. She was tempted to dig a little more on the pack thing but decided against it. After the quick answer he'd had to her first question, he'd probably be prepared and already have a logical answer to whatever other questions she asked about his team.

"How did you end up in SWAT?" She nibbled on another cheesy fry. "Did you go straight into that when you became a cop, or did you do something else for a while first?"

"Actually, when I first moved to Dallas, I worked as a paramedic." He picked up his bottle of beer. "I was a combat medic in the army for almost six years and was sure that's what I wanted to do for a living after getting out."

She'd known he was in the army before becoming a cop because that had been in the personnel record she'd been able to put together on him. But she hadn't known he was a paramedic. "What changed your mind?"

He fell quiet for a moment, the crease in his brow making her think maybe she'd brought up something he didn't like to talk about.

"I found out that just because you can do something, it doesn't mean you want to," he said softly. "Hell, at one point, I thought I'd make a career of the army. In fact, I was only a few weeks from reenlisting when things changed."

She sipped her iced tea, not wanting to push. While she wanted to know everything she could about Trey, forcing him to talk about something that obviously upset him didn't sit well with her.

"I was in a firefight in Afghanistan," he murmured, pausing to slowly eat another fry before continuing. "I was hurt bad and my best friend was injured even worse, but somehow, we both made it out. The army wouldn't have let me re-up even if I'd wanted to— they had concerns about internal damage if I ever tried to do another airborne jump—so I got out and joined Dallas Fire and Rescue. The first time I showed up at the scene of a major car accident, every injury and death I saw in combat came back to me, and I realized I'd made a mistake. I left DFR the next day, but I still wanted to be able to help people, so I joined the DPD. I did about a year in patrol before my SWAT commander suggested I join the team."

Samantha didn't say anything as the server placed their plates of food before them. Part of her wanted to know what had happened to Trey in Afghanistan, but the other part didn't. The thought of him being hurt made it hard to breathe.

Not trusting herself to speak right then, she concentrated on biting into her burger. It was juicy and perfectly grilled with the perfect ratio of cheese to beef.

"I can understand why you wouldn't want to be a paramedic anymore, but I heard somewhere that you're one of the SWAT medics." She glanced at him as she dunked her cheeseburger in a pile of ketchup. "That means you treat your teammates' injuries, right?"

Trey looked confused for a moment and Samantha hoped she hadn't slipped up and said something she shouldn't have. "I read in the paper that you've received several commendations for using your paramedic skills to treat your teammates' injuries," she added.

He shrugged. "It's different when it's my teammates. Time has helped blur some of those old memories, too. It's not as bad as it used to be."

"I'm glad."

Samantha had never known anyone who'd been in the military, but she could imagine the atrocities Trey had seen in the army. No one should have to experience that stuff.

"You were right about this place," she added, hoping to lighten the mood. "These burgers are awesome."

As they ate, Trey talked about what it was like to be part of SWAT. While she didn't learn any deep, dark secret that might explain any of the weird crap that had gone on around the team, she learned enough to know Trey did some really dangerous stuff, he adored his job, and he loved his teammates.

His pack.

She didn't realize they'd been talking for hours until she looked around and realized that it was almost closing time. The burgers and cheddar fries were gone down to the last little nibble. Heck, there wasn't even any cheese left on the plate to scrape up. A warm sensation swirled inside as it dawned on her that she'd never been on a relaxed, effortless date in her life. And even though she'd eaten more than her share of cheese fries to go along with her burger, when Trey asked if she wanted to go for ice cream, she didn't even consider saying no.

There was an ice cream shop just a few blocks away that made fancy desserts using liquid nitrogen. The place looked like a lab, complete with billowing steam coming out of the high-tech mixers. There were so many flavors on the menu and toppings to go with them that it was difficult to choose, but she and Trey finally decided on double scoop waffles cones with cheesecake-flavored ice cream mixed with pieces of Oreo cookies.

As they sat on a bench in front of the shop, eating ice cream, Trey told her about his family and growing up on a soybean farm in North Dakota. From the warmth in his voice, it was obvious he loved the wide-open spaces and working the farm with his family, but he admitted the idea of becoming a farmer like his parents, brothers, and sisters hadn't been something he wanted to do.

"That's why I joined the army," he added. "I wanted to see some more of the world, and once I did, there was no way I could go back. I mean, I go back to visit my family on the holidays, and they've come down here to visit me a few times. But it's hard for them to get away from the farm for long, so I mostly make the trek to see them."

She smiled. It was nice to hear he was close with his family. "I can understand not wanting to move back to North Dakota after traveling around the world for six years in the army, but what brought you to Dallas? Were you stationed in Texas when you got out of the military?"

Trey didn't answer and when the silence continued to stretch out, Samantha got the feeling he wasn't comfortable discussing it. Maybe it was too personal. Or maybe he'd finally caught on to the fact that they had spent the whole night talking about him. She hadn't necessarily intended to do that, but whenever he'd posed a question about her background, she found herself steering the conversation back to him.

"You don't have to tell me why you settled in Dallas if you don't want to," she said softly, finishing up her cone and realizing that his was long gone. "I get that some things are too personal to talk about on a first date."

"Yeah, I guess they are." His mouth curved into a small smile. "Is that your way of asking me out on another date? You must be eager to use up your second favor."

Samantha laughed, relieved she hadn't messed anything up beyond repair. "Do I need to use a favor to go out with you again?"

She hoped that wasn't the case. And not merely because she still wanted to learn whatever it was he was hiding from her. The truth was, there was something special about this man. Something that attracted her to him like the proverbial moth to a flame. And she desperately wanted to know why that was.

"No, you don't need to use another favor to get a second date," he murmured, his gaze becoming more heated by the second. "You just need to say yes."

"Yes," she said without hesitation.

Then Trey was slipping a hand into her hair and tugging her closer on the bench, his very warm mouth coming down on hers. The kiss stayed casual and chaste for all of two seconds before his tongue slipped between her lips. She couldn't stop the moan that came out. He tasted delectable. And it had nothing to do with ice cream or what they'd had for dinner. There was simply something there she couldn't seem to do without.

He deepened the kiss with a groan, nipping and biting lightly on the tip of her tongue and her lower hip, tugging and teasing until she had to wonder if lip-gasms were a real thing.

She had no idea her fingers were in his hair, yanking and pulling him exactly where she wanted. Not until she heard him growling. Crap, he was *growling*. A deep, rumbling sound that vibrated up through his chest and right into her soul.

No. Actually, those vibrations settled between her legs—right there where all good vibrations belonged.

Samantha was damn close to climbing into his lap right there, on a busy street in front of the ice cream shop, when Trey suddenly pulled back. He was breathing as hard as she was, his eyes reflecting the yellow glow of the nearby streetlamps. It only made him that much more mesmerizing.

"Tomorrow night…five o'clock?" he whispered, his warm

breath tantalizing against the sensitive skin of her lips. "I'll pick you up at your place again?"

It took a few moments for her rattled mind to figure out what he was even talking about, but when she did, all she could do was nod. He wanted to see her again tomorrow night. Yes, that was exactly what she wanted, too.

Taking her hand, Trey stood, taking her with him, and they walked back to his Jeep. As he helped her into the passenger seat, then walked around to the driver's side, Samantha realized Crystal lad been right. She was being absolutely stupid to risk the chance of being with Trey simply to learn a few secrets that probably didn't matter anyway.

CHAPTER 5

"You going to fill us in on how the date went last night, or did you think we'd let you slide without telling us anything?" Connor asked from the far side of the tables they'd shoved together in the training room.

Trey looked up from the STAT file he'd been reading for the past few minutes to see Connor, Trevor, and Hale sitting in front of file folders of their own, scribble-filled notepads near at hand. Tuffie, the team's resident pit-bull-mix mascot, sat off to one side, while Kat perched on the table beside Connor, looking over his arm like she was actually reading the documents Alyssa had left them. Which, considering this particular cat, was a distinct possibility.

The four of them had come to the SWAT compound early that morning to go through Alyssa's files on the three dead victims, hoping to find some kind of connection between them. Trey didn't know about the others, but so far, nothing obvious was jumping out at him.

"The date was amazing," Trey said, unable to keep the smile off his face.

"What'd you guys do?" Trevor asked.

"We went out for burgers and then ice cream."

His buddies regarded him expectantly, clearly waiting for more details. But there was no way he was going to tell them about the kiss on the bench in front of the ice cream shop. No, that memory—of the most perfect kiss he'd ever had in his life—was for him alone. He still had a hard time believing it had been real, even if it had left him lying awake all night reliving it. Even now, all he could think about were Samantha's pillow-soft lips and the way her skin had smelled like cherry blossoms and spring air after a light rain.

Of course, he had no idea how to explain the fact that, in all the time he and Samantha had been around each other over the past two years, the moment on that metal bench had been the first time he'd picked up that scent. Considering the way everyone else in the Pack who'd found their soul mate had made such a big deal about picking up their unique scents right away, he didn't quite know what to make of his experience.

"Sounds like the perfect date," Hale observed.

"It was perfect," Trey said, what he knew was a dopey smile slipping across his face again. "Oh, who am I kidding? It was better than that. I haven't been able to think about much of anything but her since dropping her off at her place last night."

Connor exchanged looks with the other guys before leaning forward. "Do you think Samantha is *The One* for you?"

"Dude, they've been on a grand total of one date," Trevor pointed out. "How is he supposed to know if she's his soul mate yet?"

"Because he's been crushing on her since the first day he saw her," Connor said, as if that should explain everything. Then he looked over at Trey again. "So is she?"

Trey almost laughed at the eager expressions on his pack mates' faces. He should have known the question was coming. Over the past two years, more than half of the Pack had found their soul mates—aka that one person who could love a werewolf in spite of what they were. Every time he or any of the other single guys went out with someone, everyone automatically assumed they'd found *The One*. That was the way it seemed to work lately. He'd be lying if he said he hadn't been wondering the same thing when he'd knocked on Samantha's door last night.

There was just one problem.

"I wish I could tell you definitively that she is," he said, shocked at how true that statement really was. He hadn't realized until then exactly how much he wanted what most of the other members of his Pack had already found: a future of more than merely searching and hoping.

"But?" Hale prompted.

"But I think Samantha might be playing me."

Trey sighed, something twisting in his gut at the notion of thinking something like that, much less saying it out loud. He hadn't gone to bed with these doubts floating around in his head, but they'd relentlessly started popping up as the morning dragged on and he began to overanalyze every single minute of last night's date.

"I can't shake the horrible feeling that the only reason Samantha wanted to go out with me is because she's looking for dirt on the Pack," he continued. "You know she's been sniffing around our crime scenes for years. And after all the crap that got swept under the rug with that delirium case, I have no doubt she knows we're hiding something."

His pack mates looked at him dubiously.

"You think she knows we're werewolves?" Trevor asked.

Trey shrugged. "I don't know. I hope not, but you have to admit, the timing of all of this is strange. The two of us have been flirting with each other forever, and then out of the blue she asks me out? You don't find that at least a little curious?"

"Not really, no," Hale said. "Is it so shocking that Samantha got tired of waiting for you to ask her and decided to take things into her own hands? This is the twenty-first century, you know. Women are completely comfortable going after what they want."

"Maybe," Trey admitted. "But you weren't the one sitting across from her as she asked me question after question."

Trevor laughed. "I may not be the greatest at the whole social thing, but isn't asking each other personal questions what people normally do on a date?"

"Yeah, personal questions I get," Trey answered. "But almost all Samantha's questions were about how I got into SWAT, what kind of work we do, how tight I am with you guys, and how well I know all of you. And every time I tried to steer the conversation in her direction, she turned it right back around on me. After a while, it was like she was grilling me for information."

His friends were quiet for a while, considering that.

"So what are you going to do?" Connor asked.

"What can I do?" Trey ran his hand through his hair exasperation. "If I'm right, and the only reason Samantha is going out with me is to dig up dirt, then every minute I spend with her puts the Pack at risk. If I walk away now, and it turns out I was wrong about her, then I'd be giving up my chance at a soul mate."

"You can't do that," Hale said firmly. "Walking away from a shot at finding *The One* would be insane. Nobody in the Pack would expect you to do that."

"I know," Trey murmured. "That's why we're going out again tonight. It feels like I'm playing with fire, but the thought of walking away makes me sick to my stomach."

As they sat around, the files in front of them untouched, they talked about how much Samantha might already know, in between his buddies giving him suggestions on where he should take her on their second date. Connor was of the opinion that if things went well enough, maybe Samantha would give up her snooping and realize she was his soul mate. Trey thought that might be a little optimistic, but he couldn't stop himself from hoping his pack mate was right.

It was Trevor who finally pointed out they'd been talking about Trey's love life for the past hour, instead of finding clues on who was murdering men and leaving mummified remains at the city dumps.

"Never let it be said that I'm the adult in the room," he added. "But maybe we should actually get back to looking at these files, especially if STAT is right about the MO and there's a good chance the killer is going to strike again this weekend."

Trey couldn't argue with that logic. Pulling his pad full of notes a little closer, he flipped through the pages of scribbles he'd written. "I don't know about you guys, but I haven't found anything earth-shattering yet. Maybe we'll get lucky and find something STAT missed."

"STAT has an army of intelligence analysts on this, not to mention criminal profilers, data-mining and predictive analytic software tools, and loads of experts with experience dealing with supernatural killers," Hale pointed out. "You honestly think we're going to find something they missed?"

"We don't need a miracle here," Trey said. "Just something that will give us a place to start looking."

With that, Trey and his teammates spread out the papers from the three folders. Well, actually, two of the folders. Trevor was still sitting there holding one in his hand, his expression thoughtful.

"There's not much on the body found in the McCommas Bluff landfill. We know from his bone structure that the guy was approximately thirty years old. STAT says he was likely killed last Saturday or Sunday," Trevor said, holding up a piece of paper. "But they haven't IDed the body yet."

"All right," Trey said. "With so little on that one, let's set him aside for the time being and focus on the other two."

Grabbing photos of the other two victims, Trey stood and walked over to the whiteboard at the front of the room. After hanging them up with some magnets, he picked up a marker and turned back to look at his pack mates.

"Let's start laying out everything we know about these two guys," he said, motioning at the "before" pictures. "Give me everything you got. No detail is too small."

"The first body, found in the truck at the Fair Oaks Transfer Station, was a man named Demario Harris," Connor said, skimming through the file. "He was twenty-seven years old and worked as a commercial plumber."

"Alden Cox was the one found at the DFW Landfill. He was a supervisor at a UPS distribution warehouse," Hale added. "Twenty-nine years old."

His teammates kept going like that, calling out information on first Demario and then Alden, helping Trey by focusing on equivalent data points. Trey didn't pay much attention to what he wrote, instead listing everything the files had on the two victims—home addresses, education, work history, bank accounts and credit cards balances, police records, nearby relatives and close friends, how often they went out at night, where they went when they did, sexual preferences, even the type of women they hung out with.

As they quickly filled the whiteboard, Trey decided it was more than a little creepy how much personal information STAT had been able to dig up about the two men, most of it probably coming straight from social media and other open sources.

After he finished writing, Trey stepped back to regard the whiteboard. While there were still no obvious slam-dunk connections, seeing everything laid out this way allowed him to realize the two men were surprisingly similar in many ways.

"We might only have these two victims, but I think we're already seeing a pattern," Hale said. "Both of these guys were physically fit, around the same age, attractive, and, if their social media accounts are any indication, extremely active on the club and party scene, which means our killer has a type."

Looking at what he'd written about Demario and Alden, Trey had to agree with Hale's assessment. According to the date and time stamps on their social media posts, both had gone out to a club almost every night in the weeks prior to their deaths, including the weekends when they'd been killed. But as he continued to compare the two men, he realized they had more in common than their social lives.

"These two were perfect victims," Trey said. "Neither seemed to be close with their families or have any close friends. Their interactions seem limited to casual acquaintances and a series of one-night stands."

"Yeah, and I'm willing to bet the killer picked them specifically because no one would notice them leaving a club or bar with a complete stranger," Trevor said.

"So we're all leaning toward the killer being a woman, right?" Connor asked.

"Or a man and a woman," Hale said. "The woman might be the bait. Her partner could be someone waiting for her to lure their victims outside."

"The guy we found yesterday did have his pants down around his knees," Trevor remarked. "That definitely supports the theory a woman enticed them to leave the clubs with the offer of sex, then whoever she's working with took them down while they were distracted. It's cold-blooded but effective."

Trey sighed. "While we're probably right about all of this, it doesn't help us much. STAT had their analysts go through both men's social media accounts. There were no women—or men—in common between them. There also weren't any bars, clubs, or restaurants in common, either. Whoever the killer or killers are, they're smart enough to stay away from any cameras. That's going to make it damn hard to find them."

"We could ask STAT to use their fancy computers to create a list of all the places the two victims spent time in the weeks before their deaths, then start hitting all of them with photos of Demario and Alden. Maybe we'll get lucky and someone will remember seeing something suspicious."

Trevor and Connor both groaned at that idea.

Trey didn't blame them. "With only the four of us and the number of places those two guys frequented, that might take a while," he pointed out.

He left out the part about there being a good chance someone out there could get murdered this weekend, if they hadn't already.

Unfortunately, they had nothing really to go on when it came to stopping it from happening.

"You're right," Hale said. "We need a way to cut down the list of potential locations. If not, we could be canvassing clubs and bars for the next month and still never find anything."

They studied the board again, running through every detail they'd listed, wondering if there was something they'd missed. It wasn't until Trey went through the files again that he caught sight of a picture of the garbage truck where Demario's body had been found.

"Maybe we can use the fact that the killer appears to use dumpsters to dispose of the victims to our advantage." He dug through the photos until he found some from the DFW and McCommas Bluff sites. "I doubt the killer would have lugged those bodies very far after the murders. If we're right and the men were killed close to the bar, restaurant, or club where the killer picked them up, maybe it's as simple as looking for dumpsters positioned close to those kinds of places."

Trey could practically see the light bulbs going on as his pack mates picked up on his reasoning.

"We could have STAT dig into the landfill records," Connor suggested. "See if they can figure out where the trash came from that the bodies had been found in. It should be easy for the truck that unloaded at Fair Oaks Transfer Station. Probably a little harder for the body at the DFW site. Once they have an ID on the body from yesterday, they could do the same for him. If they can figure out where the trash came from, they could compare that to the list of places the men went. That should give us a list of clubs, bars, and restaurants that have dumpsters nearby. It should cut way down on the number of places we have to check out."

"That theory depends on the killer being too lazy to haul the bodies anywhere before dumping them in the garbage," Trevor said. "That's one hell of an assumption, but at least it gives us a place to start. It might even lead us to the actual places the men were killed."

They spent a few more minutes talking before Trey called the number Alyssa had left for him.

"We'll have your requested info within twenty-four hours, if not before that," the woman on the other end of the line said. "I'll send the spreadsheets to each of your phones."

Trey frowned. "I'm not sure I can read spreadsheets on my phone."

The woman laughed. "You can now. I've updated your phones with the app. It's already been installed and authenticated. All you have to do is tap the document attachment when you get the email. Call if you need anything else."

As Trey hung up, he wondered if he should be worried that STAT could apparently get into his phone and do anything they wanted, whenever they wanted. Then he decided it wasn't worth his time to care. He had other stuff to worry about now that he and his pack mates had a plan to find the killer. Like figure out where he was going to take Samantha tonight.

Maybe he should have asked STAT if they could have helped with that.

ACKNOWLEDGMENTS

I hope you had as much fun reading Harley and Sawyer's story as we had writing it! Since our STAT series is international, we thought it'd be fun to make Sawyer an MI6 agent. Since she fell so fast for the hunky British werewolf, Harley clearly agreed. By the way, Caleb is the next werewolf to find The One, and you aren't going to want to miss the girl he falls for!

This whole series wouldn't be possible without some very incredible people. In addition to another big thank-you to my hubby for all his help with the action scenes and military and tactical jargon, thanks to my fantastic agent, Courtney Miller-Callihan, and thanks to my editor and all the other amazing people at Sourcebooks, including my fantastic publicist and the crazy-talented art department. The covers they make for me are seriously drool-worthy!

Because I could never leave out my readers, a huge thank-you to everyone who reads my books and Snoopy Dances right along with me with every new release. That includes the fantastic people on my amazing review team!

And a very special shout-out to our favorite restaurant, P. F. Chang's, where hubby and I bat story lines back and forth and come up with all our best ideas, as well as a thank-you to our fantastic waiter-turned-manager, Andrew, who makes sure our order is ready the moment we walk in the door!

Hope you enjoy the next book in the STAT: Special Threat Assessment Team series coming soon from Sourcebooks and look forward to reading the rest of the series as much as we look forward to sharing it with you.

Also, don't forget to check out the action-packed series that started it all—SWAT: Special Wolf Alpha Team!

Happy reading!

ABOUT THE AUTHOR

Paige Tyler is a *New York Times* and *USA Today* bestselling author of sexy, romantic suspense and paranormal romance. She and her very own military hero (also known as her husband) live on the beautiful Florida coast with their adorable fur baby (also known as their dog). Paige graduated with a degree in education, but decided to pursue her passion and write books about hunky alpha males and the kick-butt heroines who fall in love with them.

Visit Paige at her website at paigetylertheauthor.com.

She's also on Facebook, Twitter, Tumblr, Instagram, Tsu, Wattpad, and Pinterest.

Also by Paige Tyler